JESUS WAS A
TIME TRAVELER

D.J. Gelner

Orion's Comet

To Mom, Dad, Grant, Jenga, and Sully

CHAPTER ONE

"Shlama, Bar Enosh!" I stroked my now richly-bearded chin.

"Better! Much better!" Avi Naris beamed. "Of course, I have no idea why you want to greet the Son of Man, but—"

"Just a Bible nut, is all, I suppose," I hoped some of my English charm would disarm the swarthy, ex-Israeli commando-turned Aramaic scholar who now sat across the table.

"Hey, whatever floats your boat, buddy," the man was surprisingly good-natured despite his student's shortcomings. "The person who's bringing me in here must think it's worthwhile, for what they're paying me." He gathered up the various tablets he had scattered across the desk.

"Yes—quite. About that..." I waited several uncomfortable moments for Avi to say something, but his expression remained stony as his eyes focused on mine with the intensity of one of the nearby tunneling lasers. "You're fired."

Avi glared at me for one of the (to that point) tensest moments of my life. Just when I thought he was about to smash his tablet over my head, he shook a phony smile onto his face.

"Hey, no problem, my friend! I was meaning to talk with your boss about this, anyway. With what your Benefactor has paid me, I can afford to take an extended vacation. But indulge me on one thing; may I ask why? Why hire me? Where might you be going where you'd need to know ancient Aramaic?"

"No, you may not," I tried to project as much firmness with the man as I possibly could, despite my sheer terror only moments before. Avi stared at me, mouth agape. For a brief moment, I thought he might bolt from behind his chair and snap my neck. I cooly took out a roll of hundred dollar bills and snapped off four or five.

The smile returned to Avi's face, "I got it, I got it. Super secret spy stuff, right? Well, if you're going to the Middle East, be careful, my friend. Fallout is nothing to fuck around with."

"Goodbye, Avi," I extended my hand along with a curt smile and a nod. The Israeli took it and grinned. He whipped an expensive-looking pair of Ray Bans to his face with his off-hand.

"Goodbye, Finny." He walked to the large set of double-doors that led to the long hallway outside of my lab and exited. The heavy, steel door crashed shut with a satisfying "ka-CHINK." I followed Avi and put three steel bars across the doorway before I engaged the magnetic lock. My Benefactor always said that you could never be too careful, and though I had often poo-poohed the eccentric old-timer, as the zero hour drew nigh, I was beginning to think that he had a point.

Before I go any further, allow me to introduce myself. My name is Phineas Templeton, and though you should know my name, unless you're a close family friend, you're probably as blissfully unaware of my existence as everyone else in this world.

I write this little travelogue not for fame or fortune; I'm well aware that it will be somewhat less than successful, either due to poor sales or some mishap that will befall the poor courier carting this manuscript to its intended destination. That's just the way the universe—this universe—works.

Nor do I write this screed as an indictment of others whom I have met along the way. Though there are those toward whom I bear some ill will, and understandably so, dear reader, as will soon become apparent, I have never been the vindictive sort. Jealous? Sure. Arrogant? Perhaps at times.

But vindictiveness is a special type of response, a reaction that combines jealousy and rage with some necessity of action. It is that compulsion with which, outside of the field of advanced theoretical physics, I was not born. Or rather, I should say, I wasn't born with the capacity to follow vindictiveness to its natural ends.

No, I write this book as a purely selfish endeavor. The first aim of this story is an attempt to achieve some sort of catharsis, some measure of solace despite all of the slings and arrows suffered by my rather fragile frame and ego over the past several months.

But perhaps more importantly, I write so that hopefully someone out there will finally discover the truth. As unassailable, static, and unforgiving as that truth may seem from my point of view, know that even when the mysteries of time and space have apparently been all but unraveled, when the man behind the curtain has been exposed as a charlatan, there are still bits of the *truth*, not as a space-time construct, but as the absolute, "this is what happened" concept that may still leak through the cracks.

In return, I ask only for three indulgences on your part. First, forgive my manner of speech and cadence. Though I was born an American, and that is where my life and laboratory reside (or reside*d*, I should say), I grew up in London for many years—until university, actually—and I still consider myself a Britton, thus though my accent is decidedly English, my speech (and spelling, for that matter) is a somewhat bastardized combination of American colloquialisms and lapses into the King's.

Secondly, I have visited three separate doctors within the walls of this fine university, and after a battery of tests involving all manner of flashing tablets and poking and prodding electrodes and rods, I have been diagnosed with a condition referred to as "hyper vigilance." Though you will receive the benefit of this dastardly illness in the form of my mind's tape-recorder-like precision in recalling places and conversations, do know that it is a positively dreadful way to go through life. I've never been able to sleep without the benefit of eyeshades, a pair of foam earplugs, and perhaps a nip or two of fine scotch. And yes, I've even tried the new holoprograms that profess to help such a condition by thoroughly depriving the senses. For whatever reason, when I'm in one of those ghastly, coffin-like chambers, I can't shake the feeling that someone is watching me.

The third allowance is connected to the second; if you haven't been able to tell as of yet, I do have a propensity to go off on the odd tangent or two. I apologize in advance if this is disconcerting, but do know that I have thoroughly edited this manuscript by hand (as I'd surely be locked up in an asylum should I have provided it to a proper editor for review), and only those deviations that are absolutely necessary to the story and its veracity have been left untouched so that you may enjoy better context for my (at times questionable) actions.

I suppose your first question is likely what the devil was Avi doing in my lab? I'm not Jewish. I say that not as a slight or indictment, simply as a fact that is, and one that may allow you to better flesh out my tale. Far be it from me to try to editorialize as far as "who shot first," but I firmly maintain that the war was no fault of the Israelis. At any rate, it's not like Avi is a guy with whom I'd pal around on my off-hours under usual circumstances. He's more than a little uptight, and his phony-baloney "my friend" routine is as transparent as a whore's raincoat, though judging by his rather offensive odor, he could afford to be caught in a storm with said whore.

Personal failings aside, Avi happened to be one of the foremost scholars of ancient Aramaic in the world. After his stint in the Mossad, he decided to take up (of all things) archaeology, and, being a rather intense fellow, threw himself into the study of all things old and Assyrian—know your enemy and whatnot, I suppose.

When the shit *really* hit the fan in the Middle East, Avi bolted to America; say what you will about the Americans, but their lavish military spending finally seemed positively prudent after the Battle of Mecca. That's why they remain one of the truly safe places in the world, and why I relocated my research at the behest of my Benefactor to the relative safety of Johns Hopkins University in Baltimore.

Back to Avi—he set up a rather successful "security consulting" business (which I fear may have been a front for organized crime of some sort), and, when the price was right, taught ancient Aramaic to mad scientists with wealthy Benefactors on the side.

4

Let me back up once more: my father was a banker. I was born before the turn of the century, and raised during the "Great Correction" of the late aughts. My father kept his job because he had relocated the family to London when his bank asked him right around the dawn of the millennium. Unfortunately, my mother was a bit more of a free spirit, and got into the Neo Boho scene and eloped with an artist she met on the street in Spitalfields when I was quite young, named "Varden" or "Mannix" or some such sort.

My father was devastated, but threw himself into his work with renewed vigor. He was wildly successful, and was able to retire at forty, though soon thereafter he suffered a rather severe heart attack, and died at a tragically young age.

Through the early years in London, we had been inseparable; I would often sit in on calls where he would lounge in his chair, chain smoke, and scream at and berate whomever was on the other end of the line. I would be left asking innocent questions at the end like, "Daddy, what's a cocksucker?" I distinctly remember that he would often take a deep breath, force a smile, and swing me around the room wildly until he thought I had forgotten the question.

I never did.

His lone "hobby," if you want to call it that, was ancient history; Egyptology and the like. On Sundays, we would take long, circuitous walks to the British Museum by way of the Thames. He'd engineer the enterprise so that we'd pass the same stretch every week, right by the candy floss vendor, so that my father could "indulge" me with a treat. In an alleyway nearby, the same beggar would sit, week after week, pitiable in his shaggy beard and decrepit clothing. "Any spare change, pop?" the bum would ask.

My father would invariably use the episode as a teaching moment, "Now Finny, that's a bum. You work hard because you don't want to end up like him." Right in front of the wretch's face! And for some reason, the filthy begging bastard would always smile and nod like an idiot, even though my father never passed him a single schilling.

But as I grew older and my father's responsibilities compounded, we drifted further and further apart. He had his finance, and I had my physics, and apart from the holidays, when we would send each other rather merriless Christmas cards and exchange a brief phone call to check in on one another, I didn't have much contact with the man. It was a bit of a running joke that we'd travel together to see the pyramids "someday." Of course, our schedules being what they were, there was precious little time to take off, and our "low periods" seemingly never aligned.

When he died, though, I felt a profound sadness, like a part of me had also if not passed away, then passed me by. I had never married, and he had never had a chance to see any grandchildren. All of those "firsts" that I had never had a chance to share with the man, first graduation, first grant proposal accepted, first new discovery—all of those possibilities that fathers so often share with their sons, were blinked out of existence in a single, silent moment, by a clogged artery that refused to fire any longer.

They say that daughters eventually end up like their mums given enough time. What they don't tell you is that the same usually applies to fathers and sons, if not in looks, then most certainly in comportment. Maybe I was already "too British," stiff upper lip and all that, but the sadness passed, and eventually I was back to working too hard in the lab, fully aware of the irony. What can I say? Those walks by the Thames had quite an impact on young Phineas.

My father left me with a small fortune, and a roomful of antiquities and journals that he had collected over the course of his life. In cleaning out his flat, my love of history was rekindled; it wasn't so much that I was interested in the numerous masks, tablets (*stone* tablets, I should clarify), and the odd sarcophagus or two, beautiful as they may be. Rather it was the information that those items represented, the stories behind them, and all of the history associated with them that we would never know. Those are the kinds of things that would make my mind race like only physics could at the time. I would pour over some random carving to memorialise a Sumerian nobleman's wedding and wonder "What were these people like? Were they so different than you and I?"

As only a fool might, I spent countless nights pondering the course of my research, how I could bring my two loves, physics and history, together in one grand, unifying, brilliant project that would overshadow even the greatest titans in the field. Newton? An idiot with an apple tree. Einstein? A mere stepping stone to my greatness. No, one day, people would use "Templeton" to mean the apex of human achievement, the ideal of the human mind to which others may only aspire. It would be a fitting tribute to my father, if I could only decide on what course of research to pursue.

And, one night, after perhaps a couple too many refills of scotch, with the force (and in hindsight, bad luck) of a lightning bolt, it hit me.

Time travel.

No one in history (aside from Dr. Ronald Mallett, to whom I am eternally grateful for his pioneering research) had ever tried to harness the power of time itself. No one attempted to bend the stream of time to his will, to master and control it, then release it on its new course like a wound-up car.

My research had already bordered on focused laser space-time tunneling in the most tangential way possible, but I would have to refocus all of my energies on the matter, and dip into my now rather considerable resources to tackle the problem. Once I had mastered space-time tunneling, I moved on to rotational mechanics and alternative propulsion, and the picture began to come into focus. (I discuss this, dear reader, so as to prove that I'm not entirely a quack; should you wait until a later date to find out for yourself, you will see how eerily close I am to the mark).

Fifteen years (of my thirty-six in all) of hard work and sacrifice. Fifteen years and countless experiments on arcane, extraordinarily theoretical concepts like antigravity and string theory, a decade and a half of trying to manifest the impossible as possible.

Most of my colleagues thought I had lost my mind. Eventually, as my coffers ran low, I even questioned my own sanity. I called in a favor from a friend, who was happy to give me lab space at Hopkins if I agreed to serve as an "Adjunct Faculty Advisor," which consisted of their full-time faculty being granted one hour a week to ask me questions of their own research. It wasn't much, but it gave me a place to spend my rapidly-dwindling cache in relative peace.

Enter my Benefactor.

For all you know at the moment, dear reader, "he" may not be a man at all, nor may "he" be old. "He" could be a fabulously wealthy bikini model with a keen interest in theoretical physics. Regardless, my Benefactor is obviously a bit of a recluse, and had his reasons for wanting to unlock the secrets of time-travel; something about manipulating time to create some sort of financial windfall for himself. It is only in hindsight that these types of moments can be seen for the "chicken-or-the-egg" types of paradoxes that they truly are. Before you ponder the concept too deeply, know that your universe doesn't care about such "trivial" matters.

Also, if you're waiting for a singular "Aha!" moment from my research, I can break the suspense, and enlighten you that there was not one. Rather there were a series of amazing breakthroughs, each made all the more awful by the fact that I could never claim credit for any of them, per the terms of my agreement with my Benefactor. The results of my research were for him, and him alone. Besides, I always thought that if I was ultimately successful, I could just go back in time and prove my brilliance to the world by showing up in a bloody time machine.

If only it was so simple!

The end result of all of the experimentation sat neatly in the corner of my laboratory, protected from the great unwashed masses only by the three steel bars and magnetic lock on the door, as well as the sheet I haphazardly threw over the curiosity whenever Avi or another potential lookie-loo would stop by.

After I was sure that Avi was gone, I walked over to the large sheet in the corner. I gripped the fabric in my well-worn hands and gave it a quick tug to reveal...well, nothing, I suppose. The craft's cloaking device had been engaged for quite some time, which, in hindsight, would have made the hovering sheet far more remarkable should anyone else have occasion to remove it.

No matter; I engaged the button on the temple of my smart spectacles to reveal the cloaked ship and invisible access panel. I ran my fingers across the smooth surface to reveal a touch pad, and placed my hand on the pad to reveal an open door on a remarkable contraption, straight out of a forties, pulp sci-fi novel; a perfect, brushed alloy disc with counter-rotating, magnetic halves that could manipulate gravity on a whim.

One year ago to the day, I had completed this most modern of marvels, an honest-to-goodness, working time machine. At least, at the time, I *thought* it worked; I hadn't yet tested it in great part due to the particular peculiarities of my Benefactor, who insisted that he would not pay for a shakedown flight when I had a far more important initial destination, one that could answer thousands of questions that had been asked for centuries should I take the time and effort to learn the language and customs:

Ancient Judea.

My goal was to meet Jesus Christ.

What a capital idea it was by the Old Bird! The man whose name has been damned more times than all of the sinners in all of time, who has been invoked by the bearers of countless flags throughout history in their offensives seeking to secure more territory, and yet a man whose honest actions have provided a simple, basic moral code for the rest of the world to live by for two-plus millennia. A man who would be able to answer so many questions about the Bible and its meaning. And my Benefactor wanted *me* to be the one to meet him! Not only would I eventually be able to publish my treatise to redefine the laws of physics as any human understood them, but I'd also have occasion to write a memoir about my conversations with Jesus Himself (though I thought *Conversations With Christ* would have been a catchier title—it later went unpublished for what will become obvious reasons).

So my Benefactor hired Avi and a few other teachers to school me in ancient Aramaic, Hebrew, and several other ancient languages, in case the gravity drive and tunneling laser missed their mark and I had to make do sometime else. Weeks of lessons culminated in this moment, the evening of July 6, 2032, a date which would eventually reverberate through history with the force of a thousand church bells.

"It's important to blend in, ya know," my Benefactor had pulled me aside and said to me one day. "Butterfly effect and all. Don't wanna screw up the future for the rest of us!" (Pardon my barbaric print rendition of an American accent). As he spoke, his secretary, Helene, invariably would spill coffee or scotch on me and pardon herself.

Damn you, clumsy tart! I would think.

"Think nothing of it," I would say with a dismissive wave of my hand.

Indeed, though, my Benefactor was right. One slip-up, and I could set a chain of events in motion that resulted in the Nazis winning World War II, or a vast totalitarian government controlling the entire world; there were countless ways that, were I not careful, could result in our already dire world becoming positively unlivable.

I removed my lab coat and cast it aside, so excited was I that "best lab practices" were all but forgotten. I giddily stripped down to my underwear and, after a pause for unnecessary modesty, slipped those off, as well.

Naked as a jaybird, I ran back to the table where I had been studying with Avi not but moments before and opened the drawer to reveal a locked case. I picked up the key (which lay, in hindsight, rather carelessly next to the metal box), inserted it into the lock, and turned it.

The lid popped open to reveal a standard military-issue Baretta nine millimetre in a shoulder holster.

My hands trembled as I secured the holster around my torso; though I was loathe to admit as much at the time, I was terrified of handguns, and found the idea of discharging it to be repulsive. One could never be too careful, though, and I took solace in the fact that should the need ever arise to fire it, I would likely end up destroying all of space and time through the cascading reverberations of the very Butterfly Effect of which my Benefactor warned that would change all of history from that point forward.

10

Once my holster was secured, I wrapped a simple, linen undergarment around my waist, and then threw on a similarly-crafted linen tunic, specially-made and devoid of any tags. I fashioned a beige keffiyeh out of a cotton-wool blend, and wrapped it around my head before I secured it with a modern Saudi headband (don't ask how I had it smuggled into the States). I then laced up the Roman-style, upper-calf sandals that I had procured via eBay, completing the image of a confused Middle Eastern tourist at "Romanland" or some similarly ghastly amusement park in pre-War Dubai.

I punched a sequence of buttons on the frame of the time machine and entered. The interior was rather spacious, if I do say so myself. The cabin was maybe sixty feet wide and occupied most of the saucer's interior. A set of bunkbeds was situated in a small room off to the right behind a sitting area, and an equally economical head was located opposite the quarters. To the left, a pantry and kitchen were tucked behind several walls, stocked with enough foodstuffs to last me several years. In front of me was a flight deck with a single chair and several touchscreen panels that could be switched to holodisplays, though I found the holograms dreadfully tiring, and after a while my aching shoulders would beg for the more conventional, two-dimensional setup.

I sat in the chair with a satisfied "whoosh" as I pulled off my spectacles, which would have surely drawn some unwanted attention in ancient Judea, and placed them in the spacious glove box under the dash, which was really a large recessed cabinet that I had designed more out of a sense of familiarity and convenience than anything else. I double-checked its contents; a "file" with numerous changes of clothes, vacuum-wrapped and era-specific, with all identifying tags removed, a simple canvas drawstring bag filled with gold that had been pressed into near-exact replicas of Roman coins, one universal charger for all manner of modern gizmos I may bring along, one First Aid kit, complete with laser omni-tool for suturing and decontamination, as well as Purell, bandages, and other dressings should the omni-tool fail, one digital tape recorder, should I wish to interview anyone discreetly, and several paper books, including an updated and annotated version of David Macaulay's book, *The Way Things Work*, as well as an historically annotated almanac, a guide to basic Aramaic that Avi had been paid to put together, and, of course, a copy of the Bible, King James edition. I also had thousands of other books preloaded on my tablet, but just in case it was destroyed or lost, I wanted to ensure that I had some way of surviving in the past should all else fail.

I then checked at the locked armory cabinet at the rear of the cockpit and took a quick mental inventory. There would be the reinforced sword, the updated colt revolver, several other pistols, as well as some more modern weaponry like two fully automatic rifles and even the prototype laser pistol that I had designed on a whim while researching my thesis on hypermagnetic tunneling laser containment, which now seemed like such a quaint pursuit all of those years ago.

The engine had been running for quite some time; not only did it need to run for the cloaking device to remain engaged, but it's also rather difficult to prevent a matter/antimatter fusion reaction from occurring once the switch is flipped and the magnetic containment on; to do so could end the Earth as we know it!

This is all a roundabout way of noting that I didn't have to turn any kind of ignition, which was, in hindsight, perhaps a bit of a design flaw. No, instead, I merely spoke a quick command to the computer, and shifted the mechanism into gear, which caused the dash to produce one of my finer creations; the omni-yoke. When controlling a craft that is unbound by traditional physics and can travel in literally any direction, a simple joystick just will not do, as it's far too "two-dimensional" to control something that requires a third (and fourth, as we shall see) dimensional input. Nor would a traditional airplane yoke be able to fully realise the amazingly acrobatic maneuvers of which this craft was capable; it relies far too heavily on momentum and other concepts, which have no bearing on my time machine, unbound by the restraints of bothersome gravity.

As loathe as I am to admit it, the answer to this problem lies in holograms. The omni-yoke is a horizontal representation of a ball floating in the middle of a cubical grid. Simply "grab" the ball and move it in whatever direction you want the ship to go, and the ship follows suit. In this way, you can make the craft travel in straight, zig-zagging lines, or wide, regular arcs in any direction; the choice is entirely up to the driver. Though I agree that I generally prefer to control a vehicle by some means physically attached to the craft on the rare occasions where the government hasn't legislated such simple joys as "driving oneself" out of existence due to the supposed "safety" of self-driving vehicles, the omni-yoke was the only discernible way to deal with the rather complex problem of controlling the craft. Besides, I wasn't nearly as concerned with "where" the ship was going as "when," a factor that would solely be controlled by the touchscreen consoles located comfortably nearby.

One half of the screens flashed with the current time and location. The other contained a simple "dial" imprinted on the OLED screen, which I could manipulate clockwise and anti-clockwise to adjust the date that was imprinted above. Though I hadn't much time for television over the past decade or so (as most of my free time was occupied with turn of the century American cinema—one thing the Yanks actually do well), I'd be lying if I said that *Star Trek: The Next Generation* wasn't an inspiration for the panel designs, both in color scheme and font (SWISS 911 Ultra Compressed BT, if you must know).

I turned the digital knob anti-clockwise and the years ticked away, slowly at first, and then more quickly as the "dial" built up "momentum." Somewhere behind the panel, the quantum computer performed an amazing number of calculations per second to flesh out the position of the Earth, not only within the solar system, but also accounting for progression relative to Earth's gravity well. I'm sure this is all terribly boring to some of you, but it's wonderfully fascinating to me, so bugger off.

I slowed the rotation of the dial as it approached the single digits, then fine-tuned the date to "31 A.D." A map of the world flashed in the bottom left corner of the display, and I pinched to zoom in to the Middle East. Another thing I'm terribly proud of; I (or I should say I guided the quantum computer to figure out how to—and, to be fair, that likely goes for far more of these discoveries than I give the stupid thing credit for) even programmed the little map to account for continental drift should the need arise.

I selected "Nazareth" and the edges of the screen pulsed with light (it's a better "busy" indicator than a flipping hourglass). The upper right corner scrolled through numbers with a prominent percent sign at the end, and after several moments settled on one single number:

"99.9%"

These were the odds of successfully plotting a course to that exact date and time. And why shouldn't it be so high? After all, I had designed the damned thing with that moment and those coordinates in mind. Those were the very calculations that the computer was calibrated around—in fact, I was more than a bit peeved at that missing ".1%."

I eyed the bright red "Engage" button that appeared in the middle of the console. *Is this really it? The moment that my entire life has been building toward?* I thought. I gather it's what most footballers feel on the eve of…whatever the big football championship is…"Euros" or some such thing. Never been much of a fan of sport.

I realised that I was squinting, and produced a pair of contact lenses from the glovebox. I hated the dastardly things, as will become apparent later, but needed them to see, so poor was my eyesight without correction. I wrangled with them for several minutes before I finally jammed the plastic discs onto my eyes, and was able to see once more, albeit uncomfortably.

I went through one final mental checklist. *Coordinates…supplies… guns…door…* The door! I hastily re-opened the glove box and pulled out a rather archaic-looking bodge of a garage-door opener. Though such devices had long since been integrated with smartphones or vehicles themselves, my preference for tactile feedback led me to have workmen install a rather simple retractable ceiling on my workshop, complete with a motor and chains. I pressed the large button, and the ceiling rolled off of the building to expose the clear Maryland sky above. I could only see a sliver of the starry night from my current vantage point, but I found the sight to be simultaneously ominous and intoxicating, like the first whiff of insanely expensive scotch while on holiday in Las Vegas.

I picked up my tablet, which was synched up with the craft, and with a few swipes of my finger, selected a fitting soundtrack for this first flight: *The Rolling Stones'* "Start Me Up." It was between that and *Steppenwolf's* "Born to Be Wild," but in case of a tie, my British heritage was always going to be the determinant.

As Mick Jagger's voice strained in the background, I buckled myself into the seat and hit the bright red button with a flourish. The cloaking device disengaged (as much power as an antimatter reaction may provide, I am confident telling you that it's not enough to both cloak the ship and travel through time), while the window in front of me paradoxically appeared to expand to the ceiling above, though this, too, was an illusion, as the saucer would appear solidly metallic from the exterior (provided all systems were nominal).

The ship took off and floated upward, casually as a cloud meandering through the stratosphere. Though the inertial dampeners should make such a feeling impossible, I still imagined I could sense the floor begin to rotate in one direction as the top portion of the saucer rotated opposite. For a few blissful moments, I looked upward and saw the starry night sky, with so many orbs that hung so tantalizingly close. With any luck, I'd be able to re-jigger the time machine for reliable interstellar travel within a decade of my return, but that would be a project for another day.

Suddenly, the craft shot straight up in the air at an incredible rate of speed. It was all that the machinery could do to keep my body together until the artificial gravity could compensate. It must have been quite a sight in the greater Baltimore area, though I may have failed to mention that the craft wasn't exactly FAA-legal; though it had running lights, I had turned them off for the time-being, lest some slack-jawed yokel report a UFO sighting in the vicinity of my lab. I swiped a finger across one of the consoles and two displays came into focus on the window; one nightvision, the other infrared. Either would be enough to fly the ship.

Eventually, the deep navy blue of the sky and the whisping clouds that parted as I zoomed by were replaced by a stark blackness with specks of brilliant, twinkling white light. Though I had always dreamt of being an astronaut, I could now truthfully say for the first time that I was one, and in a way that no human being had ever experienced before…unless one would count my ostensible rematerialisation in ancient Judea, as it would, by necessity, have to have occurred at some point in the past.

The time machine hovered at the edge of the Earth's gravitational envelope for a moment and re-calibrated before I piloted the craft to a safe distance away from the planet below.

The mechanics involved in time travel are obviously incredibly complex, as I'm sure anyone reading this book can imagine. For the uninitiated or slow-witted, though, perhaps the best way to explain how it works is by way of an analogy. Imagine that the known universe is a simple, cardboard coffee cup. Inside of that cup is boiling hot tea (I refuse to use coffee just to give a proper "bugger off" to the Yanks reading this), just sitting there, for our purposes relatively static in any one location, but always pushing up against the sides of the cup.

The mechanism that I devised uses the gravity drive and tunneling lasers as a "stirrer" of sorts; as an artificial gravity semi-singularity (a temporary almost-black hole, to the layman) spins spacetime, and draws it inward, the result is that the very fabric of spacetime itself is brought closer together, like two points on a tablecloth that are drawn nearer when the cloth is formed into a cone.

Amazingly enough, though one may think that such an arrangement would make interstellar travel all the simpler, due to the vagaries of how space and time are arranged, before one can build up enough gravity to travel long distances, the lasers create a rip in the fabric of spacetime. Depending on the force of the singularity, its

16

location, the intensity of the lasers, et cetera and so forth, I (or the computer and I) can pinpoint the exact date and position in the universe to which a given rift will lead, give or take one tenth of one percent.

Another "button" came up on the console, this one brilliant and green. The words "Time Shift" flashed in futuristic lettering above it. The take-off hadn't really given me pause; after all, I had fleshed out the advanced "normal" physics of the whole thing years ago, and checked them and re-checked them numerous times.

The time travel physics were so utterly new that I had to trust the quantum computer to re-check my work, and ensure that everything on board was in working order. Classic cinema buff that I am, I couldn't help it as visions of HAL from *2001: A Space Odyssey* danced in my head, though I always imagined the "QC" as a wise-ass Irishman; not the cold, calculating serial-killer type, but that's neither here nor there.

I closed my eyes and braced my jaw for an impact that never came as I lowered my finger to the blinking green button.

And that's the last time anyone from my time, my home, cared about Phineas Templeton.

CHAPTER TWO

Travelling through a temporal wormhole is initially a thoroughly wondrous and invigorating process. On the one hand, that first wormhole represented a tangible manifestation of decades of hard work. On the other, it's fantastically beautiful; colours that I've never seen before on this planet jumped out at the ship as it passed by as if trying to impart hue and tenor to the well-brushed alloy, succeeding only for brief flashes against the reflected light of billions of stars.

On the third hand, my knuckles lodged themselves in the ends of the armrests as I nearly messed my pants with terror.

Eventually the chromatic operetta outside of the craft ceased as I cautiously opened one wrenched eye, then another. In front of me, little larger than the bottom of a pint glass, was the same Earth that I had just vacated, though the shimmering lights of cities and satellites had disappeared. No, this was a new, virginal Earth, unpocked by centuries of man's influence.

"And I'm about to run a hand up her skirt." I said to no one in particular.

Not by plowing into the planet at full speed or causing some kind of environmental catastrophe, mind you, but rather I felt dirty by simply *being* there, in a time where I didn't belong. My capacity for disrupting the time stream was at that time virtually limitless, and I was determined to prevent myself from blinking...myself...and countless others out of existence with a wayward glance or a poorly-timed fart.

I pushed the button on the console to activate the omni-yoke, and guided the craft back toward the blue orb that hung in front of me. As inexperienced as I was with the damned contraption, I managed to stutter the ship along with several jolts punctuated by abrupt stops.

Once I had guided the ship in range, the computer once again took over, and the ride became significantly smoother. I watched as entire continents soared by, first the Americas ("watch out for those ruinous Europeans!" I wanted to cry, half in jest), followed by the Continent and Africa beneath it. Just to the right and above was my target, the Middle East, still sporting the Arabian Peninsula as the light brown rhinoceros head looking to butt into India (at least that's what I always thought it looked like).

Thankfully, I had enough power available to engage the cloaking device as I descended above the harsh, craggy Judean landscape, dotted only by the odd tree or two.

*It looks so…dusty…*was my first thought.

My second was that I should have added sunscreen to the glove box.

Finally, as I saw the mud-baked houses and clear blue sky, my mind came to terms with what I had just accomplished.

I had become the first time traveller in human history!

What a mind-boggling feat, but one so befitting all of the hard work and sacrifice I had put in to that point! It had worked, and done so beautifully. Gone was the horrendous fallout and bombed-out landscape. The tan rocks looked positively *pristine* compared with what I had come to associate with this part of the world.

The only remaining question was how accurate I had been.

I looked for an out-of-the-way cave that could accommodate the time machine, but couldn't find one. I settled instead for an out-of-the-way patch of desert several hundred yards from the nearest town; I presumed that a cluster of trees would be unnecessary for cover, and might only attract more visitors seeking shade from the unforgiving sun.

I could barely contain my excitement! Eager to leave, I had to remind myself to bring a number of coins from my "Roman" cache with which to barter. I thought for a moment before I decided to keep the Baretta on my person, though, in hindsight, by doing so I disregarded all of the fears and lectures about timeline pollution that my Benefactor had impressed upon me.

It turned out those were to be the least of my worries.

Satisfied that I had enough supplies to last me until the evening, I made my way to the exit of the craft. I inhaled deeply and took my first step into a new era.

I wonder what Neil Armstrong thought? was all that ran through my head at the time.

I practically skipped from the craft to the walls of the city, so giddy was I to finally make contact with some of the locals, time stream pollution be damned. The village consisted of a large central square, which gave way to a larger, central building, where a bustling throng of people milled about. I was astonished to find that I stuck out like a dislocated elbow due to my height; I towered over the denizens despite being only slightly above-average in height in my own time. My stature drew several gawks from passers-by, which threw me into a momentary panic; what if my presence was already affecting the timeline?

I darted into an alleyway between two shops and eyed the rest of the square. A somewhat smaller building stood next door to the impressive one, and counted many children of various ages among its patronage. Around the edges of the square, shopkeeps' cries created an awful din of hard "ch" sounds, followed by streams of words that were even unintelligible to me despite my hyper vigilance and Aramaic-slash-Hebrew lessons.

Beyond the shops, several layers of decrepit houses completed what I must admit was a rather unimpressive scene, topped by the horrific smell of a mass of humanity and free-flowing sewage baked into the ground by the unrelenting sun that seemed to be omnipresent in this town, a scent which even now causes me to gag.

It was then that the realisation struck me: this might not be where Jesus ben Joseph was at all.

20

He could be hundreds of miles away, ministering to masses in another similarly foul-smelling town. To compound matters, the residents of this city may not even know who Jesus was, nor ever had any contact with the man. Judaism, though a respected cult, tolerated by the Romans at the time, was still that; a cult. There was no guarantee that this was a Jewish town. I began to sweat as much from the midday sun as from the epiphany that I may be staring down a long, arduous process of trial-and-error.

To make matters worse, as I gained my bearings, a particularly gruff-looking denizen covered in warts emptied a chamber-pot all over my feet, without apparent regard for any form of decorum or standards.

"Slikha?!" I yelled the Hebrew word for "sorry" at the man, momentarily forgetting my Aramaic; thankfully I didn't lapse into the King's. The warty fellow glared at me, one eye swollen shut by some awful disease, the other maddeningly open and round, as if to balance his awful, pock-marked face.

"Raaaugh," was the approximate "harrumph" that he made at me, and continued on his way.

Add Purell to the "day pack," I thought.

I shuffled my shit-covered feet through the dust to soak up some of the slime as I made my way to the crowd gathered around the large, impressive building. As I approached it, I made out a large Star of David carved into the exterior, and I knew I was in luck.

"It MUST be Nazareth!" I thought aloud, sadly in the King's, hopefully only a whisper among the din of the shops.

There were few entirely Jewish enclaves at this point in Roman history. Fewer still had this many people shoved into such a small space, owing to the fact that the city was located near more populated cities in Galilee. The combination of the large synagogue and throngs of people indicated that I had found my intended target, after all. Or I should say that the QC had found it.

My hopes renewed, I looked to the mob gathered around the front of the temple, but only found an older Rabbi giving a sermon in Aramaic. The Son of God was nowhere to be found.

Frustrated, I decided to make my way to one of the shops along the fringe of the square to ask about the Son of God's whereabouts. I'm actually rather proud of myself that the first shop I thought of stopping at was a finished wooden goods store; after all, whom better to ask regarding the whereabouts of a carpenter?

I ducked through the doorway, guarded only by a coarsely-woven cloth, and emerged in a dark room filled with chairs, cribs, and all manner of furniture. The shopkeep was (of course) short and bald. A well-worn robe covered his stocky frame, and a disheveled beard framed his rotund face. Despite the lack of hair atop his head, I thought that he bore more than a passing resemblance to Avi, and wondered if the two may have been related.

"May I help you?" The shopkeep asked in Aramaic (I'll translate to appropriate English phrasing from this point onward).

"Thou tellst me, fair shopkeep, what town doth I have the pleasure of enchanting?" (Avi's skills, though unparalleled for the time, may not have been as practical in dealing with actual ancient Aramaic-speakers).

This garnered a raised eyebrow from the shopkeep.

"Nazareth."

I strained to hide the smile that begged to cross my face. I approached the counter at the far end of the room.

"Yay, thou seest. Doth thy know one carpenter, goeth by the name Jesus ben Joseph?" The shopkeep replied with a blank stare.

I began to wonder if such inquiries were handled in much the same manner then as they are now. I fumbled with the purse attached to my belt for several moments before I produced one of the faux-patinaed, Roman coins and flung it cooly at the shopkeep.

The shopkeep picked up the coin and eyed it for a few moments before he turned it over. A foul, bothered look washed over the man's face as he eyed me again, though this time with far more disgust.

In one motion, the man flung the coin back at me, spit in my face, grabbed my hand, and brought up a scimitar, which hovered over my outstretched forearm.

"Blasphemer!" The man yelled at me. My pulse beat like a terrified drum inside my head as my mouth went dry. I tried to pull my hand away, but the stout fellow was surprisingly strong for his size and would not relent. I squirmed and may or may not have let out a bit of a shriek in a moment of rushed terror.

"Easy, Yacob!" An easy-going, but firm voice stopped the sword dead in its tracks.

I turned around, fully expecting to see that a kindly Roman soldier had saved my hide.

Instead, it was a spindly fellow, perhaps a bit taller even than I, who looked pale, but handsome in a way that no one else I had seen to this point had. His beard was shaggy, but still much better-groomed than the shopkeep's. What stuck out most were his teeth, as white and straight as two rows of chicklets, and the kind, almost intoxicating smile on his face. And suddenly it all came together:

"Jesus Christ," I muttered, almost under my breath.

CHAPTER THREE

"What's it to you, Yeshua? This man uses blasphemous money!" The shopkeep kept his grip on my hand, but picked up the coin (while somehow maintaining hold of the scimitar) and flung it at the Son of God.

Jesus eyed the coin for a moment before he looked at me intently. He moved around me a number of times and even took the fabric of my clothing between his fingers for several seconds. He turned his back to the shopkeep and raised an eyebrow before he cocked his head downward, toward his midsection.

I followed the cue, and saw his left hand separated into three parts, an outstretched thumb, with pointer and middle fingers joined together, and ring and pinky forming a third digit.

The Vulcan "Live Long and Prosper" sign from Star Trek? I thought.

The look on my face must've been suitably blank, as Jesus furrowed his brow and his mouth went taut with annoyance. He affixed a rather phony grin to his visage as he turned toward the shopkeep.

"Worry not, dear Yacob—a Roman traveler who knows not our customs. I shall teach him our ways and ensure that such a misunderstanding does not occur again."

"You had better," the shopkeep spat the words at me, "lest this Roman dog's HAND be cast asunder from his arm!"

Jesus shook his head, "He is a child of God, my son. Same as any Israelite or beggar, and as such so deserves our pity."

The shopkeep looked over the Son of Man suspiciously before he broke into a broad smile.

"Indeed you are right, Yeshua. Go, take your Roman dog and 'enlighten' him as to our ways."

"Thank you, dear Yacob, for being so understanding." Jesus nodded at me slowly, urging me to take the hint.

"Thankest thou, fair shopkeep, for not splitting mine arm in twain—" Jesus interrupted my clumsy attempt at gratitude by grabbing me under my arm and dragging me from the shop around the corner into the alleyway. I was caught between the natural urge to run away from such discomport and my state of general awe at being pulled by the Son of Man.

"Dude, what the *fuck*?"

I tilted my head. I thought the words had come from the man who was presently dragging me, in English, plain as day.

No, no, must be a trick of the ear, you dolt, I thought. *Be more careful lest you let such an utterance escape the confines of your own mind!*

Jesus pulled me into a doorway, which led to a simple mud room. Various wooden devices were scattered about that made the room look like an Inquisition-era torture chamber, a sentiment that was not lost on my sense of irony. The spindly carpenter placed me in one of the dozen-or-so chairs that dotted the dwelling and pulled over another seat to face me.

"DO...YOU...SPEAK...ENGLISH?" Jesus asked slowly, with the intonation of a California surfer.

I was stunned. I had no idea how to respond to such an inquiry. For so long, I had geared up for having a long, drawn-out conversation in what now appeared to be "Old Aramaic," that the words hit me like a brick to the face.

"Uh...hablas Español? No, wait...I should probably use the formal Usted—" Jesus continued.

"You...you speak ENGLISH?" My eyes bulged from their sockets with the question.

"Uh, duh, bro," he looked at *me* incredulously. "What the hell is ChronoSaber thinking? I mean, your costume is *terrible*—the

25

headdress is simply atrocious! And those sandals! But the coins—that shit could get someone killed."

"I *beg* your pardon?"

He flipped a coin at me, which was identical to the one I had used, save for a smooth side where the Emperor's face had been.

"It's not cool to use money with the Emperor's face on it in a Jewish town, bro. Something to do with 'worshipping false idols,' or some bullshit like that. Did they, like, *want* you to die?"

He let the words sink in for a moment before he rose from his chair and walked over to a nightstand-like creation, which featured several warped planks and irregular nails, and pulled it over next to him, "Look, I know, I know, I have a bunch of fans," Jesus opened the drawer and took out a glossy sheet of paper. He produced a Sharpie from one of the drawers and scrawled a signature over it quickly before he threw the headshot at me. "Here you go. Man, those ChronoSaber guys were such hard-asses when *I* came back, but now I guess they let any old asshole jump in a time machine."

As he continued to lecture me (*he lectured* ME*! About* time travel*!*), I began to sweat profusely. The beads pooled on my forehead and sent a shiver down my neck.

"You're a...you're a...you're a *time traveller?*"

Jesus rolled his eyes, "Uh...yeah man. Isn't that why you're here, too?"

I struggled to compose myself, "Well good man, then today *you* are the one in good luck, for I am none other than Phineas Templeton, the father of time travel!" I raised my right hand reflexively as I built toward the apex of my proclamation. "And though I may not have any 'head shots,' though I should *certainly* look into getting some, I suppose, it is my great pleasure to meet someone so touched by my creation." I stretched a lean hand out toward the man, with as broad of a smile as I could muster at the moment.

He looked me over once more before he shook his head, "Naw. No way, man."

"What? What the devil do you mean?"

"You're not Commander Corcoran."

"Commander *who?*" I felt the colour drain from my face.

"Sorry bro, you're like, way too gangly to be him. Good try, though—you had me going for a minute. Nobody ever tried that one on me before."

"Now see here, sir, would you take me for a li—"

"Whoa, whoa, calm down, bud," he took me by the shoulders and sat me in one of the (I must say in hindsight: poorly-crafted) chairs. He sat facing me, "Now what did you say your name was again?"

"Phineas Templeton," I ground the words out through clenched teeth. "Who the hell are *you?*"

"Name's Trent," he stuck his hand out. I grasped it only out of bred English politeness. "Trent Albertson. Originally from Denver, but I've spent the past…oh, I don't know…ten? Twelve? Fifteen? How long has it been?" I could virtually see the cannabis smoke waft across the interior of his head through his pupils. "Anyway, you probably know the story, right?"

"Refresh my memory," I hoped my glare suitably conveyed my level of frustration.

"Dude, seriously? Wow, I haven't been asked this in a while. Let's see…" he looked up at the ceiling for several uncomfortable moments as if hoping that the answer to my simple question might just fall from the sky and rattle around whatever remained of his brain. "I…uh…well…hmm…" he snorted once, "I was at school in Boulder for like, *ten* years, man…oh yeah! So, like time-travel had just been de-regulated, and I—"

"De-regulated time travel?!" I couldn't help but interrupt.

"Yeah man," Jesus…sorry, "Trent" said.

"But what of the timeline? What the devil have you done—are we doing to it? Have we changed all of history? Did the Nazis win the war? Is there even a future to which I can return?" My chest tightened and heaved with deep, choking breaths as the distinct possibility that I had, to use a scientific term, "royally fucked things up," lodged itself in my mind.

Trent nodded, "Slow down, bro—everything's fine. The Nazis were still dicks and we still beat them."

27

My pulse slowed measurably. "Ah...well...that's a relief," I said far too awkwardly. "But how is that possi—"

"It's like," Trent preempted my question, "It's like the ChronoSaber guys explained to me—whatever happened, like *happened* already, you know?"

I made sure that my stare informed Trent that I most certainly did not.

"Okay, think of it this way; what year are you from?"

"2032," I replied tersely.

"Right on. Great year." He looked at me with a blank veneer.

"Please, good sir, to the secrets of the universe," I tried to spur him on.

"Sure thing, bro. So, after Commander Corcoran came back from his first time jump, it started to become clear that nothing had changed. At least, that's what Commander Corcoran said. Everything was exactly as he had left it, no matter what he did, and this was, like, *vericified* by everyone that came after him. Whatever happened...*happened*."

My head swirled as I began to feel faint, though not at Trent's malapropism, "So you're telling me that the timeline is *static* throughout history?"

"Eh, naw, it's pretty clear, at least by 2038, where I'm from," he said, his expression hopelessly vacant. "But no matter what any of the time travelers did, they would always come back to their time. They did all kindsa stuff to make sure they were right; they sent back stuff, buried it, and dug it up in the future. They took camcorders to make sure that the time travelers did what they said they were doing, but in the end, nothing changed. History was as it always, like, *was*."

I cocked my head to the side, "So, you're telling me that whatever happened happened?"

Trent nodded proudly, "You're getting it, man!"

"So you're telling me that if I were to *kill* you, right here, right now, history wouldn't change at all?"

Trent was unfazed by my morbid thinking aloud, "No way, bro. *Something* would stop you from doing it. Either you couldn't bear to do it, or a legionnaire would appear out of nowhere to stop you, or maybe you like, just…die before I do then. No matter what, it doesn't happen that way."

"But…I mean…you *do* realise…" I struggled for words before I decided to go another direction. "So how *exactly* did you become *Jesus Christ?!*"

Trent grinned, "Riiiight! So I was at Boulder, on a bit of an 'extended studies' plan since the old man was—"

"The old man?" I hoped perhaps he was referring to my Benefactor.

"You know—my dad? Pops? Anyway, pops is…was…will be…whatever…footing the bill, so I could afford to be a little…picky…as far as my major was concerned. I tried a bunch of stuff; earth sciences, theater, film studies, and even hard stuff like anthropology and history. But all of them just so epically *blew.*

"Then one day, in year like seven or nine or whatever, I saw this totally *slammin'* chick, killer bod, you know? Ass like an Indian drum—"

I cleared my throat.

"Sorry, bro, *Native American* drum," Trent replied. "Anyway, so I follow this smoking hot girl to her next class, and lo and behold, it was Aramaic. Now, I know what you're thinking—"

You have no possible way to fathom, I thought. *No concept, not even a shred of—*

"I don't seem like the 'academic type.' Well, this girl's name was Madison, and I totally got in good with her, you know, on a personal tutoring basis." I couldn't help but roll my eyes. "Turns out she was actually pretty smart and…uh…good at teaching Aramaic, too and stuff. I graduated with a degree in Ancient Linguistics a few years ago.

"Unfortunately, it's like, kinda tough to get a job with that degree, given, you know, the war and everything. So I decided to stick around Boulder and get my masters.

"Then, like my second year of my masters, the government decided to de-regulate time travel. And I thought that was totally, you know, cool and stuff. And this was before all of the historical tourism and stuff, so *I* came up with the idea: what if I went back in time and just *lived*? And then one night, I fired up the Brainenator, and—"

"The Brainenator?" I interrupted.

Trent stood up and walked over to the far left corner of the room and removed a worn, dirty linen cloth from along the floor, revealing an enormous cannabis water pipe contraption, as that's the only way I can explain it.

"The Brainenator, bro—you know, 'cuz it—" he hoisted an imaginary automatic weapon to his hip and "rattled off" a few imaginary rounds, "totally terminates brain cells, but in a good way. Anyway, my buddies and I were rockin' this thing one night, and we were talking about time travel and we thought, 'wouldn't it be kinda cool to go back and like *be* somebody? Like, you know, take over for them, like their *life* and stuff?"

I marveled at the man's articulation. "So you formed the basis for an entirely new industry while smoking copious amounts of cannabis with your degenerate friends one evening?"

"Exactly!" Trent lit up.

"So then why Jesus Christ Himself?" I asked.

"Well, you know, I've always admired his...*my*...gentle way, and how he preached love and not war, and how he was just a cool dude about the meek inheriting the Earth and all that stuff. So that's cool. Plus I'm one of the few people that knew Aramaic, before the holotran came about, and—"

I cringed at the thought of asking for another explanation from this stoned hooligan.

"Holotran?" I could barely force myself to croak out.

"Yeah bro, the holotran, the patch that you put on your neck that translates what you're saying and what you hear into whatever language you want, and synchs up a hologram with your mouth to make it look like you're speaking the same language the other person is speaking? God—" he sighed with exasperation. "You really *are* from way back in the past, aren't you?

"Anyway," now *he* rolled *his* eyes. At me! "I knew the language, and I figured that I kind of looked like Jesus, at least the pictures I had seen and stuff, so I conned dad into loaning me some money for 'books' or 'housing' or something like that and went to the ChronoSaber branch office in Denver, and signed up to come back here, and so here I am."

I rested my elbow on my knee, and my chin on my hand, unconsciously forming the "Thinker" pose.

"So what happened to the *real* Jesus?" I asked.

Trent shook his head, "You're looking at him. He's me."

"No, you dolt—not *you*, the *real* one, the man whom you have replaced."

He beamed, "That's the beauty of it—there wasn't one! Some of these poor dudes and chicks go back in time and have to try to kidnap the guy or chick they want to replace, or even try to kill them, but that's always a risk because the universe sometimes has, like, its own ideas about stuff. People go back in time and disappear, never heard from again. Somebody gets to them before they can do what they want to do, or they flash around too much cash and get robbed and left in the gutter. Or, this one's kinda popular now, the dinosaur eats *them*, and they don't get to have, like, a stegosaurus dinner and come home with their T-Rex trophy."

I didn't even want to touch the last one for the moment.

"So you're telling me that there never was a Jesus of Nazareth before you? No manger scene, no virgin birth, nothing of the sort?"

Trent shook his head, "Nope. Well...actually, sort of, if you mean that I tell them that stuff happened."

"Huh?" My head began to throb.

"Like, it's like I say it happened, so it happened, you know?" He opened the drawer with the headshots again and pulled out a leather-bound, hotel bible. "This is the perfect script, you know. I just, like, do what the book says for the most part. Except for that forty days in the desert part—that's fucking bullshit, man. I just went off to Sepphoris and relaxed for a while, and told everyone here that I had, like wandered around the desert for forty days."

"But that's a paradox!" I shot out of my chair and turned away from Trent.

"No, man—it's how it happened!"

I walked over to Trent, picked up the Bible, and shook it vigorously at his face.

"You are *writing* the Bible by *reading* the Bible! Where did the idea come from in the first place? Thin air? It's a chicken-or-the-egg paradox! It simply can't be!"

Trent laughed, "And yet here we are! Look, I don't pretend to be a physi…physi…physics guy," he frowned. "But all I know is that they said it's fine to bring whatever I want, and do whatever I want. And it's not like I'm gunning down people. I'm improving lives, performing miracles, for *my* sake! Now, granted, most of it is like technology and stuff, but whatever, I'm making a difference, and for good!"

"But…the water into wine?"

"Technology. Micro amino-acid synthesizer or something like that. Got it at Williams Sonoma."

"The loaves into fishes?"

"Same deal."

"Healing the sick? The lame? Raising the *dead*?"

Trent laughed, "Dude, that's like the *easiest* thing, bro! Modern medicine is *so* far advanced compared to bleeding and leeches and shit. And I don't even know if they're that far along yet; all I know is one medigel or even a few Advil and these people think that I'm the Messiah."

"Medi-what?" I asked.

Trent opened the drawer and tossed me a packet of greenish goo, with a red cross imprinted on the side.

"Medigel. This stuff's the fu—this stuff's the *bomb*, man. Heals anything: cuts, infections, even like broken bones and stuff. It's, like, a disinfectant combined with something that, like, focuses your body's own healing mechanisms and shit. Totally awesome. Go ahead—keep that one. I have tons of the stuff."

I pocketed the souvenir as I furrowed my brow, "So you're a Charlatan! An utter fraud?"

Trent shook his head, "I *am* Jesus, bro. I help people, I do heal the sick, I do all of the good stuff. Why's it such a bad thing that I'm from the future?"

"You parade around as the Son of God, for one thing," I shot at him.

"But aren't we *all* sons of God? Daughters of God? That's Jesus's message in a nutshell, and now it's, like, mine too."

"Let me ask you this, though, Mr. Albertson—"

"Whoa bro—Trent, please. Mr. Albertson is my father."

"Uh…yes…Trent…aren't there other individuals that would later have the same idea that you did? That would try to come back in time and kill *you* and take *your* spot as Christ?"

Trent laughed, "I guess so, but for whatever reason, that's how the universe shook out this time. I *am* Jesus. If anyone else had come back to try to be Jesus before me, then, like, something happened to them. If they would come here *now*, then something would happen to them. I know it's a mindfuck, but that's the way the universe operates—there's something totally *elegant* and *awesome* about it, don't you think?"

"But that's my point—history remembers it as—"

"Ultimately, however history remembers it is how it happened, from the future dude's point of view."

I was caught off guard by the harsh poeticism of the man's statement.

"So history …*doesn't* remember me then?"

He shook his head, "Sorry man, can't say it does. Maybe you decided to live your life here with me for the rest of your days. I only have like ten apostles right now—that means there are a couple of openings left…"

The day I follow this wretched asshole is the day I'd just as soon go back and be eaten by a dinosaur!, I thought.

"No, thank you," I said. Damn my British manners!

"Well, anyway, maybe you found another time to chill in, or destroyed your machine for all of the '*evil*' you think it can do. Maybe you decided to jump ahead of my time, though that can be, like, a problem."

"What in the hell do you mean?" I asked, my eyes narrowed.

"Well...it's like this," he sat down and motioned for me to re-take my seat, which I did. "It's not always just so easy to get to go exactly where—when—you want to go, especially over long stretches of time."

"But that's impossible! I designed the program myself, the quantum computer will—"

"Again, I'm like, not a computer guy, but quantum computers have some limitations, as you know. It turns out that even in *my* time, a few years after yours, quantum computers throw a wrench in the works sometimes. They use like, probability and stuff to make calculations, but whatever genius set up the things didn't properly account for...uh...'frame of reference,' or something like that, whenever they coded it out or whatever. So the further you go back or forward in time, the wonkier things get, and the lower the chance that you end up where you want to."

My heart sank into my bowels. *Of course.* It was the one variable for which I hadn't accounted. My Benefactor was so adamant that I get the machine ready to go to *this time*, this one specific moment, that I hadn't considered the cascading effect of multiple quantum computer calculations on one another! How could I be so *stupid?*

To put it in relatively understandable terms for the layperson, think of the space-time continuum as a pond, and time travel as a rock cast into that pond. After the rock enters the pond, though you may be able to see the ripples on the surface, you have no real idea of where the rock ended up under the water. The ripples give you an approximation of where the rock is, but the quantum computer itself is an imperfect device that relies on some assumptions. The further you throw the rock, the more likely it is that it ended up somewhere away from the initial ripples, and the less the quantum computer has to go on to get you safely back to your time period.

I had made it safely to the year 31 A.D. because I had programmed the computer to get me to this point in time. Sadly, even the short time I had already spent in this period would have an adverse effect on the computer's ability to return me home.

It was so clear now, but I damned my haste and my willingness to blindly follow my Benefactor's advice; though I can't recall whether I questioned his intentions at that moment, at some point it became clear that perhaps his own motives may be to blame for my not receiving proper credit for the invention of time-travel.

"Yeah, it kind of sucks, bro. ChronoSaber has the most advanced computers ever, and even then they can only give you an idea of when and where you'll end up, and a percentage of likelihood of success. My chance to get back was supposed to be a month ago or so, and they said it would be, like, eighty percent, or something like that. Bastards never showed."

He sighed, "That's why I'm just going to stick around and ride this one out. Who knows if I'd be able to ever make it back? There's another chance for me to hitch a ride in India, but it's like decades away."

My eyes bulged, "So you're going to *die* on the cross?"

Trent nodded, "Yeah, I suppose so. Though," he pulled another package of the fluorescent turquoise goop out of the drawer and held it up, "I think the resurrection is going to be pretty *epic*, bro."

I put my head in my hands. Here I was, facing eternity damned to wonder through time, searching for my way home like Dr. Samuel fucking Beckett on *Quantum Leap* (though sadly it didn't appear as if I'd enjoy many of his sexual exploits, nor did I particularly care to with any of our shorter, more troll-like and disease-ridden ancestors).

I stood up and offered a curt smile toward Jesus, "Thank you for your hospitality, sir, but I simply must get going."

"What's the rush, man? After all, you did, like, invent time travel, right?"

I considered backhanding the Son of God in the face.

"That may be, but I've clearly made a mistake, and I must simply be going. Another wasted minute and I may never be able to return home."

"Whoa, whoa, whoa—slow down, bro." Trent clasped a hand on my shoulder. "You need to *relax*. So your time machine may not make it all the way back right now. Big deal, man. Learn to *enjoy* the past, enjoy the *ride*, man. If you want to do something interesting, then do it. If you spend the rest of your life trying to create a perfect wormhole to make it to *just* the right time, what good is that going to do? What good is it to live life if it's a life with no purpose other than an end?"

Again, I reeled from the stoner's apparent poeticism. *You know what, though? He might be right, Finn,* I thought. *You've spent two solid decades building this damned thing. Why not enjoy it a little? Why not visit your heroes and some important time periods along the way?*

And suddenly, I had an idea.

"My dear Christ," I said, as I clasped an arm around Jesus. "You said that getting exactly where I wanted to go could be problematic for the quantum computer, correct?"

"Yeah. Totally."

"But even though the computer relies on probability to create some of its calculations, some destinations will be easier to reach than others, correct?"

Trent smiled, "Yeah bro—that's exactly right."

"So indulge me for a moment—might there be a way for the quantum computer to chart a course through several different time periods, each jump alone highly probable, but designed to ultimately arrive me at my home time period?"

I looked at Trent, but he had already cast his eyes skyward.

"Uh…sure, man. Whatever. Like I said, I'm not really a computer guy. I don't think ChronoSaber does that sort of thing, but hey, if you *did* invent time-travel, then maybe you could, like, be smarter than them…and stuff."

I beamed, finally happy to hear what came out of the degenerate's mouth. I stuck out my hand.

"Wondrous! I mean, wonder*ful*! Thank you Trent...err...Jesus—"

"Whatever," he shrugged and offered his own smile. "Thank *you*, man—you've, like, totally blown my mind."

"Quite. Cheerio." I took a couple of brisk steps toward the doorframe before I turned back to Jesus once more. "One other thing; when I first came here, you flashed me the Vulcan 'Live Long and Prosper' sign from *Star Trek*."

Trent grinned, "Yeah bro."

"What's that all about?"

"Well, you see, ChronoSaber had to come up with a way for time travelers to recognize each other if they cross paths in the past, you know, so we can look out for each other and stuff. They settled on the Vulcan symbol for some reason—I don't know, maybe because, like, it's new and recognizable and stuff. Anyway, if someone flashes that at you," he winked and gave me a thumbs up while making an odd clicking/sucking sound with his mouth, "you're *golden*."

I couldn't help but smile. At least these "ChronoSaber" folks involved *Star Trek* in these bizarre expeditions in some manner. It was heartening to know that such a quaint little show could serve as such an inspiration across time.

I nodded at Trent. "Indeed. Thank you, Jesus."

"Later bro," the Son of Man replied.

CHAPTER FOUR

I returned to the time machine in the hopes of getting back to work straight-away, and solving this mess created by the "what happened, happened," conception of time that Toasted Trent Albertson (nee "Jesus Christ") had leveled upon me.

Before I started, though, I fancied myself a swallow of scotch and a cup of tea, though I struggled with my preferred order of taking down each beverage for several moments. Eventually, the scotch won out (it always does, doesn't it?) and I removed the bottle of Macallan eighteen year from its place, strapped to the small bar near the galley. As I poured it over rocks, I noticed a bright, red envelope hidden behind the bottle. The envelope was made out of heavy artisan paper, and smelled faintly (I thought) of smoking embers.

"Finny" was written on the outside in large, almost calligraphy-like gold print, and the back was sealed by a proper wax stamp. Whomever had prepared the letter had taken great pains to show a rather proficient level of decorum, which I always appreciated.

I broke the seal and opened the envelope, only to find two thin, almost rice-paper sheets, with the following message:

"Dearest Finny,

I trust that you're reaching for this rather wonderful bottle of scotch because you have just met Trent and are perhaps somewhat troubled by what you have found about your inability to return to the future.

Though it is regrettable that I could not inform you of my wishes ahead of time, it was the only way that I could ensure that you would respect my orders with regard to the full scope of the mission.

Trent was indeed correct that the quantum computer can have a devil of a time processing jumps back to the future. Sadly, this is partially by design, as the computer that I provided you was constructed precisely so that you could only make a number of jumps *in seria* in the order that I preferred. I knew that, had this been a parameter of our original agreement, you would have been somewhat less inclined to go along with it, though I hope by now your natural curiosity and intellectualism will get the better of you, and allow yourself to forgive me in the future.

I have enclosed a list of specific places and time periods that, if visited in the precise order given, will result in you being able to eventually return to your rightful place in 2032. Should you deviate from this list…well…perhaps that's the reason that Trent knew nothing about you. Or perhaps I told him to feign ignorance should a foppish British scientist come poking about.

Along with the coordinates and times, there is a one-line description, which should, in context, provide you with enough information to figure out exactly what you're supposed to do in a given place and time. While you were busy spending your time and my money on all matter of technical details to get the machine ship-shape, I had a small team of experts pore over the requirements and the quantum computer to ensure that you got from place-to-place safely and in one piece, as this is utterly *critical* to history. As a result, you need not worry about how much time you spend in any given time period, other than the 20 hours (*Twenty-one hours, six minutes*, I thought) required to recharge the gravity drive and tunneling lasers. Know that you *do* have a specific task to accomplish at each stop, and each task should not be taken lightly. Shirking said tasks will only make things more difficult on us all, and result in all manner of backtracking and doubling around to accomplish these goals, and allow you to assume your rightful place in history, which, I assure you, is quite extensive, no matter what Trent may have said.

If you have any questions, I suppose you will have to figure their answers out yourself, or pose them to the quantum computer, though I've heard the thing can be positively unreliable at times. But you're a capable fellow; I have my full trust in your abilities! Though things may get difficult at times, please do remember that 'however history remembers it is how it happened, from the future dude's point of view.'

Do take care, and I will see you in good time.

Humbly Yours,

Your Benefactor"

I could feel my heartbeat thunder through my head with the regular metronomy of a war drum. I was too angry to ball up the letter, nor to scream nor cry (again, Limey and whatnot), and could only manage two, spit-out words from the bowels of my soul:

"Fucking prick," I said.

I wished the old bird was around so that I could smack him around a few times, maybe with his own gold-tipped cane, but seething at the moment would be of no use. Instead, I poured a full draught of Scotch, and took out the second piece of paper, which had the following on it:

"2-4-1666: Woolsthorpe-by-Colsterworth, England: Share port with IN

23-1-65,132,571 B.C.: Isla Yucatan, Mex.: Dine w/ TR

6-9-932.: Chichen Itza, Mex.: Save R.C., S.B.

31-12-1985: St. Louis, MO, USA: Communicate w/ VB

13-3-325: Nicaea, Turkey: Witness C's skepticism at the FEC

18-4-1738: Leipzig, Germany: See the only show in town

17-6-691: Jerusalem: Corner and Deal With T V

6-2-1943: Paris: Seek out VS

6-7-2032: Baltimore: HOME"

I wanted to ball up the list and tear it to shreds as soon as I read it—what did all of the initials even mean?

"Why would I want to visit the Federal Election Commission in Turkey in 325—" I said to no one in particular, though I stopped myself as I realised how ridiculous I sounded and smacked myself squarely in the face with the butt of my palm.

And who was my Benefactor to lay out such an audacious list for me before I even had tried to make a jump back to the future? In a huff, I stormed off to the control console and dutifully keyed in the coordinates for the last jump on the list:

"Baltimore, Maryland, USA, July 6, 2032."

Then the odds of success flashed on the screen:

"1.8%"

One point eight percent! I slammed the metal panel on top of the console as forcefully as I could manage, though I seem to recall that it hurt somewhat more than I would have thought, and found myself vigorously shaking my hand for several seconds to dissipate the pain.

Okay, Old Bird, I'll play your game, I thought. Or perhaps I whispered it—in either case, it was the thought in my mind at the moment. *I'll go on your little 'scavenger hunt,' but I will find you, and when I do, the result won't be two friends celebrating over a glass of scotch!*

I took a long drag off the whiskey glass and savored the warm liquid as it burnt my throat on the way down; even I can appreciate the subtle hint of smoke and utterly smooth finish that defined the Macallan Eighteen, which was, coincidentally, from the same year that I had finished my doctorate at age eighteen.

"You're nuts," my father said when I told him of my intention to make physics my profession, in his starkly frank, American way of saying things. "There's no money in that."

41

Oh, if he could only see me now! Sipping some of the finest scotch in the world in a time machine that would have bankrupted more than a few countries and companies to create!

I collected myself and dialed in the coordinates for the first jump:

"Woolsthorpe-by-Colsterworth, England, United Kingdom, April 2, 1666."

Sure enough, the display almost instantaneously flashed:

"99.9."

Damn it all! I thought. It continued to fluctuate between 99.9% and 99.8% for quite a while, before it finally settled on 99.9% and stayed there.

Resigned to my fate, I took another long pull off of the scotch, and decided that since time was no longer "of the essence," I would get properly leathered; after all, such a good bottle of scotch shouldn't go to waste, and though there was a crate of the stuff in the pantry, who knew when I'd have time to enjoy any more?

"What am I thinking?" I definitely said this part, "I have all the time in the universe!"

I spent the rest of the evening drinking as I gazed out on the ancient Judean landscape. At twilight, it was almost as if looking upon another planet, eerie and harsh and unforgiving all rolled into one. Though I've come to learn that there's a term for such disoriented sensations ("temporal disassociation"), such a condition does not undermine the very powerful thoughts and feelings I experienced as I looked around the landscape.

At one point, I felt positively randy, and decided to set all of the walls of the ship to "one-way transparent," so that I could look around in all 360 degrees. As I did so, I experienced a moment of panic (and, in hindsight, levity) as a rather hideous little fellow rode his camel full speed into the side of the cloaked time machine. Or I should say that the camel stopped short of the craft, and the little bearded fellow flew out of his seat and slammed into the side of the ship. He staggered to his feet and felt for the outer surface of the machine before he screamed some dialect of Aramaic for the equivalent of "bloody murder," as far as I could gather. I had half a mind to activate the ship's external intercom and really give him a show, but I thought the better of it, lest I attract undue attention and have to open up the armory. Once the fellow left, I did move the ship several hundred yards away, in case he decided to come back and visit the site of the "miracle" once more. I poured one final glass of the wonderfully smooth scotch, and allowed myself one of the cigars in the pantry as a celebration of a first step in the mission "accomplished" as I placed the Doobie Brothers' "Takin' it to the Streets" on repeat over the ship's internal loudspeakers (for those of you questioning my rather archaic and eclectic selection in music, I'd proudly suggest that you fuck right off). The last thing that I remember from that evening was hammering the tambourine beat from the song on top of the command console.

I passed out in the command seat and woke to a symphony of finely-tuned jackhammers inside my brain, each note of...what was this dreadful song again? No matter...I cursed myself for destroying so many of my extremely valuable (and much-needed) brain cells in a fit of emotion. The view was still in 360-degree mode, and I ordered the view to return to "standard," and for the customary "window" pane at the front to darken. My next order of business was to turn off that dreadful noise, the appeal of which I may have overestimated in my drunken stupor.

I surveyed the damage to the cabin. I had dug into the food stores, though I'm proud to admit that my own personal "autopilot," as it were, gorged on the perishable items first, the baguettes and cheeses that were loaded into the galley.

As I made my way to the larger table next to the galley, though, I noticed the smoldering remains of what appeared to be a sheet of rice-paper.

In a panic, I fumbled through my robe, and realising that its pockets only contained the medigel, I rifled through various drawers

43

throughout the cabin. I finally found a similar piece of rice paper, but it wasn't the list; rather it was the Old Bird's condescending and bombastic letter, which I could easily do without. My slightly-sunburned skin went pale with the realisation that I had no map to reach the future; though I probably had a good enough memory to piece the places and years together, I still had no idea what I was to do upon my arrival. I was a Bedouin, a wanderer, forever condemned to meander through time to try to find my way back home!

I needed to relax, and though the Scotch once again sounded appealing, I nearly vomited at the thought of going on another bender. No, I needed something soothing and familiar, something that would calm the nerves and steady the mind. I needed my customary cup of tea (always Earl Grey, always hot).

I staggered over to the tea service in the galley and removed the first box of Earl Grey from its resting place. As I did so, another red envelope, with the same style of paper and embossed with identical calligraphy as the one from the day before, practically jumped out at me from behind the tea box. I cocked my head to the side as I destroyed the seal and greedily tore into the damned thing, and began to read the contents:

"Dearest Finny,

If you're reading this, I trust that you've already destroyed the first list in a fit of drunken rage and debauchery, or at least as much debauchery as a man can manage by himself (I trust that you'll give the head a proper cleaning). I've enclosed another copy of the list, seeing as though that as smart as you may be, you were too dumb to not photograph it into your tablet and save a copy to the ship's memory banks. DO NOT FUCK THIS UP AGAIN! There are no more copies to save your ass this time. You have been warned.

Humbly Yours,

Your Benefactor"

This time, I could only manage a single word, two syllables that conveyed my thoughts perfectly.

"Wanker."

CHAPTER FIVE

Too often we take linear time for granted, and along with it the idea that every day millions of souls will take their final gasps, and forevermore go silent. Each passing day is but a weigh station, a short stop on the road to that final moment that ultimately defines us all, and makes us move in time with whatever reality we currently occupy.

When you're a time traveller, each of those days has no meaning, or should I say no greater meaning outside of oneself. Of course *I* am one step closer to that final milestone of death we all shall one day embrace, but all sense of generation, of shared experience and memories, any idea that you're tethered to *this time*, this moment, this *instant* is gone. You are a nomad wandering the wastelands without a compass or map, forever damned to cross the same river and name it a thousand different things.

Unless, of course, you have a fabulously wealthy Benefactor who apparently had the benefit of knowing the future (and the past, and whatever), and the foresight to provide you with the very map needed to get where you needed to go.

Truth be told, once I found that second map, I was actually grateful to the Old Bird for including it; though I initially had been appalled by the presumption of it all, absent that map, I would be similarly lost to time, even more of a footnote to history than I already am. I recorded it in every way that I knew how; I even scanned a picture into my tablet and re-wrote it in triplicate in the margins of the old paper Bible.

It could be worse, I thought. *I could've tried to make a low-probability jump in my drunken stupor.*

I cringed at the thought of being cast adrift in space, which would have more than "complicated matters," before I took another sip of tea and studied the list once more:

"2-4-1666: Woolsthorpe-by-Colsterworth, England: Share port with IN"

Perhaps the Old Bat had thrown me a bit of a bone. I was enough of a student of history to know that the "IN" that my Benefactor referred to was likely none other than Isaac Newton. The dates worked rather well, and despite my rather off-hand and regrettable comment in the first chapter, Sir Isaac remained one of my foremost heroes.

After all, how many men had contributed so much to so many different disciplines, and had such a profound effect on the world? Calculus, optics, mechanics; all areas utterly revolutionised by Newton. Outside of Da Vinci, he was perhaps the greatest Renaissance man in history. Only time will tell if, eventually, someday, "Templeton" takes its rightful place among this group of peers, though I most certainly have my doubts.

I knew that this was the man my Benefactor wanted me to meet, but I felt a flutter in my chest; what if he wasn't? What if I was to meet "Ignatius Newcombe" or what if the "IN" didn't refer to a person at all, but rather a thing, or a direction to share port "in" something? Regardless of the Old Bird's intent, I thought that I would start with Newton—it was the best lead I had, after all—and move on from there.

Besides, I thought that given his somewhat unorthodox views on Christianity and the church, Sir Isaac might rather enjoy hearing about my run-in with our friend Toasted Trent Albertson.

"Computer: what type of dress would be appropriate for England, 1666…nobleman," I said. I thought I was rather clever; after all, I'd have a much easier time meeting Isaac Newton (even pre-knighthood, I suppose) as a noble rather than as some member of the rabble. Not to mention that I gathered that the noble clothing was more likely to be made of silks and satins, and hence far more comfortable.

The computer opened the glove compartment and flipped to one of the pre-packaged outfits: a rather fancy-looking purple silk waistcoat with a crisp white, frilly shirt, and matching purple pantaloons. Long, white socks and polished, black, buckled shoes completed the ensemble, which I found to be rather gaudy, even if it belied a simple elegance that has somehow vanished through the centuries. I put on the clothing, an activity far more time-consuming than I would have imagined.

Perhaps the Old Bird hates me, after all, I thought as I looked in the mirror in the head. I especially didn't like the *2001*-esque coldness with which the computer complied with my request, which aroused a new round of paranoia at a potential HAL-like computer takeover. Alas, nothing nearly so exciting was to be the case as of yet.

Though my hangover had begun to fade, my usually crystal-clear mind was still foggy and dull like a London winter. I eased my way into the command chair, and was delighted to see the coordinates for the time jump already loaded into the console from the night before. I allowed myself a smirk as I cautiously raised a finger over the red, flashing icon and quickly pressed it.

The machine immediately came to life, as each half rotated in an opposite direction and the gravity drive kicked in. The ship shot off toward the town as the cloaking device disengaged, now visible to everyone in all of its shiny, metal splendour.

Much to my amusement, the machine's autopilot took us over our earlier landing site, where the curious, squat little bearded fellow with the camel gesticulated wildly toward several of his friends, attempting to explain his run-in with the ship the day before. One of his friends pointed at the craft, eyes wide as if I was sure to obliterate them with a death ray, and all three ducked as the ship buzzed overhead. I wonder what came of those three fellows? Everyone probably thought they had gone positively mental when they later described the scene.

Eventually, the autopilot shot us straight up, out of the atmosphere, and a comfortable range away, in the outer range of the Earth's gravity well. I won't bore you with the specifics of the actual time travel since I believe I adequately described it in the first chapter. I will add the addendum that I'm sure that one of the reasons that Trent enjoyed the experience of time travel so much was trying to put "the Brainenator" to use while the miraculous colours jumped out of space—it must have been quite the trip (pun most certainly intended).

Fortunately, when the ship emerged from the wormhole and came to a stop, the Earth still hung in front of me like a big, blue marble. I was transfixed for several moments by the scene; it sucked me in and hypnotized me…until the collision alarm sounded and it was all I could do to hastily activate the omni-yoke and yank the ship downward rapidly (though in hindsight the autopilot likely would have guided us safely past, I was terrified at the time). I looked up to see the moon, far more massive than I would have thought, thunder by (and yes, I fully realise that it should have swung past asonically, but I will swear until the day that I die that moon roared past with the noise of a thousand jet engines).

The satellite no longer a threat, I reengaged autopilot, and the craft cruised elegantly toward the planet. The North Sea appeared, followed by the Motherland, and, as truth is my primary endeavor in this travelogue, I must admit that the atmospheric recyclers must have been a bit overwhelmed at the moment, because I could have sworn that it got more than a little dusty in the cabin. How else could one explain the manner in which my eyes welled up, and nearly shed a tear upon seeing Jolly Old England once more? (One explanation? The bloody contacts I forced myself to wear in lieu of my spectacles. Damned things are still a menace to this day. And no, I absolutely *will not* allow my eyes to be butchered by a laser like a common article of cattle; test all you want, but put away your ghaastly lasers, you deranged opthalmic surgeons).

We glided in, once again unhindered by the orbits of satellites (or I should say *man-made* satellites) and came to rest behind a lonely haystack, away from its peers in a field otherwise dotted with the damned things. Though it was a typical April day in England, the sun peeked through the clouds every so-often to bring the normally-muted landscape to life, and honour it with its proper verdant hues.

The console flashed the words "Jump Successful," as I unstrapped myself from the command chair and headed for the exit. Immediately before I disembarked, I remembered that I didn't have any money, and grasped the bag which held the "blasphemous" coinage from my last stop, and attached it to my waist. As I was about to exit once more, I remembered that I had forgotten something else, and, after fumbling through the glove box for several moments, emerged with a tiny bottle of Purell, lest early English hygiene resemble that of the Nazarenes.

As the door opened, the cloaking device engaged automatically. It must have been quite a sight: this tall, gangly (if quite handsome, if I do say so myself) nobleman emerging from behind a haystack in the middle of Woolsthorpe.

A stout, pudgy-faced woman tended some plants close to a rather tall, striking stone house over a hill in the distance. She didn't appear to notice me as I approached, though I did think the better of walking in from the fields, and quickly moved toward the road so that it would appear as if I was just another wayward traveller looking for a spot of tea.

Even as I came within five metres of the woman, she didn't cease pruning the rose-bushes that surrounded the structure. After the "signature" smell of Nazareth, I especially enjoyed the pungent, familiar aroma that the flowers provided.

"Uh...excuse me? Madam?"

The woman looked up at me momentarily, her gaze a bit cross-eyed.

"What of ya'?" She asked curtly.

"Pardon me, madam, but I'm looking for a local resident. Perhaps you know of him? Si—err...the scientist Isaac Newton?"

50

The woman rolled her confused eyeballs and marched over to the thick wooden door.

"Isaac! You 'ave another visitor!" She screamed at the top of her lungs. Someone from inside replied something unintelligible, and she stood aside from the door. "'Ee'll see you now, but if you even think of spreadin' that bloody black death around 'eese parts, I'll—"

I couldn't help but chuckle, "Madam, I assure you, I'm most certainly *not* carrying the plague. Rest easy, you and your family will be safe."

She squinted at me, "Yeah—'at's what 'dis one said, too!" she motioned inside the door. Curious, I followed her hand motion to see through the (particularly well-appointed for the day, I thought) kitchen, and into a small study. One man was seated at a desk; he furiously scrawled notes on paper as the other one leisurely lounged against a chair and snorted.

"So, numbskull, does thou see how *moronic* thou canst be at times?" The lounging man's accent seemed a bit off. More than that, he was taller, though much shorter than I was, and had smooth, unpocked skin, other than the bristly mustache above his lip. His hair was grey and cut in a stylish manner, even if it was somewhat obviously a comb-over, and he held a coffee mug in his hand. A pair of black-rimmed glasses framed his somewhat round, dorky face.

I couldn't believe what I saw next: as the poor man in the chair continued to scribble, his tongue curled around his thin lips, which complimented his steadily bobbing square (if pudgy) jaw, and the prominent, English nose attached to his face.

"Isaac Newton?" I asked.

The man in the chair stopped writing momentarily and turned around.

"Who wishes to know?"

I took a step back; if the man in the chair was Newton, then who was—

"Verily. Now, Isaac, if thou doth please, thou hast work to do!" The lounging man pushed off of the table and walked toward me. As he looked me over and saw that I towered over even him, the expression on his face changed from one of arrogance to a meek, near-cowardess. His lip trembled as he raised his right hand over his stomach and flashed the "Live Long and Prosper" sign at me.

Now that I finally knew what it meant, I returned the gesture. The man offered a weak smile.

"Very good, Isaac, now thou shallst work on the...?"

"On the..." Newton replied, without a hint of sarcasm.

"We just hath worked on the *first* law of motion, so verily the next one is the...?"

"The..." Newton echoed the man once more.

The other man rolled his eyes, "*Second* law of motion!"

"Second law of motion!" Newton tried to speak contemporaneously, but came up a bit short, and trailed the man with the mustache by a half second.

"Indeed, now I'm going to have a word with this traveller over here, so keep mulling that priceless realisation over in thy head until my return."

"Verily, master teacher," Newton replied.

A smug smile crept across the mustached man's face, as he turned toward me and raised his eyebrows. He punctuated the gesture by throwing a dorky "thumbs-up" my way, which I must've responded to with a frown, as the timid look quickly returned to his face.

He ushered me outside the house and into the yard, opposite the side where Mrs. Newton trimmed the hedges, under a familiar-looking apple tree.

"Son of a gun! I can't believe it—another time traveler!" The man's accent was decidedly American, and though his voice was a bit nasally and grating, it was balanced with a gravelly, lower-pitch that made him seem a less-than-complete coward.

"Um...yes...indeed, good sir. Phineas Templeton," I extended my hand, hoping to get the hero's welcome that Trent hadn't given me.

Instead, all I received was a dead-fish hand in return.

"Hank Fleener, physics professor, St. Mary's High, nice to meet you, Phineas."

I couldn't help but chuckle, though I wouldn't tell this "Mr. Fleener" everything…not yet, at least, "Physics professor, eh? I know a bit about the subject myself. I'm tenured as a faculty consultant at Johns Hopkins—"

Hank did a double-take, "Wow, really? That's great. I mean, I expected anyone from the future to know more than that dim bulb in there, just by the fact of the ChronoSaber introduction and whatnot, but to have a real, kindred spirit, it's…just wow!"

"You do realise that you're speaking about one of Britain's national heroes, a man whom you and I owe a great deal to in the pursuit of our—"

Hank waived a palm at me before he let out a guffaw, "Pffft! How amazing! I used to think the same way that you did, Phineas. Can I call you Phineas?"

"Finny is fine," I offered a weak smile.

"Well, Finny, you know how it is, right?"

"How what is, Hank—I may call you 'Hank,' correct?"

He waived off the question, "Of course, of course! Not a problem at all. No, I mean, how 'it' is. You know…teaching."

I decided to tell the truth; and to tell *you* the truth, I was just happy to be able to converse with someone else from near my time whose main hobbies didn't previously include eating Funions and playing X-Box.

"I suppose I don't. I generally only advise tenured faculty members, though I hear that their tantrums can rival even the most temperamental children."

Hank rolled his eyes, "That may be true, but you haven't dealt with anything until you've tried teaching physics to American kids. Talk about entitled; these kids want you to do everything for them except wipe their asses after they take a shit. Then you have the parents, who always try to annoy and cajole me to improve their kid's grades, always threatening lawsuits and whatnot, you must at least know *that*, right?" He looked at me for approval and I nodded.

"And *that's* of the ones whose parents care! Then you have all of the metal detectors and school shootings and all kinds of other crap, and I'm teaching a bunch of bored kids in the middle of a war zone. They might as well ship me off to the Middle East! I mean, I thought the draft might help some with getting these kids in line, but it's still the same old shit, you know? The ones left behind still just couldn't care less about anything other than their holomessages, you know?"

"So…instead of dealing with those spoiled high schoolers, you decided to come back in time and…berate Sir Isaac Newton?" I tried to maintain a dry tone.

Hank chuckled again, "Hardly! You think I wanted to try to teach this putz all of the most important theories in our field? I was coming off a divorce, the bitch—sorry, ex-wife—made me sell the house, and all I got was a lousy hundred grand, with almost that much in credit card debt. No wife, kids hated me, pension in the dumper, and teaching was getting more and more horrible by the year.

"Then, the government de-regulated time-travel, and I *knew* that was the answer. I'd burn through my life's savings to get back here, to converse with Newton and pick his brain, to get some kind of inspiration for what I should be doing with my life, you know?

"So I forked over the $100,000 to ChronoSaber, took their introduction for a week, and before I know it, here I am, at Newton's mother's house, finally face-to-face with the 'master.' Well, wouldn't you know it, but the guy's a dull blade! He's dumb. He's an I-M-B-E-C-I—"

"I think I get the point," I said, with a curt smile.

Hank reared back like a frightened kitten poked one too many times with a stick, "Uh…yes, well, regardless, this guy didn't know ANYTHING. And I mean the basics. Fortunately for him, I brought a copy of the *Principia*, in its original Latin, and—"

"And so now you're helping him write his own books?"

Hank gave a skittish nod, "Something like that, yes. Gives me purpose, you know? I always dreamed of coming up with my own theories like his, and advancing humanity that way, but if this is how I can best serve mankind, by educating Newton and giving him the resources to become the man he will some day, then by all means, who am I to interfere?"

As I momentarily savored the irony of Hank's comment, Newton staggered out of the house. His puffy cheeks looked more drawn in and sunken than I remembered from the various portraits I had seen, but his visage was unmistakable, especially for someone with a British public school education (Eton, if you must know). I struggled to keep my mouth from falling to the floor as he approached Hank.

"Master Fleener, I've looked at the second law of motion, and I can't say I completely understand what it doth mean."

Hank tilted his head for a moment, "Isaac, cannot thou seest that I am entertaining at the moment?"

"I do apologize, Master Fleener, but I could use some—"

Hank sighed deeply, bent over, and picked up a couple of the apples scattered on the ground before he offered Newton a terse smile.

"You—sorry—'thou' wants something to ponder?"

"Verily," Newton replied.

Hank threw one of the fruits in the air in a high arc. Both Newton and I marveled at the irregular-shaped red object's flight through the sky.

Oh my God! Is this the *moment?* I couldn't help but wonder.

Just as the apple began to fall back to Earth, Hank wound up and (with rather poor form, might I add) winged the other fruit not but six inches from Newton's head before it splattered on the stonework behind him.

"There! Thinkest thou about that!" Fleener said in his most authoritarian, firmest voice possible. The now-skittish Newton cowered as he retreated back into the house; he never turned his back to Hank for the rest of the day.

As soon as Newton had disappeared, so too did the rage from Hank's face. He even let out a good-natured chuckle as he shook his head. "Kids will be kids…"

"That was a bit harsh, don't you think?" I asked.

Hank raised his eyebrows, "Harsh? Harsh is having your school on lockdown when some wacko kid is running around, gunning down everyone in sight. What you just witnessed—*that's* respect!"

"He's terrified of you!" I pled with Hank.

Hank laughed again, "You mistake fear for reverence. That's what I so missed about teaching. When I started out, there was a real…respect for authority, for those older than oneself. But each passing year just got worse and worse—'teach to the test,' 'you can't berate the kids anymore,' 'they'll get a complex.' And even when we handled them with kid gloves," he looked around and moved his head toward mine to whisper, "they still *bitch* and *complain*. Everything is owed to them; it's not 'what can I learn?', but rather 'teach me NOW.' It wouldn't even be so bad if, underlying all of it, the kids actually cared. They don't. How anyone can teach in that environment is beyond me."

Fleener raised a finger skyward, "Ah, but Isaac, he's *eager* to learn. He may not yet be the greatest mind in the world, but he does have an insatiable appetite for knowledge, for information about how the world works, and he's willing to ask the questions and put in the long hours to figure it out."

"Even if you're putting his own books into his head?" I asked. Though Fleener was doing his best to be endearing, I still found his prosthelytising and his abhorrent treatment of Sir Isaac Newton to be utterly annoying.

"*Precisely*, Finny. Pre-freaking-cisely."

"So why not just become Newton then? Why not tie him up somewhere, or—"

Hank shook his head, "Because I *wasn't* Newton. Newton exists—he's here, right up there, actually," he pointed at the house. "Though he may be a dolt now, he's going to grow up to be one of the greatest minds ever, and revolutionize the world in countless ways. I don't share his charisma or his youthful curiosity, anymore at least. He's more than just a scientist, you know: two stints in Parliament, Master of the Mint—"

"I'm well aware," I offered Hank a curt smile.

Fleener nodded, "All I can do is teach him what he's supposed to know, give him the tools, and live out my life comfortably in Jolly Ol' England, away from my numerous creditors in the twenty-first century." He looked whistfully into the distance for a few moments before he shook the view out of his head, "So what's your game? Just another Newton fan, come to see the 'master' at work?"

"Something like that," I said. I decided to test the waters. "What if I told you that *I* invented time travel?"

Hank looked at me blankly for a moment, "Commander Corcoran?" he asked.

"I'm afraid not," I said, "that's the second time that's happened to me, though. I previously went to see another historical figure who ended up being a time traveller, and *he* asked me the same thing."

Fleener shrugged, "Well, I can't help you with that one, buddy. I have no way of telling if you're right or wrong, all I know is that Commander Corcoran gets credit in the history books. Some kind of top-secret military project. Still very hush-hush. Not many details known even when they declassified little parts of the story right after they announced that time travel was no longer regulated. Very strange."

"So nothing about Phineas Templeton then?"

He shook his head, "No, not really that I can remember. You'd have to have some kind of proof to convince anyone of that, though."

I smiled, "Come with me."

CHAPTER SIX

Lacking my spectacles, I felt around the invisible ship for a few moments before I located the hand panel, and disengaged the cloaking device on the machine.

"My God…it's…your own machine!"

I told you so, you twit! I thought.

"Indeed," I said.

"This is remarkable! Do you know how much these things cost? No one can buy their own, and no one's ever stolen one. ChronoSaber has quite the nice little monopoly on it." The panicked look returned to Fleener's face, "Assuming you didn't steal it—"

"I assure you, that's hardly the case," I interrupted.

Hank wasn't fazed, "This is just so insane—do you realize how fortunate you are?"

"I doubt fortune has anything to do with it," I replied coolly, "Though presently I appear to be quite the prisoner of my own success."

I explained the situation with my Benefactor, and the pre-planned jumps.

"That's curious," Hank said. "So you've never heard of Commander Corcoran?"

"I'm afraid I haven't."

"Hmm…" Hank stroked his chin, "Well that does leave a limited number of hypotheses. It could be—"

"That I end up destroying the machine, yes, or that I meet my untimely demise at some point, I know."

"I was going to say, could you *be* Commander Corcoran?"

"What do you mean?" before the words were out of my mouth, I knew exactly what Hank meant.

"Assume *his* identity. Take credit for his accomplishments. Or maybe that's a code-name you developed in the first place."

The wheels began to turn inside my head. Though I had no designs on stealing someone else's identity at the moment, little did I know how crucial those words (spoken by pitiful little Hank Fleener, no less!) would become in due time.

"Eh, I don't know..."

Hank spent the better part of a half-hour trying to convince me of the various virtues of becoming Commander Corcoran, but I waved each of his advances away with a suitably English "harumph" of some sort or another.

I gave him a tour of the ship, always careful to keep my distance behind the fellow, in case he should obtain designs on stealing the thing, but Fleener proved to be as harmless as a fruit fly, at least if you weren't one of his students.

When we had finished, we made small talk outside of the ship for a bit, talking shop about my solutions to all manner of common physics issues, until we came to an awkward pause. Like a couple of teenagers on a first date, I sensed that Fleener wanted me to say or do something to him, though I couldn't for the life of me figure out what.

"Do you...err...want a lift back to the future?" I finally asked.

"What? Oh no, I'm fine here. No, as I said before, I have a greater purpose than teaching high school physics, and the creditors can't very well reach me here. I suppose they *could*, but why would they want to shell out the cash, y'know? Besides, the whole 'what happened, happened,' thing comes into play, so I know I don't set myself up with a lot of cash from some adventure we have, or from buying a lot of low-priced stock in the sixties and putting it in a trust, so what's the point? Also—"

That was all the response that I needed as I zoned out for the rest of Fleener's lengthy explanation as to why 1666 was a better "time fit" for him. It was a curious concept; a debtor taking a windfall to head back in time and escape his creditors. Even more bizarre was the idea that a person who "didn't fit" in a given time period could actively go out and try to save enough money to travel to a time and place where he would cease to be a curious anachronism, and could become a happy, functioning member of society. I wondered if Trent would have proscribed such a system to some nonsense about it being the "wishes of the universe," even though I knew deep down that it was far more likely a product of nostalgia and wish-fulfillment than anything else.

As the sun set behind the smattering of hay stacks in the field, Mrs. Newton started to prepare dinner. I had to wait several more hours for the gravity drive and tunneling lasers to recharge, so to pass the time Isaac, Hank, and myself built a fire outside to sit around. Hank forced poor Isaac to break out some fine port that he had been saving for quite some time, despite my offers to get another bottle from my collection in the time machine, and we sat around getting positively pickled for the next several hours.

If you think I'm a lightweight, then Fleener could barely keep his feet on the ground, such a teetotaler was he. After a couple of drinks, the man became positively blotto (or, as I've often suspected since that evening, he pretended as much for the attention that it afforded). At some point, the teacher wore a goofy smile on his face as he addressed his student civilly for the first time.

"You know, Finny over here is a time traveler?"

"Psssh!" Newton still had his faculties about him, or at least he appeared to to the two of us.

"Now Isaac, what hast I taught thee about listening to me?" Fleener's expression darkened. "Thissun's got a silver time machine and everything."

On a normal night, I probably would have played my cards a bit closer to the vest. Unfortunately, I, too had a few pulls off of the cask, which loosened my tongue a bit.

"Yep," I said.

"Verily, thou both doth seek to make a fool of me!"

"It isn't...tisn't true...whatever the hell you *morons* talk like now!" Hank laughed, and I couldn't help but follow suit.

"Yep, I'm from the future." I calmed down enough to form the words before I had to stifle another booming belly laugh.

"Verily? Then tell me, fair traveller, what doth I accomplish in the future?" Newton asked.

"Ha! That's easy. If you listen to your mentor, Mr. Fleener over here, then I think you're in for quite a lifetime. You'll revolutionise physics, optics, mathematics, and that's all before your forays into politics and even printing money!"

Newton smiled, "Perhaps the man is more veracious than he initially appears."

Hank laughed for a moment before he became "asshole Hank" to Newton once more as he picked up a stick and poked the man with it, "See there! Listen to Master Templeton! He knows—listen to me and *great* things are in store!" I laughed, but Hank didn't follow suit.

Newton's skin paled and reflected more of the flickering firelight, "Indeed! Indeed!" he turned to address me, "So what other times hast thou been to, Master Templeton?"

"So far? Hmm...let's see..." I paused for effect. "Ever heard of Jesus Christ?"

"Balderdash!" Newton couldn't believe it.

"No, no, it's quite true. Except..."

"What?" Newton was deeply interested.

"Ah, I really shouldn't..."

"No, no—I want to know!" I mean, the man practically *begged* me to tell him, and I knew that Newton was a bit "unorthodox" in his religious beliefs. In fact, he was what they may have called a "heretic" at the time, and been burned at the stake had he not kept his views on the non-divinity of Christ hidden.

"Well...okay!" I finally gave in. "The thing about Jesus Christ is that his name isn't Jesus Christ at all. It's Trent Albertson. You see, Trent is very much a time traveller like myself, but he decided to go back in time and *become* Jesus Christ. He performed all of the miracles, hell, he even used the Bible as his own personal road-map.

I've actually been meaning to broach this topic since I arrived since I know that you hold rather 'interesting' views about the man."

Newton looked as if he had seen a ghost, "I hadn't prior, but now I do," he looked at Hank, "Is this true, Master Fleener? Doth Master Templeton speak the truth?" Hank shrugged with a sly smile. Newton continued to fret, "This information is of great interest to me; you see, as a Fellow at Cambridge, I'm required to take Holy Orders sometime in the next few years. This wouldn't be of great concern, were it not for the vow of celibacy that was included in the right." Fleener burst out laughing, and I couldn't even stifle my chuckle.

"That's a big sacrifice to make to a religion that preaches false orthodoxy," Fleener said.

"Oh, I don't know," I said. "I think the lessons of Trent—sorry, Christ—are good morality tales no matter if the person that professed them was some half-wit stoner from Boulder. I've had a couple of days to think on this now, and ultimately, I've come to the conclusion that it doesn't matter who delivered the message, but rather what people do with it, to what ends and purpose they put that message. A lesson is only as good as the student who implements it."

Hank poked Newton with the stick once more.

We debated all manner of physics, and spoke of all of the fanciful inventions that would one day be made possible by Isaac's "discoveries." The odd part was as we continued to speak of his contributions to society, it was almost as if the firelight made its way into Newton's belly. His cheeks lost their puffiness, and the fire ground the gears inside of his head.

"Thank you both, so much," Newton said as he shook both of our hands at the end of the night.

"Thou aren't going to get rid of me that easily!" Hank said. "We still have much work to do." Hank turned to me, "Goodbye, friend!"

"Goodbye…you!" I shook his hand vigorously.

"If you ever stop by again—" Hank had snapped out of his stupor for a moment.

"I'll be sure to look you up," I lied. It wasn't that I didn't like the man, but I had little desire to see one of the towering geniuses and intellects in history be bullied around by Hank Fleener any more than necessary.

"Si—uh, Scientist Newton, it's been a pleasure," I caught myself; some surprises didn't need to be ruined. I shook hands with one of my heroes, and practically skipped through the field back to the ship behind the haystack. As I opened the door, I wondered if Newton saw the light escape from the cabin and illuminate the night sky.

And until the day I die, I'll wonder who had more of an impact on Newton's life: Hank Fleener, or me?

CHAPTER SEVEN

I spent the night in the small quarters in the cabin. The Newtons had gracefully offered to put me up for the evening, but I figured that a bed of straw and lice may not be the most conducive to proper rest, which I sorely needed given my scotch-addled escapades from the previous evening. It was nice to sleep in a proper bed again, though I had several horrific nightmares about a giant apple that chased me and poked me with a stick.

I awoke the next morning refreshed and reinvigorated, though I had to strain to remember whether Hank Fleener had exposed me as a time traveller to Sir Isaac Newton before I figured that even if he had, there wasn't much to do about it now, and "what happened, happened," right?

I figured that whatever last night had been was my task for the time period, and sure enough, as I sipped my tea and the gravity drive "recharged" indicator lit up the screen, I pulled up the display on the console. I entered the next coordinates:

"23-1-65,132,571 B.C.: Cozumel, Mex. : Dine w/ TR"

This was the jump that I had most been dreading since opening my Benefactor's insane list. Over 65 million years in the past? If what Trent said was accurate, then this was sure to be the most harrowing part of the journey. Future quantum computers couldn't even process such large jumps in time without significant errors; how was my lowly, first-generation model supposed to get me there and back safely?

Then again, *if* the time machine could make it all that way, then I was about to live every young boy's dream:

Dinosaurs!

Though I had outgrown my preoccupation with dinosaurs years before, I still remember my father handing me a number of the figurines shortly after we had moved to London, perhaps to calm my mind and ease the transition. Naturally, like any other young lad, I took to the terrible lizards like a duck to water. I learned everything I could about the great beasts and stuffed the information into my comfortably oversized young brain.

On a lark, I changed my mind and entered "July 6, 2032, Baltimore, Maryland, USA" in the console. After several moments, the computer returned the probability:

"2.1%"

More resigned than frustrated, I entered the Benefactor's coordinates, and (surprise, surprise) the console read "99.9%" once again. I shook my head; perhaps Trent hadn't been correct after-all. Maybe this was a wild goose chase set up by my Benefactor for reasons beyond unknown to me.

Or maybe, this is where you're destined to die.

The thought had occurred to me; with my Benefactor in possession of all of the technology I had created, my lab, my notes, and bloody hell, even Avi, perhaps this list was designed for me to meet my bitter end, and leave all of the "loose ends" neatly tied up. I cursed my curiosity for having gotten the better of me, and my stupidity for not having tested the machine properly before jetting off in it to times unknown.

I opened the glove box and, once again, asked for suitable garments for this leg of the trip. The computer spat out the vacuum-sealed bag with my "normal garb," which consisted of a long-sleeved, Brooks Brothers shirt, slimly-tailored knickers, and a navy sweater-vest, as well as a pair of comfortable loafers. One piece of clothing that certainly was *not* from my usual ensemble was the camouflaged flak jacket that was at the bottom of the package.

That's odd… I thought, before I realised that any humans during this time period would most certainly be from the future, and thus would wear similarly modern garb. The flak jacket was, of course, for protection in the event that whatever nasties inhabited the Earth 65 million years in the past wanted to get a better look at me, or fancied me as their supper for the evening.

The red button glowed on the console and illuminated the dimmed cabin. It was an eerie effect, a klaxon of red light that seemed to prophecise impending doom, though I fully admit that my trepidation about the time shift may have had something to do with my thoughts on the matter.

I had brought my tea over to the console, but, thinking the better of ruining literally billions of dollars of equipment with one jolt that might slip by the inertial dampeners, I dutifully placed the cup over in the galley before I returned to the command chair, strapped myself in, and hit the red icon.

The ship hovered above the ground for several moments. I noticed that Isaac and Hank had come out to see me off despite the chilly, dank weather that hung over the farm. Mrs. Newton tended the plants in front of the house, and though she looked up, and though the cloaking device wasn't engaged, she didn't even so much as perform a double-take as the shiny metallic saucer lifted into the sky.

I had grown quite used to the ascent by this point, and was for once able to enjoy the view as the British Isles grew smaller and smaller against the calming blue of the North Sea. Whisps of white clouds obscured the view as I approached the edge of the atmosphere, but somehow I found it fitting, and thought they added to the beauty.

Clear of the atmosphere, the ship bolted away from the Earth and away from my new celestial nemesis, the moon, to the edge of Earth's gravity envelope. The green button flashed on the console, and, after steadying myself with a deep breath, I hammered it with my fist.

The tunneling lasers did their thing, whilst the gravity drive began to pulse as it tugged, pushed, pulled, and nipped at the very fabric of spacetime itself. I began to fret after several minutes; the first two jumps had taken far less time, but the gravity drive bravely soldiered on. The strain on the poor thing must've been incredible; though there were no bolts to come flying out of pipefittings or boilers to burst open with pressure, there was an odd, metallic "groan" that started at a low hum, and eventually came to reverberate through the ship.

It's happening! I thought. *We're making a black hole.*

Normally, this would be a fantastic scientific achievement; an artificial singularity? Yes, I'll take that Nobel Prize, thank you! But when the black hole's epicenter is the time machine in which you've invested decades of your life, and it's near enough to Earth to cause a bit of a snafu, then *you* see if your shorts stay dry!

Fortunately, at the last possible moment, the noise ceased as the ship jolted forward through the wormhole. Decorum prevents me from wholly confirming or denying what I said above regarding the condition of my shorts, but needless to say, though I was shaken up, I was glad to still be in one piece, especially since that one piece wasn't a string of spaghetti with infinite length (little physicist-black hole inside joke there).

As soon as I had regained my wits, I surveyed the cabin, and instinctively ducked, fearing another stealth flyby of the moon that never came. The autopilot engaged, and I hurtled through space toward the now-familiar hanging blue orb. This time, upon closer inspection, the planet actually *was* different. I could make out the various land masses, but they were at the same time familiar and different, eerie precursors to the well-known and map-worn shapes that they would become, made even more alien by the lack of ice caps and correspondingly higher sea levels, which sanded away many of the rough edges of the continents.

As the time machine descended into the atmosphere, the sky turned a pinkish, almost Martian hue. Active volcanoes dotted the landscape, as plumes of smoke drifted skyward toward the craft.

Though such a thought was utterly insane, I was glad that the time machine didn't rely on such an archaic means of conveyance as a jet engine, lest the volcanic debris clog the intakes and leave me hopelessly vulnerable and stranded in this most foreign of lands.

The ship jolted as something connected with it. I ordered the three-hundred sixty degree view from the computer, and saw an honest-to-God-damned six-foot wide dragonfly in a momentary daze before it dropped toward the Earth.

A collection of pterosaurs coasted in front of the craft, and for the first time in many years, I felt my childlike reverence for these beasts return. My father, voracious "apex predator" that he was, loved the cretaceous and all of the T-Rexes and allosaurs that populated it. Truth be told, my gentler sensibilities were often more piqued by the majestic, plant-eating beasts of the jurassic such as stegosaurus, though I also had a soft spot for triceratops and ankylosaurus, those gentle vegetarians that had the temerity to stand up to those bullying, savage killing machines of the same era.

Oh, for the days when I longed for nothing more than to write an entire treatise about these animals! Though admittedly said book would be in crayon and half of the letters would be backwards not for any use of Greek or Cyrillic characters, but rather for want of the author's proper instruction in English penmanship. Six-year-old Finny was absolutely obsessed with the "terrible lizards," and would have been happy to make a campfire and dwell alongside these beasts for years at a time. Now, I fretted over which one of them was hungriest, and thus most likely to dine upon me that evening.

Perhaps oddest of all was the lushness of the jungle as the ship approached what appeared to be an inundated Mexico. Layers of green canopy covered the landscape as far as the eye could see, as pterosaurs of various sizes, shapes, and even colours (for the feathered ones, at least) soared above the rainforest. What was the ceiling for most creatures was these soaring beasts' carpet; a veritable verdant sea that the flying lizards dipped into from time-to-time to hunt, or otherwise rest their weary wings.

The machine flew right past the edge of the landmass, and for a moment, I thought my Benefactor had consigned me to a watery grave some 65 million years in the past. Fortunately, an archipelago appeared over the horizon, a collection of large-sized islands similarly covered by flora.

One of the islands contained a clearing, and I surmised that must be our ultimate destination. Sure enough, the metallic disk floated right above the treeless patch for a matter of moments, allowing me a look at the scene below. Instead of the bare earth or tall grasses that I had expected, the space was consumed by a thoroughly modern complex. A good half-dozen helipads were occupied by a fleet of half-as-many polished, metal disks, each one similar to my own but, as became apparent upon descent, many times larger again. A flat, bunker-like building stood next to the "saucerpads," and was remarkable in its utter lack of remarkability.

A man dressed in green camouflage held out an odd-looking wand, and aimed it directly at my craft. I thought it may be a weapon of some sort and engaged the omni-yoke, which lurched the disk into a deep left dive. A moment later, the time machine stabilised and a calm, but firm, female voice filled the cabin.

"Unidentified craft, this is Chronobase Alpha, identify yourself and your native time period or we will be forced to open fire pursuant to 55 U.S.C. 4402 regarding unidentified time travelers in restricted airspace, please advise, over."

I raised an eyebrow and stared out of the window blankly for a moment. Any thought of escape was mitigated by the fact that their time machines were superior to mine, which would seem to indicate that my machine was likely not a match for whatever superior weaponry I might find in their arsenal; for all I knew, they had a gravity drive generator of their own that could crush my craft like an aluminum (pronounced the proper, British, "a-loo-minium," of course) can, or worse, an antimatter containment field destabiliser, which would have potentially disastrous effects.

I decided to respond the only way I knew how; via the external speakers that I had ever-so-briefly considered using to scare that fellow with the camel back in Trent's time. I pressed a button on the right console, which lowered a microphone from the cabin's ceiling.

"Uh...Chrono...Base...Alpha, my name is Dr. Phineas Templeton, and I am the originator of this time device from Baltimore in 2032, by way of England."

The seconds of silence ticked away on the other end, each one punctuated by several of my heartbeats, willing away whatever ghastly demise these individuals may have in mind for me.

"Dr. Templeton, please be advised you are clear for landing on pad six, over." The far left rear landing pad illuminated with some sort of blue holo lighting, which extended toward my craft and provided a glidepath.

"Err...roger that, over!" I tried my best to mask my relief with professionalism.

I guided the ship in using the omni-yoke, though "guided" may be too artful a term for the jerky, "still-learning-on-the-job" route with which I piloted the vessel. Despite the elegance of the gravity drive, I dropped the machine out of the air with a resonating "CLANG" that struck the Earth like a gong.

Several green camouflaged, heavily-armed individuals surrounded the craft. I hadn't the faintest idea of what to do for a number of moments: unlock the armory? Provide them a peace offering of one of the other fine bottles of scotch on board? Throw myself at their feet and beg for mercy?

I finally decided on the last option, and took a deep breath as I approached the doorway. I ordered the computer to lower the gangway, and the door to the external world opened with a satisfying "WHOOSH."

Four soldiers greeted me and cocked their weapons. A cacophony of odd, bird-like noises from the jungle were punctuated by the occasional deep, saurian roar that likely could have shattered normal glass.

I took another deep breath through my nose, and took in the heavy ozone smell that pervaded this jungle. Terrified, I held my hands in the air and froze. My brain went into overdrive for a few moments, as the fresh air heightened all of my senses, as well as my terror.

Then, a sensation of increasing calm cascaded over me in waves. I began to feel lighter than any of the pterosaurs, which had curiously disappeared from the skies above the clearing.

"Don't shoot!" I opened my mouth to say, but instead could barely outstretch an arm to break my fall, as I collapsed onto the cold, unforgiving metal gangway, out like a burned-out light.

CHAPTER EIGHT

I awoke to find myself in an amazingly modern hospital bed, marked not by the futuristic gizmos that surrounded it, but rather the decided lack thereof. A single holo-emitter hung in front of me. The non-judging eye measured the subtle changes in my breathing and exposed skin to detect any abnormalities. As you pasties (Damn me, using their contemptible slang, I know, but it's the quickest and most elegant way to refer to you past-dwellers, so pardon my impoliteness) may understand, it was rather like being attached to a constantly-monitoring MRI, or at least that was the way the whole set-up was eventually pitched to me.

A beautiful, but stern, woman with a caramel complexion stood at the foot of my bed. Her posture was impeccable, her black hair wrapped meticulously into some kind of a braid or bun (as you can perhaps tell, female fashion is not nearly as much of an area of expertise of mine as, say, rotational anti-gravity physics). A single beauty-mark kissed the arch of her high cheekbone, the only blemish on an otherwise flawless sample of skin. Had she been smiling, I would have wondered if I was in the midst of the most pleasant dream of my life.

Instead, her face was rigid; her stare bored through me with halogen intensity.

"Phineas Templeton?" She asked it as if my very presence bothered, or even offended her.

"Yes." I offered.

"Sophia Sanchez, Commander, Chrono Base Alpha," she said with a perfect American accent, to the point that I thought her diction might be overly-practised. She extended her hand for an incredibly formal and professional handshake.

"Pleased to make your acquaintance," I said.

And simultaneously absolutely terrified, I thought. I hoped that the quickening pace of the subtle "BEEP"s in the background that indicated my heartbeat didn't betray my feelings.

"Dr. Templeton, rest assured, you're not the first time traveler who's succumbed to hyperoxia upon his arrival, though I thought I had trained my soldiers to do better than to let an innocent traveler pass out like a greased pig in heat," For some reason, I didn't think the idiom was meant as a joke. "On behalf of ChronoSaber, I apologize for any inconvenience caused by your brief hospital stay." She saluted *me* (!) and, after a confused moment, I returned the gesture.

"Quite. Thank you, Commander Sanchez."

"Permission to speak freely, sir?" She stood, unblinking for several moments. *Why is she treating me like her superior?* I thought.

"Uh...granted?"

"Look," she bent over and placed one hand on the bed, the other pointer finger extended directly in my face, "I don't know who you are, or what you're doing here, but first you show up in an old-model time machine, non-ChronoSaber, as far as I can tell, but then word comes down from command that you're to be extended every courtesy of a superior officer while you're here. Forgive my language, *sir*, but that's fucking bullshit."

I raised my eyebrows as sweat began to bead on my forehead, "I...uh..." Did I mention that I've never been particularly good with women? Particularly that vexing creature that is the beautiful woman in power?

"We're to show you around, even take you on a hunt if you like, but we aren't to ask you or answer any questions other than typical pleasantries or background information, nor are we to search or scan your vessel. I don't know about you, but when my job is to ensure the safety and security of this base, no matter how trivial its existence may seem to you or anyone else from the future, I have a bit of a problem with that, okay?"

I was again momentarily at a loss for words. "I…uh…wow…" Commander Sanchez looked at me with a knowing eyebrow; apparently she frequently inspired this kind of reaction in others, or at least other members of the opposite sex. "So, this base…you…ChronoSaber?" I was able to cobble together the faintest hint of a complete sentence.

She rolled her eyes, "Forgive me, I forgot. You're from '2032.'" Her tone made it clear that she already had trouble believing my story. "Do you want me to explain it, or will a holovid suffice?"

In hindsight, oh what I would give to go back and listen to her read from a phone book! But for whatever reason, in the heat of the moment, my curiosity about seeing an advanced piece of technology, even something so loathsome as a holovid, got the better of me.

"Holovid," I said.

She sighed with relief, and the first hint of a smile curled her lips.

"Excellent." She took out her mobile and pointed it at the holoemitter. It continued to monitor my vital signs, but otherwise I was immediately transported, flying toward a city skyline that was oddly familiar, though I couldn't place exactly where I had seen it previously. One incredibly modern building towered over smaller, but equally new and impressive structures surrounding it. At the top, a stylized logo read "ChronoSaber" in a sleek, sexy font, with the "C" turned into a clock face, and the "S" forming its hands.

"Baltimore!" I blurted out reflexively. This drew another eye-roll from Commander Sanchez.

As the bed appeared to move toward the tower, it built up speed, and barreled onward toward the top floor. I put my arms up to shield my face as the "glass" panel of the building exploded into shards that shimmered in the air around me like a daytime constellation. Everything about the video seemed slick; the effects were some of the best hologram work that I had ever witnessed, though my aversion to the medium has accounted for a decided lack of consumption of holovids previously. In fact, I hate to admit as much, but I may have giggled like a schoolboy as the tiny crystals danced around me in the sky.

Unfortunately, the scene inside the building was decidedly not slick. A generic conference room housed a generic conference table, around which any number of historical figures (or, in this case, low-budget lookalikes) gathered. Leonardo DaVinci hobnobbed with someone dressed as an Egyptian pharaoh, while Gandhi and Socrates played chess at one end of the table. In an unfortunately campy touch, a human-sized, somewhat cartoonish, computer-generated version of a dinosaur dressed in a short-sleeved dress shirt and tie, and wearing comically large glasses told a joke, at which Mao Tsedong, Winston Churchill, and Abraham Lincoln laughed uproariously. Ben Franklin, at the end of the table that didn't house Gandhi and Socrates, glared at the group, and banged a gavel to call the meeting to order. A typical oversized, underdressed American-looking tourist next to Franklin snapped several shots of the action with his camera phone.

"Imagine a world where all of your problems are worked on by history's greatest minds." A voiceover began.

"Should Frank's wife apologize for calling him a fat slob? Socrates?" Franklin called out. The actor playing him had obviously watched too much of Dana Carvey's impersonation of John McGlaughlin of "The McGlaughlin Group" fame on those delightfully classic episodes of *Saturday Night Live.*

"What do you consider the perfect human form?" It bugged me that "Socrates"'s accent was thoroughly English.

"Nadia Tyrell, I guess," the touristy fellow answered. The table laughed, though apparently the reference was lost on me.

"And what is man other than the pursuit of betterment and perfection?" Socrates continued.

The tourist over-pantomimed the "deep in thought" pose that involved him furrowing his brow, looking upward, and placing his pointer finger on his chin for a moment, before having his "aha!" moment and raising that same finger in the air.

The camera cut to the dinosaur, "I think that Frank looks great—just good enough to eat!" The good cheer of the table died down as Frank and the dinosaur were transported to a landscape very similar to the one I had just witnessed. The anthropomorphized dinosaur burst through its shirt and tie as it grew exponentially, and let out a resounding "ROARRR!" in the face of the viewer, who was, presumably, meant to be Frank.

Scared for a moment, Frank reappeared and tightened his jaw, resolute as he picked up a rather powerful-looking laser rifle of some sort and began to fire on the King of the Lizards.

"Or what if you could live every fantasy—" The dinosaur fell and twitched for a moment while Frank stood over it triumphantly before the viewpoint cut to Frank surrounded by a harem of female historical figures, ranging from Helen of Troy to Cleopatra to Hillary Clinton.

Suddenly, Frank's "wife" entered the frame, clutching a rolling pin, furious with her husband for his dalliances. The lack of any sort of tact or attempt at subtext was positively jarring.

"Hold on, ladies," the voiceover continued. "We'll take care of you, too." Tom Brady, Tommy Lee, and (most curiously) Tommy Lee Jones surrounded the woman, who immediately dropped her kitchen weapon and let down her hair.

"Sign us up!" Frank and his wife uttered with groan-inducing false enthusiasm.

"Since a joint project between the U.S. Army and ChronoSaber scientists cracked the secrets of time travel, ChronoSaber has been the world's foremost provider of chrono vacations. In fact, we're the only provider!" The scene flashed to a typical "busy, but smiling, drones" office sequence which my father would have likely recognised, absent the happiness.

"Experience history through any number of our vacation packages, each one custom-designed to fulfill your every whim."

The office became a desert, as poorly-costumed aliens forced starving actors in rags to push large pyramid blocks into place, "Want to see how the pyramids were *really* built? We can take you there!" The scenery changed to the harsh, unforgiving Judean landscape that I had visited only a few short days ago. To my amazement, Trent's familiar face greeted me, though he had an arm around each of Frank and his wife. Both of Trent's hands were extended into the Vulcan symbols over each one of their shoulders.

"Want to meet Jesus? He's a time traveler, too!" The narrator churned the contents of my stomach with his overenthusiastic cadence. As if to emphasise the point, Trent leaned in and winked at the camera while Frank and his wife gave a "thumbs-up."

Another moment, and I was in the middle of a busy laboratory.

"Here at ChronoSaber, the world's foremost scientists work hard, day-after-day, struggling to ensure that your time travel experience is as seamless as possible. Anywhere you want to go is fine with us; just make sure we can get you there and back." The scientists huddled around a smaller version of my own time machine and waved as it disappeared, only to moments later shrug at one another when the disk failed to re-appear.

As slick as the holovid had been earlier, even the editor couldn't disguise the jarring jump-cut back to the cartoonish dinosaur, who addressed me with a thoroughly English accent, and was surprisingly articulate.

"If you're viewing this vid, that means you must be at Chronobase Alpha, one of our finest and most popular destinations. Though you've already been thoroughly briefed that no matter what you do, the future won't change, we've chosen this site in the rare event that you have a last-minute 'crisis of morality.'

"The station is built on Isla Yucatan, which will eventually become ground zero for the asteroid strike that will destroy us dinosaurs some five years from now. Rest assured, you're completely safe from any planetary debris, but us dinosaurs are not. We'll suffer much less by dying a noble death by your hand than in a firestorm of unimaginable magnitude should we survive until the asteroid strike."

"Yes, I'm sure being lobotomised by a laser rifle of some sort is far more pleasant than being vaporised by an asteroid," I looked at Sanchez, who only nodded back curtly toward the holovid.

An older gentleman appeared in front of me. He looked somewhat like the actor Ernest Borgnine in his later years.

"Hi, I'm Zane Garrett, CEO of ChronoSaber. I'd like to be the first to welcome you to the ChronoSaber family. Remember, at ChronoSaber, it's always our mission to make sure that you have the time of your life!" He smiled and extended a hand as if to shake mine.

"Time Travel is an incredibly complex scientific concept with many moving parts. ChronoSaber cannot ensure your safety during any of our excursions, nor can they ensure your safe return. All depictions of historical time periods and historical figures are meant for illustrative and parodic purposes and are not meant to be an accurate representation of what your time travel experience will be like. You may pay a premium for time travel services outside those offered by ChronoSaber, but don't expect ChronoSaber to offer a guide or a full travel package. ChronoSaber disavows any and all liability with regard to its products, foreseeable or unforeseeable." The voiceover hurriedly listed the requisite disclaimers.

The image in front of me went blank. I couldn't help but notice that Commander Sanchez actually smiled in the corner of the room.

"So, what did you think?" Sanchez asked

"That was...err...interesting..." I said.

"Our marketing department felt that adding a little humor to the presentation would lighten the mood, maybe get folks' minds off of the dangers inherent in time travel."

"What dangers? Like timeline pollution?" I decided to have a bit of fun with the lovely lady.

The famous Sanchez eye roll reappeared, "Don't tell me I have to give you the lecture about—"

"Of course not," I cut her off. "I was just winding you up a bit, having a laugh, that sort of thing." I chuckled nervously.

Sanchez met me with a glare, "Dangers meaning going too far back in time, too far forward, missing your rendezvous, inserting yourself into an overly hostile situation, or even, I don't know, the whims of what we've figured out is a finicky universe, you know, *real* dangers."

"Too far back or forward meaning either end of the universe?" I asked.

"Not...exactly," Sanchez's expression grew more grave. "Too far back meaning too far to reliably calculate the trip back."

"But we're tens of millions of—"

Sanchez interrupted me with a sigh, "There is...a beacon, of sorts, I suppose you could call it. We brought it back here since the dinosaur package was so popular. Don't ask me how it works, but somehow it makes trips here and back more reliable."

While my mind raced with the physics involved in the very notion of such a device, I decided to occupy her with another question.

"And too far forward?"

"That's the more troubling problem. Anytime we send people farther in the future than April 20th, 2102 they don't make it back."

"What do you mean 'don't make it back?'"

"As in, they don't return. We don't know if they can't return, or if something cataclysmic happens, or if something wonderful happens, but no one has ever made it back from further than that in the future. People have made it back from the 19th of April just fine, and everything was normal, or I should say as normal as it can be in the future. But even if someone's scheduled to come back the 19th and misses the rendezvous, we never hear from them again, which is odd, since we usually can just send another machine from the future back to their—"

"Own time?" I tried to complete her thought, probably in the hopes that it would impress her.

"Exactly," It did not. "The worrisome thing is that the same thing happens with 9/11, or the start of World War II or World War III; people drain their life's savings to try to go back and stop these events, but for whatever reason, they're ultimately unsuccessful. We try to convince them that they're wasting their time, money, and lives, but they insist on going on these stupid errands to nowhere.

The universe has a funny way of ensuring that what should happen happens."

"Quite," I decided to see if perhaps history in the further future might be more kind to my own plight, "Yet you've never heard of me? Phineas Templeton?"

She furrowed her brow, "Can't say that I have, sir. Honestly, something's terribly fishy. HQ wants you treated like a king, but something in all of this just doesn't add up. It feels like you're—we're—being used."

"I know exactly what you mean…" I said. I thought Sanchez hit the nail spot on the head with her assessment; it was almost as if I was floating through a play, assuming a role while dutifully saying its lines and hitting its marks.

"So there's no chance you can take me back to 2032?" I asked.

She shook her head, "Sorry, most of our missions are resupplies from 2041. Even if we could, I'm under strict orders to not allow you passage on any ship other than your own."

"Headquarters?" I asked with a frown.

"Exactly."

"And about this Commander Corcoran—"

She shook her head, "No one really knows. He was kept in quarantine for a while, and the Army did all they could to keep the discovery under wraps for years. They even put out a few different versions of events just so no one would actually know what happened."

"And this 'ChronoSaber?'" I asked.

"Sorry, sir—that's classified."

I could no longer hide my exasperation and shrugged, "So one of the greatest accomplishments of all time, a startling jump forward for the human race, an entire new industry sprung out out of the ether in the blink of an eye, and you don't know, or more accurately, won't tell me the story of how it happened?" I felt my eyes narrow at poor Sanchez, though I shouldn't characterise her as such.

"Look, *sir*, it may seem odd to you, but to us, it's completely normal. I know the war was winding down when you left, but afterward, as you can imagine, security got a bit tighter. R&D programs went completely black, and intel went through four or five different iterations, sometimes purposely filled with disinformation to prevent the enemy from figuring anything out. So yes, though Commander Corcoran may be a genius, and a bit of a rake, he took an oath to keep the details of his journey secret, and he's honoring that oath to this day."

Her gaze was measured and steely; this was a woman who could obviously more than take care of herself. It was clear that though she had been ordered to answer (some of) my inquiries, she regarded it as a chore, one of those "official duty"-type errands that individuals in positions of power dreaded.

I tried to meet her stare, but my eyes widened as my skin went pallid and damp. I would like to say that I wasn't frightened by her, but all indications were to the contrary.

Rather than suffer any more verbal beatdowns, I decided to ask one final question.

"I do say, thank you, Commander. One final thing—is there someone in your outfit with the initials 'T.R.'? Perhaps a Torrance or Terrance, or Thomas, or Tyler, or—"

She smiled curtly, "Dr. Templeton, of the forty-seven soldiers and employees on base, we have a Tom and a Tiffany," I gulped as I realised I hadn't included any females in my ridiculous list, "but neither has a last name beginning in R. Why do you ask?"

"Well, you see, I have a rather curious list of tasks to accomplish, and my errand for this era is to 'dine with T.R.'"

Sanchez snorted as the grin returned to her lovely face.

"I think I know *exactly* what you need to do."

CHAPTER NINE

"The LR-15 Laser Rifle is one of the most efficient and deadliest killing machines of all time. It accelerates a bolt of halogen plasma to the speed of light at the rate of one hundred fifty rounds per minute. This ain't your daddy's hunting rifle." What made this speech more surreal was the fact that it was being delivered by a petite black woman named Alyson ("with one L and a Y") who had greeted me with a sweet "hello" and warm smile moments before.

"You are not to point your rifle at any human targets during engagement. You are only to target saurians, and even then these rifles cannot guarantee success. T-Rexes are mean sons of bitches, and before you know it they'll be on you and using your femur as a toothpick. Am I making myself clear?"

I nodded, though the flak helmet covering my head dipped in front of my eyes when I did so. Apparently though the future had terrifying automatic laser guns and time machines, they still couldn't solve the problem of properly-fitted headwear.

"Good. Now, Templeton, you'll be in the back of the rover. She might not look like much, but she's got some get-up and go. Accelerates to eighty-eight in under three seconds. It is, to use a technical phrase, some 'serious shit,' but Liam over here," Alyson pointed to a lanky, blonde bloke with aviator glasses, "is one of our best drivers. He knows the paths, and he knows how these things think. If you trust him, you *might* make it back here alive.

"Stay in the back of the buggy at all times. If you exit the buggy, we *will not* come back for you—you'll already be sloshing around, dissolving in one of these damned thing's stomachs." I grimaced; the thought had already crossed my mind. "Keep your gas mask on at all times. We wouldn't want you to faint again."

"It was hyperoxia, I can't really—" I interrupted, but was cut off.

"You're the only one scheduled for today, since it was supposed to be our day off," she lowered narrowed eyes at me. "But orders are orders, and these came from HQ, so you must be someone pretty goddamned important. I'll be riding in the back of the second buggy, with Jayden, just in case anything goes wrong. If the shit *really* hits the fan, remember: *return to base.* We have all kinds of nasty firepower we can throw at these things.

"Any questions?" Alyson asked as the sweet smile finally returned. I was quite taken with the petite, yet extraordinarily capable young lady. It was all I could do to blush and shake my head.

She snorted, "Well, guess I covered anything then. It really is pretty simple," she raised her rifle toward the force-field at the end of the long hangar. "Just point, and pull the trigger. Aim for the brain—granted, it's a small target, but I've seen little old ladies knock these things out." She fiddled with a device on her wrist for a moment, and, sure enough, a holopic of a grandmotherly-looking sort popped up in front of us. The look on the woman's face was positively Rambo-esque as she posed with a T-Rex head that looked like a prop from *Jurassic Park*, save for the fact that this one had a sizable hole of singed flesh where its right eye should have been.

"If there's nothing else..." she paused to allow me to interject, but I really couldn't think of anything at the moment. I had never really hunted for sport before...though I suppose I had never hunted for meat, either.

This was a different kind of hunting, though, something dare I say beyond sport, purposely going out into an extraordinarily dangerous scenario with a very real chance of death. I had never been much of a risk-taker previously, save for trusting my Benefactor and using a time machine without taking it for a test run, but I had to admit, this was *exhilarating.* I don't know if it was the strong, independent, beautiful women with whom I had been in contact at the base, or the extra oxygen that no doubt still coursed through my veins, but for some reason, deep inside my brain, below countless physics equations and tidbits of historical trivia, there was a very base layer that very much wanted to kill one of these giant lizards, perhaps the greatest land predator in the planet's history, to show that, yes indeed, I could engage in as manly of pursuits as anyone in history.

Of course, having the holopic of the ordeal would also be pretty neat. Not to mention that I was getting an experience that normally cost several million dollars for nothing.

I followed Alyson, who covered a surprising amount of ground for someone of her size, and Liam as we made our way to the first buggy. A uniformed black man ran to us, and smiled. Alyson met his look with a scowl, but the newcomer simply shrugged.

"Templeton, this is Jayden Washington, the other driver. Late as usual," Alyson said through gritted teeth.

"It was my day off!" Washington protested, but Alyson's scowl remained.

We made our way to the first rover at the far end of the hangar. It was a curious little contraption, like a compact dune buggy, but with the added benefit of powerful laser weaponry.

Liam put on his helmet and protective gear toward the front of the vehicle.

"I, err…so you're pretty good at this?" I asked.

He shrugged, "Been here since we opened. Ain't dead yet. Can't say the same for some of my colleagues, though."

"So it actually *is* dangerous then. That wasn't all poppycock ginned up to scare me?"

Liam laughed and shook his head, "Hell no! We have billionaires that have become giant, T-Rex cowpies. Ever heard of H. Houston Mifflin?" I must've met the question with a dazed expression. "Of course not—you're 'from the past.' Anyway, guy made a fortune in robotics. One day, he decides he's going to hunt dinosaurs. Real gung-ho guy, but kind of a prick. We get out there and this guy decides he wants to face the thing down mano a mano, capice? Some kind of wild west, showdown at sundown bullshit, I don't know. So he unbuckles, gets out, and before he can hit the ground, the bastard has him in its teeth. Wasn't a pretty sight."

"And you're positive this happened? It's not some urban legend designed to—"

"Who do you think was driving?" He lifted up his sunglasses as his eyes fixed on mine, his jaw clenched, unflinching.

I gulped. *What am I getting myself into?* I thought. Perhaps my bravado was just that—*false* courage. Once more, I was certain that my Benefactor wanted nothing more than to send me to my doom.

I hopped in the backseat and strapped myself in. I turned my attention to the LR-15. It wasn't nearly as sleek as any "ray gun" in a science fiction series. It was probably twenty to thirty pounds of brushed metal tubes and gas, an odd sculpture that was almost as ugly as it promised to be deadly. Had I not known any better, I would have guessed that it was some sort of deranged miniaturisation of a long, thin city's waterworks. Instead, it was the only thing that would stand between myself and certain doom at the otherwise humorously tiny hands of the T-Rex.

"You ready?" I heard Liam through my helmet's radio.

"I suppose I am. Why not, eh? I always say—"

The buggy jolted forward, as I almost lost the laser gun from my loose grip around its stock. It was a curious sensation, like being dragged behind a boat, backwards, at an incredible rate of speed. When I came to my senses, I noticed the oddly-matched sounds of Credence Clearwater Revival's "Up Around the Bend" blasting through the speakers in my helmet. The music softened for a few moments.

"Sorry there, buddy; probably shoulda warned ya, but hey, this was way more excitin', wasn't it?" he chuckled. "How's the music treatin' ya?"

"Quite fine, thank you." I hoped my voice wasn't too tremulous as I yelled through the microphone.

Liam laughed again, "All of these millionaires seem to eat this shit up. Gets their blood pumping or, hell, Christ, I don't know, their dicks hard. I'm more of a Bieber fan myself, especially once he ditched all of that teeny bop shit. Real classic shit that really has an edge, you know?"

"I...err...well...I suppose..." Truth be told, I couldn't stand most of the rubbish that passed for "rock music" nowadays. Especially Justin Beiber, whom I found to be particularly reprehensible.

"Awright, well, I s'pose we'll be in T-Rex country pretty soon. May wanna get your rifle all set up and ready to go." I gripped the stock of the rifle, which seemed rather plastic and cheap compared with the rest of the sturdy (if cumbersome) collection of metal pipes and gizmos.

"These paths are set up in a set of joined concentric circles, all the better to confuse the stupid things if something goes wrong. We're headed to the middle right now. Once we're there, get ready to see somethin' that'll blow your fuckin' mind."

I nodded, though in hindsight I don't know why; my back was to his, and we had no way of viewing one another. I thought I might have another minute or so to process that I was actually *hunting dinosaurs sixty-five million years ago*, but the buggy covered ground extraordinarily quickly, and before I knew what exactly was happening, we stopped in a large clearing, probably several miles from the base. It was as Liam had described it; a large, roundish area, perhaps a half mile across. Four paths radiated out from the middle.

What was rather extraordinary, however, was that a "family" or "pride" of stegasaurii grazed not but a hundred feet in front of me!

"I thought this was the cretaceous!" I couldn't help but exclaim.

"Yeah, lots of folks get a kick out of that. 'Stegosaurus was a *jurassic* dinosaur!' Like they have any clue!" Liam laughed again. "All I know is that when we got here, it was all triceratops, T-Rexes, and these characters, and then a bunch of different little beasties I didn't recognize."

"They are *marvellous* creatures, aren't they?" I said. One of the larger stegosaurii snorted on cue as it tore off a bunch of low-hanging greenery and chewed it, rather like an enormous cow.

"They're dumb as shit," Liam laughed, "And smell about as bad—be thankful for that gas mask of yours. But they're ultimately harmless...to us. Damn if it isn't fun to see them fuck up a T-Rex proper, though."

Alyson's buggy pulled up alongside ours. "Well Templeton, you're in luck," her businesslike voice chimed in over the headset. "Looks like you might get to see a real spectacle today. Jayden, the drones!" She commanded. Immediately, two holograms launched from her buggy, and two more followed shortly thereafter from our vehicle.

"Drones...?" I half-asked.

"They're meant to get the attention of the big beasties," Alyson said. "Not that it should be much of a problem with these stegos here, but—"

Suddenly, a shudder. Then another. This wasn't Spielberg's ominous, approaching thunderstorm, but rather the fastest cyclone that the world had ever seen, each "CLAP" closer and louder than I thought possible in nature.

"Lock and load!" Alyson yelled. Liam made a tight turn as the buggy's treads tore through the soft, thin layer of soil and threw up a cloud of debris. When the dust settled, I was able to make out what appeared to be a small bird on the horizon, its brightly colored feathers swirled into a tornado of colour not unlike that of the wormhole, though much smaller and more focused.

Each successive "BOOM" brought the form closer, like a thousand howitzers firing in rapid succession. As it gained on our position, the only thing that I could think was *T-Rex had feathers?*

As if he read my mind, Liam came over the intercom, "It's a nice surprise we like to try to keep. Now get your fuckin' rifle ready to go!"

The mighty feathered creature gained ground as the earth shook violently. I may or may not have needed another new pair of knickers at that moment. What punctuated my thought was the gleaming, ivory-like tusks for teeth that the thing had; it was a machine designed to process flesh, tear it from bone and turn it into nourishment, feeding so that it could kill more, and continue the cycle.

Then came the first roar. My God—that roar! If I hadn't voided my bowels by then, that would most certainly have done the trick. I can say with great certainty that the reprehensible barrister in the *Jurassic Park* movie wouldn't have bothered to have exited the vehicle, entered the W.C., and sat there with his pants around his ankles; how much time that would take when the terror was so present, so gnawing at one's mind even from a distance that I thought it may drive me to utter madness!

"Get ready!" this time it was Alyson, who was perhaps twenty feet to my right. I glanced at her vehicle, and the difference was startling. She sat, steady as a rock, unwieldy laser gun propped on her shoulder, laser sight honed in on the target. Here I was, soiling myself in fear, and this tiny woman was a regular John Wayne.

I couldn't possibly find a woman more irresistible!

"Open fire!" She yelled over the intercom. A torrent of laser bolts exploded at the T-Rex from the buggy next to me. Trees crashed down as the surrounding forest was singed and felled by the focused plasma.

I leveled the weapon and followed suit. The rifle kicked back like a bucking mule as I sprayed the sky with all manner of laser bolts. Alyson's cover fire didn't do anything except anger the great beast, which finally burst into the clearing, taking a number of trees with it.

The stegosaurii immediately lumbered into action. The larger ones formed ranks around their smaller counterparts and brayed and swung their tails wildly. I sat, mouth agape for what must've only been a split second, but felt like at least a minute.

"Fire!" Alyson screamed. I hammered the trigger once more and struggled to wrestle the gun toward the T-Rex. Instead, the rifle cast bolts wildly about above the stegosaurs, which directed their braying at me.

This gave the T-Rex an unfortunate opening; it snatched one of the smaller stegosaurii in its jaws and shook it about, like a dog roughhousing with a toy. A larger stego bleated as the smaller one's cries reverberated around the clearing. The bigger one jumped into action; it swung its tail wildly and connected with the T-Rex's midsection, which sent the predator reeling.

The T-Rex shuddered away in pain and flung the young stegosaur to the ground. We moved again in order to get a better shot at the T-Rex, which had a difficult time righting itself, since it couldn't easily push off of the earth.

"Circle around back, Liam!" Alyson shrieked.

"Roger that. Templeton, fire that thing right up its [STATIC] hole." The radio crackled, though I had a pretty good idea what Liam said.

"Uh...roger that!" I cried. I was relieved that the smaller stego had (possibly?) been saved, but terrified at just how close we were getting to the T-Rex. Its legs kicked up clouds of dark earth into the gunners' seats of the buggies. Its head heaved and its tail snapped like a whip as it fumbled around on the ground.

My heart pumped increasingly quickly as its beat thumped in my head. Coincidentally, it was the only sound that I heard as time finally began to slow down. I leveled the rifle on my shoulder and squeezed the trigger.

A violent explosion rocked the animal in front of me. A shower of miniature lightning bolts ravaged the lizard's body, and for a moment, I felt the slightest pang of remorse as its flesh seized and singed. I allowed myself a wild, primal scream as I continued to pump the poor thing's body with an unending stream of laser bolts; each one elicited a low, glutteral roar from the fallen beast.

Then, it stopped. I released the trigger and surveyed the carnage that I had wrought. The lower half of the dinosaur was an utterly mangled mess of burned flesh and knotted tendons that clung to singed bone. Liam circled around to the front of the animal, and any second thoughts about killing it were expelled from my mind. Its eyes were wide not with fear, but with an eerie hunger. Its sharp teeth were still stained red with the smaller stegosaur's blood and flesh. I looked around to see the "tiny" (though it was still about the size of the buggy), injured animal limp back toward one of the larger stegosaurs.

"Well ain't that—hey Alyson, you ever see anything like that?" Liam asked.

"Sometimes, I love this job!" Alyson said. She punctuated the sentiment with a hearty sigh. Her buggy was positioned in front of mine, and she had a great view of the scene which, from my angle, was to the right of and behind the T-Rex. Dare I say it was the first time she had seemed human, other than the kind smile she had offered me when I first arrived on the hangar deck.

As I looked upon this rather touching scene, I didn't notice the yellowed, bloodshot eye of the T-Rex blink twice. Nor did I notice its chest begin to rise and fall once more, forcing the oxygen-rich air through its lungs.

Suddenly, the T-Rex seized up again. Its powerful jaws clamped down on Alyson's buggy and lifted it into the air as the killing machine attempted to shake the life out of its newest victim. Alyson and Jayden's screams shook my helmet. My eyes went wide and the blood drained from my face. Wordlessly, instinctively, I leveled the rifle on the creature. I hesitated; I was aiming at its head, and just as likely to kill Alyson and/or Jayden as I was the terrible lizard. I re-calibrated and pointed the laser rifle's barrel right at the middle of the giant, feathered beast's torso and unleashed a flurry of shots, all of which missed their mark. They did succeed, however, in drawing the animal's attention toward my buggy.

"Fuck, fuck, fuck!" Liam screamed over the intercom. He jammed the pedal furiously, but one of the buggy's wheels was caught on a tree trunk that had been felled by laser or dinosaur. The T-Rex dropped the other buggy to the ground and tilted its head to one side, curious about this new threat. It swung its head down until its eye was level with my own.

"Shut up—stop it! Don't move!" I hissed over the microphone. The T-Rex's head was right up on me as it struggled to move without any legs. Its large eye stared at me as I sat up, so still that I worried that I might begin shaking or screaming wildly any minute. I waited until I had a can't miss shot, until the pupil in that giant, unblinking eye was but five feet from the barrel of my gun.

"Say goodnight, darling," I smirked as I pulled the trigger.

Nothing came out of the barrel.

I yanked the trigger again, to no effect. I could've sworn I saw those same jaws that were eager to tear me to shreds smile, like a lion must grin at a gazelle before snapping it in twain.

The T-Rex seized up and spread its jaws. I wondered why my life wasn't flashing in front of my eyes, or why I didn't get that serene sense of peace that so many describe right before their own erstwhile demises. As the dinosaur's tusk-teeth bore down on the buggy, I prepared for the worst and covered my head. The T-Rex's roar shook the earth and I felt its warm breath soak my face even through the plastic of the gas mask.

I braced for the inevitable impact, the devilish pain and suffering that was in store for me all because I was damned fool enough to create a time machine in the first place…and felt nothing.

Instead, I heard a "WHOOSH" over the roll cage of the buggy, followed by the sensation of being covered by a quick, cool shadow. The tail of the largest stegosaurus struck the T-Rex squarely on the face; one of the protruding spikes landed right in the damned thing's eye. This time, there was no doubting it; the T-Rex's body went slack. The stego had hit its small target.

The stegosaur shook what remained of the T-Rex's head from its spiky tail with what sounded like a satisfied "harumph," and (perhaps most remarkably of all), without any further fanfare, returned to grazing lazily on the greenery at the base of some singed trees.

I was utterly befuddled, but then remembered Alyson and Jayden. I unfastened my restraints (which set off some sort of an alarm, but I didn't care) and rushed over to their sides. As Liam was marginally faster than I, he arrived first.

Their buggy was a mess. The roll cage was twisted into an unrecognisable sculpture. Alyson sat, her body cast aside like a rag doll within the gunner's seat. A rather large puncture wound in her midsection oozed blood. I rushed to her side.

"She needs a medic!" I exclaimed.

"No shit, pal!" Liam kneeled next to me. "Here, help me with—"

Someone groaned over the radio.

"Jayden!" Liam yelled. He hurried to the front of the vehicle and began flinging debris wildly about the clearing. Liam stopped, his eyes widened with fear and incredulity. He bent over and offered a hand to Jayden, or I should say what was left of him. Only Jayden's original head and chest were intact, though that probably sounds more gruesome than it was. In reality, his right arm and leg, both clearly cybernetic implants, still whizzed and groaned with strain as he staggered to his feet…err…"foot."

Jayden took deep breaths as he placed his arm over Liam's shoulder and limped toward me.

"Take him—I'll get her!" Liam barked. Before I could offer assent, Liam threw Jayden on me in a heap. I nearly collapsed under his weight; in hindsight I'm not exactly sure why I expected him to be lighter.

"Got him!" I did have the man, but just barely. Liam bent over and swung Alyson onto his shoulders in a fireman's carry.

"We have to hurry—that thing's—"

The silence was punctuated by another roar. Though it was far off, it already shook the ground with more force than even the T-Rex's death throes.

"That…thing's…?" I heaved out the question between gasping limps.

"Mother!" Liam yelled without turning to look. I glanced over my shoulder at one of the long vertical paths and found a terrifying sight; another brightly-colored, feathered T-Rex on the prowl, though this one made the first one look positively tiny. The earth vibrated in grand undulations as the creature gained ground even more quickly than the first one.

Fortunately, we were only several metres away from the buggy. I jumped in the gunner's seat; to my credit, I grasped Jayden's robotic hand before doing so and hauled him up into the seat on top of me

92

with all of my strength. Jayden crashed down on me with a thud and an unintelligible groan.

I tried to buckle the restraints around us, but despite my sleight frame and Jayden's missing limbs, I wasn't able to secure the shoulder straps.

"Hang on!" I could barely hear Liam above the rapidly-approaching T-Rex. It appeared angrier than its predecessor...or son...or whatever the first one had been. Everything about it was as ferocious and fierce as the first one, but on a far grander scale; larger teeth the size of doric columns, larger, yellower eyes the size of serving platters, and even (in hindsight) humorously tiny arms that were the size of small tree trunks.

Liam jammed the pedal and churned the stuck wheel against the errant log, to the point that smoke billowed from beneath the vehicle. As the larger T-Rex reached the clearing (and I considered, ever so briefly, to pray to Trent Albertson to save us), the buggy jolted underneath us and took off. I hung onto the roll bar with one hand, and desperately tried to corral Jayden with the other.

"Gun..." Jayden muttered, seemingly drugged and obviously nonplussed by the buggy's sudden (and dare I say erratic) movement.

I was glad to hear the badly-injured driver speak, though I shook my head.

"Out of ammo!" I cried.

"Gun!" he managed to yell. This startled me, and I hoisted the gun onto his right shoulder. "Safety!" his voice was beginning to regain some of its tenor. Sheepishly, I clicked off the safety, which had likely been the reason the gun had not previously fired. I cursed myself for having been so stupid as to make such a grave error that nearly cost us our lives.

I barely ducked my head to the left just before a flurry of laser fire blasted in the general direction of the terrible animal. It sidestepped the beams like they were of little more annoyance than firecrackers left carelessly in its path.

The chassis of the buggy shifted as Liam turned onto one of the circular portions of the path.

"Where are we going?" I screamed over the intercom.

"It's blocking the way back to base!" Liam yelled, clearly annoyed by the question.

"Fucking...backseat...drivers..." It was good to see that Jayden hadn't lost his sense of humor.

The T-Rex crashed around the corner and began to catch up; though the buggies were fast, I gathered that on a curve they likely couldn't reach top speed as quickly. Jayden let loose another flurry of laser fire, and though some bolts hit their marks, they hardly carved flesh wounds in the creature's leathery, feathered skin.

Liam made a sharp left, and then a sharp right as he took us to the second level of this maniacal roundabout. The T-Rex tore through the layer of jungle and emerged directly in front of us. It was all I could do to continue holding Jayden despite how violently the quick bursts of fire shook him.

The T-Rex snapped at the buggy, but Liam made a last-minute change of direction and spared us, though he nearly cast both Jayden and myself from the gunnery perch.

"Almost there—one more turn. Hang—"

Liam didn't complete his thought as the buggy's wheels tore through the soft earth. The chassis teetered at a forty-five degree angle for several moments; I thought for certain that we were about to meet our doom. I shifted my weight in the other direction and pulled Jayden that way with all of my might.

The buggy crashed back down, firmly on its wheels. The T-Rex snapped again, but Liam was quick on the throttle, and we jetted off down the straightaway. The base was finally in sight, as were the four large laser turrets that guarded the hangar bay.

"Mayday, mayday, this is Dino Alpha requesting emergency assistance. We have a broken lizard, over. Request backup!" Liam shouted into the mike.

Immediately, the barrels of the laser turrets began to glow and hum. Each one let out a sharp shriek as they unloaded on the terrifying creature. I cheered with glee as the first bolts of focused energy stopped the beast. The T-Rex staggered forward, but the gunners opened up on it and subdued it in a deadly hail of laser fire.

We headed toward the purplish energy shield of the bay door, and I fully expected Liam to slow down, but he kept his foot on the accelerator.

"Liam? Liam!" I shouted as we hit the energy barrier at full speed. Immediately the whine of the engines died down as several nets ripped over the top of the roll cage; each successive net slowed the craft more than the previous. After several of these nets had deployed, Liam slammed on the brakes. All I can say is that I feel fortunate that my loose-fitting helmet bore the brunt of the impact, both for myself and Jayden.

As we came to a halt, emergency lights flashed and klaxons whined throughout the bunker. A team of soldiers surrounded the craft with fire extinguishers and sprayed it with what I assume was fire-retardant foam. I removed my gas mask and noted that the smell was antiseptic and cold.

"Medic. Medic, goddamnit!" Liam screamed into my headset, over and over again. "Get me some fucking medigel!"

CHAPTER TEN

The next few hours were a blur. I assured the medics that I was fine, but they still confined me to a hospital bed for twelve hours. I pled desperately for some news as to Alyson and Jayden's conditions, but each entreaty was met with suspicious eyes and blank stares. At some point, one of the staff members brought in a rather delectable-looking steak with large, unidentifiable vegetables.

"What is this?" I asked.

"Stegosaurus." The attendant replied.

I initially cringed at the thought that perhaps they soldiered out and collected the poor, dying little stegosaurus that the smaller T-Rex had torn into. Then I realised that such thoughts were absurd; one stegosaurus likely could feed the entire base for a month, and, starving as I was, I tore into the meal.

Not bad, I thought. *Tastes like…bison?* It most certainly did *not* taste like chicken.

The hours passed as I had little to entertain me other than the collection of movies that the holoprojector could play. I've previously mentioned my aversion to the technology, but depending on what era you're from, what you may not realise is that a holoprojector can also create a "screen" in front of you, on which it can project a proper, two-dimensional film. Of course, they had all six *Jurassic Park* films, but I was in no mood to relive the activities of the previous day. I settled on *Dumb and Dumber*; crude as it may be, it is a true classic, and you know what they say about laughter being the best medicine and all that.

The LED lighting in the room was dimmable, yet no matter how "warm" it was designed to appear, I couldn't shake the notion that the lights were sterile and cold, and gave the room the "sickly" feel of a hospital.

Finally, Commander Sanchez entered the room wearing a weak smile.

"Professor," she nodded curtly. "How was your hunt?"

"How was my—? You know damned well how my hunt went, Commander! How are—"

She shook her head, "Jayden will be fine. The doctors have already fitted him with another pair of prostheses. Fortunately, any damage was contained to his limbs and not his..." she looked down toward her groin, which induced a wince.

"And Alyson?"

She turned away from me. "Alyson...didn't make it. Her injuries were too severe to be repaired by medigel."

I felt as if someone had sent a pick axe through my chest. Though I had known her for mere minutes before the hunt, she was dead as the result of my (and my Benefactor's) actions. That sweet, bubbly, yet almost frighteningly capable and intense woman was snuffed out in an instant because of *me*.

Sanchez took a deep breath, "She knew the risks when she came back here. That's why ChronoSaber pays so much—everyone knows it's more than likely a one-way trip. Alyson's family has a better life because of the sacrifices that she made."

"She had a family?" I asked. Tears welled in my eyes.

Sanchez nodded, "Her parents were indigent. She entered the corps precisely so that they could enjoy their later years, so that they could escape the grips of poverty."

I wanted to scream a thousand different things, about how it was wrong that this woman sacrificed so much for people who didn't have terribly long left in their lives, about personal responsibility and my father's "lessons" with the bum on the Thames, but more than anything I wished to curse this damned Pandora's Box of time travel that I had unleashed on the world. I would say "for better or ill," but at this point, aside from soiling myself in history's most ridiculous trophy hunt, most results appeared to be for the latter.

I fought back the tears—again, Brit and whatnot—and merely nodded instead.

"You're free to leave whenever you wish. I regret that you had to experience these unfortunate events at a ChronoSaber facility. Please do not allow what occurred to sully your opinion of ChronoSaber or any of its employees in the future."

I want to find that Zane Garrett and give him a proper tongue-lashing, I thought.

"On a more personal note, don't feel guilty. This happens more often than you think. It's not your fault. Blame those damned T-Rexes. *They're* the true menaces." Sanchez saluted smartly, and I returned the gesture half-heartedly before she exited the room, and I was left to ponder her last several words.

I got dressed (my clothes had been laundered) and slowly slinked toward the landing pad. I thought about asking Commander Sanchez whether I could appropriate one of the LR-15s for my collection, but eventually decided against doing so; I wasn't particularly capable with the weapon, and was therefore only all the more likely to start a war in the past than provide myself with any sort of tactical advantage or other tangible benefit.

A war that will be fought no matter what you do... I thought.

I *did* pass the commissary, and *of course* I asked for several prepared dinosaur meals to go. Apparently it was a frequent enough request that they had the meals waiting for me. I carried them onto the ship and put them in the freezer in the kitchenette.

I heaved myself into the command chair with a satisfying grunt. I weighed whether or not to take a nip or two off of one of the remaining bottles of scotch in my collection, but decided against doing so; I really had no desire to stay in this time period any longer than necessary. I wondered if the beacon would make it any easier to return to "Chrono Base Alpha" should I wish to, and cursed myself for not having tried to key in the coordinates previously. Then, a glimmer of hope: perhaps there were other beacons in other time periods to allow for easy access. I frowned as I realised that even if there were, finding them would be akin to finding a needle in a haystack. More importantly, based on my previous unsuccessful attempts to key in coordinates to 2032, the year of my departure apparently didn't possess such a beacon, now or ever.

As I had surmised, the gravity drive had recharged and was ready for liftoff. I powered on the vessel and began fiddling with the controls.

"Templeton One, this is Chrono Base Alpha control, over, please state your intended destination."

I sighed and turned on the loudspeaker.

"Chrono Base Alpha control, this is Templeton One, I'm heading to…" I read the list, "6-9-932, Chichen Itza, Mexico. Save R—" I hit myself in the forehead; no need to alert these future dwellers that a proper madman had been amongst them!

The moments ticked by, "Roger that, Templeton One. You are cleared for take off. Have a good time, over."

"Roger, thank you, over and out." I felt like a proper pilot! I had always thought about becoming one, though where was the excitement in that? Crappy pay, stewardesses that grow grumpier by the year, flying puddle jumpers for years before you graduate to larger jets, and able to reap the reward of flying interminable intercontinental flights over the same stretch of nameless, indistinguishable ocean? No thank you! I was just fine becoming one of the greatest physicists this world has ever seen, known or not.

I flipped the speaker off and set about entering the coordinates into the computer. "Save R.C. and S.B." Finally, something a bit more concrete! People needed saving, and the newly battle-hardened Phineas Templeton was going to be just the man for the job.

The only problem was, clearly I wasn't. I hadn't been up to saving Alyson, nor had I played any great role in ensuring Jayden's survival. I was weak, impotent, a great mind, to be sure, but trapped inside a frail, cowardly body. Though I had helped to kill (murder?) a T-Rex, I needed a high-powered, futuristic laser rifle to do so. It instantly became clear to me that were it not for that asteroid, mankind very well could have never existed at all.

I brooded as the computer went through its calculations and flashed up a solution:

"99.9%"

Big surprise, I thought. I shook my head. Though the shock of Alyson's death had largely passed, I still felt that stone lodged in the middle of my chest, a gaping wound not unlike the one her torso had suffered from the pike-like jaws of the T-Rex.

"Computer, play us some uplifting takeoff music, please?" I asked.

The speakers blared the first line of Aerosmith's "Don't Want to Miss a Thing."

"No, no! I said uplifting, damn you!"

The staccato beat of "Lee Harvey Super Model" by the Inklings started up. Fair enough. Not my favorite, but it would do.

I then asked the computer for proper clothing for the next stop.

"Request denied—current clothing is suitable," the console read.

I shrugged, and realised that the computer was probably right; what did it matter *what* exactly I wore? Unless the populace believed me a warlock of some sort (and given the time period, that was a distinct possibility) and thought it best to kill me or sacrifice me or make me a part of some other appalling practice, then I supposed I would be okay, after all.

I sighed. My fingers floated over the red button. Though I wanted nothing more than to leave this place at that very moment, I hesitated. With the horrors that this jump had dredged up, what kind of fresh hell awaited me at the next turn? For once, I yearned to be back in my relatively safe, quiet lab, even if it entailed getting yelled at by Avi for butchering some ridiculous pronunciation of some ancient Aramaic word, which, by the way, *wasn't even how they spoke in Ancient Judea!*

My hand quaked. I felt like the rat that I had tormented in my early career by placing a button in its cage. Whenever it hit the button, it was rewarded with a pellet of food, and punished with a shock. The rat knew it needed the nourishment, but invariably after several weeks of mixed stimuli, it would refuse to push the button any longer. And it would die.

My curiosity was similarly crucial to who I was, who I *am*, yet here I was, hesitating like one of those horrible rats in a cage all those many years ago.

Wouldn't it just be easier to give up? I thought. To be honest, this was the first time the thought ever crossed my mind. I could just stay at the base, perhaps hitch a ride to the future and tell *them* about my legacy.

Or 'headquarters' could change their minds and throw you out into the wild, I thought. No, far better to be making progress toward my own time on my Benefactor's terms than to be at the whim of someone else's, though I was beginning to think that my Benefactor might have a few more hands in the workings of ChronoSaber than I had initially imagined.

I sighed again and my tremulous pointer finger landed squarely on the red indicator on the screen before it slid off to the side (did I mention I was sweating a bit?).

The familiar hum of the gravity drive kicked in, and before I knew it, I was off once more. I thought it was a nice touch that Sanchez herself came out to the launchpad to give me a proper send-off. Then her form flickered: a hologram. My smile turned to a scowl in the blink of an eye.

The ship made its way through several families of pterosaurs as I once again admired the oddly eroded surface of the Earth. Obviously, the dinosaurs hadn't a clue that some advanced creatures were coming back to hunt them any more than they realised that a gigantic asteroid collision would begin a chain of events that would exterminate their ilk in the coming years. I wondered if the same could be said for Isaac Newton, or the innocent folks of Nazareth whom Trent continued to bilk. Did they appreciate the many influences exerted on their lives by advanced beings, whom you could even venture were an entirely different species? Or were they similarly blissfully unaware of the external factors that had preordained the outcomes of their lives?

I shook my head as the ship exited the atmosphere. Though the planet could differ from period to period, complete with a gaggle of different sights, sounds, and smells, the one thing that stayed constant was the cold, unforgiving, blissfully empty nature of space. Though, the more I thought about it, even *that* assessment wasn't true; in a few short years, this space would be filled with an asteroid about to obliterate the creatures below. Even the moon could make a surprise appearance, as my near-miss with it had shown. Even in space, everything was guided by the invisible hand, though that hand wasn't so much human as...something else. I was beginning to see what Sanchez meant by "the universe has a funny way of ensuring that what should happen, happens."

Or as Trent might say, "What happened *happened*, bro."

Again, the ship sailed what felt like half-way to Mars, even though I knew that we were just outside of the Earth's gravity well. I pressed the flashing green button, the gravity drive ramped up, and the tunneling lasers did their job. Before I knew it, I was in the same, extraordinarily long wormhole as before. This time, thoughts of creating a black hole and finally receiving my sweet release coursed through my mind.

Alas, 'twas not to be. Though the cabin vibrated for quite a while, eventually the craft emerged on the other end of the wormhole, unscathed. Instead of marveling at the blue marble in front of me, I took the omniyoke and, in a trance, pushed it forward to maximum speed. Maybe this time period would finally provide some answers. Or, at least, a safe respite from the horrors of the last one.

As the machine approached the Earth and the autopilot took over the controls, I was caught off-guard a bit by the familiar shapes of continents and the ice caps below. As I got closer still, everything seemed to be in miniature. The trees weren't as tall, nor the wildlife as gargantuan as sixty-five million years before; a simple fact, I know, but one in which I took great solace at that moment.

Just good old, ordinary devilish people *here,* I thought.

My pulse quickened as the time machine flew over the same area that had served as my hunting grounds those millions of years before, but which had been in reality only a short day ago. I wondered if those individuals shepherding time travellers to-and-fro ever got a sense of temporal vertigo, and found it difficult to keep track of exactly how old they were. Even I couldn't remember what "day of the week" it technically would have been had I stayed in the "normal" course of time in Baltimore, and never embarked on this most foolish of fool's errands in the first place.

Several clearings dotted the thick jungle, but one was of particular interest. It was a smoldering crater carved into the otherwise lush, full canopy. While several stone buildings dotted the fringes, a number of metallic beams were strewn about the surface of the crater. More curiously, the time machine approached the crater instead of the clearing, and set down on the far edge, furthest away from the burning debris.

A couple of figures trotted out from the underbrush. Both wore camouflage body armor and pants with plain green undershirts. One of the forms waved at the ship; I quickly engaged the cloaking device. The figures yelled something at the ship, but I couldn't make it out. I engaged the external mikes.

"Over here!" One of the voices yelled in a heavy, southern drawl.

"Thank God!" The other sighed with a nasally whine.

"You're a soldier—act like it!" the first voice hissed.

I patted the Baretta holstered snugly against my chest as I made my way toward the ostensible gangway. I pressed the panel next to the ship's entrance, and the door opened with a "WHOOSH!" The figures ran toward me.

"Finally! You the rescue party?" The first man asked, surprisingly not out of breath after his sprint. He was handsome, if not dapper, with a well-chiseled jaw coated by a thin layer of stubble. An unkempt, overgrown sandy blonde crew cut framed his recruiting poster face.

"Are you 'R.C.' and 'S.B.'?" I asked, more than a little thrown.

The second man stuck out his hand. He was more than a bit out of shape with curly black hair, and a smooth, boyish face betrayed by a thin whisp of a mustache.

"Specialist Steve Bloomington, United States Army, Sir," the portly fellow said.

The handsome man extended a gloved hand and caught mine in an iron grip.

"Commander Richard Corcoran, United States Navy. Happy as hell to meet you." A sly smile crept over his face.

"You can call me Ricky."

CHAPTER ELEVEN

Part of me wanted to see exactly how much punishment that well-crafted jaw could take. Another part wanted to ask a thousand questions of the man who would some day, somehow, appropriate my accolades for his own.

"Commander Corcoran? Commander Corcoran!" I could barely contain my rage.

"Like I said, you can call me Ricky," he flashed that smile again.

"Indeed I can, Richard."

"Ricky," he said one more time as the smile perked and faded.

"Commander..." I corrected myself. "And apparently, yes, I am the 'rescue party,' as it were."

"And your name is...?"

"Doctor Phineas Templeton, but you can call *me* Doctor Templeton."

"Pleased to meetchya, Doc," Corcoran extended the gloved hand once more, which I grasped out of politeness. The man's grip was firm, dare I say crushing, even.

"Before we go anywhere, though, you're going to answer a few questions." I said.

"Sure, no problem," Corcoran grinned and nodded. He took several steps toward the cloaked vessel.

"What do you think you're doing?" I asked.

"I figured we could do this...you know...in your little ship over here."

"What *ever* gave you that notion?" I asked.

"Look, we've been stranded here for a full week now. We've tried to respect Order One, but these natives are pretty nosy little bastards. They come at us with their spears and want to use us for all of their voodoo rituals and all of that crazy shit, so forgive me if I'm a bit on edge out in the open. Not to mention that we've done God-knows how much damage to the timeline—"

I shook my head without thinking, which stopped Corcoran in his tracks.

"What the hell was that?" he tilted his head toward me.

"What the *hell* was what?" I asked.

He looked at Bloomington, who arched an eyebrow in reply. "Wait a minute, who the hell are YOU?" Corcoran reached for his sidearm and I pulled mine. The pistol quivered in my uneven grip.

"Listen very carefully. My name is Phineas Templeton. I created time travel at the behest of my Benefactor—"

"Bullshit you did!" Corcoran yelled.

"—In the year 2032."

Corcoran blinked. It took every ounce of my restraint to not kill the man right here, though I was certain that he would do the same to me given the chance.

"2032? Twenty years?" Bloomington asked.

Corcoran nodded, "That's impossible."

"Twenty years?" I looked at Bloomington, though I kept my gun firmly trained on Corcoran. "In the future?"

Bloomington eyed Corcoran sidelong and nodded.

"Twenty years...in the past." Corcoran said. "In *your* past. Project Omega's base year was 2012."

"But that's imp—" I had launched into a premature attack, and Corcoran's words hit me squarely on the jaw. "Did you say 2012?" I asked.

"Yeah. 2012. Not what you expected?" Corcoran snorted. Our guns still were trained on one another.

"No...no, most certainly not." The colour drained from my face and I began to sweat cold beads. I reeled backwards, caught only by the same soil that had washed over me some sixty five million years before, one short day ago. I dropped the pistol to my side, and Corcoran cautiously holstered his own weapon.

"2012? But how—?" I asked.

Corcoran sighed, "Project Omega took off from Montauk Naval Base in Long Island in base year 2012, with a mission to conduct time travel experiments. Bloomy over here was the project's chief scientist. I'm the mission's commander."

"How the devil did the Army build a time machine in 2012? I mean, compared to all of the breakthroughs that I've had to make—
"

"Aliens," Corcoran deadpanned. He locked eyes with me for several moments before he broke into a broad smile. "I'm just messin' with ya'. To be honest, Bloomy here is your man in that regard; I just oversaw the program."

"Well...it's pretty complicated stuff..." Bloomington rubbed the back of his rather hirsute neck.

"I'm all ears," I said.

Bloomington sighed, "Project Omega was the culmination of a number of Army Black Ops projects that have been in place since the 1947 crash of an unidentified flying object outside of Roswell, New Mexico."

"So...you're telling me it *was* aliens?" My eyes must've been wider than pound coins.

"No...well...we don't know...but if they were aliens, they looked an awful lot like us. None of those shittin' little grey things that people are fixated on," Bloomington said, with more than a tinge of disappointment.

"After sixty years or so, we realized that it wasn't a spaceship at all. It was a time machine," Bloomington said. "Sure, the gravity drive could be appropriated for interstellar travel," Corcoran rolled his eyes at the pudgy nerd, "but that would take years, decades even. Once we figured out what it was, it was much easier to reverse engineer and figure out which pieces went where."

"But...inertial dampening? Tunneling lasers? Wormholes? Quantum computers?" I asked, incredulous that they would have this technology as well.

"I know, right?" The portly little wise-ass mocked me. "All of it was there. We...uh...worked around the quantum computers. You ever heard of quantum entanglement?"

"No, I built a time machine from scratch in my lab, but I've *never* heard of anything of the sort." I repaid his sarcasm in kind.

"Hey, some of us 'preciate the physics lesson," Corcoran interjected.

Bloomington grew annoyed, "Quantum entanglement is the idea that information can be passed between two molecules that have been 'entangled' with one another, over vast distances, seemingly in violation of relativity, r-tard." I cringed at Bloomington's lack of tact. "Someone on the team postulated that if this arrangement exists through space, then why couldn't it work through time, too?"

It was an interesting theory, and one, quite frankly, that I hadn't considered in my experiments.

"So, we had a highly experimental, super powerful computer in 2012 that would theoretically interact with the time machine through these temporally-entangled pairs of molecules."

"Theoretically," I lowered my eyes at Bloomington.

He shook his head, "Of course, we somehow ended up *here*, which is centuries away from where we were headed, so—"

Corcoran shot Bloomington daggers as he interrupted, "—I s'pose that plan didn't work so well. We lost power pretty quick after we got back here, and control right after. We crashed in the jungle, and I guess we just assumed you were here to rescue us. 'Course, by now the timeline's probably so fucked that Bloomy here doesn't even exist."

"Hey!" Bloomington yelled.

My face finally brightened a bit, "Well, Commander, that's one benefit of my intervention here; you'll be happy to know that the idea that anyone can pollute the timeline is absolute hogwash. What happened, happened." *Bro*, I thought, but didn't add.

What ensued was an hour-long conversation about my travels, and all the various pieces of evidence that appeared to cement that fact, from Trent to Newton to hunting dinosaurs, and the curious presence of the still-enigmatic ChronoSaber in the time-travel economy of the future.

"Well fuck me!" Corcoran finally exclaimed. "Hear that, Bloomy? We're not so fucked after all. The way you've been talking, we'd be expectin' a world where Hitler's in charge if we'd ever make it back. You eggheads and your mumbo—"

"Fucking fascinating," Bloomington cocked his chin, deep in thought. "So, you're saying that the variable model of time is false."

"Completely," I nodded.

"And the static model—the so-called *Terminator* model—" he snorted a laugh, "is how time-travel actually works."

"Indeed," I replied.

"That's fuckin' *crazy*," Bloomington removed his glasses. I didn't know if he exaggerated out of genuine wonderment, or because he meant to mock me.

"Look, are you two nerds quite—" Corcoran interjected.

"Not only that, but everyone whom I've spoken to from the future seems to indicate that you are the one credited with discovering time travel," I nodded at the Commander.

"Him?" Bloomington asked.

"RHIP, son—rank has its privileges," Corcoran nodded.

"And now, I'm afraid, credit was properly given." I finally admitted defeat. How was it even possible? Twenty years in the past? Twenty years! No wonder no one had known who I was from the future; I was the second man. I was Buzz Aldrin. The true pioneer was this rather rough around the edges rake, a Yank whose grand achievement was to stay alive in ancient Mesoamerica for a week with his pudgy, toadish sidekick.

"I duly give it to you," I extended my hand. I hoped that Corcoran focused on the outstretched peace offering rather than my vacant stare and quivering lower lip.

"Where are my manners?" The Commander asked rhetorically, as he removed the gloves that adorned his hands and placed them in his shirt pocket. "I don't think we have to worry about getting ebola from him, Bloomy." He turned toward me. "Do we?" I shook my head.

Bloomington raised his eyebrows at Corcoran, who gave Bloomington a subtle nod in return. Corcoran grasped my hand forcefully once more, and Bloomington followed suit.

I offered a tight smile, "Well, I suppose you gents are in luck. Quarters are going to be a bit tight, but I think I really have no choice, provided you don't mind a few stopovers along the way, and ending up in 2032."

I explained the situation with my Benefactor and the rather curious temporal scavenger hunt he had designed in greater detail. When I finished, Corcoran and Bloomington exchanged arched eyebrows.

"Well...guess it's better than the alternative," Corcoran said. He nodded in the direction of the village.

"Not the hospitable sort?" I asked.

"We've been doing our best to stay out of their way. We were under the impression that by even being in the past, we could've destroyed everything we've ever known." Corcoran glared at Bloomington, semi-serious. "S'pose that all's out the window now."

Corcoran waited for a reaction from his partner, but found only a blank stare in reply. After several seconds, the pudgy scientist fell over in a heap. A sharp obsidian axe blade stuck out of the body armor in his back.

"Steve!" Corcoran yelled. He pulled his pistol, and I followed suit, though I gather my aim and disposition weren't nearly as professional or practised as Corcoran's. There was movement in the underbrush nearby. Fortunately (though that does seem rather grisly in hindsight), the Mayan warriors were streaked with rather obvious, turquoise paint, and wore leopard skins that stuck out like a hitchhiker's thumb against the greenery of the jungle.

One of the Mayans jumped out of the underbrush. The look on his face was what I would call a "practised madness." His mouth twisted into a primal scream as he fiddled with some kind of a contraption that appeared to be a sling-shot, with a long, obsidian-tipped spear as the ostensible ammunition.

Corcoran didn't hesitate. He aimed and pulled the trigger three times. The three slugs found their mark in a tight formation around the poor bloke's midsection, though I don't take too much pity on the man because had Corcoran not felled him, I could have easily fallen victim to the curious spear-throwing device. The Commander fired two more shots in the air, which scattered several other Mayan warriors from the jungle in our general direction.

One of the Mayan soldiers was over-eager and readied his own spear slingshot. Corcoran wasted no time; he turned and fired on the warrior. This time, the Mayan succumbed after only two rounds found their target.

"Anybody else?" Corcoran asked of the remaining warriors. Realising that they likely had no idea what was going on at the moment, let alone what Corcoran was saying, I quickly dropped my own sidearm and put my hands up to show the warriors what Corcoran expected of them.

"That's right—thunderstick go 'boom,'" Corcoran pointed the gun at each of the group of five men in turn, and each one took the hint and dropped his own weapon. I muffled a groan at the Commander's outburst.

With the situation under control, I picked up my weapon and rushed over to Bloomington. I checked for a pulse. Thankfully I found one, albeit weak.

"He's alive," I said. "But he's losing a lot of blood. We need to stop it, lest he go into shock."

"We're fresh out of first aid supplies, Doc." Corcoran deadpanned.

"Keep them under control," I nodded to Corcoran as I rushed back into the ship and retrieved the first aid kit from the glove box. The laser suture wasn't perfect; Bloomington had lost so much blood already, I worried that "stitching" him up would be in vain, but it was the best I could do given the circumstances. I grabbed the curious little device, and as I was about to disembark, I remembered the medigel I had received from Trent, which seemed like eons ago, both literally and figuratively. I raided the hamper in the living area and found the simple robe I had worn in Judea. I practically tore the packet of greenish gel from the crude pocket I had fashioned and sprinted toward Bloomington.

The toady fellow had begun to convulse. He flopped around on the ground like a marlin on the deck of a boat, gasping for water.

"Better hurry, Doc—he's hurtin'!"

I produced the packet of goo, and Corcoran's eyes went wide.

"What in the sam fuck?" he asked no one in particular.

I gripped the axe handle, which gave a bit in hand, slick with sweat.

"This may hurt a bit," I gritted through my teeth, though in hindsight I'm not quite sure why. I jerked the axe out. Bloomington yelped and gasped before he resumed his shivering convulsions.

I took the packet and attempted to tear it in vain for a number of moments. I cursed the individual who would think it wise to create a first aid device that was packaged so thoroughly. Frustrated, I gripped the pouch in my teeth and tore a corner off. In the process, I accidentally digested a portion of the stuff, which I remember tasted rather like pineapple.

I emptied most of the bag's contents on Bloomington's back, which spewed forth blood like a geyser. I held my breath as the goo just *sat* there, and didn't do anything for several moments. Corcoran's jaw was slack, almost as if he wanted to say something, but didn't know exactly how to phrase it.

Suddenly, the blood stopped pouring from the wound. A moment later, the gel had sopped up most of the errant erythrocyte-laden fluid and congealed into a semi-puddle of deep purple goop. As the seconds ticked by, the pool shrank as the substance seeped into Bloomington's wound.

His tremors lessened. The gasps for air turned to great heaving sighs that were, nonetheless, more controlled. After several minutes,

Bloomington stopped convulsing entirely and the deep breaths died down. His body lay there, still, no signs of life. I checked his pulse, for a moment furious that the charlatan Trent's "treatment" hadn't worked.

"His pulse is fine—" the shock showed in my tone. "—*Strong* even. It's remarkable, it's unbelievable, it's…"

"A miracle?" Corcoran asked. He pointed the gun at the warriors several more times as he made his way to his companion's side.

"Steve? Steve you okay?" Corcoran asked, with what appeared to be genuine concern.

"Oooh…my back…" Bloomington grabbed at the small of his back with mock concern.

"Re*mark*able!" I said.

"Son of a *bitch*!" Corcoran let out.

The Mayans all around us had dropped to their knees and bowed at us…bowed at *me*, I should say. Unfortunately, there was no time to bask in the adoration; I hurried over to the warriors whom Corcoran had previously taken out. One had already gone cold and blue, but the other, though not breathing, appeared to be in better shape. I squeezed the remnants out of the package as the turquoise gel oozed out into the man's bullet wounds.

I waited anxiously. I hoped against hope for some sign of life, some indication that this man, too, could be saved.

"Bullets must be in his vital organs," Corcoran appeared over my shoulder, finger outstretched toward the man. "Sorry, Doc—not much I could do. It was either us or—"

I offered a terse smile and a nod, "I'm well aware, Commander Corcoran. Thank you."

"Kul..Kul Kan?" One of the older Mayans asked.

I pointed at the commander, "Corcoran. And I am Templeton."

"Kulkulkan," the man pointed at the commander. "Tepeu," he turned his attention to me.

"Cor-cor-an," Corcoran's eyes betrayed his annoyance. "Doc Templeton," he motioned to me.

113

"Kulkulkan tun Tepeu u tan Chichen Itza." The man's eyes lit up. He dropped to his knees and began to bow, unable to contain his tears. I looked at the others, who were similarly emotional.

Then it happened: the warrior whom I had squeezed the remnants of the medigel onto, struggled to his feet.

"Kulkulkan! Tepeu!" The men began chanting our very odd, Mayanized names. I basked in the glow of the attention and adoration for several minutes, soaking up as much as I possibly could.

"Uh, Bloomington," the reanimated scientist interjected. Though I had only spoken with him for a brief while, his expression was far darker, and his tone more bothered than the relatively harmless nerd with whom I had conversed minutes before.

"Bol-um-yak-ti?" One of the warriors asked quizzically.

"Okay, that's enough, folks." Corcoran was somewhat less enthused. "Hey, chief, give us some room, okay?" The Mayans didn't relent, and now worked themselves into a frenzy. They violently threw limbs akimbo in what I can only imagine was some form of worship.

Corcoran pulled his sidearm and raised it in the air. The Mayans cowered with a chorus of meek yelps. Corcoran smiled and lowered the weapon, only to raise it once more. Much to his pleasure, the Mayans again cringed.

One of the younger warriors was undaunted. He dropped his weapons and cautiously stepped toward us. When he was five feet away, he motioned toward the village, off at the far edge of the clearing.

"Taal," the brave man said, with a wave of the arm.

"I do believe he wants us to follow him," I said. I took a couple of steps toward the man before Corcoran's heavy hand gripped my shoulder.

"Not so fast, Doc," he said. For a moment, I worried that I would be next on his list of victims before I turned and a sly smile crept over his face.

"Wait for us."

CHAPTER TWELVE

"What? That's ludicrous!" Bloomington staggered to his feet.

"Why? Doc over here said that we can't change the future, right? So why not have a little bit of fun with these folks?"

I nodded, "I'm afraid the Commander is correct. No matter what we do, the future simply will not change. We have the time anyway, may as well see how these people live."

"And…you're basing this on what? Some nut guy claiming to be Jesus, and a douchehead high school physics teacher in the sixteenth century?" Bloomington asked.

"Don't forget the dinosaur hunt gone awry," I said, dryly.

"Look, Steve, even I know that stuff Doc had wasn't exactly 2012-era." I nodded, well aware of the irony that the medigel wasn't even from my own time. "If not for him, you'd be dead."

"Maybe I should be! Ever consider that?" Bloomington worked himself up. "We both took an oath, that we wouldn't interfere with the timeline, an oath that—"

"An oath that's a little…inapplicable," Corcoran interrupted. "The man was hunting fuckin' dinosaurs! He has a miraculous…gel…pack…thing… that saved your life! Don't make me pull rank on you, specialist." Corcoran glared at Bloomington for several moments as he allowed the words to sink in.

"Yes, sir." Bloomington offered with a mock salute. Even this minor subordination raised one of my eyebrows, though Corcoran either hadn't noticed or didn't care.

We were led to a large village with a spacious town square. Several stonework buildings dotted the plaza, and mud huts were packed more closely together on the outskirts leading into town. Though impressive, I must admit that none of the monolithic stone buildings with which I'm familiar from Mayan architecture were anywhere to be found.

Corcoran kept his hand cautiously dangled over his sidearm in his hip holster like some damned fool gunslinger from the Old West. Bloomington limped along behind us; though the medigel had apparently regenerated most of the vital tissues, they were still not completely healed. Fortunately, the axe had missed his spine, which only meant that his lungs and/or kidneys needed some time to mend, probably the former judging from his irregularly-staggered breaths.

Much like in Judea, these people were short, and dare I say rather distasteful to look at. There were some exceptions, of course, but Corcoran and myself towered over virtually everyone that we encountered. Even the sturdier Bloomington was taller than most of these feistier miniature humans.

Fortunately, the smell was somewhat better around Chichen Itza; as a pungent aroma of corn covered up most of the most offensive odors that we would normally be subject to in a place without proper hygiene. I reflexively reached for the bottle of Purell that I had stashed in my pocket and gave my hands a good slathering of the stuff. For once, I relished in the antiseptic, hospital-like scent, which actually smelled "clean," and not overly-medicinal.

The men brought us to the largest stone building at the far side of the clearing, a rather crude, haphazard structure that was nothing like the pristine, well-fitted-together Mayan masonry work with which I was familiar. There was a small door that we had to bend down to enter, guarded by two men with the spear-tossing contraptions.

In the middle of the room sat a rather ghastly fellow, more rotund than most of the others but with a face full of ornamental piercings that made his head look like a pincushion. The man's eyes went wide as we entered the room, then narrowed as he tried to reclaim control.

"You must be the chief," Corcoran said. He extended a naked hand to the man seated in front of him. The guards reached for their weapons, but I anticipated as much and moved my hand over my own sidearm, now stashed safely in my waistband. The warriors flinched and backed down as I smiled, fully self-satisfied for the first time in quite some while; I felt positively badass.

To his credit, Corcoran never wavered. He held out his hand to the rotund man in front of him, who eyed the appendage skeptically. After several contemplative moments, the chief grasped Corcoran's hand. The chief's momentary wince let me know that Corcoran gave the same hard, alpha male handshake to this peculiar little man as he had me earlier.

The chief smiled and began to speak. Unfortunately, I can't recall exactly what he said, since to my ears the long string of Mayan words was gibberish.

When he was finished, Corcoran and I raised eyebrows at one another.

"Well?" the Commander asked.

"What?" I replied.

"Say something!"

"How am I supposed to respond to *that?*" I asked.

"I dunno, you're the guy from the future. Don't you have any kind of a...gizmo or something that can talk to these folks?"

"I...well...I...uh..." I looked from Corcoran to Bloomington as both men stared back, now hoping that *I* could somehow produce the same "magic" that they had used to wow the Mayans.

Instead, I began to pantomime my journey here, as well as what I understood to be Corcoran and Bloomington's voyage. I used my fist to represent the earth, and my pointer finger my vessel as I "lifted off" the surface of the planet, and built to the ship as it "zoomed" through the wormhole. I had no idea how to convey time travel, nor did I have any real desire to do so. After all, why did the Mayans need to know that we were from the future? I suppose "alien being" would have to do for the moment.

The Mayans sat, utterly enthralled. With each flourish I added to the story, they let out wondrous gasps and "oohs" and "aahs." I hadn't ever much considered public speaking my forte, outside of presenting muted, dry, low-level research for other physicists in Hopkins' physics department, which was utterly soul-crushing, a mere annoyance that took a valuable hour or so of my time every few months to justify my rather extravagant lab space.

But this experience, telling the story to a rapt audience, was far more exciting and, dare I say, fun. I delighted in eliciting any kind of an emotional reaction from the onlookers, especially since the crowd was made up largely of erstwhile stone-faced, brutal warriors that didn't understand a lick of English, King's or otherwise.

I had just finished acting out my adventure being chased by dinosaurs when I had a bit of an epiphany.

"Hold on one minute," I said to Corcoran as I rushed past him.

"Hey, wait, whereya goin'?" He asked as I worked up to a sprint. "Where's he going?" His voice receded rapidly as I gained distance from the hut. I raced through the clearing to the spot where the time machine was parked. I fumbled around the exterior for several moments before I found the panel and placed my hand upon it. The disc and open doorway appeared and I rushed inside.

I hurried to the glove compartment and opened it to reveal my tablet, carefully filed away behind the various vacuum-sealed outfits.

"Computer, any chance you can pull up ancient Mayan language patterns and place them on the tablet as an app?" I stared at the screens on the console for a moment in anticipation of a response.

"404 - The Page Cannot Be Found." Both screens filled with the familiar error message.

"Wise ass," I muttered under my breath. Of course, there would be no internet in ancient Mayan times; how could I have been so careless?

Then, another thought. "Computer, is there any chance that the Mayan language patterns are pre-loaded on the tablet?"

The screen went blank for several moments before an animation of the tablet came up. The computer showed a cartoonish hand switch to the tablet's search function and type in "languages." A hidden folder popped up with a note:

"Dearest Finny,

I take it you haven't solved the language problem yet. This is only a temporary solution; you *must* figure out what to do by the end of your next jump or you will be utterly lost. Please do not try to take advantage of my generosity.

Humbly Yours,

Your Benefactor"

"Clever old devil," I said. I looked at the folders that popped up on the facsimile of the tablet: "Mayan, Latin, Arabic, French, German."

Looks a tad more permanent to me, I thought. I pulled out the tablet and followed the instructions to pull up the Mayan folder. I tapped the icon and an old-timey microphone popped up on the screen.

"What in the hell?" I asked no one in particular.

"Ba'ax ich Xibalba?" The tablet parroted me with a warm, female, vaguely mechanical voice, presumably in Mayan.

I smiled and shrugged as I jogged briskly back to the King's hut. I giddily held the device out toward Corcoran.

"What is this? Some kind of fancy iPad?"

"Ba'ax lela'? Ts'iiboltik iPad?" The tablet responded.

"Very cool," Bloomington finally lit up a bit.

"Hach siis," the tablet responded.

"Stop it!" Corcoran shouted at the device.

"Haual!" the tablet barked.

I held my finger up to my lips as Corcoran was about to take possession of the device and smash it to bits. I addressed the chief.

"Noble chief, we come in peace," I began. "We have travelled a long ways through space and time to visit you, and bring you

119

knowledge and good fortune." I said. The tablet dutifully spat out a string of Mayan.

The chief responded, "This is not good Maya. Some words, okay. Others, not. You are spacemen? Warlocks?"

Corcoran opened his mouth but I preempted him.

"Spacemen," I said as I lifted my eyes to the ceiling. The chief followed my lead, then was jolted as he spoke once more.

"Wonderful spacemen, welcome. I am chief Pacal of the great city of Chichen Itza. We welcome your otherworldly knowledge of the gods."

"What are you doing?" Bloomington whispered in my ear.

"Having a spot of fun," I said. "Care to join?"

Truth be told, I had rather enjoyed the rush I got from play-acting my strange journey to the rapt crowd in the stone hut, and we still had ten hours left in the time period, so I decided to give the Mayans a show they would never forget. Perhaps I was blinded by arrogance, or even hubris, but more than anything else at that very moment, I wanted this group of people to think that I was the smartest being they had ever met.

Unfortunately, I doubted that even the brightest Mayan would be able to understand isolated gravometrics, or advanced laser tunneling theory. Compounding the problem was that I didn't have an internet connection, and the vast majority of apps on my tablet relied on being tethered to the cloud in one way or another, or at least most of the ones with useful information to impart did.

I exited the translation program and scrolled through the list of apps, searching for something stand-alone, yet utterly useful. I settled on the "Night Sky" app, which defaulted to the current view of the cosmos. Even without an internet connection, one could enter any relevant date and the app would calculate the position of stars, planets, and even the exoplanets that had been discovered as of my latest sync.

As soon as the star map came up, another round of "oohs" and "aahs" resounded through the crowd. I entered that evening's date and pinched and pulled through various constellations and stellar phenomena. The Mayans sat in rapt silence. I did my best to explain the various concepts in simple English terms, as the translation app apparently didn't work in tandem with others, but by-and-large, I think the Mayans were content to sit through this most curious of presentations.

One person who seemed anything *but* content was Bloomington, whose body had regained enough rigidity for him to stand in a corner behind me and shoot me daggers during the entire affair. Perhaps it was a case of scientific envy, or the childish manner in which I had handled being told that I wasn't, in fact, the inventor of time travel, but whatever the case, whenever I addressed his corner of the room, his paunchy little face was twisted into one of the sourest pusses I had ever seen.

I continued for several hours, enjoying the attention much as before until my voice hoarsened, at which point I finally put the tablet down. The guards let out sharp gasps and raised their weapons.

"Maas!" the chief's eyes were alight with anger.

"I think they were enjoying the show, Doc," Corcoran allowed himself as he reached for his weapon. This time, the guards were resolute.

I fumbled through the tablet's search function quickly to pull up first the hidden folder, followed by the Mayan translator.

"Maas! Maas!" The crowd had joined in with the chief.

"More! More!" The tablet repeated in its monotone, soft female voice.

"I think we knew that already," Corcoran said with a smirk.

"They want more?" It was Bloomington, softly, over my right shoulder. "I'll give 'em more." He cleared his throat.

"It all began with a big bang, billions of years ago..." Bloomington recounted, slowly and deliberately. "One moment, one explosion, that ignited the heavens and created the building blocks from which we all were created." It was oddly stirring and poetic, and absolutely not what I would have expected previously from the odd little toad. He continued to detail most of the important events in human history, complete with dates, at least as accurately as he could remember them. I was amazed by the man's seemingly photographic memory and recall, which I couldn't help but think was rivaled only by my own keen intellect.

The tablet dutifully (presumably?) spit out the Mayan translation of whatever Bloomington said. After a few minutes, the chief called some of his warriors over and dispatched them out to the village. They returned with several harried, even smaller men led at spearpoint. Each one carried a brush and several hastily-prepared pots filled with paint. These men began sketching glyphs on the walls of the "palace" as quickly as thye could manage.

Bloomington spewed forth information for a good long while, well past the hour of the setting sun. Once more the Mayans sat, enthralled, particularly when Bloomington referenced any sort of war. Though I didn't notice that he particularly tried to focus on conflict, there was certainly a lot of it, and the Mayans, being a war-like lot, I surmise, enjoyed hearing about the advancements as far as humans deciding to end one another's existence.

"Let's see...then London will host the Olympics, and then, after that, we left on our journey and arrived here."

"Why?" The chief asked without hesitation.

"PACHOOM!" Corcoran put his hands together to form one fist and "exploded" them slowly apart, much like Bloomington had done to open this odd little history lesson. I must've done a double-take.

"What in God's good name are you doing?" I hissed at him, fortunately softly enough not to be picked up by the tablet.

"Having some fun," Corcoran said.

"When will this happen?" The chief demanded to know.

"December 21, 2012," Corcoran said. The tablet calculated and spit out the Mayan translation as the Commander turned to me, eyes locked on mine. "Same day as we left."

His gaze was even, unflinching. My eyes grew wide and fearful momentarily. Then I narrowed them at Corcoran.

"Seriously?" I asked.

Corcoran only nodded.

I looked at the chief and the others, whom still practically leered around the room at one another, mouths agape.

"That's not true! I'm from even further in the future than this man!" I blurted out.

The chief's eyes narrowed and he began to speak.

"No offense, noble Tepeu, but Kukulkan is the wielder of thunder and life and death itself. You are a great giver of life, but only Kulkulkan would know something about the destruction of the world."

"Wonderful," I said. Corcoran could only smile. "Do you bloody well know what you've done?" I asked him.

He shrugged in reply.

"Well, I don't know about you, but I'm exhausted. Time for some shut eye." Corcoran yawned for effect and stretched as he turned to exit. He was met by two spear tips, leveled at his chest.

"Aw, *come on*, guys. Don't make me—" he reached for his sidearm, but the men jabbed their spears at him. Corcoran shoulder rolled away from the warriors and came up in a kneel, pistol leveled at the two guards that had just tried to stab him.

"No blood today, pal," Corcoran said as he cocked his pistol, "'cept for your own."

The tablet dutifully translated the phrase. Two guards had flanked me as the chief approached. The stout man nodded at the tablet, which I now clutched at my chest.

"Give," the tablet barked as he kept repeating the Mayan equivalent.

"Leave him the fuck alone, Paco," Corcoran nodded at the chief before he aimed squarely at the fat noble. Bloomington stood in the corner of the room, hands raised in the air.

The guards did not take kindly to Corcoran threatening their leader. The soldier was undaunted; he trained his gun on each armed man in the stone hut in turn. I slowly moved my hand toward the pistol in my waistband.

"Noble chief, if you do not cease immediately, we will be forced to use magic to—"

"Do not threaten *me*, spaceman," the tablet said in its feminine monotone. "I am Pacal, king of all of Chichen Itza, ruler of—"

"Fuck this," Corcoran said as he dropped both men at my sides with two well-placed shots each. I hit the floor as the shots found their marks, made all the more impressive that Corcoran only had the glow of the tablet with which to guide the projectiles. Bloomington waddled toward the door quickly, like a duck with its arse on fire as I pushed myself up and followed suit.

Corcoran already had leveled his gun on the other guards, who had raised their spears and hesitated. The scribes and few women in the hut screamed all around us as Corcoran's gaze bore down on the warriors. Another must've made a move toward one of us as Bloomington and I made our escape, as four more shots rang out. Once we were clear of the door, Corcoran turned and followed. Though it was dark, the sounds of spears flung through the odd catapults surrounded us. Corcoran turned and provided cover fire every so often as we scrambled toward the clearing.

I had never been so glad that I had maintained such a trim figure in all of my life. Unfortunately, I couldn't say the same for Bloomington, who lagged behind, and, quite frankly, put Corcoran in harm's way since he forced the far more capable soldier to cover his ample arse. How things may have been different if one or both of them had been felled by the Mayans!

I suppose fortunately both of them survived and sprinted toward the time machine as I frantically searched for the entrance panel. Finally, my hand connected with a non-metallic surface, and I heard the familiar chime signal acceptance of my handprint, and the craft, as well as the doorway, appeared in front of us. I scampered up the steps and heaved myself inside, utterly exhausted.

Corcoran raced ahead to take a position on the ramp leading to the entrance and fired more covering shots at the pursuing warriors (he must have reloaded at some point during our escape). Bloomington thundered toward the rectangle of light in the middle of the dark jungle and (it seemed to me, at least) took his sweet time loading himself into the craft.

"Computer, close door." I asked firmly, but politely.

Nothing happened.

"Computer, close the door." Again, silence.

"Computer, please close the fucking door, right fucking now!" I was beginning to lose it.

"Runnin' low on ammo here!" Corcoran yelled from the ramp as he fired two more rounds.

I forced myself up and fumbled with the armory lock while Bloomington made his way to the glove box, still open from my giddiness getting the tablet earlier.

"What are you doing?" I asked him off-hand.

"Helping the Commander," he replied, matter-of-factly. He took two objects out of the glove box and rumbled to the doorway.

"Nothing valuable!" I yelled after him.

"It's not!" He screamed in reply. I heard two loud thuds outside of the vehicle. Almost immediately, the ramp relented and sealed up the vehicle.

"Finally!" I screamed. "Cursed machine! Engage cloak, engage 360-degree view. And external light."

This time the computer complied post-haste. The walls of the vehicle seemingly disappeared as the external light engaged, and, sensing movement, turned to face our pursuers.

Five flung spears appeared in mid-air. They rapidly gained on Corcoran and Bloomington; even Corcoran flinched as he braced for impact.

Suddenly, five sharp "clangs" in rapid succession ringed the air, as each spear fell harmlessly to the ground.

"They're going to have to do a spot better than that to bust into this girl," I said.

"Too cool!" Bloomington exclaimed, almost like a kid in a sweet shop.

I smiled tersely. "By the way, what did you throw at them?" I asked.

"Just a couple of thick books that I found in that glove box. They were the heaviest things I could find on short notice."

My jaw involuntarily dropped as I rushed to the spot that normally became the gangway when lowered. In front of me, two of the warriors held up *The Way Things Work*, as well as the *World Almanac* that I had brought should my tablet fail. The men looked at one another as they shielded their eyes from the bright light in the middle of the jungle, exchanged some Mayan words, and retreated cautiously into the wild darkness that surrounded us.

CHAPTER THIRTEEN

"Are you quite *mad*?" I asked Bloomington. I put up my dukes in proper Eton fashion and faced the man.

"What? I just spent hours telling all of those mouth-breathing Mayan *hard-ons* secrets about the future, and you worry about a couple of innocent books? In English no less?"

"I worry about the books because they might be our only way to survive should this machine crash to bits and leave us stranded in the past!"

"Hey, knock it off!" Corcoran raised his pistol at both of us. "No use caterwallin' about what's happened. What happened, happened, ain't it, Doc?"

I met Corcoran's eyes for a moment, and when I had turned back, five flabby, sausage-like excuses for fingers brushed me alongside the jaw.

"Goddamn it, Bloomy!" Corcoran yelled as he pulled his partner off of me.

"You pimp! You fucking pimp and rogue!" I screamed at the man.

"Fuck off, you fancy fuck!" He spat the words at me and I wanted to get one shot in, just one good punch to teach this little shit what was what.

Unfortunately, that wouldn't be proper—wouldn't be English.

"Hey, Doc over here's done a lot for us," Corcoran said. "Without him you'd still be fightin' off Paco and his band of merry Mayans back there."

"First of all, it was *Pacal*," I corrected him.

127

Several moments of silence followed.

"Aw, kick his ass, Bloomy!" He released his friend at me and I landed a rather clean overhand left square on Bloomington's jaw. His flabby face bounced like jell-o as the (admittedly not incredibly strong) force of my fist connected flush. The specialist's head turned on a swivel away from his momentum as he reeled backward, and crumpled in a heap.

Corcoran immediately rushed over to the man, "Serves you right!" he yelled at his friend before he turned to face me. "All right, now you've got it out of your system, Doc. That'll be all, for *both* of you!" He directed the last statement at both myself and Bloomington. "Am I clear?" As if I needed any more incentive, he patted the sidearm in his hip holster.

I nodded, though I like to think not incredibly meekly.

"Very good. Tell your pudgy little friend to mind his manners next time!" I couldn't resist getting one final dig on Bloomington before I took a few deep breaths to calm down.

"Fair enough," Corcoran said. "Now…do your thing to get this machine ready to go."

"I'm afraid we still have several hours until the gravity drive is recharged," I said.

"What?" Corcoran asked.

I rolled my eyes, "The…engine won't be ready to go for another six hours or so. Do you really want me to explain—"

Corcoran shook his head, "Unnecessary. Alright then, we'll all rest up and get ready for the jump."

"Just so you and your friend don't get any ideas, remember that this craft will only jump between this point and the next one on the list. Besides, the computer is locked to only identify my voice-print commands, so if you have any designs on—"

Corcoran shook his head, "No offense, Doc, but if I wanted to hijack this thing," he patted his sidearm, "I would've already. We get it—this thing needs you to go anywhere. Got it. You're safe. I'll protect you. You have my word."

I sized the man up for several moments before I nodded my assent.

"Good. Great. Wonderful. Now you take whatever bed you want, and Bloomy and I'll find a corner somewhere to lie ourselves down."

"Nonsense," I said. "You two take the bunks. I'll take the command chair."

Unfortunately, the soldier didn't offer the usual courteous protestations to which I was accustomed.

"Even better. Rest up, Doc," the man placed a meaty paw on my shoulder. "Somethin' tells me we're in for a long day tomorrow."

I helped Corcoran carry Bloomington, who was only now beginning to sputter gibberish, into the quarters and shut the door. I freshened up a bit in the head, and even had a chance to take a shower, a luxury which I hadn't enjoyed since the staff at Chronobase Alpha had presumably cleaned me after my run-in with the T-Rexes.

As I brushed my teeth (which were in far better condition than most Englishmen's, in large part thanks to my Yank of a father's influence), I looked into my reflection and immediately noticed my sunken eyes, sucked into their sockets deep inside of the mirror. Though I could wash away all of the dirt and blood from these increasingly violent encounters, no amount of scrubbing could mask the very real fatigue with which I currently struggled. It was one of the increasingly nagging results of being a time traveller without a home time, destined to jump every twenty one hours and six minutes, give or take a few. My days were shorter than most, yet I still had no way to measure when the last one ended and the next one began.

Set a tablet alarm, you twit! I screamed at myself in my head, with enough force and volume that it shook me out of my trance. Or perhaps it was that I was dozing, even now, toothbrush in mouth (always post-floss, so as to rub away all of the grit from between the teeth. At least that's how pop always taught it).

I shook my head slowly and finished with my personal hygiene routine. I felt like a new man...except for one thing, which I couldn't exactly put my—

The contacts!

Of course! I could finally dispose of those wretched things. I had extras in the glove box should I need them once more, as I was utterly as blind as a bat without correction, but until now, for whatever reason, I hadn't thought to remove the bloody annoying things. I poked and prodded my own eyes with glee, eager to remove the offending plastic discs from their temporary homes.

When I removed each one, I held it close enough to my eye to see all of the dirt and grime caked across its surface. It was the oddest thing; that little piece of plastic was caked with millions of years worth of different types of particles. It was an archaeological relic, something that future geologists would literally kill to get their hands on.

And here I was, about to throw it away! Instead, I made my way back to the command chair and opened the glove box. I found a specimen bag in the compartment and carefully lowered each lens in turn into the plastic receptacle. I then filed the bag carefully behind the various sets of clothing, presumably for historians of the future to catalogue and celebrate.

Though my conversation with Commander Corcoran, or "Ricky," as I would soon begin to call him, had been somewhat heartening, I still didn't completely trust either of my fellow time travellers, especially in the wide-open cabin.

"Computer, set up a proximity perimeter at the edge of the cockpit...entry only." The console flashed with a confirmation message. Despite the presence of a trained killer and a man whom had tried to engage me in fisticuffs mere minutes ago, I was exhausted from the day's events and fell asleep easily.

The next morning, I awoke before Commander Corcoran or Bloomington and was able to relieve myself before the others. Unfortunately, upon my return to the command chair, I had forgotten about the proximity perimeter, which the computer triggered in what I like to think of as another one of its persnickety, wise-arsed tricks.

Corcoran bolted out of the quarters, ready to fire at whatever intruder was lurking.

"Computer, cease alarm!" I projected above the screaming claxon.

"Jesus, for a moment, I thought that Paco's boys had come back for more," Corcoran said, with what I thought was a twinge of regret. Bloomington, for his part, staggered out of the room still in a bit of a daze; I suppose that's what he deserved for daring to engage the two-time fifth runner-up at the annual Eton boxing championships in a round of pugilistic exploits! All unofficially conducted, mind you, but I convinced myself that I packed quite a wallop nonetheless.

"I assure you, the cabin is quite secure," I told the American Commander.

Corcoran's face turned serious, "Bloomy has something to say to you."

Bloomington's fat form staggered forward, "I'm sorry for being such an asswad last night. You're right, those books could be useful down the road, and I'm sorry I threw them at the Mayans."

I wanted to tell the little toad right off once more, but I was able to maintain my composure.

"Apology accepted. I, also, apologize for perhaps…overreacting a bit."

Bloomington mumbled something.

"What was that, Steve?" Corcoran asked.

"Thanks." Bloomington said once more, more audibly.

"Good. Now that you two have kissed and made up, can we get the hell outta this place and back to civilization?"

I thought the better of cracking wise that had I kissed Bloomington, he had most certainly *not*, in fact, turned into a prince, and instead nodded. I grabbed my tablet (thank goodness I hadn't dropped *that* during our hasty retreat) and pulled up my Benefactor's scanned list to see the next destination:

"31-12-1985: St. Louis, MO, USA: Communicate w/ VB"

"VB...St. Louis...80s...Vic Burnham?" Corcoran thought aloud over my shoulder.

The name sounded familiar, but my look must have been sufficiently vacant.

"Rich guy, billionaire, one hell of an investor?" Corcoran continued.

"The Sage of St. Louis?" Bloomington offered, the words muffled through his stuffy nose. I must have really popped him one. "When he croaked, he only had the most extensive collection of Star Trek memorabilia in the entire world."

"Ah, indeed," I said, with a smile. As a bit of a Trekkie myself, I knew I had heard the name somewhere before. His collection was filled with all manner of rare props and other bric-a-brac. "He was quite the stock picker, wasn't it now?"

Corcoran nodded, "Damned straight. My mom worked in the same building as his company, Burnham Herrington."

"You grew up in St. Louis?" I asked.

"Sure." Corcoran said. Both Bloomington and I looked at him with an arched eyebrow. "The suburbs." Corcoran tried again. This only increased our skepticism. "All right, all right, maybe a little beyond the suburbs, but the point is, the guy made a fortune picking stocks, starting in the sixties, all the way through the mid aughts. Made a big splash sometime in the—"

Corcoran stopped himself.

"In the...?" I had the distinctly unpleasant experience of feeling like Hank Fleener browbeating Sir Isaac into an answer.

"The mid-eighties. Announced one day, New Year's Eve, that he was going to donate his entire fortune to a charity after his death, give it all away. One hell of a nice guy."

"Well then," Bloomington wheezed, "I think we have our man."

No kidding, genius, I thought, but once again held my tongue. Of far more import to me at the moment was the thought that without Corcoran on board to flesh out the details of the rather notorious life of Victor Burnham, I would have wandered around downtown St. Louis of the late eighties, foolishly asking prostitutes and drug addicts where I might find "VB," though I imagine the prostitutes may hear the initials somewhat differently and make an offer of their services. Though I had an inkling that these little "coincidences" that I had been experiencing were, in fact, nothing of the sort, it did seem rather convenient that this soldier was from the place we were about to visit (or at least thereabouts).

I checked the indicators for both the gravity drive and tunneling lasers. Both were green. I dialed in the proper time and set the coordinates to St. Louis, Missouri. I must admit, I knew little of the town outside of some of the more radical urban redevelopment proposals of the city's young mayor, Titus Yeardling, over the past several years, though I suppose that's another tale for another day.

"Computer, ready ship for time travel." I said. The right console flashed green. I hit the flashing red "Engage" icon on the left panel and the familiar humming and whirring of the gravity drive kicked in.

"What in the hell...?" Bloomington asked.

"What? Didn't you two come here in a time machine?" I asked.

"Sure we did, just nothing quite so—"

"Advanced?" I said with pride.

"*Loud*," Bloomington said. I forced a grin.

"What's the expression, computer?" I looked skyward, "'You Ain't Seen Nothing Yet?'"

Thankfully, the QC didn't have one of its momentary lapses and the sounds of Bachman Turner Overdrive's hit flooded the cabin. Corcoran and Bloomington looked at each other and shrugged.

"Don't tell me that you two of all people don't appreciate some classic rock!" I said with a genuine grin. "The first two individuals from the recent past that I meet and neither can—"

Bloomington shook his head, "This isn't classic rock!"

"Beg your pardon?" I asked.

Corcoran nodded, "He's right, Doc. Stones, Zeppelin, Stooges, even Ozzy or I'd give you Clapton, but this? No thanks."

"Well, it's considered classic where *I* come from…" I tried to recover.

"Twenty years in the future?" Bloomington asked.

"Computer, please go to three-hundred sixty degree view." I said, eager to prevent this "ganging up" from going forward. The cabin walls shimmered away as the craft hovered above the wide expanse of jungle below. It was an expanse marred only by the crash crater from which we presently rose, as well as the rather dowdy version of Chichen Itza in front of us.

Curiously, as we hovered overhead, a number of the villagers looked up and pointed. More still fell to their knees and bowed.

Then I remembered that the cloaking device automatically disengaged upon takeoff, and their wonder was somewhat more understandable. It appeared as if they were screaming something toward the heavens at this vehicle of the "gods" who had supplied them with amazing knowledge and technology.

Against one of the village walls a more grizzly scene played out: four of the warriors who had ostensibly been involved in the previous day's altercations lined up several otherwise unremarkable individuals. A rotund figure commanded the soldiers from the rear. The round man looked skyward and pointed at the peons along the wall. Spears shot out of the odd slingshot contraptions in the warriors' hands and pinned the villagers to the wall. The warriors seized upon the men, clawing at their wounds, not to stem the tide of blood, but rather to increase its flow.

I flinched at the sight and wanted to wretch.

"Well I'll be damned…" Corcoran said over my shoulder.

"They're…they're *slaughtering* each other!" I let out a panicked whisper.

"Why would they do that?" Corcoran asked, eyes still wide with wonder.

"Isn't it obvious?" Bloomington said in his clogged voice. "They're trying to appease us."

"Beg your pardon?" I asked once more.

"Or I should say, they're trying to appease the Commander."

Of course…all of the killing and blood that had been spilled when they angered the "gods." Corcoran's cold, calculated demeanor. The hopeful portion of me wished that somehow the "miracle" I had performed in the crater might somewhat lessen the famous bloodlust of the Mayans. Instead, all of our actions, ostensibly for attention and "on a lark," had served to help create one of the most brutal, advanced cultures that the world had ever seen.

More troubling than anything was the hopelessness I felt about it all. What could we do? Land the craft and implore them *not* to sacrifice others? Hardly. We had been lucky to escape two armed confrontations without any casualties among the three of us, and that wasn't counting the axe that formerly stuck out of Bloomington's back. Though I didn't particularly care for the man, he deserved better than dying a nameless, faceless, time traveller's death somewhere in the hidden bowels of history.

The craft ascended more rapidly and exited the atmosphere. Though Corcoran and Bloomington had seated themselves in the small dining area next to the bar and pantry, they couldn't mask their astonishment at being among the stars once more. I have to admit, I didn't share their admiration, so fed up was I with this nearly intolerable, ridiculous scavenger hunt.

When we had reached a safe distance away from the Earth, I hit the green time-travel button, and the tunneling lasers carved up space and time outside the vessel. Though I thought the vibrations were positively benign compared to the previous couple of jumps, Corcoran and Bloomington exchanged worried glances several times as if they thought the ship might burst in twain at any moment. I secretly seethed at the notion that my craftsmanship (along with the nano-assemblers and three-dimensional printers, of course) was anything but of the highest quality.

The jump itself was shorter this time, and somehow seemed more routine, loathe as I am to use the term since I was a veteran of all of four time jumps. Though I caught glimpses of Bloomington pointing out various star formations to the far less science-literate Corcoran (albeit with several unnecessary profane outbursts interspersed in the lecture) out of the corner of my eye, I couldn't help but notice that Corcoran appeared to stare past anything Bloomington pointed out, to a point so far away that it appeared to me that he was staring into his own soul.

And as I saw the Commander's reflection in the brushed "glass" of the wall, the normally sly grin turned taut and humourless, his eyes drawn and dull. I knew that he most certainly didn't like what he saw.

CHAPTER FOURTEEN

As the blue marble turned into first a cricket ball, then a basketball in front of us, Corcoran and Bloomington didn't stand rapt, looking over my shoulder as I thought they might.

Rather, Bloomington fixed himself a nip of scotch, while Corcoran assaulted the armory.

"What the devil are you doing?" I asked.

"Tryin' to get some more ammo. The Mayans emptied me out, remember?" Corcoran replied

"Not you," I said, gesturing toward Bloomington, who held the Macallan Eighteen in his hand like a secondary schooler looting his father's liquor cabinet. "*Him.* That's very fine scotch you're pouring for yourself, Specialist Bloomington."

The man clutched the glass toward his chest and glared at me for a moment like Smigol before he smiled and lilted into his hoarse, ugly, snorting laugh. He allowed himself a guzzle and lowered the glass, allowing remnants of the quaff to drip down his chin.

"Eh, it's okay, I guess." Bloomington said. He polished off the liquor and set the empty whiskey glass down on the counter with a self-satisfied sigh.

My face reddened with anger, but instead of giving in to my near-murderous urges, I decided to calmly approach the bar, pick up a glass for myself, and enjoy a quick swallow of the stuff.

"A little better than 'okay,' don't you think, Steven?" I allowed any hostility to boil harmlessly off my skin. "Notice the subtle notes of peat and caramel, the smooth finish that belies the almost indescribable complexity that—"

"Little help?" Corcoran interrupted from the armory. I glared at him for several moments before he jostled the lock and shrugged. I exhaled deeply and carried my glass of Macallan over toward him. I produced the armory key from my pocket and unlocked the cabinet. Corcoran flung open the door as he surveyed the contents within. His gaze fixed on the futuristic-looking laser pistol prototype that I had included.

"Probably don't want to take that old gal out here—want to stay inconspicuous and whatnot," I said.

"Right..." Corcoran said. "What the hell was I thinkin'? Especially since, you know, what happened, happened."

"I know it may seem odd, but just because whatever we do has been pre-ordained, so to speak, doesn't mean that we should go around waving a laser pistol in a major city in the 80s."

"Why not?" Bloomington asked. He actually held his liquor fairly well. "I just got done explaining all of human history to a bunch of batshit Mayans through a tablet app."

"Yes, I'm well aware," I said through gritted teeth. Would he hold that over us for the rest of our time together? "But what if you lost it? Someone else finds it?"

"Isn't that what was supposed to happen, then?" Corcoran asked.

"Yes, but it's not what *I* want to happen. That's the only prototype I have, and I would be remiss if it would go pilfered or lost. Besides, I doubt we'll need the stopping power."

"You ever been to St. Louis in this time period, Doc?" Corcoran asked. I shook my head. He leaned a skeptical eye toward me, "You never know."

The autopilot had brought us well inside of the Earth's atmosphere, with more than a few changes in direction to deal with a new hazard, satellites, that had gone unnoticed by us due to my pioneering work on inertial dampening. We emerged from the clouds into a fairly clear sky, though there was a dustiness to the air, an underlying layer of grit that took away from the bold, almost shimmering sky blue to which I had become accustomed.

As we glided down gently, a jumbo jet raced beneath us at an odd, diagonal angle. I believe it was a 747, and judging by our location and the red tail markings, my guess would have to be TWA. As the craft remained visible, I sincerely hoped that some nosy, hyper-vigilant member of the flight crew hadn't witnessed our descent, and alerted the tower.

The tower! Air traffic control; a new obstacle, considering that I had only visited pre-flight and post-time travel societies thus far.

"Computer, divert all nonessential power to the cloaking device and raise cloak as soon as is computerly possible." Corcoran and Bloomington eyed me skeptically. "What? It's faster than 'humanly possible.'" I said.

We descended to the point where the unmistakable profile of the Gateway Arch shimmered in front of us. I had never seen the thing in person, as I tend to avoid visiting monuments for the sake of visiting them. Monuments always seem to have a way of only *just* meeting or falling well short of expectations.

The Arch, though, was one of those rare structures that surpassed my (admittedly modest) anticipation. It was much taller than I had ever imagined, and stood like a sentry as if it guarded the various office towers of the city from whatever ills may await it on the other side of the Mighty Mississippi.

When I finally looked past it to see what it guarded, however, I was shocked. Buildings with painstakingly-crafted architectural details crumbled and lay in decay. Skyscrapers covered in soot and shit and badly in need of a power-washing. Eyesores like a new shopping mall under construction amidst it all.

"It's a...a...a pit!" I exclaimed.

I expected my declaration to be met with impassioned resistance and protestations from Corcoran. Instead, the Commander nodded gravely.

"Not the city's finest hour," he said. "Crime, graft, corruption—all right at their peak. Cards were doin' pretty well, though, 'least until

Denkinger gave 'em the old fuckaroo. Burnham was the only one who made this city go. Well, him and the brewery, I guess." Corcoran spoke to no one in particular. "It's better now, but this is no joke here, fellas."

"Two days ago, I was being chased by a T-Rex. Yesterday, I outran a bunch of bloodthirsty Mayan warriors. I think I can handle a few gangbangers and aggressive panhandlers,'" I said with as much bravado as I could muster. Perhaps unconsciously, at that moment I patted my sidearm, now safely tucked away in my holster.

"See what I mean?" Corcoran said.

It was about then that the cloaking device indicator finally lit up on one of the panels. I breathed a silent sigh of relief as the computer guided us down gently toward a rather pitiful-looking abandoned lot somewhat north of the main business area.

"Do I get one?" Bloomington asked.

"I believe you've already had a couple," I said, as I tilted back an imaginary glass.

"A gun, dickhole." Bloomington snorted.

"Sorry Bloomy, you know the rules. Only I, and I guess Doc over here, get to pack heat."

"But if this place is as dangerous as you—" Bloomington protested.

"It's not *that* bad; can't you take a joke?" Corcoran asked. "It's actually a little charmin', once you get used to it," Corcoran said as he chambered a round into the pistol, cocked the safety, and holstered the weapon in the hip holster under his jacket. That reminded me to put on my own camo jacket that the computer had so graciously provided.

"Good idea, Doc," Corcoran said. "Doubt the hoi palloi'll wanna tango with Uncle Sam."

"Precisely," I said.

"Or the Queen, or Monterey Jack, or whoever you Limeys say over there." Corcoran said with a grin.

"*Union* Jack," I replied, with a smile of my own. I nodded at the Commander and Bloomington in turn before I took several

140

measured strides toward the egress ramp and asked the computer to lower the gangway. This time the mechanism worked perfectly, and soon enough we were sauntering through what appeared to be the war-torn streets of northern downtown St. Louis.

Perhaps I'm exaggerating a bit, but not by much. The sun hung nearly directly over our heads, and yet as we looked around during disembarkation, there was no one to be found.

What was immediately noticeable, though, was the distinctive smell of the brewery that permeated the air. It was as if hops and barley had been soaked, vaporised, and lit ablaze, as if the stale air from a thousand pubs had been concentrated down to its essence and propagated throughout an entire town. I couldn't decide if the aroma was repulsive or utterly intoxicating.

Corcoran surveyed the scene with one arm tucked inside his jacket. Having not identified any threats, he waved us toward him.

"This way," he said, and began the walk south.

We walked along a street named "Broadway" for quite some while, though it was nowhere near as elegant as its identically-named counterpart in *Monopoly* might lead one to believe. After roughly a quarter mile, we encountered our first pedestrian, a man who wore a similar camouflaged jacket to our own, though his looked far worse for wear.

"Spare change, misters?" he asked. We ignored him and soldiered on.

Eventually, foot traffic increased around us as business people scurried to-and-fro, presumably during their lunch hours. Humourless trench coats hid stark cotton white shirts and woolen suits. Only the odd person dared to wear the colourful plaid pants or jackets that were still "barely-in-fashion" at the time. Women wore their hair in a poufy, remarkably unattractive manner accentuated by the tell-tale angularity of the shoulder pads in their blazers and long skirts. Men and women alike were a rather dowdy lot, though a welcome change from the horrors of ancient times; at least these individuals (presumably) bathed more than once per month.

Though the majority of the skyscrapers were indeed tired and half-sitting, one was under construction along this thoroughfare. We crossed the street and came alongside a smallish (perhaps twenty stories or so), distinguished-looking building, fully refurbished. The dark slate tiles of the eaves matched the stark red bricks rather nicely. It was, in fact, so tasteful that it stuck out like a sore thumb compared with the odd jumble of pre-modernist and what I can only describe as "horribly Epcot-ish" buildings that otherwise pocked the skyline.

Though there was no signage on the building proper, a marker in front of the edifice read as follows:

Burnham Herrington Investments (Floors 5-20)

Proops & Gardner, Attorneys at Law (Floors 3-4)

Simons Innovation, Inc. (Floor 2)

Obviously, Burnham Herrington was in much larger lettering than the others. We entered the revolving door and emerged in a well-appointed, marble lobby. The security desk sat empty to the right of the revolving doors, and a bank of three lifts faced us at the other end of the room. In the middle was a familiar-looking fountain, though I suppose the same can be said of any number of water features in corporate offices around the globe.

We crossed the lobby and pressed the "up" button on the bank of lifts. The brushed metal of the lift doors appeared to be ahead of its time, though the floor-by-floor indicator atop each bank of doors was decidedly retro.

The chime from the lift on the left indicated its arrival. As we sauntered over to the opening doors, a dour, yet striking, young woman emerged from the lift wearing a large, Kentucky Derby-style hat and oversized sunglasses, which I couldn't help but think were horribly anachronous. Her raven-dark hair had been straightened and tied up underneath the hat's impressive canopy, and her red dress was cut in a thoroughly "modern" fashion, though it brought out her bright, almost emerald-like green eyes.

Oddest of all, I couldn't shake the idea that I had met her previously.

She passed us, and didn't even so much as nod in our direction.

"Do I know her?" I asked my companions. For a moment, I thought I gleaned a similar sentiment of recognition from Corcoran's face.

"I don't know, but I sure want to," Corcoran said with a grin.

Bloomington clammed up; his lack of comfort with the opposite sex made me seem like a regular Tiger Woods.

I shook the thoughts out of my head and we entered the lift.

"Which floor?" I asked, though as I said it, I noticed that Corcoran had already pushed the button for twenty.

"Which floor would you be on if you were the boss?" Corcoran asked rhetorically.

The lift ascended amazingly quietly toward the top floor. Within moments, it opened upon a rich, mahogany-clad space with green carpet that screamed "country club." Two capable-looking women with matching red, plastic-rimmed glasses busied themselves clattering away on first-generation Apple MacIntoshes while conversing over the telly.

As we approached, one of the women sat down her receiver.

"May I help you?" she asked. She was a middle-aged, though attractive, black woman, who lowered skeptical eyes at us.

"Uh, yes…we're here to see Mr. Burnham." I said.

The woman smiled gently. "Of course. Do you have an appointment?"

"Um…perhaps…" I stammered. "Phineas Templeton?"

She thumbed through her appointment book for several moments before she shook her head.

"I'm sorry, I don't see a Templeton in here. Being New Year's Eve, Mr. Burnham has a very limited number of appointments today, so perhaps you were scheduled to see him a different day?" She frowned understandingly.

"How about Corcoran?" the Commander asked.

She smiled, "Certainly, Mister—I apologize…" She looked at the rank insignia on the Commander's jacket, "Commander Corcoran. It'll be just a moment." She excused herself and ducked behind the corner of the wall.

I glared at the Commander, and he offered a weak shrug in reply. For his part, I believe Bloomington was attempting to disguise the fact that he was picking his nose.

The receptionist emerged from behind the wall several minutes later with a pleasant-looking, middle-aged fellow with large, coke-bottle-like lenses inside of horrendous-looking, black-and-amber tiger-striped plastic eyeglasses frames. He was short, shorter than Bloomington, actually, but exuded a remarkably kind, understanding disposition.

"Gentlemen, hello!" The man extended a hand toward first the Commander, then myself and finally Bloomington, though I cringed when Bloomington extended the same hand that had moments earlier been engaged in nasal excavation. The little man in front of us shook each of our hands enthusiastically, though with the odd-fitting, apparently off-the-rack suit that he wore, it was tough to believe that this man could be a billionaire.

"Good to see you, good to see you! I must admit, this is a bit irregular; Doris over here tells me that you have an appointment, though I specifically remember asking for the day to be booked off. You're quite lucky that I'm putting the finishing touches on a speech I'm to give to my guests at my New Year's party this evening, or I'm afraid you would have been out of luck."

"And a great speech it shall be," I said. "A watershed announcement, where you'll announce you're setting up a charity with your vast fortune."

Burnham stared at me, his eyes burrowing into my skull.

"How in the hell? Did you speak to her—I mean, no one could possibly—" he grew flustered before he regained his good cheer.

I smiled, "Just a few fans, hoping that we could have a few moments of your time, sir." I raised my hand into the Vulcan "live long and prosper" gesture, as Trent had taught me.

Burnham's eyes widened for a moment, the smile washed from his face as he struggled to regain his composure and good cheer.

"Fellow Trekkies? Star Trek fans?" He asked with a chuckle.

"No," I replied, deadly serious. "Fans of yours."

I met his gaze for several moments, as beads of sweat formed on his brow.

"*Speak* for *yourself*," Bloomington whispered in my ear before he also adopted the Vulcan hand-sign, though I'm sure for very different reasons.

The colour and smile returned to Burnham's face, "I…uh…of course! Of course, my fine English fellow! Doris, Nancy, please hold all of my calls, for as long as these gentlemen are in here."

"Of course, Mr. Burnham," Doris smiled as she took her seat once more. I don't think that the phone resting against Nancy's ear could have been surgically removed.

"Follow me, Gentlemen," Burnham said as he led us around the corner, which led to a short hallway. The door at the end of the hallway was adorned with a plaque that read, "Victor U. Burnham, Principal." Burnham opened the door and held it for us.

"After you, please, I insist," he said with a broad, grandfatherly grin. We made our way inside to find a large mahogany desk and suitably plush chair across from us. Three couches were arranged in a "U' shape around a modern coffee table to our right. The rest of the otherwise tasteful office was adorned with all manner of Star Trek memorabilia, including props, models of ships, and all manner of other merchandise. I think Bloomington and myself took a moment to marvel at the collection, while Corcoran couldn't help but stare in shock and horror.

"Have a seat, please," Burnham motioned over to the couches, and we followed his hand toward them.

No sooner than the door had closed did the kindly smile and warmth drain from Burnham's face.

"Just what the *fuck* was that?" Burnham thundered. "'No more time travelers.' That's exactly what I told ChronoSaber, and yet, here you idiots are, bruising my fucking asshole!" He turned to Corcoran, "Just what the *fuck* are you looking at, slim?"

"Ricky Corcoran, pleased to meet you," he extended his hand.

Burnham stood, mouth agape. "Ricky...Corcoran? *The* Ricky Corcoran? Commander? Well fuck me sideways!" The smile returned to his face, though it wasn't the warm, grandfatherly smile of before, but rather the grin of a shark eyeing a bleeding seal carcass. "Ricky Corcoran! American hero, come to visit me? Outstanding. Just fan-fucking-tastic!"

Corcoran raised his eyebrows at me.

"I assume this is your coterie? Your entourage?" Burnham asked.

"Somethin' like that. This is Doc," the Commander nodded at me and I cleared my throat. Corcoran broke into a terse, thin smile. "I mean, *Doc-tor* Phineas Templeton." His affected English accent was remarkably well-practised for such a presumptive hayseed.

"Charmed," I extended my hand with a hopefully not-too-phony smile.

"And this over here is Bloomy—Specialist Steve Bloomington," He corrected himself before the toad had a chance.

"This...is...*awesome*," Bloomington stared around the shrine to *Star Trek*. "I'm, like, dying now. You are a *God*."

Burnham waived away the praise, "You think I actually *like* this stupid shit? Morons flying around in spaceships in horrible costumes, solving boring, bullshit mysteries one week after another?" Burnham huffed. "Fuck that. I only keep up the ruse in case those assholes over at ChronoSaber ever disregarded my wishes and created one of their damn-fool time tourist traps to visit me. No fucking thank you. $11.7 million dollars spent on this shit, and it *finally* pays off."

Corcoran, Bloomington and I eyed each other with varying levels of awe and disgust.

"Like with Albertson?" I asked, innocently enough.

"What the fuck about him?"

"Time tourism. Albertson? You know, he's—"

"Albertson!" Burnham screamed at the door. He realised that no one was forthcoming, so he hustled behind his desk and hit one of the array of buttons at his disposal.

"Albertson!" He failed to lower his volume.

"Yes, sir." The receiver buzzed.

"Get your ass in here!"

"Right away, sir."

Not but five seconds later, the office door cracked once more to reveal a young, dapper, clean-shaven man who couldn't simultaneously be more different than the man I had met as "Jesus Christ" in Ancient Judea, and yet possess enough similar facial characteristics so as to promote the rather obvious notion that the two must be related.

"Ever meet these guys before?" I wished we would see the paternalistic grandfather once more, but it was not to be.

This Albertson looked us up-and-down like a spectator at the world yo-yo championships.

"No sir, I don't believe so."

"Very good," Burnham paused and stared at Albertson. "Dismissed, dummy!" he hissed at the young man before he threw a (rather elegant, I may add) coffee mug at the door. The whole scene was suitably Hank Fleener-like to give me a distinct feeling of deja vu.

"What the fuck are you talking about? Albertson doesn't know you. He's from this time," Burnham thundered.

"Not him—his son. Or maybe grandson..." I saw that Burnham's anger didn't abate and decided to change my strategy. I shook my head, "Never mind. We aren't here to bother you or ask for autographs, or to ogle your, and I must say rather impressive, collection of Star Trek memorabilia," I looked at Bloomington, who still hadn't the good sense to shut his maw. "Rather we've been engaged in a somewhat tiresome temporal scavenger hunt put on by a reclusive billionaire."

Several moments of silence followed.

"Well, don't look at—" Burnham grew indignant.

"I assure you, it's *not* you, Victor." I did my best to keep an even tone. "We do have the unenviable task of 'communicating' with you here, and I believe it has something to do with the speech you're about to make this evening."

"Well? Communicate away!" Burnham yelled. "So I'm giving away my fortune. Hoo-fucking-ray for me! What a hero I am. Another feather in my cap that'll keep the wine and women a third my age flowing until I finally croak."

I spent several moments with my head cocked to the side pondering if the angry little man had just misspoken or not.

Bloomington and Corcoran looked at me, so I continued to probe.

"I suppose I should ask 'when' you're from, then?"

"See, this is *exactly* why I didn't want to have to deal with this. You're just like the goddamned rubes in this town asking where someone went to high school. *When are you from? When did you get here? Why now?* Spineless English prick!" He turned to face the floor-to-ceiling window at the back of the room.

"Actually, I'm an American citizen," I replied. "Dual citizen, really. It's complicated—"

"Of course it is! Of *course* it's fucking complicated. Gentlemen, we're *traveling through time*! Humans aren't *supposed* to be able to do that. We're fucking with the very fabric of existence, with the fate of the universe itself. That's why I told ChronoSaber, 'one way, no one follows.' Every small-minded hustler and lottery winner would have the idea to do what I did."

"Play the market?" Corcoran asked.

Burnham laughed. "You think that's how it started? No, my good Commander, in my own time, I was a sharp. A hustler. A pro gambler, living the okay life out in Vegas. You know, a couple mill, nothing too much, not starvin', but not livin' the good life, either.

"Eventually, news of the good Commander's successful mission leaked out, and I start to hear from some of my sources that ChronoSaber's about to go deregulated. So I pull some strings and I get to the front of the line. Have to put up my whole nest egg to do it, but I figure fuck it, it's a sure thing."

"I thought the only sure thing in a sports book was the ajax?" I interrupted. I received blank stares for my trouble. "The beeswax?" More stares followed. "The...oh, what the devil...the vigorish!"

Burnham shook his head and balled up his fist, as if he wanted to take a swing at me. "You've obviously not been to enough sports books, you dumb Limey bastard! Since history was found to be immutable, that meant that the outcomes of games were fixed. And here I was in the future betting on games that were in question like a sucker!

"So my ingenious plan was to go back in time and bet a bunch of games, make easy money, and retire to a tropical island filled with beautiful women." I wanted to tell Burnham that his plan didn't appear to be particularly unique given my experience, but I let the old man continue.

"I dug up an old paper sports almanac and went back to the sixties. Just like that asshole from *Back to the Future*, but with a little panache and a lot more discretion."

"Two." Bloomington finally said something.

"What?"

"*Back to the Future II* is the movie where Biff appropriates Marty's idea to steal a sports almanac and take it into the past, thereby creating an alternate—"

The spry old man took two quick steps at Bloomington and reared back to hit the squat nerd. Bloomington flinched, and Burnham's fist stopped just short of its target.

"SHUT...THE...FUCK...UP!" Burnham screamed. "Christ, isn't anyone else in the future *normal*? Except for you, Commander, of course. You're as American as football and apple pie."

I decided the better of engaging the man in a discussion of whose country properly used the term "football" given Burnham's current mental state.

"Aw shucks," Corcoran said with not-so-thinly-veiled false modesty.

"At any rate," Burnham gritted his teeth, "Sadly the Vegas of the sixties isn't quite as 'warm and fuzzy' as the Vegas I know. I tried to be discreet, vary my bets, change casinos, the whole nine, but word got around fast back then, and the mafia sure as shit doesn't like some wise-ass messing things up for them. One night, they worked me over pretty fucking good, took all of my cash, left me penniless.

"So there I was, stuck in Vegas, my return trip not for another five years. Hitchhiked my way back east, and eventually found myself in St. Louis. This was the city's heyday, by God—old Busch was still being built, the Cards were good, Budweiser flowin', fuckin' fantastic, I tell you. I decided it was as good of place as any to set up shop."

"So what did you do then?" Thankfully Corcoran asked.

"I wasn't doing enough of a job connecting the dots to your liking, *Commander?*" Burnham practically spat at Corcoran. His narrowed, beady little eyes were magnified through the thick lenses of his spectacles. The billionaire realised what he had done as his eyes went wide. "Sorry about that, just used to schooling your moronic goons here in a little respect."

"No offense taken," I couldn't help myself.

Fortunately Burnham ignored me. "I got a job at a soda fountain and started saving my money. I knew I could do something to fleece the past, but I hadn't figured out what or how. Then it hit me—stocks! Glorious stocks. Companies like GE and Coca-Cola weren't going anywhere, and could make me a healthy living until an Apple or Microsoft came along.

"I also thought that once I got set up, I could start making these," he opened a drawer in the desk and pulled out a handful of what appeared to be plastic-wrapped nicotine patches.

"Smokin' problem?" Corcoran asked.

Burnham laughed, "I forget—you guys are practically from the dark ages. I'd hardly call it a 'problem;' just vaporize some medigel and goodbye lung cancer! No, these, my good Commander, are called Holotrans."

My mind raced back to those several (more than several?) days ago when Trent had explained the concept to me.

"You mean the universal translator with a speaker and holo-emitter to synch your mouth with the other person's language?" I offered.

Burnham beamed and looked at Corcoran, "And here I was thinking this one was the dumb one. Tell me, how did you figure that out, my boy?"

"You're far from the first time traveller from the future that I—we've met." I said.

"Well, that's exactly right. Put this patch on your neck, and presto, you speak whatever language that the other person does. Not to mention, it translates what you hear into English. I wanted to make these in China and flood the market, but turns out that they require some sort of special nano-tech or some bullshit like that—like I said, I'm a sharp, not an engineer."

He casually tossed each of us one of the devices, which caught me off-guard.

"Go ahead—take one each. I have a drawer full of 'em. Turns out it got me in good with the Japs. Someone has to help 'em take over this country this decade, am I right?"

"I, uh...thank you." I said.

"Thank *you*," Burnham said.

"Whatever for?" I asked.

"For letting me finally get this shit off my chest. Do you know how tough it is to go around, playing the kindly old grandpa to the world," he put on his practised, warm smile and gave a token wave, "let alone keeping all of this future talk bottled up? It gets to a guy. Pardon my language, but fucks him up a bit in the head, you know? This has been therapeutic, refreshing, invigorating! Now if you'll excuse me..."

I still had hundreds of questions for the man, but it was obvious that he had said his peace and he was done.

"Aw, already?" Corcoran's "already" may as well have been "shucks."

Burnham grinned, "I apologize, Commander, but I'm a busy man. The world isn't going to take over itself. I would love to chat more, but I'm afraid that the best I can do is to offer some VIP tickets to you and your friends for my New Year's Eve Party tonight. Hell, I'll even throw in a suite at the Adam's Mark—that's where it is, you see."

"We...erm...aren't dressed appropriately," I said as I surveyed our sorry collection of what appeared to be military surplus and articles from a J. Crew outlet.

Fortunately, Burnham waived the concern away, "No problem at all." He pounded on the button once more.

"Albertson!" the old man growled again. "Albertson!" he released the button. "Fuck! Little shit always does this when I throw the mug." He depressed a different button, "Garrett!" though the volume didn't change.

"A moment, please, with my compatriots?" I asked.

Burnham looked at Corcoran, who nodded.

"Of course! No rush!"

We huddled up quickly.

"Are we quite sure that we should be doing this? Shouldn't we just rest up for the next jump?"

"Aw, come on, Doc—can't you relax? Have a little fun?"

"Yeah," Bloomington chimed in with an air of unearned superiority.

I raised my voice somewhat, "The last time we 'had a little fun,' I nearly got a spear in the back of my throat for the trouble!"

Over my shoulder, Burnham cleared his throat.

"Is that some kind of...code phrase or something? You know, not that there's anything wrong with that..."

"Why you prig-covered bollywort!" I stepped toward the old little man, eager to make him pay for his little display of homophobia. He responded by lowering his eyes just above the rims of his frames toward Corcoran in an "I told you so" gesture.

"Hey, whoa!" Corcoran yelled before he let out a shrill whistle. Everyone stopped and turned to look. "Mr. Burnham, we'd be honored to be your guests at the party tonight."

152

"Stupendous!" Burnham clasped his hands together. "A real-life celebrity, but one going incognito—the guests will be none the wiser! It'll be a terrific way of 'winding the guests up,' as your people say," he nudged me with an elbow in the ribs.

The door flung open to reveal a youngish fellow, with a smooth face that looked to have never seen the sharp side of a razor blade. His red hair blended almost seamlessly with his flush face, which was somehow familiar.

"Yes sir," the young man said.

"Have these men fitted for tuxedos in the ancillary suite at the Adam's Mark. And not the cheap shit—go to the Italian guy, not Huang. Capice?"

"Yes sir, Mr. Burnham!" As the young man spoke the phrase, my mind raced back to Isla Yucatan. Three short "days" ago, but by now it seemed a lifetime. I imagined I was in the hospital bed suffering from hyperoxia, and watching that dreadful holovid that ChronoSaber put together.

And just like that, the CEO's face flashed in front of me once more.

Nice to meet you, *Zane Garrett*, I thought.

CHAPTER FIFTEEN

"Here you go—the 'ancillary' suite at the Adams-Mark," Garrett opened the door to a cavernous room with high ceilings. The furnishings, though I'm sure considered ornate for the time, seemed ancient and more than a bit gaudy. Garish red fabric upholstered the gold-rimmed furniture in a manner that I'm sure some of my fellow countrymen could only appreciate. Don't get me wrong, I'm a sucker for English tradition, just not when it interferes with a crisp, clean, modern modality of decor.

Garrett looked at us as if he expected a series of whistles and cat-calls, but I think even Corcoran and Bloomington felt let-down judging by the hang-dog looks on their faces. Though to be fair, Steven always walked around as such despite cheating death not but one day before.

"Very nice," I said with a tight smile as I turned toward Garrett. "Mister…Garrett, is it?"

"Yep. Zane Garrett—pleased to meetchya." He extended a hand, and I accepted it. Sadly for him, he also offered it to Corcoran and Bloomington, and received a crushing grip and various germ-caked phlegm remnants for his trouble.

"May I call you Zane?" I asked.

"Sure thing, Mister…"

"Templeton," I said. "Phineas Templeton. You can call me Finny. Don't worry, though; I've heard every *A Separate Peace* joke there is."

His face, of course, remained flat, as did Corcoran's and Bloomington's.

"Not big readers, I see," I said.

"No, I've read it," Corcoran said.

"Me too," Garrett said.

Bloomington remained noticeably silent.

I shook off their blank looks and removed the rather heavy camo jacket. Though it seemed as if the door had shut mere moments before, a knock cracked the silence like a whip.

Garrett opened the door to reveal a well-dressed man with slicked-back, peppery hair and large bags under his eyes.

"Gentlemen, this is Alfredo Manetti, Mr. Burnham's personal tailor. He must've been quite impressed with all of you."

Or unimpressed, judging by the quality of his own suit, I thought.

"Please, call me Freddy," Manetti said, stopping only momentarily to raise a tape-measure-filled hand toward us.

"Hey Freddy," Corcoran was all smiles once more.

"So, Zane, how did you come to be in Mr. Burnham's employ?" I was determined to continue probing, even as Freddy knelt down to do some probing of his own around my groin area.

Garrett shrugged, "Not sure, really. Lucky, I guess. Went to Mizzou, graduated last year, before I know it I'm starting here as Mr. Burnham's assistant."

"He hand-selected you, then?" I asked.

"Turn around," Freddy said. I complied.

"Eh. He came to a job fair. Of course, it was a big deal at the time. Everyone wanted to get their start with Burnham Herrington. Some of the guys were prepared to do anything—and I mean *anything*: kill, maim, steal—to get the job." Garrett's eyes narrowed as he bit his lip.

"Arms out," Freddy commanded. I complied once more.

Garrett smiled, "Fortunately, it didn't come to that. Met with Mr. Burnham, and I told him I thought it was great, you know, the work he was doing with the Japanese, and how Japan was the future. He wasn't scared to ship stuff over there, and talked about how he'd be lauded as a visionary twenty years from now." Garrett grinned, "It also probably didn't hurt that I knew he was a *Star Trek* nut, and flashed him this when I first met him," Garrett's fingers trembled as they struggled to contort into the familiar Vulcan hand signal, which held very different meaning for him than us.

"So you're from Missouri then?" Corcoran asked.

"Yep," Garrett answered. I exhaled with relief as Freddy moved on to Bloomington, satisfied that I had removed an inch or so from the waist and chest measurements he had obtained.

"Whereabouts?"

"Poplar Bluff. Little town down south. You?"

"O'Fal—uh...unincorporated St. Charles county."

Garrett smiled warmly, "You're practically a city slicker compared to me then. It wasn't farm life growin' up, but it was close. Simpler times back then, don't you think?"

The fresh-faced young redhead stared down each of us in turn, a cold, measured stare that was either meant to be a tip off, or a suggestion to not pry any further into his past.

"Hee hee, that tickles!" Bloomington giggled. Now it was Corcoran and myself who shot icy glares at him.

"Anyway, if you'll excuse me, gentlemen, I do have quite a bit of business to attend to, with the party and whatnot. Freddy here will set you up with some tuxes once he has your measurements. I'm afraid that they won't be custom-fitted due to the time-sensitive nature of this order, but—"

"Pretty damn close," Freddy said, through the stick of tailor's chalk gritted between his teeth.

I'm sure, I thought. I hope the sentiment didn't show across my face.

Garrett smiled his semi-weasily smile once more, "Exactly. I'm sure I'll run into you gentlemen tonight. Until then, make yourselves at home, relax, help yourselves to minibar, room service, whatever. Mr. Burnham was very specific that you are to receive the utmost in luxury during your time in St. Louis. Farewell."

Before I could stop Garrett from leaving, the heavy hardwood door closed with a hard "thud," and the man was gone.

Freddy had finished with Bloomington, and predictably the portly little pig had his mind on only one thing:

"Minibar!" he exclaimed. He raced (with far more speed and alacrity than he had showcased in Mayan times, might I add) to the rather archaic looking mini-fridge and flung it open, and eagerly shoveled armloads of horrific-looking junk food into his pudgy, greedy little arms. Once he had appropriated all that he could carry, the little porker gleefully pranced to the couch and, in one motion, cast himself upon the davenport, grabbed the remote, and fell comfortably in place as the snacks showered down upon him.

"You realise the ship has a fully-stacked pantry, don't you?" I asked. The only answer I received was the loud "click clacking" of the remote as Bloomington searched the archaic-looking telly for something interesting. Something interesting to him, at least.

"Let him go," Corcoran said as Freddy took his measurements. To his credit, the Commander didn't so much as flinch.

"How do you dress?" Freddy asked as he measured the Commander's inseam.

"To the right," Corcoran said without skipping a beat. Freddy's eyes widened momentarily as he motioned for Corcoran to turn around.

"I beg your pardon?" I asked.

"What? Now you want to know which side I tuck my c—"

"Not that!" I shook my head. "*Babe* over there wallowing in his own luxuriation."

"Come on, Doc—the guy nearly died little over a day ago. I think he's earned the break. So have you—we all have. That Mayan business took its toll on all of us. Not to mention—" he waved me closer, and I obliged, "—Bloomy hasn't been exactly…right…since you put that goop into him to fix him up."

"How do you mean?" I whispered.

"He was always a little bit nerdy, a bit of an odd duck, as you Brits might say, but nothing quite like this. This is…something else. It's like he's forgotten how to function in society."

"And here I was thinking that he was merely ill-bred!" I punctuated the comment with a tight smile.

"Shhh!" Corcoran was unamused. "I think that goop is fuckin' with his mind a bit. Look at Burnham, too—cussin' like a sailor without his rum. Something's up with that stuff, Doc. I just don't know what to make of it."

"Look, maybe Steven's just getting comfortable now. Maybe his 'near-death experience' has made him see everything in a new light. Staring death in the face has an odd way of—"

Corcoran raised his eyebrows at me, "Look who you're talking to."

"Nevertheless, all I have is your word for it, and, much as I'm loathe to admit it, I have no reason not to trust you thus far. I'll continue to monitor the situation using my eminently and thoroughly rational mind," I said.

Corcoran shook his head, "Whatever. Thanks, Doc. You want some free advice?"

"I'm all ears."

"Take the afternoon off and do the same thing. Take a nap, or do…whatever you do for fun."

"Movies."

"What?"

"I watch movies. Classics, mostly, though in your time they may not be considered as much. American cinema, 1985-2020."

"Great. Do that then."

I gestured toward the useless lump of semi-humanity on the sofa.

"Eh, go out, catch a flick then," Corcoran said.

"I suppose they may still be showing *Back to the Future*…" I stroked my chin. "But I must say, a nap in a real bed sounds positively delightful right now."

Corcoran motioned to the three sets of double-doors in front of us.

"Looks like we each have our own room, Doc. Go ahead—we'll wake you up when it's time to get ready."

I smiled a weary grin, "Very well then. I'll be in my room." I straightened my posture and took easy, deliberate steps toward one of the sets of doors. I tried to open the left door for several moments, and failing to yield it, instead gingerly pulled on the right one. This time it gave, and I walked inside and shut the door lightly behind me.

Safely away from the rest of my suitemates' prying eyes, my shoulders slumped as I staggered what seemed like an impossible number of steps toward the baroque-looking bed in front of me. The last thing I remember is throwing myself at the mattress before I passed out, face first, utterly gone to the world.

"KNOCK KNOCK KNOCK!"

"Hey Doc, you alive in there?"

If the Commander's handshake was firm, then his manner of knocking was positively bone-chattering.

I shot up, still only half on the bed.

"Err...just a moment." I collected myself and stood up.

"Well, hurry up, wouldya? Garrett just called, and we're supposed to be down in the ballroom in fifteen minutes."

The revelation startled me. I stormed over to the door in a huff. This time, I unsuccessfully tried to open the right door for several moments before I opened the left with a jolt, only to find Corcoran on the other side.

"I thought you were going to wake me up when it was time to get ready?"

"I tried! I've been bangin' on the door for a good fifteen minutes. Bloomy wanted me to call the cops." He held out a hangar draped with a particularly cheap looking rubber-polyester cover. I snatched it with a toned-down snort of indignation.

"Fifteen minutes, Doc."

"I'll be ready," I said.

Twenty-five minutes later, I emerged from the shower and began to dress. I appreciated the irony that a time traveller, of all people, had asked me to be prompt.

I finally tied my bow tie and took a look in the mirror. I would be dishonest if I didn't admit that (much like any other Englishman worth his salt) I gazed into the mirror and pantomimed holding a gun in the air.

"The name's Templeton. Phineas Templeton." I said to the man in the mirror.

"Come on, Doc! We're gonna be late!" Corcoran thundered through the door.

"Err...'coming!'"

I straightened my tie once more, and we were off to the ballroom.

The ballroom was actually a collection of ballrooms on the ground floor of the hotel. As tony as Burnham had tried to make the scene— his cronies had covered old bits of torn wallpaper and shoddy carpeting with balloons, streamers, and carefully-placed fabric— there was still no disguising the fact that we were in a hotel ballroom in St. Louis, Missouri in 1985.

Nonetheless, throngs of well-dressed partygoers (and hopeful party-crashers) clogged the entrance to the grand ballroom, where the festivities were already in full swing. To my great surprise and joy, the usual big band music was replaced by a proper Huey Lewis and the News cover band. Somehow, I thought it fitting that "Power of Love" was playing during this most surreal of scenes, even if "Back in Time" would have been even more appropriate.

Five large bouncers guarded the entrance, and repeatedly cast away all but the most stunning young beauties the town had to offer, whom were themselves done up in their pouffiest hair and with their oddest wardrobe choices. As slovenly as Bloomington appeared in his tux, Corcoran and I knew how to wear ours rather nicely, and we cut through the masses to make our way to the front.

"Name?" One of the neanderthals asked.

"Templeton. Phineas Templeton," I said. Somehow it didn't come out nearly as confidently as it had in the mirror.

"Try Corcoran," the Commander said. "Richard, Ricky, whatever Corcoran."

The bouncer flipped through pages upon pages of list, well past where the "Cs" should have ended. The look on the guard's face added to my impression that the whole ordeal was like a dog trying to read Dickens, but eventually he came to something that he at least pretended looked like the Commander's name.

160

"There it is. Corcoran, plus two." He looked behind the Commander, saw us, and couldn't help but show the shock on his face. "Uh, have fun...gentlemen." He said with narrowed eyes. Between Burnham's crack earlier and this Cro-Magnon's off-hand remark, I had had more than my daily dose of low-level gay-bashing.

"Come on, fellas—let's go find us some ladies!" Corcoran winked at the security guy, whom nodded satisfactory assent at the Commander. Apparently, Ricky had picked up on the same vibe.

I had to hand it to Vic Burnham; he really did his damnedest to throw a thoroughly modern, entertaining affair. I soon discovered that the Huey Lewis and the News tribute band was *actually* Huey Lewis and the News, which particularly tickled my fancy, seeing as how large of a fan of theirs I was. Various table games dotted the sides of the room as middle-aged men had women less than half their age blow on dice before they launched the white-and-black cubes toward the end of the craps table. Though ostensibly the games were for charity, I saw a decent amount of actual currency make its way onto the tables over the course of the night.

Booze flowed freely from the bars located in every corner, stocked with enough high-end liquor and capable bartenders so as to prevent all but the shortest of lines. We made our way over to the nearest bar, and I was positively tickled to find eighteen-year Macallan as one of the options. I had the bartender pour me a double.

"And for you, sir?" the bartender asked Corcoran.

"Make it a Budweiser." Before the Commander could finish, a fresh bottle of the iconic beer sat open in front of him.

"And you, sir?" the bartender turned to Bloomington.

"Vodka red bull." I could barely keep my hand from smacking myself in the forehead. It was all I could do to force a firm elbow into Bloomington's back.

"Vodka what now?" The bartender asked.

Bloomington sighed with annoyance, "Whatever. Make it a vodka coke then."

Just when I think someone can't possibly get any more annoying, I thought, *Bloomington always steps in to demonstrate a new low in decorum and common decency.*

We spotted Burnham along a side wall and he surprisingly waved us over to chat.

"Gentlemen!" the grandfatherly fellow that had greeted us at reception the day before had returned. "How are you doing?"

"Extraordinary," I said.

"Thanks for the tuxes. Freddy knows his stuff." Corcoran said.

"He's the best," Burnham said.

If you say so… I thought as I tugged on my right sleeve, which was a good half-inch shorter than the left.

"I do love these parties, though." The billionaire leaned in closer to us and whispered, "My doctor told me a couple years ago: no more blow. Something about how my heart was gonna explode. So, I decided then and there to give it up; except for New Year's. You guys want any?"

Corcoran and I immediately shook our heads and offered a polite, "No thank you." Reflexively, our attention turned toward Bloomington. We knew the response before he had said a word.

"Sure. Yeah. Why not? Fuck it." The portly scientist said.

"Fan-fu—" Burnham stopped himself. "Fantastic. Gentlemen, we shall return."

Corcoran and I eyed each other skeptically.

"Hey, maybe it'll even him out a little." Corcoran said.

"Are you quite mad? You're trying to rationalise this? Steve Bloomington doing coke with a billionaire in his mid-sixties? What possible good could come of this?"

Corcoran shrugged, "Beats the shit outta me. All I know is that he needs something to get on track. Maybe a line or two'll shake some sense into his head. I mean, I never touch the stuff, but to each his own, you know?"

All I could do is shake my head.

"'Course, you seem like the uptight type who's never tried anything."

I stood in silence.

"Oh, come on...nothing? Not even a 'puff on a spliff' in prep school or anything like that?"

I raised my glass and swirled the scotch inside.

"One vice is plenty, especially when it likely costs more than the cocaine that Bloomington is presently doing."

"But you're not denying that you went to prep school, then?"

"Eton, if you must know. And yourself?"

"I was a bit of a wild one," Corcoran said. "My folks shipped me off to the Missouri Military Academy when I was in seventh grade. Think they held a party when I left. Turns out it was the best thing they ever coulda done to me."

"You learned discipline, sacrifice, yada yada yada," I interjected.

Corcoran chuckled, "Bull-*shit*. Turns out Mom and Pop had a shitty furnace that was leaking carbon monoxide into their place. Croaked in their sleep three months after I had left."

"Commander, I'm terribly sorry for my flippant re—"

He took a long swig of his beer and waved me off, "Don't worry about it—it was their own damn-fool fault for not fixin' it. Fortunately, the Military Academy picked me up on a full scholarship. Once I graduated, I figured my trade was bein' a soldier. So I enlisted in the Navy. Grunt initially, went to SEAL school, elite ops, that sort of thing. Served over in the Gulf, Kosovo for a bit, then Afghanistan for who-knows how many tours. Made Lieutenant Commander, then took the controls of our helo after the pilot had been shot by those Mujahideen pricks. Crashed it away from a school. General Carter from Army black ops apparently took note, and next thing I know, I'm supervising Project Omega."

"So, they just pulled you out from combat and put you in charge of the greatest human technological achievement of all time?"

"Guess they saw some kind of leadership potential there, didn't they?" Corcoran took another swig of his beer. "And it worked out okay, didn't it? Here I am, sharin' a drink with a genuine time traveler in 1985."

"You'd still be stuck in Mayan times had I not shown up, though," I reminded him.

"And for that, I'm forever grateful," the Commander offered his bottle in a toast. "To happy accidents."

"To happy accidents," I said, and clinked my glass with his bottle.

"So what's your deal? Grew up in England, then what?" He asked.

"I'm afraid it's terribly boring, really, compared with your story. Father transferred to England when I was still young. Graduated from Eton by fourteen, Oxford by seventeen. Had my PhD in advanced theoretical physics by nineteen. Always have had a knack for making that one insight that pushes a project past the wall, and makes it doable."

"When did you start working with the government?" Corcoran asked.

"Beg your pardon?" I asked.

"How else could you have gotten your hands on our research?"

My eyeballs nearly exploded, "*Your* research? *Your* research? I'll have you know, Commander, that every breakthrough I made with the quantum computer was mine alone, based on my *own* research into areas that you couldn't possibly even begin to—"

"Try me," Corcoran said.

I sighed, "The time-travel mechanism is activated—"

"—Via a matter, antimatter reaction contained by an advanced superconductor-keyed forcefield." Corcoran said.

I tried to hide my shock.

"You don't think they give the program director the broad strokes? Truth be told, I wasn't supposed to be the one going back in time. Unfortunately, our original pilot went into rehab a little while before the first flight—something about the stress of it all getting to her. Probably wasn't really cut out for it anyway, if that was the case. So I stepped in. Now, we didn't have quite as many fancy gizmos as you do, but the concepts are similar enough that I can talk shop."

"And Bloomington?" I asked.

"Mission specialist. Given a provisional commission to operate the time machine, fix 'er up if we got stranded. With the crater that thing left, though, there wasn't much to fix."

I felt a hand on my shoulder and turned to find Bloomington's sweaty, but otherwise in-good-spirits visage.

"Hey, Professor! How's it going? I'm feeling great—just *great!*" Bloomington said. He took my hand and shook it vigorously before he stood up straight for once and offered Corcoran a crisp salute, "Commander."

Corcoran's eyes grew wide, but he returned the gesture.

Feedback rung out over the loudspeakers, and we turned to see Burnham wipe his nose as he set up the microphone at the podium.

"My fellow revelers, good evening!" Burnham's congenial, grandfatherly disposition had returned. If the drugs had given him an extra bounce to his step, he hid it well.

"Good evening and welcome to the twentieth annual Burnham Herrington New Year's Eve celebration!" Wild applause filled the room.

"As you may know, I have a wild announcement to make this evening, one that bodes well for the city of St. Louis, as well as similarly struggling cities around this fine country.

"Burnham Herrington is doing better than ever. Once again, our share price rocketed upward and now sits comfortably north of $6,500 per share!" More cheers from the crowd.

"Yet, in the face of all of this wealth, in spite of the mountains of capital that should be flowing through the streets of St. Louis at the moment, we're left with a city that's rotten at its core." Shocked murmurs replaced any residual merriment.

"Not the people, mind you, for the most part anyway. Sure, there will always be a few bad apples that try to spoil the pie, but I find that to be more a reflection of our failing schools, which, intentionally or not, reflects an attitude that the less fortunate than us shouldn't be able to rise above the circumstances in which they find themselves and be able to attend a function like this, down to the last man and woman."

Is this the same man who was calling us every variation of "fuck" imaginable and throwing coffee mugs at his underlings several hours ago? I thought.

"And St. Louis isn't alone in its plight. Cities from Kansas City to Cleveland to Pittsburgh to Baltimore all are experiencing the same, sad fate. Poor schools. Few jobs. Crumbling infrastructure. And, as a result, skyrocketing crime.

"Various charities do their best to stem the tide of these problems, but they're but a single sandbag in the deluge of poverty-related causes that plague our once-great cities. Try as it might, a charity cannot create jobs on the scale needed to lift a city out of its dire milieu. A charity cannot make decisions that are in its best business interests in order to take on projects that can simultaneously rebuild a community, employ its residents, and lift the rest of the world into a loftier position.

"No, to do that requires a true company, one that can make beneficial business deals to improve infrastructure, one that can hire and train employees to improve the cities around them. But simultaneously one that will also have a charitable purpose baked into its corporate charter.

"Ladies and Gentlemen, I have founded such a company. I'm endowing it with a sizable donation of Burnham Herrington stock, with the balance of my fortune to be put in a trust under its control in perpetuity upon my death. Ladies and Gentlemen, I give you, the St. Louis Area Burnham Executive Rebuilding Corporation, or as I like to call it, SABERCorp!"

My jaw went slack, my tongue numbed at Burnham's proclamation.

"Well fuck me with the devil's dick," was all I could muster.

Corcoran glanced over at me, "Say, wasn't there something that Burnham mentioned about a ChronoSaber, something like that?"

Yes! Yes you fucking dolt! I thought. They're *the reason we're on this sick, twisted temporal scavenger hunt, I'm sure of it! That fresh-faced nincompoop that brought us to the suite will run it some day, and then they can pin a fucking medal on your rube chest while no one ever acknowledges the advancements that Phineas Templeton has provided the world!*

"Indeed," I said.

I could remind Corcoran about whatever details of ChronoSaber's existence that I had been able to glean thus far a few minutes from now. For the moment, I needed to get at Burnham, which would be no small task. As the applause died down, and Huey Lewis of all people took over the role of M.C. and got the crowd back into the swing of the festivities, I made my way over to the curious little man who dawdled off the stage.

"Mr. Burnham!" I called out to him. "Mr. Burnham! A word, please?" Burnham met my gaze and smiled slyly. He waved away the guards who flanked him and escorted me over to an area along the wall.

"What in the *hell* are you doing?" I asked

"What the fuck do you mean?" Burnham must have still been in good spirits; otherwise I fear I would've received a gut punch for my trouble.

"SABERCorp? ChronoSaber? Don't you see the connection?"

"Now that you mention it…" Burnham said with a wry smile.

"You knew that you were going to do this! And why haven't I heard of SABERCorp before?"

Burnham raised his eyebrows playfully, "Questions, questions. And so little time for answers. What am I saying? You have all of the time in the universe! Come now, my dear Doctor Templeton," he lapsed into what seemed to be an incredibly-practised English accent. "Do you think that either the kindly grandfather or the hillbillied yay-hoo that you've met this evening is what I'm really like?"

Though I had been chased by a T-Rex and nearly killed by Mayan warriors over the past several days, it was the first time that a pronounced chill leaked down my spine.

"As far as SABERCorp is concerned, they have instructions to stay largely behind the scenes as a cadre of shell companies and fronts do their work for them until a very specific date, one that you're no doubt unfamiliar with as of yet, at which time a 'corporate consolidation' will once again bring SABERCorp to the forefront, as well as a number of subsidiaries with which I'm sure you *are* familiar."

"But you—you're *not* Victor Burnham then?"

He laughed a haughty English laugh, "Who is? The poor bastard who was killed in Vietnam whose identity I assumed? I'm just as much Victor Burnham as Trent Albertson is Jesus Christ. Which is to say simultaneously not at all and always. And who are you, dear Templeton? Someone lost to history? A man without an identity? Tell me now, what does that make you? A fucking *ghost*. Poof!" His hands radiated outward quickly, "and you're gone." His brow reddened as sweat poured off it.

"Can you stop this? Can you call off this scavenger hunt I'm on with Corcoran and Bloomington? Can you send me home?"

Burnham chuckled, "Can I prevent World War II? Can I warn the passengers who got on those planes on 9-11? Sadly, I cannot. What I *can* offer you is a warning." His eyes turned pale and grave as he placed a hand on my shoulder, "You're involved in a conspiracy more dangerous than you can possibly imagine. A pawn in a game for Rooks and Queens. Always remember that, no matter what, no matter how indelible things may seem," he paused to loosen his collar, "*you* make the choices. You've...*always*...made the choices. And you are doomed to make those...same choices..."

Burnham's full weight collapsed on my shoulder.

"...again," he spat out as his body went slack. I stared, mouth agape, for several moments as I looked down at the bald spot on Burnham's head.

"Medic!" I yelled. "Doctor! Is anyone a doctor?"

CHAPTER SIXTEEN

The room descended into chaos as Burnham's guards threw their weight around in a vain attempt to clear the area.

"The old cuss finally bit it," one onlooker said with a bit too much glee. I imagine he had been a bitter business associate.

One of the guards flung Burnham over his shoulder like a sack of meal and waded through the crowd. The hulking bouncer signaled Garrett, who sprinted toward the microphone.

"Ladies and gentlemen, please!" the fresh-faced young ginger said. "Please calm down!" He brought both hands out wide and attempted to calm the room. "It appears that Mr. Burnham's blood sugar has dipped a bit low. Nothing to be alarmed about—I assure you, he will be fine in the light of day." His smile was a bit overbroad, in that way that a parent tries to conceal bad news from a child.

Corcoran glared at me, clearly thinking that Burnham looked to be far from okay.

"Stock price," I mouthed. The light went on in Corcoran's head. He promptly shook it off.

Bloomington buzzed next to him, "No fucking shit, man. That guy did a fuck-ton of blow. I'm surprised he lasted that long."

Now it was my turn to glare, "I thought you said that he died in the mid aughts?"

Bloomington shrugged, "Yeah, I mean, I think so."

I widened my eyes and raised my eyebrows at the portly scientist, and he returned the gesture as if to mock me.

"If he dies tonight, doesn't that throw a wrench in the whole 'whatever happened, happened,' business?" I asked.

Almost on cue, a hushed gust of noise rose like a cresting wave from the exit. Burnham's previously inanimate body stuck up a hand, contorted into the universal symbol for time travel, or the "Live Long and Prosper" sign, as these hapless fools would understand it. I thought it to be one final twist of the knife by Burnham aimed at us, but as far as the crowd's mood went, concern melted to a chorus of cheers and applause as the room went wild. A hearty breeze blew over my face; I thought it was likely a collection of top Burnham Herrington shareholders exhaling simultaneously.

Garrett applauded vigorously into the microphone, to the point where the obnoxious noise buzzed and stung my ears. It rather seemed like something that Bloomington might do, just to wind me up.

"You see? He's okay!" Garrett swept a hand toward the exit. "Well, now that Mr. Burnham has made one of his trademark exits," a brief pause for a round of phony guffaws, "We can get back to the task at hand, which, as I'm sure you're all well aware, is to par-tay!"

Another token round of cheers and laughs was followed by applause to chase Garrett away from the stage. As soon as he was away from the microphone, Garrett's smile darkened into a scowl as he motioned at Huey to start playing once more. Huey cringed visibly, before he brightened and approached the mike.

"All right everybody! Good to see Mr. B's okay. Let's get things rockin' again! 2, 3, 4!" As Burnham's choked-out exhortation rattled inside my head, "Back in Time" boomed from the loudspeakers. I suppose I shouldn't be surprised at how many of the partygoers shrugged the whole deal off, and went back to their drunken carousing without skipping nary a beat.

What did surprise me, though, was that two of the said coterie of revelers were Corcoran and Bloomington.

I suppose that's not an entirely accurate sentiment; it didn't surprise me that the utterly-stoned Bloomington was one of the first to pick up a random drink from a nearby table and guzzle it down when the music restarted.

Corcoran, though, was another matter entirely. Before I could even turn to relay the specifics of my conversation with "the real" Victor Burnham (as much as his identity could be ascertained due to the vagaries of time travel), Corcoran had hooked a slinky-looking blonde around each elbow. As reluctant as I am to admit as much, each one was rather attractive despite the curious fashion choices of the day.

Frustrated, I tapped Corcoran twice on the shoulder.

His clenched jaw when he turned betrayed his own feelings.

"What now, Doc?" he asked.

"I have something to discuss with you of a rather urgent na—"

"Oh, come on. What could possibly be so urgent *right now*."

I nodded at each of the women in turn.

"I apologize, ladies; lovely as you both may be, it's a conversation of a decidedly private and confidential nature that I must have with the Commander here."

"I didn't know that you're in the Navy!" one of the blondes exclaimed with a bit-too-practised naïveté.

"Somethin' like that, darlin'." Corcoran's own "country boy" affectation was in full force.

"Commander, I must insist—"

"Oh, lighten up already, Doc." He gritted his teeth into a scowl and glared at me before he turned to each woman in turn and grinned. "Ladies, can you excuse me for just a moment? My colleague and I need to have an 'impohhhtant and confiden-chial conversaaaation.'" Corcoran drew out the last part in an (admittedly, pretty good) stodgy, mocking British accent of his own.

The ladies laughed at my expense (as has so often regrettably been the case) and Corcoran grabbed me by the arm and dragged me off to the side of the stage.

"This better be fucking—"

"Burnham is an Englishman." I decided the direct route to be best.

"What?"

"His whole backstory is a fraud. He's an Englishman, sure as I am."

"I thought you said you were born in America?"

"I…never mind that. For all intents and purposes, I'm still—"

Corcoran shrugged, "So what?"

"*Pardon?*"

"So what if he's a Brit?"

I literally took a step back, "You mean you don't find it the least bit pertinent or odd that this old billionaire made it a point to lie to us for a half hour earlier this afternoon as to who he was? You don't find it the least bit suspicious that—"

"Look, you said it yourself, people come to the past to escape their old lives. So what if he's not a hardened, Vegas hustler?"

"You mean, so what if he's a fraud?"

For a moment, I thought Corcoran may hit me.

"HE'S ALREADY A FRAUD!" It was all Corcoran could do to keep his voice at a hissing whisper. "Don't you get it? He's conning everyone here! He's no 'self-made' millionaire."

"Billionaire," I corrected him.

For this transgression, I did receive a quick slap on the cheek from the Commander.

"That's not the point. The point is, what does it matter if he's English or American or Martian?"

"I just think that it might have some bearing on how the whole ChronoSaber mess affects me—us." I quickly corrected myself.

Corcoran shook his head, "Why did I need to hear about this *right now*?" He asked. "Can't you see I'm busy here? We're stuck here until around noon tomorrow, aren't we? Tell ya what, I'll chat up these lovely young ladies for the rest of the night, *you* stay the fuck outta my way, and tomorrow you can tell me all about what the old cokehead told you just before he collapsed from a heart attack, okay?"

I opened my mouth to rebut, but before I had a chance to respond, Corcoran patted me twice on the shoulder and bolted off to take his rightful place between the two fetching women.

Had the time machine been ready to go, I would have gladly left Corcoran and Bloomington to their own devices in the eighties, content to do all of the cocaine and zonked-out groupies that they could afford.

Unfortunately, that wasn't the case. I instead opted to make my way over to the bar, where the capable bartenders were presently overwhelmed by the "post-death-scare" demand. One of them had carelessly left a full bottle of Macallan Eighteen on the edge of the bar. After all of the rubbish that Burnham had put me through, I felt but a small twinge of remorse as I carefully lifted the bottle from the edge of the bar.

Perhaps because I was still shaken up by the whole ordeal, and precisely because I was trying to be so suave, I fumbled the vessel and it fell to the ground with a thud. I experienced a moment of sheer panic when I saw that perfect, pure bottle of scotch (from 1967, mind you!) tumble to the ground. All I could think of as it connected with the floor was that had I somehow smuggled it into the future, it would be worth potentially thousands, even though it would likely taste little different than the Macallan eighteen being served in 2032.

I cringed, and anticipated the loud crash and shattered glass. Instead, the bottle let out a sharp "PING," muffled by the din of patrons ordering drinks. I released a hearty sigh and picked up the bottle with far less panache than before. I found a glass and a seat at a table somewhere near the bar and began to pour.

This is where my usual hyper vigilance fades away to something far less comprehensive, that wonderful creature that I've heard referred to as a "brown out." I remember the next hour or so, as I spent he first portion commiserating with an elderly Jewish couple about the state of politics in the Mideast in 1985, and whether the "current" war between Iraq and Iran would potentially escalate into something catastrophic for Israel. Instead of inducing what would surely be a second heart attack that evening in either the shrunken little fellow or his wife by explaining the full extent of what was in store for the region in the coming years, I listened patiently and intently, and did my best to steer the conversation toward other topics.

Eventually, the couple excused themselves and a fortiesh brunette sat next to me. Her expression was downcast, her curly hair puffed out to the very limits of hairspray, and her mascara racooned around her eyes. She looked like she could use a drink, so I offered her one.

"Huh? Oh, sure. I mean, 'yes, please.'" she said.

"Rough night?" I asked as I tilted the bottle toward her glass and gave her a generous pour.

"You have no idea."

"Oh, I have *some* idea," I said.

"I sincerely doubt that."

"Try me."

"Well...sure, why not?" she sighed as she let out an exasperated laugh. "Who better to tell all of my problems to than some random Brit at Victor Burnham's party?"

"Sometimes strangers have the most objective point of view, and thus the best advice to offer," I said.

"And sometimes they're some kind of...serial killer...or..."

"Time traveller?" I offered.

She nodded as she downed a gulp of whisky, "Or 'alien,' or other whack-job, looking to make your hair into a wig."

I chuckled, "However would I do that? I don't even have a decent razor." I rubbed a hand over my unkempt stubble.

This elicited a chuckle from Cynthia, and she allowed her shoulders to relax in the chair a bit.

"Okay, but I'm warning you—you asked for it."

"Indeed I did," I replied with an arched eyebrow.

"My husband left me last week. Some bimbo secretary of his could do...things I wasn't willing to do." I found her modesty to be rather refreshing. "So he just up-and-left. Packed up his stuff and hopped the next flight to Aruba with Sucky McGee," I nearly spat out my drink. "It wouldn't be so bad if it wasn't the holidays, and I get so lonely now that the kids are out of the house…"

"I'm sure you're not lacking for male attention," I said without thinking. "Beautiful young woman like yourself—"

"You think I'm beautiful…and young?" she asked. She batted her eyelashes at me several times.

"I…uh, well yes, I do. I find runny mascara to be utterly intoxicating."

She laughed and grinned. It was a wonderful, bright smile, though oddly familiar; a smile that bubbled to her face from deep inside, and washed over me like sunlight on a warm spring afternoon.

"You're sweet," she said. Her eyes lingered on mine for several moments as neither of us dared to break the other's gaze. We were forced to as a waiter stopped by and placed a full champagne flute in front of each of us.

"Two minutes, folks. Two minutes," he said.

Cynthia began to sob.

"My dear, I—"

She took out a handkerchief and waved it at me, "I'm so sorry—it's just, I haven't been alone for New Year's Eve in…as long as I can remember. Maybe twenty years now. It's usually such a great time for a fresh start, but—"

"But isn't that exactly what you need right now?" I asked. I tried to appropriate Corcoran's rakish grin as my own.

She laughed between choking sobs, "I guess so. But who would want—?"

"I'll make a deal with you," I said. "My friends abandoned me as well." She leaned in, expecting more information, but I shook my head, "They're not important. But what do you say that I agree to be your friend for the evening, and, in return, you can be mine?"

She brightened once more, "Okay," she said, softly at first. "Okay, you've got a deal. I'm telling you, though, you have no idea what you've gotten yourself into."

"Nor do you," I said, as I raised both eyebrows. I offered my glass toward her for a toast. "To fresh starts," I said.

"To fresh starts," her eyes twinkled in the light of the wonderful, antique crystal chandeliers.

Just then, a faint chant began to build from the crowd.

"Eleven...ten...nine..."

"This is usually my favorite part. But however will they do it without Ryan Seacrest?" I asked.

Eight...seven...

"You mean Dick Clark?" she asked.

...Six...

"What?" I said.

...Five...

"Who?" she replied.

...Four...Three...

"It was a joke, you see—"

I didn't hear two or one as Cynthia grabbed me by the lapel and pulled me in for a kiss. Now, as inexperienced as I may be with women, I'll have you know that I was no thirty-six year old virgin, though it had been so long by now that I sometimes thought of myself as much.

I puckered up and shivered as my lips met hers, a surge of electricity rocked my body as we held each other. The room must've been louder than ever, though to me, it seemed empty and hollow at the moment; the only "real" things were the woman in front of me and the Burnham-proclaimed "ghost" who was currently kissing her.

After several wonderful moments, the make-out session ended. My face must've twitched several times out of sheer giddiness and excitement, while her eyes were still the same kind, wonderful oasis of blue in the generally red-appointed room.

"Wow," she said. "You're one hell of a kisser."

"Indeed," I said, thoughtlessly, before I realised what she had said and shook myself straight, "You're quite ravishing, or I should say 'ravish*able*' yourself."

"I could use a drink," she said, as she shook her empty glass right by those wonderful eyes of hers.

"As could I," I replied.

"What's your name?" she asked.

"Templeton. Phineas Templeton," I said. I like to think it was far more James Bond than Phineas Templeton earlier that evening.

"Cynthia," she said. "Cynthia…Hess. Sorry, I apologize, it's tough to go back to my maiden name after all of these years. You have to admit, it sounds better than the old one, though."

"Really? What was it?" I had never damned my curiosity so much as right after the question left my lips, since it was that moment that I realised why that smile seemed so familiar.

"It was stupid…*but*…Albertson." She said. "Cynthia Albertson. My son, William, works for Victor. As you may be able to tell, I'm so proud. Something tells me he's in for great things some day."

I poured the bottle into my own glass until it was full to the brim, downed it, and checked out for the rest of the evening.

CHAPTER SEVENTEEN

As had become customary on this excursion, I awoke the next day to a splitting headache. I wondered for several curious moments if the events of the past several days had all been a dream. Maybe I was still in my lab at Hopkins, perhaps taken feverish, and had conjured up all of the insanity that I had recently experienced.

Instead, I found myself, alone, in my bed in the suite at the Adams Mark. I grasped at the far side of the bed as I searched for whom I could only imagine was Jesus Christ's grandmother, and was simultaneously relieved and dismayed when I found it vacant. I sighed, and reached for my glasses on the nightstand. After putting them on, I noticed a piece of paper from the notepad folded in half into a tent, with an elegant "Phineas" printed across the front.

My heart raced, both out of suspense for the contents of the note, and because I hadn't remembered more than a minute of 1986 until this very moment. My quivering hand reached for the note and I unfolded it as I felt a suffocating weight fill my chest.

"Dearest Phineas,

Thank you for a wonderful evening. It was great to spend the best New Year's ever with someone who can be such a giving friend (and more…). Don't be a stranger next time you're in St. Louis!

All My Love,

Cynthia."

Her phone number was scrawled in that wonderful, sweeping script. I sighed and savored the note for a moment before my jaw dropped and my eyes bulged.

"And more...?" I asked myself. "And more...?" I repeated the mantra incessantly as I paced around the room, and even into the bathroom as I showered and shaved. Had we...done *it*? Had I slept with Trent Albertson's grandmother?

And if so, why was I so furious that I didn't remember a second of it?

"And more...?" I put on the creased tux pants and did my best to beat the wrinkles out of the ruffled shirt that Burnham had provided.

"And more...?" I tucked in the shirt and tied my bow tie in a clumsy knot. I looked at myself in the mirror and sighed.

"And more..." I shook my head.

As reckless as my behaviour may have been the previous evening, I couldn't rattle out the nagging thought that I was most upset that I hadn't my full faculties to remember the experience. As disheveled as she may have been, Cynthia was a wondrous creature, and through the incessant pounding in my head, I seem to remember bits of intriguing conversations as the night went along. I just hoped that I hadn't told the woman that her grandson would some day become Jesus Christ Himself. I chided myself for forgetting that ultimately, even if I had spilled the beans on our entire time travel excursion, not only did it not matter a whit as far as the timeline was concerned, but also that it had proven endearing, a fact to which the note was testament .

I studied the note for several more minutes before I folded it and placed it carefully inside my coat. I staggered to the full-length mirror in the corner of the room and assessed the damage from the previous evening. Though the bags under my eyes that became more a part of my face with each passing day were still present, and my skin was a bit pale, I thought I looked rather good, all things considered.

179

If nothing else, I projected an air of confidence that had been sorely lacking within me previously. Don't get me wrong, of the many adjectives used to describe my personality, I'm not so naive as to think that "arrogant" isn't in the top three. But there's a marked difference between "confidence" and "arrogance," insomuch as the latter is usually used to mask the absence of the former.

As I approached the door, I entertained briefly the idea of leaving Corcoran and Bloomington in the past and absconding with the machine to take on the rest of this horrid scavenger hunt by myself. As improbable (nay, impossible) as such a notion may have proven to carry out, I was still upset with the two acquaintances from the preceding evening. Bloomington because he was Bloomington, and Corcoran because of his cavalier attitude toward my very real concerns regarding Victor Burnham.

Any thoughts of escape were dashed as I exited the room to find Corcoran at the door, fully dressed in blue jeans and a non-descript (if faded) maroon t-shirt. He kissed one of the bimbos from the previous night and bid her farewell with a pat on the ass as he shut the door behind him and smiled.

"Whoo-boy. Helluva a night, eh Doc?" He pursed his lips and blew out a mouthful of air. "Wow. Worked out pretty well for everyone. 'Cept for Bloomy, I guess. He just sorta locked himself in his room and has been out like a light."

"You remember what happened last night?" I asked.

A sly smile, "How could I not, you dog? You were givin' it to that brunette chick pretty good. I say good for you, Doc; finally let your hair down a bit. Maybe you won't be such a tight-ass from now on."

My initial instinct was to chastise Corcoran for the comment, but instead I felt a swell of pride in my chest and mustered a chuckle.

"I suppose you're right. Perhaps as Trent Albertson said, I should enjoy—"

"That guy who works for Burnham?" Corcoran asked.

"What? No, no not at all. No, the guy who's parading around in the past as Jesus Christ, remember?" Corcoran responded with a blank stare. "We went over this back in Chichen Itza, outside of your smoldering wreckage?"

He affected a knowing grin, "Oh yeah, *that* whole deal," Corcoran said.

"Yes, *that* 'whole deal,'" dare I say my tone was only slightly mocking. "And we still have to discuss how all of this—Burnham, Albertson—both of them," I interrupted Corcoran before he could flood the room with more brilliance, "fit in with ChronoSaber. Now if only—"

I looked toward Bloomington's room precisely as the doors opened. One of the benefits of maintaining a rather unkempt style and pudgy physique was that the scientist hardly looked worse for wear despite his drug-fueled bender from the previous evening.

He took two steps into the main area before he obnoxiously sniffed the air deeply.

"Stinks like sex in here," he said with a broad smile. I shot daggers at Corcoran as he offered a wry grin and a shrug.

"He's kinda got a point, Doc."

"Come on, I'm kidding, I'm kidding." It was about as effusive as I had seen Bloomington since before his brush with death. "What a hell of a night though, eh dickheads?" I opened my mouth for a witty retort, but Bloomington preempted me, "I know, I know, sorry Doctor Templeton for being such a mess recently. Until I took down a couple of rails last night, I just had been feeling like shit. I think the coke pretty much evened me out."

Corcoran simply nodded as if Bloomington had said he was going downstairs to get the paper. I suppose in hindsight it's easy to say that Bloomington's erratic behavior was due to some kind of reaction with the medigel or withdrawal after a full week of not using whatever it was he was on, but I figured that no matter how wrong-headed the man's logic, I already much preferred this Bloomington to the one who had been along for the ride thus far.

"I...uh...see..." was all I could muster before I collected myself and offered a tight smile, "Glad to hear you're feeling better."

"That makes two of us," Corcoran nodded at Bloomington.

"Good," Bloomington nodded. "Now if you'll excuse me, I have to run the water in the shower to cover the sounds of my masturbating." Even I chuckled a bit at that one, and Corcoran practically guffawed, but Bloomington remained stone-faced as he turned and re-entered the room.

"Told ya' he was a better guy than he was letting on," Corcoran winked at me.

"Indeed," I said. "Well, I suppose we have about two-and-a-half minutes to spare, so what do you say that we tackle this Burnham quandary?"

I relayed the last conversation that Burnham and I had to Corcoran, who looked lazily around the room as I spoke.

"So? What do you think?" I asked him.

I expected the Commander to try to cover his ass with any number of vagaries, but was shocked when he abruptly turned and looked me in the eye.

"Isn't it obvious? At some point, Garrett gets put in charge of SABERCorp, or whatever the hell you said it is now. He makes the decision to get into time travel. Everyone makes a shitload of money, including this Albertson character, which then allows his son to get in the game as Jesus Christ."

My mouth must've almost dropped to the rather stiff burgundy carpet.

"I suppose that's as good of a working hypothesis as any," I tried to hide my shock. "But still, there's something missing here. Burnham's final comment was '*you* make the choices. You've *always* made the choices. And you are doomed to make those same choices again."

"So? Doesn't that fit into the whole 'what happened, happened' thing?"

"Yes, but there was something *more* to it. The way he said it, his tone, his cadence, it was very ominous."

Corcoran shook his head, "The man was having a heart attack. Of course it sounded ominous."

"All done," the door to Bloomington's door flung open and the pudgy scientist stood in the frame, true to his word dry as a bone.

"Good. How we lookin' on time, Doc?" Corcoran asked.

"The machine should be ready to go, provided we survive the trek back there."

"Aw, come on, it's New Year's Day. No one'll be out yet."

"No witnesses," Bloomington offered.

Corcoran shook the thought out of his head. "We'll take a cab then."

"I hope they take gold," I reached in my pocket and flung the bag of Roman coins at Corcoran.

He frowned with annoyance. "Steve, you got any—?"

Bloomington shook his head. Corcoran cringed again. "Well, I guess it's up to Mr. Garrett, then." He picked up one of the ornate (if gaudy) expensive-for-the-eighties phones and waited for the operator.

"Yeah, this is...uh...the suite. I'd like to get in touch with Garrett..." he put his hand over the receiver and widened his eyes at me.

"Zane," I whispered.

"Garrett Zane...err...Zane Garrett....awright." He looked at me and mouthed, "Put me on hold." Despite how I had perhaps previously underestimated the man's intelligence, he was apparently rather adept at making it possible to do so.

"Yeah, hi, Mr. Garrett? This is Ricky Corcoran, how the hell are ya?" He winked at me once more. "Good. Listen, I'm embarrassed as all get-out here over at the Adams Mark, but it looks like none of us have money for a cab handy. Is there any way...good. Great. Fantastic. Oh yeah, and how is...? Oh, great. Well that's wonderful. Sure, sure—totally understand. All right, thanks a bunch, Mr. Garrett. Okay...you too...bye now." He set down the reciever.

"We're to tell the front desk that Mr. Burnham's going to take care of everything, set us up with a gen-u-ine Lincoln with a driver and some spending money."

"As gracious as that gesture may be, I doubt that they're going to have a currency exchange in fourth century Turkey," I said.

183

"It's the thought that counts," Corcoran replied with narrowed eyes.

"How's Burnham?" I asked.

"Good. Surprisingly good, really. They said he's gonna make a full recovery."

"Wonderful," I offered a tight smile. "Any way that we could—"

"Sorry Doc," Corcoran shook his head. "Garrett said no visitors."

"Jesus, with the way that guy sucked down that blow, I'm shocked he's alright," Bloomington said.

"Maybe it's the same way you could take an axe to the back and still be alive?" Corcoran asked.

"Through body armor," Bloomington snorted. Corcoran and I shook our disapproval. I was almost certain that Burnham had used the medigel to heal himself, though in the event of a heart attack, I didn't see how that was possible through any conventional method of application. Perhaps he had rigged a syringe with the stuff to fire directly into his veins, or perhaps his security had been instructed to inject him.

I collected the casual eighties garb that Burnham's people had provided. As I pondered the precise mechanism that Burnham had used to reanimate himself, I shuffled along practically on autopilot first into the Town Car, all of the way until the limo pulled up next to the abandoned lot where we had parked the time machine.

"Thanks," Corcoran said with that winning smile of his as he handed a wad of bills to the driver.

"Thank *you*, sir." The greedy driver waited, palm outstretched, angling for gratuities from Bloomington and myself. Even had I the currency to do so, the man's brashness would have assured that he received none.

We exited the car only to find a couple of children who threw rocks at the invisible time machine. They laughed with glee as the projectiles appeared to dance and turn abruptly in mid-air, scattered by some magical, unknowable force.

"Now see here, children!" Though the alloy that comprised the machine was far too strong to be damaged by rambunctious tykes tossing stones, I thought the better of having to explain the mysterious invisible shape that clanged with every rock hit.

Corcoran patted me on the shoulder and held up his other hand. He casually ambled over to the children and spoke to them, though I couldn't hear what he said. He pulled several crisp hundreds out of his pocket, which produced ear-to-ear grins from the children. They greedily grabbed the bills and scampered off into the urban wilderness.

"Just needed a bit of motivation, that's all," Corcoran said. I likely would have been flustered with the ease with which Corcoran had dispatched the boys normally, but in my lingering post-coital afterglow, I simply smiled and nodded.

I pressed the smart spec button on the temple of my frames, and the enhanced vision display jumped into view. I easily located the entry panel, and placed my hand upon it to lower the gangway and provide the entrance.

We settled into our usual spots, as I manned the controls, and Corcoran and Bloomington settled in to the dining area next to the pantry.

"Any chance we can get that full-angle view again, Doc?" Corcoran asked as he absentmindedly struggled to place his billfold in his pocket.

"Computer, three hundred sixty degree view, please," I said. The walls faded away, leaving a panorama of the crumbling vacant lot surrounding us. A family of rats scurried into one of the sections of remaining masonry walls that skirted the edges of the parcel.

"What a view," Bloomington deadpanned. I quite liked the new and improved Bloomington already, despite the rather questionable means he had employed to arrive at his current disposition.

"Some of us got a soft spot for the old gal, Bloomy," Corcoran looked at me, "And others of us just like the city."

"Now just one moment, Commander. I'll have you—"

"Relax, just a little joke. That chick you were with was a total cougar, man. Just," he let out a low, long whistle, "All kinds of all right."

"Thank you for your approving commentary," I said through gritted teeth. Perhaps the afterglow was beginning to fade.

I programmed the computer, though more out of curiosity than anything else, I checked the odds on returning to my time (1.8%) and Corcoran's time (0.2%) before doing so. Momentarily amused by the fact that the craft was "eight times more likely" to return to my time period than it was to theirs, I pulled up the list memorialised in my tablet and keyed in the coordinates for our next jump.

"13-3-325: Nicaea, Turkey: Witness C's skepticism at the FEC"

I was somewhat ashamed that my own knowledge of ancient Turkey was likely as limited as Corcoran's or Bloomington's. Sure, my father had procured several antiquities from the general area and similar time period, they were mostly "lesser" pieces as far as I was concerned, not because they were any less ornate or polished than others, but because they were of the type of goods that did not lend themselves well to drawing inferences as to the story behind them. A clay jug containing simple drawings memorialising even the most mundane occasion at least had some history behind it, something that would unleash my imagination and allow it to run wild; what had these people been like? What purpose did this jug serve?

Unfortunately, any pottery in my father's collection from the place and time we were about to encounter was more of the "just a jug" variety. Though I admired each piece for dutifully performing its function day-in and day-out for who-knows how many years, and surviving through the centuries against the odds, there was no indication as to its, I suppose this may sound hackneyed by now, but "rightful place in history." Whether it ever commemorated a special event or otherwise distinguished itself from all of the pottery lost to time that otherwise became shards in trash pits, studied by archaeologists, who themselves seemed little more than archaic curiosities given what we now knew of the realities of time travel.

I asked the computer to produce clothing appropriate for the era, and it provided what can best be described as three tunics, each of which was a bright, sky blue. Three pairs of simple sandals (which, for my money, appeared to be little more than discount flip-flops from Wal-Mart) were also included in the clothing package. I shook my head, then amazed that the computer knew that I'd have two other companions at this point in time, though in hindsight I should have recognised that the exhortation to "rescue R.C. and S.B." would likely necessitate such an occurrence.

I tossed two of the packages at the dining area.

"What in the sam fu—" Corcoran protested.

"Put it on," I interrupted. "We don't want to draw undue attention next lifetime, do we?"

"And here I was, thinking it was casual Friday from here on out," Corcoran shook his head. He peeled off the simple shirt and Bloomington followed suit. I began the somewhat more arduous task of removing the tuxedo, though I carefully folded it and placed it in the glove compartment next to the casual ensemble that Burnham had provided; I never knew when I may need such a formal garment once more, and in the event that I did, I didn't want to be caught unawares.

I patted the pockets of the tuxedo pants once more to ensure that I didn't forget anything vital, and found the small, nicotine-patch-like form of the holotran encased in clear plastic. I retrieved the amazing little device and slid it into a concealed pocket inside the tunic.

I also found an unwelcome surprise in the packet of clothing; another pair of contact lenses. I suppose fourth-century Turkey would not look kindly upon some giant stranger sporting spectacles, though I may have muttered a curse or two as I put the damned uncomfortable things in.

The red "Engage" icon flashed on the left console. I looked back at Corcoran and Bloomington, who were deeply immersed in a conversation as to which American football team had a better chance to win the Super Bowl during the season in which they had left (for the record, I believe they were debating between Atlanta and Houston). I allowed myself a stifled chuckle as I hit the icon and the ship began its machinations, and hurtled us noiselessly, forcelessly toward the heavens.

CHAPTER EIGHTEEN

I'll spare you the particulars of our arrival in Nicaea, other than to say that it was surprisingly green and lush compared to the arid desert for which I had prepared myself. The city was a small, but thriving community on the eastern shores of a body of water that I would later discover was known as Lake Iznik, and something about the calm waves as they gently lapped against the shore was so utterly peaceful and picturesque compared with the rotting urban core we had just visited that I fancied that I could return to the city in my own time for a proper spa vacation, were I not concerned with such benign matters as "war" and "fallout."

We touched down on the outskirts of town in between a row of olive trees. Though Corcoran had no reason to raid the armory, he sat at the table and cleaned his sidearm, lest it fail him in an inopportune moment. For once, Bloomington merely sat quietly, or I should say "more quietly than usual," as he whistled a nonsensical tune.

"Well gents...any ideas?" I decided to take charge.

"Your guess is as good as mine, Doc." Corcoran said. "I'm not exactly Mister History over here."

Not yet... I thought.

"Uh...Holy Roman Empire...anyone?" Bloomington piped up.

"What about it?" I decided to feel him out.

He paused in consideration of his next words for several moments before he shook his head, "That's all I've got."

"Lovely," I replied.

"Hey, better than what you came up with, doucheface," the toady scientist retorted.

I shook my head. Corcoran punctuated the brief silence by cocking his gun once more.

"Well, way I figure, best way to find out is to get out and ask around," he said.

There was something about the Commander's folksy practicality that was simultaneously maddening and alluring. Despite my misgivings, I nodded along with his plan, and after I cloaked the vessel, I politely asked the computer to lower the gangway.

As I caught my first whiff of fourth-century air, I was immediately taken by the pungent, pleasant aroma of fresh olives basking in the spring sunlight. Bird song showered us with warm tidings as I drank in the surrounding scenery. The entire area was in stark contrast from the overly-developed (to the point of neglect) city from which we had just come. Even Corcoran was unable to hide his smirk as he practically gulped in the fresh, sweet-smelling breeze.

The rows of olive trees led to a simple, stucco-ish hut, which was presently empty, though the crackling embers of a cooking fire indicated that it had not been left as such for more than an hour or so.

We soldiered on until the outskirts of town developed, marked by rows of small houses similar to the one out in the field, and all likewise empty. I looked first at Corcoran, then Bloomington for their takes on the situation, but each one only offered a shrug in return.

As we approached the city center, it became clear that most of the denizens had gathered outside of a large stone building protected by a number of guards wearing what appeared to be wrought-iron helmets and similar sky-blue tunics to our own. My annoyance at the designed "coincidences" that continued to pop up subdued any fear I may have otherwise felt, and I forced our way through the throng, the members of which shouted any number of obscenities in a strange language that I couldn't hope to—

The holotran! I thought. I reached inside the hidden pocket and produced the small device, and after some fiddling with the packaging and removing the plastic back, I placed it on my neck, roughly in the spot that Burnham had placed his.

I expected the cacophony of noise to be replaced by calm, measured tones of the King's, but no such breezy translation was forthcoming. I admit, I panicked a bit, and thought that perhaps Burnham had supplied us with counterfeits as part of this oddest, on-going conspiracy.

"What the devil…" I said under my breath.

Immediately, the conversations in whatever dreadful language the locals used streamed into my head, clear as a bell in plain English. I suppose it made sense that the device would need some baseline to calibrate how it interacted with its speaker, though I was nonetheless impressed with the alacrity with which it did so.

I walked toward one of the short, dreadful-looking guards holding one of the long, slender pikes at the entranceway to the stone building. My heart perhaps skipped a beat or so as I hoped that the small patch on my neck worked as well the other way as it did filtering out the cries from the square.

"Excuse me," I said. "We're on shift inside now, and—"

"What took you so long?" The short guard huffed. I decided that the lack of an answer was the best response given the circumstances, and stood, stone-faced. From the corners of each eye, I noticed that Corcoran and Bloomington exchanged startled glances.

The ugly little troll sized us up for several moments before he nodded at us. "Rumor has it that a madman has invaded the Council chamber. I trust that you will deal with him appropriately?"

I nodded as one of the ghastly, warty throng behind us jabbed me in the back. I turned to verify the perpetrator, but they all blended together in a mass of tangled, ugly humanity.

"Very well," I said. "Corc…Corcoros. Bloomoros. Follow me." I projected my most soldierly tone.

"Good luck," the horrid little troll responded.

I motioned for Bloomington and Corcoran to follow, and they dutifully did so as we made our way up the path toward the imposing structure ahead. I say it was imposing because it was all of two stories tall, and loomed over the rest of the city to the extent that it may as well have been the former Empire State Building.

Figurines were carved into the walls, and appeared to depict my good friend Trent splayed out on the cross. For some reason, I couldn't seem to shake the notion that his limbs were completely out of proportion. The pleasant smell of olives was gone, replaced by a mildewy, unpleasant aroma that reminded me of Hopkins' neglected paper library.

"What the hell was that, Doc?" Corcoran finally hissed.

"What do you mean? Didn't you gents unpackage the holotrans that Burnham gave you?"

Bloomington looked at Corcoran blankly, while the Commander fumbled in his own tunic pocket for a moment before he produced the packaged disc, tore into it, and placed it on his neck.

"Sorry Bloomy," Corcoran said. "You have one back on the ship."

Bloomington glared at his commanding officer for several moments before the light clicked on in his head and he sneered before he regained his composure and pouted more subtly.

We entered a large chamber, where a number of men adorned in brightly-colored tunics sat, rapt at attention at a large, circular table. One of the men at the far side of the room wore a well-made, fur-lined cape, which I figured marked him as the leader of this little enclave.

Opposite the fur-adorned fellow was a taller gent in a dark green tunic and pantaloons. His salt-and-pepper locks kept in an unstylish ponytail were at odds with his ghostly white, somewhat long and, dare I say, nerdy face. The forcefulness of the odd, tall man's speech and large, sweeping hand motions indicated that he was far from happy. Curiously, the tall, angry man made no show of hiding the rather plain spectacles that adorned his face, despite the four guards who stood, pikes outstretched toward him from behind.

As we approached, we could see that the taller man's gesticulations were tied to a stream of wild invective aimed at the Council convened in front of him.

"And so, Emperor Constantine," the tall man said, "You have snookered the people of the Western world for the last time. Your callous disregard of the so-called 'Gnostic gospels,' those books that you know as the 'Gospel of Judas' and the 'Gospel of Mary Magdalene,' and the like, which you are about to condemn to heresy and the depths of the most arcane scholarly analysis, deserve to be preserved in the so-called 'regular' New Testament as worthy of all other books mentioning Christ himself.

"As a biblical scholar of thirty years, I simply refuse to believe that my trek back here to convince you as much is in vain, and I simply will not leave until I hear a firm and resounding 'yes' for an answer."

The man turned from the Council and flinched as we approached. All of the usual signs of time travel were present; taller, a bit oddly-dressed, and somewhat more blowhardy. Accordingly, I offered the "Live Long and Prosper" hand signal to the man as he stood in front of who I assumed was Emperor Constantine and his coterie of theologians.

The time traveller raised a hand and echoed the gesture with a smile; apparently, he seemed to think that we were brought here as backup. Newly confident, he launched into another diatribe.

"And one more thing, *your excellency*," he nodded toward us, "you have no way of possibly knowing what effect this decision will have on countless generations henceforth. Wars will be fought and lost based on this one Ecumenical Council, a Council that, barring your selfish, shortsighted actions, would otherwise serve to help *heal* history. Would perhaps avert countless loss of life and teach humanity a kinder, gentler form of religion. In the end, isn't it about protecting your fellow man, and advancing his, or *her*, lot in life? Of building a better future for us all?

"Thus I humbly implore you, Your Majesty, to reconsider your stance on this simple issue, and to change the course of history, for the better, forever more."

The Council sat with thoroughly shocked expressions on their faces. One-by-one, they turned toward the fur-clad gentleman at the center of the room. He was tall as far as they were concerned, though not as tall as the man who stood before him, and suitably more handsome than anyone else in the room, barring myself and the Commander.

The man who I assumed was Emperor Constantine stroked his chin for several moments before he nodded at the guards behind the odd, gangly man who stood in front of him.

"I don't think so," he said, his harsh, bird-like features crinkled into a grimace.

The time traveller sighed deeply and dusted himself off before he started once more.

"Then I have no choice." He pulled a .357 magnum from the waistband of his pantaloons. Corcoran immediately reached for his holster, but I put a hand on his shoulder as the man in the green tunic pointed the gun at several guards in turn.

"By the authority vested in me by the Oberlin College Department of Religious, Spiritual, Agnostic, and Atheist studies, I hereby order you to abdicate your throne under penalty of death."

"And if I don't?" the bird-like man in fur asked with a measured nonchalance. The man in the green tunic purposely aimed high, his hand unsteady, and shot a round into the wall, which smashed one of the stone bricks to smithereens.

"I won't hesitate to use this, Your Highness. Don't make me—"

One of the guards behind the man plunged his pike clear through the gangly time traveller. My jaw dropped as the guard expertly removed the long implement from the now-gaping hole through the man and a torrent of blood poured from it. The time traveller fell immediately lifeless and slack; no amount of first aid supplies or (I doubted) even medigel could have revived the man, whose spasms ended after a few short moments.

Corcoran reached inside his tunic and grasped his gun, but fearing what may happen, I grabbed his arm and shook my head as my eyes met his.

"What the fuck, Doc?" he spat in a whisper.

I pointed at the guards that stood behind us at the back of the room. Corcoran thought of protesting further for a moment before he scowled.

"Apparently, he did hesitate to use it," Constantine stepped out from behind the table and circled toward the lifeless corpse that lay in front of him. The theologians stood and looked onward, though a lone, hacking cough punctuated the eerie silence.

The Emperor stood over the body and kicked it several times with his foot to ensure that the man who had so ardently been pleading his case was, in fact, no longer of this Earth. He picked up the sidearm from the man's lifeless hand and studied it for several moments, looking down its barrel more than once. He waved the magnum in the air and pulled the trigger several times, but fortunately the safety had caught somewhere during the time traveller's ordeal.

More troubling, Constantine turned to face us. His expression was knowing, yet innocent, like the child who had stolen a taffy from the sweet shop but had been caught, red-handed, and was desperate to avoid blame. His mouth dropped into a grimace as his eyes grew wide not with fear, but with a disconcerting naïveté that jarred me.

To this day, I don't know whether his next actions were cold and calculated, or if he decided to imitate the man whose life he had just ended, but Constantine extended a hand upward, and slowly, and carefully, without any hint of ever having done so before, mimicked the man he had just caused to be killed by forming the "Live Long and Prosper" symbol with his hand.

I tried to gulp but my mouth was bone dry. I wanted nothing more than to run far away from this building, yet I was utterly paralyzed with fear. I looked to Corcoran to stem the tide of panic that washed over me. Fortunately, the Commander was as steely as ever, perhaps because he remembered (unlike I had) that we both carried sidearms that could likely dispatch all of these pikemen should the need arise.

"You there—guards. Did you have any association with this man who dared to question my wisdom?" Constantine asked.

"No, sir." Corcoran said.

"No, what?" Constantine asked.

"No, Your Eminence," I piped up.

The man's thin lips turned upward into a smile. "Good. See to it that no other heretics make their way into this chamber."

"Yes, si—uh...Yer' Eminence," Corcoran caught himself. We stood behind the pikemen like three idiots, powerless to help the already dead time traveller splayed out on the floor.

"Well? Go on now!" Constantine pointed a long, bony finger at the back of the room.

"I think that's our cue," Corcoran whispered. For a moment of terror, I worried that Corcoran was about to pull out his sidearm and begin firing indiscriminately into the crowd of theologians.

Thankfully, he instead turned around and marched toward the entrance. Bloomington and I followed suit. We wound our way through the spartan hallways until we emerged in the crowd gathered in the town square.

"What the *fuck*?" Bloomington asked. This utterance drew some annoyed stares from the rabble, which I found curious until I recalled that Bloomington wasn't wearing a holotran.

"Shh!" Corcoran hissed at his compatriot, who was still densely unaware of the effect his anachronistic dialect was having on the crowd. Corcoran practically hoisted the portly scientist up and carried him through the mass of humanity until we emerged in a relatively quiet alley off of the main square.

I slowed to catch my breath, but Corcoran had no such intentions. He sprinted through the corridor, and Bloomington did his best to keep up. I shrugged and followed suit; though I passed Bloomington early, I didn't catch up with Corcoran until we reached the relative safety of the olive fields.

Several moments later, Bloomington huffed and wheezed his way through the maze of rows of olive trees.

"Oh my God," he choked out several heaving breaths."Seriously, Ricky, next time you're planning on doing that, remember that I practically *died* two days ago."

"I'm sure *that's* the reason for the fifty extra pounds of visceral fat you're carrying around." I clasped a hand over my mouth; I had only meant to think the sentiments, not allow them to escape into the wild.

"What the fuck, man? I thought we were cool now?" Bloomington said.

"I...uh...good natured ribbing and whatnot!" I tried to cover my own betraying thoughts. "Like we're old chums now, you know?" I chuckled in an exceedingly phony manner and delivered what apparently was a fully unconvincing smile as Bloomington remained stone-faced. "What the devil was that?" I asked Corcoran in an attempt to change the subject.

"Beats the shit outta me!" Corcoran finally let his guard down.

"They just...ran him through like a cocktail weenie," Bloomington chimed in.

"Yeah, no shit, buddy." Corcoran's anger built.

"Was that...it?" I asked. "FEC...that was clearly some sort of Council. First..."

"Ecumenical?" Corcoran offered.

"Beg your pardon?" I narrowed my eyes.

"What? That's what that weirdo said, ain't it?" Corcoran's tone was near-apologetic. "Plus, I just remembered from Catholic school, Constantine and a bunch of priests got together and figured out what was supposed to be in the Bible and what wasn't. That's the Cliff's Notes, at least."

"And you *just* remembered this *now*?" my own frustration simmered to a boil, perhaps partially at my momentary forgetfulness as to what the unfortunate time traveller had said, in large part because such lapses rarely occurred.

"Hey, it all clicked when I heard what that poor guy who got run through said, okay?"

"You didn't find it prudent to speak up at the time?" I asked.

"Not when we were so close to those pikemen. Sorry, Doc, but whatever you may think of me, one thing I'm not particularly good at is quick-draw. Never really practiced it. By the time I would've cut down one of 'em, the other two could've taken us out no sweat. Then there'd be four time traveler 'kebabs' instead of one. Not to mention, you *did* stop me, Doc."

I recalled the hand on the shoulder and shake of the head I gave Ricky in the Council Chamber as he reached for his weapon. It was another odd lapse in memory for my usually hyper vigilant, recorder-like brain. For the moment, I attributed the problem to too much scotch and not enough sleep.

Additionally, I suppose Corcoran had given me no reason not to trust him to this point. If anything, the opposite was true; aside from the drunken escapades from the previous evening, he hadn't shown many lapses in judgment. Even then, I'd say that the previous night had worked out well for all parties involved; even Bloomington was functioning on a much more "normal" level than before.

For these reasons, I simply nodded. "So…what now?"

Corcoran shrugged. "I don't know. I think that counted as 'witnessing Constantine's skepticism,' didn't it? I'm not too keen on trying to head back into that place, so maybe that was all we were supposed to do."

"I'm inclined to agree with you," I said.

"Fine by me," Bloomington nodded.

"Well, it's settled then. Back in the ship, we wait to jump again." I said.

"For what? Like eighteen hours? What the hell are we gonna do?" Bloomington asked.

"We're fresh outta books," Corcoran nodded at his companion.

"I swear to God, I am going to get my hands on a gun—"

Corcoran smirked, "Relax. Like Doc said, just teasin' ya a bit, Bloomy. I'm sure Doc has a few ideas. And you brought your iPod along, right?" Corcoran nodded at Bloomington's pocket, and Bloomington returned the nod. "Then what's the problem? Hell, we could even get some work done, write something up—a report. Memorialize the trip."

I opened my mouth, but Corcoran preempted me, "I promise, Doc, I'll put you in there. We'll get you in the history books yet."

"Thank you," I nodded at Corcoran. Though everything in my logical mind told me that it was an empty gesture, since history had no knowledge of me or my deeds, I was still touched by the Commander's generosity.

As I lacked my spectacles, I felt around the empty air and searched for the panel to let us in. One of the little pastie trolls may have wandered by as I was doing so and thought we were positively mental, but if that was the case, neither Corcoran or Bloomington alerted me to as much.

Finally, my hand came into contact with the cool, brushed alloy exterior, and worked my way around until I located the hand panel, which recognised my handprint and opened the door. Still a bit dazed by the events of the quick stop, the others followed my lead inside.

And we waited.

CHAPTER NINETEEN

Surprisingly, our idle time passed rather quickly. Bloomington and I somehow struck up a conversation about all things *Star Trek: The Next Generation*, and we actually had a (mostly) civil, engaging debate about various topics that may bore you, such as "what if Captain Picard secretly had an insatiable bloodlust that was only kept in check by virtue of the holodeck?" and, of course, "Troi or Crusher?" Predictably, I took up for the lovely Counselor played by Marina Sirtis, while Bloomington apparently had a bit of a thing for redheads.

"Are you *serious*? Are you really gonna sit here with your dumb Limey face and tell me that Marina Sirtis is hotter than Gates McFadden, douchenozzle?" Bloomington asked, ever the charmer.

I was nearly ready to pop him once more, but instead I decided to change the subject with an affected smile.

"Let's discuss something else. For example, despite your clearly misguided take on *Star Trek: The Next Generation*," Bloomington bit his lip as I said the words, "It seems like otherwise you're an intelligent enough fellow."

"Uh...*yeah*, ya' think?" he said in that grating, nasally whine of his. "I was only the youngest person to ever graduate from MIT."

"Really?" I arched an eyebrow, legitimately surprised.

He nodded, "My favorite show growing up was *Doogie Howser*, and I told my folks, I said, 'Mom, Dad, I'm gonna be just like Doogie Howser some day.'

"So they tell me, 'Well, Stevie, you better study hard and apply yourself,' and so I did. And I kept doing better than all of the other dickfaces I was in school with, and I—"

"And so you retreated to the lab, the only place you felt comfortable?" I asked, perhaps in hindsight figuring that I had met a like-minded soul.

"What? Fuck no. I got into science because I wanted to be a doctor, like Doogie. I thought Wanda was like the hottest chick ever. And since I couldn't compete with the jocks or even the drama nerds, I figured if I became a doctor, I could find a girl like that."

"But you're *not* a doctor!" I half tried to make the statement sound like a question.

"No shit, Sherlock," he chortled. "Nope; I was on track to do it. Got into MIT at fifteen, went pre-med, the whole deal, and then I took my intro to physics class, and found that I'm really good at it."

"And so *that's* how you fell in love with physics! The mad scientist, furiously scribbling out equations on the whiteboard, long after everyone else had retired to their keggers and—"

"I *hated* it," Bloomington interrupted my romantic diatribe. "Let me rephrase that; I *hate* it. It's not nearly as fun for me as being a doctor was, but my assymouthed professors kept telling me how they'd never seen a physics mind like mine. I could pull things...equations and stuff...out of thin air that some of 'em had devoted their pathetic, worthless little lives to figuring out.

"So they pushed me more and more toward physics, and I just kinda followed, you know? Eventually, close to graduation, I guess the Army caught word of how kick ass I was doing, and offered me a shitload of money to do what I do now. It sucks, but what're you gonna do? The worst part is, it doesn't even help me get chicks. Not like I can go to a bar, 'oh, and what do *YOU* do?' 'Oh, I'm building a fucking *time machine* for the dumbshit government.' Nope—that's 'top secret.' Fucking blows."

"But...you *invented a time machine!*" I hit my forehead with my palm.

Bloomington shook his head, "It's not like it was just me," he looked over at Corcoran, lounging in a chair nearby. "We had...help. Lots of help."

"Yes, yes, I know, but still...you have no sense of achievement? No feeling of, 'I built this?'"

Bloomington shook his head, "I'd give it all up to be a kick-ass doctor with a hot-ass wife...and tons of money. And...you know...I guess helping people and stuff."

I thought about debating Bloomington further, but instead just shook my head. I turned my attention to the Commander, who fiddled with what looked to be a hopelessly quaint and out-of-date "mp3 player," like the ones featured in the horribly kitschy and painfully-hoping-to-seem-retro "museums of the future" that had begun to pop up all over the country, which generally served as ironic locales for hipsters to deride the culture of the early century and make out with one another.

Though I assumed that the Commander's taste in music was somewhat eclectic, I didn't know the extent of his music ADD. Headphones in, facing us, he manipulated the touchscreen multiple times per minute, which was only off-putting due to my own hyper-vigilance.

"Impatient, are we?" I strolled over to the Commander and, for once, startled him.

He removed one earbud. "Huh?"

"You're going through quite a bit of music there."

He was unfazed, "Typing up some notes for my report. Also, trying to find some Kanye that's not '808s and Heartbreak.'"

I smiled and shook my head, "I never took you for a rap fan." I said.

He looked as if I had told him to fuck right off, "First of all, it's not rap, it's hip-hop. And second, just 'cause I may have a bit of a Southern twang and grew up outside of a big city doesn't mean I listen to Skynyrd while shotgunning Natty Light in front of my 'Stars and Bars' curtains."

I shook my head, "Of course not."

In fact, that was precisely the image of the Commander that I had developed over the past few days.

"I can like rap—hip hop—too, ya' know."

"Quite right." I offered him as kind of a smile as I could muster. Confident that I had perhaps rattled *his* cage for once, I prepared for "bed" in the command chair.

I awoke after precisely eight hours of uninterrupted sleep to the sounds of Bloomington cursing and shaving in the head, door open. I stretched and half-dazedly walked over to him.

"New at this, are we?" I asked.

"Now I know why Riker went with the beard from season three on. What a pain in the ass," Bloomington said.

I smiled at the reference. Was I actually becoming *friends* with this ugly little man? Isn't that what friends did? Share little inside jokes with one another? I must admit, though I simply hadn't the time for many friends while building the time machine, even in my Eton days. I was painfully shy and aloof. As I was advanced several grades above my own, I was also prone more to teasing than the other boys.

As my only confidant, my father took me aside during one Christmas holiday and told me in no uncertain terms, "Look Fin, sometimes you have to fight fire with fire. Give it back to 'em a bit, stir up the pot. Pop a guy in the face and tell him to fuck right off, you know? And I don't mean tell him to 'bugger off,' or whatever dumbshit British slang you've picked up, tell him to go fuck himself. Show 'em who's boss."

So I did. The next time Aaron Hardy or Andrew Percival called me "Finny Four-Eyes" or some other hilariously witty slur, I hit him right in the face and told him to fuck right off; needless to say, the Headmaster wasn't impressed. I, however, was ecstatic when the dour old headmaster called my father on speakerphone, and after he relayed the events of the day to dear old dad, my father paused for a moment before he let out an enthusiastic, "Fuck yeah! That's my boy—way to go Finny!"

Along the way, the troublemakers stopped making so much trouble, and I was able to develop my sunny, winning personality and wit without further interference.

I smiled as my reminiscent moment ended, and shuffled to the kitchen to fix myself a cup of Earl Grey before I sank back into the command chair.

The primary console read "Full Power—Time Travel Possible." As was customary by now, I once more entered my home coordinates and those of Corcoran and Bloomington, to no avail.

Why do I even bother anymore? I thought. I pulled up the list and found the next stop on our slip-shod journey through time:

"18-4-1738: Leipzig, Germany: See the only show in town"

Ah, Leipzig in springtime! Granted, it was a Leipzig filled with stunted, dirty, troll-like, foul-smelling Germans, each potentially carrying the plague or some other horrific infectious disease, but it would be Leipzig, damn it, and good to be back on the continent. I pinched and pulled and dialed the coordinates in, and the computer predictably spat back the "99.9%" confidence interval I was becoming so used to seeing when keying in my Benefactor's coordinates.

The "Engage" button flashed on the console, and without warning Corcoran or Bloomington, I hit it.

"Mother*fuck*!" Bloomington yelled from the head.

I tilted my head back toward the W.C., "Sorry." Though, in hindsight, the motion of the ship should have been, nay *was* imperceptible to the man, thus any shaving mishaps must have been due solely to his usual clumsiness.

Corcoran emerged from the bunk. He wore his comfortable eighties clothes and rubbed his eyes.

"We leavin' already?" he asked with perhaps a touch too much sarcasm.

I nodded curtly at him, "Pleasure, as usual, Commander."

"Don't you have another one of your 'classic' rock bands to play for the jump?"

He was quite right. I mentally went through all of the music I had loaded on to the ship before we had left, but found none appropriate for this jump.

"Computer, play a suitable 'classic rock' song, won't you?" I looked sideways at Corcoran as I said the words "classic rock."

Almost immediately, U2's "New Year's Day" blared over the loudspeakers. Corcoran and I looked at each other, somewhat befuddled.

"Wouldn't this song fit better last jump?" Corcoran asked.

"Yes, but we didn't play music last jump," I replied.

Corcoran raised an eyebrow, "You don't think that it's a bit suspicious that a computer more powerful than I can even fathom messed up something this simple?"

"It is curious, but not without precedent. Remember the doors outside of Chichen Itza? Quantum computers aren't necessarily one hundred percent reliable. Do you want the quick lesson?"

Corcoran considered the offer for a couple of seconds, but wisely declined.

"All I'm sayin', Doc, is it seems like one hell of a coincidence, like we went off-script."

"And...?"

"Isn't whoever's running the show supposed to know the script ahead of time?"

A light finally clicked on as I understood what the Commander was getting at. Instead of nodding or challenging him, I merely fixed my eyes on his, and hoped that genuine concern shone through my steely gaze.

"Be that as it may, there are any number of reasons why 'the script' could be 'off.' Perhaps precisely so that we have this conversation now, or to push me over the line into utter madness."

I thought this comment may elicit a smile from the Commander, but he just shook his head as he walked over to the dining area, presumably to clean his firearm once more. I swear, that weapon was so spotless it could have been used as an eating utensil.

The tunneling lasers did their thing, and as the U2 song blared through the loudspeakers, I don't think any of us stopped for more than a moment to view the otherwise wondrous colours and shapes inherent to time-travel. I suppose that's an exaggeration; I stared at "the show" for a bit, but only in consideration of the fact that much like travel by rail and air before it, time travel had already become routine, even for three "pioneers" such as ourselves.

We emerged from the wormhole to the familiar sight of the Earth hanging in the distance. I sighed with discontent as I thought about what needed to be accomplished as the computer guided us in.

"Computer, three pairs of clothing for this time period, please." The glove box opened and the odd little rolodex of vacuum-sealed clothing yielded two packages. I couldn't help but smile; they were much like the fancy getup that I had worn back during my visit with Hank Fleener and Sir Isaac, but one was an ugly, pale pea green silk-like material, festooned with various gold leaf shapes. The other was dare I say a subtle rose color, and similarly adorned with gold. The pink getup, especially tucked away in the package, seemed more fit for a geisha than for either the alpha male Corcoran or slovenly Bloomington, though I secretly hoped that the portly scientist would draw the salmon ensemble.

I was not to be disappointed.

"Costumes, gentlemen," I yelled toward the back of the craft. Bloomington waddled forward, almost like a giddy child on Christmas morning. Despite our positive chat hours before, I delighted in seeing the panic slowly wash over his face.

"What the fuck?"

"Eloquent, as always," I said with a chuckle. I shrugged, "I didn't package these outfits up. I'm afraid the person to blame is the same one who sent us on this wild goose chase through history in the first place. Hopefully you'll have a chance to meet him at some point, and then you'll be able to ask him all of the wardrobe-related questions that your heart may desire."

My little speech had little effect on Bloomington, whose reddening face belied what can only be described as his usual nerd-rage.

"You should see the getup he has me wearing; quite the fancy shade of lavender," I tried to reassure the portly scientist.

Bloomington perked up momentarily before he affected his anger once more. To his credit, when Corcoran saw the ugly green ensemble, he merely shrugged, tore into the package, and put it on. Oddly enough, both his and my overcoats had interior pockets in which our sidearms fit rather nicely.

The whirring of the gravity drive ceased. I stood in my same violet "finery" from the jump to Newton's time, dumbfounded. Had it taken so long to get dressed that we had already landed? I suppose that the alternative explanation, that the gravity drive had somehow failed and we were hurtling toward the planet at an unbelievable rate, was impossible, as we all still stood, feet firmly planted to the floor of the cabin.

"Computer, three hundred sixty degree view," I snapped, perhaps a bit unnerved by my momentary panic.

Fortunately, there had been no malfunction; the ship landed safe and sound, perhaps two hundred metres away from a rather tall stone wall. The sun barely peeked through a low ceiling of clouds and shined several rays directly at the ship.

"Computer, engage cloak," I said. Even the commands to the computer, which would have been so ridiculous mere years ago, were becoming rote and mundane as I said them.

"Open door." I may as well have been a walking billboard for any number of antidepressants. Where had the wonder of time travel gone? The endless possibilities for not only observing history, but experiencing it right alongside the historical figures?

Sadly, by introducing parameters, responsibility, and the like, my Benefactor had somehow taken all of the joy out of what should have been a thoroughly intriguing and invigorating experience. "Go here! Do this! Figure out what to do! Now, now, now!" It was a grind, a bore, simply get to the next place, the next item on the list, one step closer to home.

And what even awaited me there? A long, awkward conversation with my Benefactor, after which he'd requisition this machine into which I had soaked so much blood and sweat?

If I was really lucky, I would be a footnote in the history books, the mad scientist who had saved the real hero, Commander Corcoran, as well as his science officer, Specialist Steve Bloomington. *They* were far more likely to enjoy the fruits of our labors than I, and though I could see Bloomington as content to lay on the sand somewhere like a pasty, hairy beached whale, Corcoran was different. He was a man of action, a social creature, reliant on being around others so that he could showcase his wit, charm, and ability. I had heard nothing of his historic voyage for some twenty years; even the "history" of my near-future knew precious little about the Commander, so even if he would hop "back in the saddle," as he may say, his deeds would remain nebulous and uncertain for many years, likely guided more by legend than fact.

As I pondered these very weighty ideas, I descended down the gangway and onto German soil for the first time in years. We were in a large field outside of the large stone walls, which were decidedly harsh, angular, and thoroughly German in their appearance. The ramparts surrounded the city and provided a sense of foreboding protection, that what was to be found inside was most certainly not worth the trouble to any enterprising invaders of the day.

The city stood like a heart in the middle of the plain, as various pathways branched off as veins and capillaries from the four major entrances. We unconsciously walked towards one of the paths, then followed it toward the city, looking positively daft in our ridiculous outfits.

"What're we supposed to do this time, Doc?" Corcoran broke the silence.

"All it said was 'see the only show in town.' Perhaps a play, or a concert, or a—"

"Burlesque?" Bloomington interrupted.

"I…err…*don't* believe that to be the case," I stared at Bloomington for an extra beat, "but we can't discount the possibility." I offered a "make-good" smile, which the little gremlin returned.

"Great! So what's the plan? Poke our head around into every theatre and whorehouse?" Bloomington asked with a bit too much glee.

"Hey, it's a tough job, but…" Corcoran tailed off.

"The way the clue is phrased makes it seem as though it should be fairly obvious to us: the *only* show in town." I said.

Corcoran's lips tightened into a half-scowl, "Let's hope so," he said.

We spent the remainder of the brief trek in silence until we arrived at the gate into the city. I was immediately hit full-on by an indescribable sense of nostalgia. You see, on occasion throughout my thirties, I visited the town to consult with my good (dare I say only) friend, Klaus Thurbur, the brilliant chair of the physics department at the University of Leipzig, and one of the few individuals world-wide who could keep up with my keenly efficient intellect.

Klaus and I often would talk each other through various problems we encountered in our projects before we would inevitably retire to some dank, German watering hole and sample strong German pilsner and fine scotch well into the night. The Leipzig of my day was thoroughly European in its appearance, with glorious examples of older architecture mixed in with modern, glass-and-concrete towers.

In the past, the town was even that much more spectacular. Sure enough, there were the venerable Old Town Hall and Law Court, both bustling with activity. Even in this day, the warty little precursors to our modern Germans moved through life humorlessly and automatonically, an "It's a Small World" tableau come to life, though they replaced the insufferable cheeriness of the Disney attraction with unapproachable near-contempt.

Brightly-dressed merchants hawked their wares at the makeshift market as shoddily-clad beggars and well-adorned nobles eyed each stall. Most of what was being sold was foodstuffs and assorted goods for the preparation of meals, though there were also some more artisanal artifacts on display.

Corcoran and I were, once again, giants among the sad little throng, while Bloomington looked merely like the tallest unripened strawberry one had ever seen.

It was easy to get lost in the crowd, so we continued to observe in the hopes that we could figure out our destination without relying on the holotran to provide an accurate translation. As if sensing my thoughts, Bloomington decided it was a good moment to rifle through his pockets to produce his own holotran in the packaging, and make a big show of placing the device on his neck.

"Wurstchen!" Wurstchen!" A nearby vendor yelled as he thrust several links of rancid-looking and smelling sausages in front of our faces. "Would you noblemen be interested in Leipzig's finest sausages?" We were positively revolted until we saw the man's face, which brought us to the brink of retching. Warts pocked his discoloured visage like a particularly gruesome pumpkin, obscured only by a hoarse layer of greasy stubble. One eye looked as if it had already been stricken by cataracts despite the man's relative youth, while the other lazily stared in a different direction.

Bloomington indeed did let out a long, whooping cough, and nearly lost his supper from the evening before. I must admit, despite Bloomington's numerous faults, whenever he travelled more than one hundred years in the past, he instantly became the third most handsome man in town, provided that the Commander and I occupied the first two spots (presumably not in that order).

"No, thank you," It was all I could do to squeak out the phrase and bring a handkerchief to my mouth to contain my own round of hacking.

We looked around for some inkling as to what "the only show in town" may be, but people scurried about without apparent regard for direction or destination.

As I marvelled at the fantastic examples of renaissance architecture, church bells nearby began their rhythmic

"Clang...Clang...Clang..." to signal that the time to worship was nigh.

"Gentlemen...shall we?" I nodded at the church perhaps two hundred metres up ahead.

"Maybe we should check out the burlesque houses first," Bloomington pleaded.

"Aw, come on, Bloomy. Ain'tcha the churchgoin' type?" Corcoran asked.

"Are you?" I asked the Commander. He offered a soft frown in reply.

We pressed on toward the church, which was an odd-looking building as far as churches were concerned. In the middle stood a stone, buttressed, almost cathedral-like entryway. Everything else, though, was covered in white plaster, including the tall, octagonal spire on the left side of the building. "Tomaskirche" was engraved in the masonry over the door.

I certainly appreciated the building's uniqueness. Despite its small size, as we made our way inside, the house of worship was very clearly less than half full of patrons, each of whom appeared to be dressed far more tastefully than ourselves. The disparity drew stares from the assembled, who looked at us as if we may as well have been from Mars.

Corcoran took a step forward and jutted a thumb out toward me, "English," he said.

He must have forgotten his own ridiculous pea-green outfit.

Not that the crowd cared: half breathed sighs of relief, while the others gave some signal of understanding, either in the form of an "Oh!" followed by a laugh, or a knowing nod. Though I strained to keep the look on my face as pleasant as a spring day, internally I seethed.

See where that attitude gets you two hundred years from now, you Gerry bastards, I thought.

The crowd went back to speaking in hushed whispers in the rows of pews. One person, though, moved to the center aisle, and remained fixated on us. It was a noble-looking woman, whose face, though creased by wrinkles, exuded a practised worry, as if she had not only seen a ghost, but had long ago become accustomed to seeing them.

I looked into her eyes, each a sapphire-blue, which would be striking to anyone else for other reasons, but were even more so to me because they were the same shade that greeted me in the mirror each morning.

It couldn't be...after all these years... I thought. *No, how could she possibly—*

The woman raised her right hand in front of her body and split the fingers into that horrible, awful Vulcan hand signal with with I was rapidly becoming disgusted.

I couldn't keep the utterance down any longer. I struggled to control it with all of my might, but it was of no use. A single, involuntary word passed my lips, though in my mind it echoed with the force of a thousand of the church bells that now serenaded the village.

"Mother?"

CHAPTER TWENTY

I knew it was true as soon as I had said it.

"Finny?" the woman said. She opened her arms wide and crouched down, fully expecting me to disregard the past thirty years entirely and come running toward her.

Corcoran and Bloomington, who had made their own attempts at the hand signal (Bloomington's was perfect, Corcoran struggled with the finger placement) dropped the effort and turned their attention to me.

For a moment, tears welled up in my eyes. I had a thousand things to say to this woman who abandoned me, who abandoned *us*, who made my father's life so difficult, and why? To run off with some vagrant street artist she dug up in Spitalfields?

I was determined not to give into her. Instead of running over to her, as she wanted, I steeled myself and practically marched over slowly and deliberately before I mechanically extended my hand toward her.

"Mother...you look well."

She recoiled as if I had spit in her face.

"That's it, Finny? 'You look well?' After all of these years, that's all—"

"What do you want me to say, mother? I don't know, maybe I've resented you going on thirty years now for leaving father in such a bad way? That I blame you for his death? That I—"

"That's not fair, Finny," she shook her head, as she struggled to hold back the tears. "That's not fair at all. You and I both know that

213

your father was more married to his work than anything else. That's what killed him, not me leaving."

"He always made enough time for me," I said.

"I suppose that's where you and I differ then," my mother said as she turned away, "You weren't the widow to an already empty husk of a man at twenty-eight, consigned to cold dinners in an empty house," I rolled my eyes at her hyperbole. "Oh, sure, he'd run a hand over me every now and then," Corcoran and I briefly locked skeptical eyes, while Bloomington, true to form, licked his lips, "and bring home fancy gifts from time-to-time, but I was dying a slow death with your father, and I wasn't about to be thrown out at the age of—"

"But I was? Really, mother, that's quite touching and everything, capital job on the story and whatnot. But that doesn't make what you did any better, any more 'right.'"

Her tears streamed more forcefully, "Damn it, that *wasn't* what I meant to do. I hoped that the court would hear Manyx and I out. Would give us—"

"So, Mannix *is* his name?" I shot back.

"—With one 'n' and a 'y,' dear," a pronounced glee at correcting me momentarily broke through her grief, "Now where was I? Ah yes—full custody. Especially given that I didn't want you to end up in one of those terrible boarding schools. But your father had more money, and better lawyers, or 'solicitors,' or whatever you call them, and he won you. Much like a prize at a carnival, something that seems so indispensable at the moment that you must have it, only to have it rot in storage for the rest of your days, without nary a care."

"Glad to see you think so highly of me, mum," I said.

"Don't you get it? It wasn't you. It was *him*. *I* wanted you to be free to explore whatever you wanted to. To figure out whatever most moves you, and use it to discover what you're passionate about."

"But I did, mother! I *found* the very things that drive me. I built a *time machine*, for fuck's sake!"

"Kiss your mother with that mouth?" Corcoran whispered, unable to contain himself. I shot him a look that indicated that I would not hesitate to use my sidearm, and given his professed deficiencies as a quick-draw, I liked my chances. "Though I know I'd certainly like to," he said to her with his rakish grin.

She took an involuntary step backward and blushed. "My, my, is that…Commander Corcoran! No wonder you're such an enigmatic, charming character," she said.

"Ma'am," Corcoran grabbed my mother's hand and kissed it.

She giggled, "Though there's been tantalizingly little released about you or your mission, you certainly deserve every accolade that's been hoisted upon you."

I cleared my throat loudly for effect.

"Oh, son, of *course*, same goes for you. It's just, history is history, you know?"

"Whatever happened, happened?" Bloomington finally chimed in.

Mother smiled, "Exactly." her expression changed to one of gratitude, "Thank goodness that I've found you in the past. Here at a Bach concert, no less. I'm so glad that you appreciate the arts as much as Manyx and I do."

"So…you're time traveling concert goers?" Bloomington asked.

"That's absolutely right," mother smiled once more. "He's a bright one, isn't he?" She turned to me, so as to accentuate any potential implications that I was most certainly not in the same mental league…

…as Steve Bloomington…

"How ever did you find the—" I asked.

"Money? Believe it or not, Finny, Manyx became quite successful as an artist. Dare I say more successful than your father ever was."

Not bloody likely, I thought.

"But instead of clamoring for more, more, more, Manyx decided at a certain point—2036, to be exact—that we would be better served traveling, seeing the world. Then, once we grew tired of that, time travel was legalized, and beckoned him to find a new 'muse.' I didn't argue because, hey, how else was I going to see a Bach concert? Or DaVinci paint one of his most famous works? Or—"

I shook my head, "That's impossible. How could you jump between those time periods?"

"Well, we need to wait until ChronoSaber comes to get us, two years from now, but that's a small price to pay to see several of the greatest composers of all time, not to mention some of the world's foremost geniuses." Her disregard of my own genius did not go unnoticed.

I rolled everything that my mother had told me around my brain. Her attempt at reconciliation had served as little more than to cover a cannon shot with gauze. Not to mention that she hadn't the wherewithal as a parent to see another of history's foremost geniuses to adulthood, to raise him and provide him with other motherly things, though I secretly questioned whether her influence would have impacted my father's apparently very successful scheme for rearing me, seeing as though *I built a damned time machine on my own!*

Yet still, unbelievably, irrationally, strange emotions stirred within me. Dare I say it was pity for this pathetic creature who thought that she could find her life's calling amid the hippies of Spitalfields, yet now didn't even realise that all she had received in return was a one-way ticket to the past, doomed forever to chase down this Bach character, lest he—

Bach! I thought.

Of course! That would be the only show in town in Leipzig in the 18th century. How could I possibly be so *stupid*? I silently damned my anger for a moment before I collected myself and nodded toward Corcoran several times.

"This is it," I mouthed. The Commander whispered something in Bloomington's ear. Both appeared about as excited as a couple of children whom had been informed that Christmas had been cancelled, so upset were they that this was not a mission to sample some of Leipzig's establishments of ill-repute. I pondered whether or not we'd even want to visit such places given the general hygiene and attractiveness (or lack thereof) the denizens of this fine city had demonstrated thus far.

I turned toward mother with what must have been an amused, if slight, smile on my face, but was thrown to see a thoroughly defeated creature sobbing, though she still struggled valiantly to maintain some semblance of composure. Despite all of the injuries she had cast upon me through the years, despite her extended holiday to find herself with this "Manyx" fellow, whom I assumed was the character with the purple mohawk who sat in the seat next to the one she had vacated, though he made not even an effort to get up and make small talk, despite her casual tone that disregarded my accomplishments even now, despite all of those things, something compelled me toward her, first trepidatiously, but then with increasing speed as I plunged into her arms.

"Mother, please—" I virtually begged her.

"I'm sorry, Fin," she said. "I'm so damned sorry. You deserved better."

"I got the best," I looked into her depressed, yet somehow still vibrant blue eyes, "But I still deserved better."

I wasn't sure if she got my reference to my father's adroit attempts at raising me, or even if I was speaking about parenting at all.

Perhaps my words somehow foreshadowed events to come.

We fully embraced and the panoply of emotions that overcame me escaped my usually succinct, concise worldview to form something tragic and automatic, like a warehouse full of discarded crash test dummies. Though it would be easy to spout a platitude like, "my life had been leading up to this moment," I couldn't help but escape the thought that the previous week or more had been carefully orchestrated by powers far beyond my control.

And yet I wept.

Granted, I regained control almost immediately. And despite Corcoran and Bloomington's half-assed efforts at mock applause, the Germans appeared far more interested at the scene that developed at the front of the room. But for a brief moment, as I embraced mother, and allowed my otherwise contained emotions to slip, to be let free into the world absent any kind of check, I felt an incomparable warmth, far more intimate than casting a down blanket over myself on a cold Baltimore eve.

I looked upon mother, and the faintest outline of a smile adorned her otherwise tired visage.

"It's so good to see you again, Fin," she said.

"And you, likewise, mother," I replied, and immediately regretted the awkward phrasing and cadence I had used.

"'Pologize for interruptin', but what exactly's goin' on here?" Corcoran used the full extent of his affected charm. "Not, you know, between you two, but why is everyone here today?"

Mother offered the Commander a sly smile, "Why, my dear Commander, it's a wedding between two of the most important noble families in town! The Bauers and the Schliebens are about to cement their alliance with a union of two of their children. The Schlieben boy is as queer as a three dollar bill, if you ask me, but they're going through with it anyway. I fear they're not nearly as enlightened in this time period as we are in—"

At that moment, a cherubic little fiddler began playing a pleasant tune at the rear of the church. The people milling about took their seats; we had no choice but to do the same. Unfortunately, this meant shoehorning myself in between the Commander and my purple-mohawked freak of a step-father.

"Oy," the man practically grunted at me.

"Hello, uh…Manyx. I'm Phineas, your wife's son from her first—"

"Oy," he nodded toward the fiddler, who made his way down the aisle. Directly behind the musician was the groom's party, which was fitted with relatively tasteful attire and luxury. This only infuriated me further, as it was clear that my Benefactor was winding us up a bit with the ridiculous clown costumes he provided by comparison.

Of course, compared to Manyx's post-punk hipster ensemble, each of us looked positively dapper, Bloomington included.

I listen to enough classical music to know that the Bridal Chorus from Wagner's *Lohengrin* wouldn't be composed for over one hundred years. Though I didn't make it to many weddings, in large part owing to the fact that the typical company I keep of virgins-by-necessity like Bloomington and arrogant prigs such as myself don't tend toward the shackles of marital bliss, when I did have occasion to attend one, I always enjoyed the song, and was disappointed to realise that it wouldn't be featured.

"Ladies and Gentlemen, we are gathered here today—"

Manyx interrupted the minister with a loud half grunt, half snort.

I was horrified. Fortunately, the officiant paid it no heed and continued.

The ceremony itself was rather formal by modern standards, aside from my (ugh!) stepfather's attempts to draw attention to himself. The minister stood at the front of the church as the bride and groom kneeled side-by-side in front of the altar. There was little room for pontificating or ad libbing, as the entire thing seemed to be scripted from the get go. The only even half-way serendipitous occurrence was when the father of the bride stood up before the end of the ceremony to make an announcement.

"Ladies and Gentlemen, please join us to celebrate this joyous occasion with food, drink, and music provided by none other than the director of the St. Thomas School himself, the world-famous Johan Sebastian Bach." The crowd applauded politely, save for Manyx, who clomped his hands together as I imagine a horse might should it ever have reason to applaud. A harsh, weatherbeaten man with a thoroughly Prussian face and powdered wig stood off to the side at the front of the church and took a bow.

I leaned a skeptical eye toward mother, who smiled proudly as she joined the rest of the crowd in their approval.

"Or, should I say, *I'll* provide the food, and Mr. Bach will provide the entertainment. As many talents as the good Master may possess, I'm afraid culinary facility is not among them." Fake laughter filled the cozy church.

The minister pronounced the couple man and wife, and the gawky husband awkwardly planted a passionless kiss on the (quite fetching, at least for the time) bride, who mustered her own nervous smile. Herr Bauer signaled the fiddler to commence once more, and he struck the bow across cat gut adroitly as the parties processed out of the theater and into the street.

We followed suit, and soon found ourselves in a procession down one of the main streets in Leipzig that ended in a rather spacious (for the time) courtyard at a lovely little castle-like estate in town. God-knows how many casks of wine already lined the tall plaster walls, with any number of servants ready to wait on us hand and foot.

I figured that it was a celebration, and gladly accepted a chalice overfilled with wine. I took a swig and nearly spit the liquid out straightaway.

"No good?" Corcoran asked.

"Sweet. Far too—" I eyed Bloomington as he drained his entire chalice in two or three gulps before he wiped his mouth with his sleeve and rudely poked the next servant who walked by in the chest to ask for more. "—Sweet."

Perhaps the pudgy scientist hadn't returned *completely* to normal.

Mother wanted to take the opportunity to catch up, which largely consisted of her droning on incessantly about Manyx's various shows and all of the celebrities to whom he had sold his work (though, I must admit, I was thoroughly surprised to hear that Sunil Suniputram bought one of the freak's paintings at auction. Though as I write this, I realise you likely have no way of knowing who the "Indian Tom Cruise" is, or I should say "will be").

For his part, Manyx simply held his nose high in the air and grunted awkwardly, or otherwise drew attention to himself with a sniff or forceful nod when Mother mentioned an accomplishment of which he was especially self-satisfied.

I tried to get the attention of both Corcoran and Bloomington, but Corcoran desperately tried to convince himself that the female creatures of the era were worth hitting on, while Bloomington greedily guzzled the wine like it was grape juice (I fear there actually was little difference between the two in alcohol content; I remained far too sober throughout the festivities to withstand the utter ridiculousness of mother's continued ramblings and Manyx's annoying noises).

Thankfully, after a half-hour of such nonsense, the host clanged a couple of the goblets together to get the attention of the crowd.

"Ladies and Gentlemen, as promised, Headmaster Johann Sebastian Bach!" Polite applause followed as the same sour man who had stood up at the church now stepped forward and took a bow to more light applause. His scowl appeared to be permanent, and made him look like a shorter, fitter John Belushi, who happened to be wearing a powdered wig for an early *Saturday Night Live* sketch.

Servants carted an odd-looking contraption (which I later found out was a harpsichord) to the center of the courtyard, and the presumptive Bach sat down at the bench in front of it. He shot a look at the crowd that immediately demanded silence. Bach turned toward the instrument and cracked his knuckles before he placed his hands on the keys. I chuckled at how this custom had somehow made its way through the ages to my present day.

Bach's hands moved with a level of skill and expertness that I had rarely seen at any craft, outside of perhaps Corcoran with a firearm in his hands, or myself tearing through equations on a whiteboard. He got a full three measures into the piece, as he hammered each key precisely so as to make the twangy sounds of the instrument sing off of the tall courtyard walls.

Then it started. One painfully missed note. Then another. To the man's credit, Bach's expression never changed from "bothered grimace" as he invariably crashed several wrong keys, stopped, took a deep breath, and resumed where he left off.

Even more baffling, the crowd seemed to peg the entire thing as completely ordinary. Corcoran and Bloomington winced at the miscues, though Mother played along with the rest of the crowd, willfully oblivious. And, of course, Manyx grunted or (much to my dismay) spit loudly whenever one of the awkward silences struck his fancy.

Bach limped along through the performance for several more minutes until the piece mercifully came to an end. Mother clapped excitedly almost as soon as he had struck the final note, while Manyx engaged in his own equine style of loud applause, punctuated by snorts and grunts. I looked at Corcoran, who widened his eyes and tugged on his collar in mock embarrassment for the man, whom likely at this stage in his life was more renowned as a composer than performer, or at least that's how I rationalised this…this "display."

As the applause died down, a wretched-looking man emerged from the crowd to confront Bach, who by this time had recovered from his bows.

"Perhaps Mr. Schiebe is right when he criticizes your pieces for their lack of clarity or higher purpose," the man said in a haughty tone.

Bach's face reddened, not with embarrassment, but rather anger.

"Ernesti, you hack! *Dare* you criticize me once more? I believe this crowd thoroughly enjoyed themselves this evening, did they not?" Bach motioned toward the reception. It was the first bit of showmanship we had seen from the man, but it was met with a tepid, if polite, smattering of applause.

To Bach, it must have seemed a veritable torrent of support. He nodded his head at this "Ernesti" fellow with a flourish. The composer's eyes bore through the man like the pike through the time traveller in Nicaea.

"That's no tone to take with me, you miserable old coot!" Ernesti brandished a dagger from his waistcoat and the crowd erupted in low murmurs and high screams. Corcoran instinctively reached for his holster , but was stopped by the father of the bride, who interjected himself into the argument.He unsheathed his sword and levelled it at both potential combatants. Ernesti thought about challenging the otherwise jolly paterfamilias, but I suppose he realised that it was imprudent to bring a dagger to a sword fight, and backed down.

Sword still in hand, and without skipping a beat, the host smiled broadly and motioned to the dour-faced musician, who still stood in front of the harpsichord.

"Ladies and gentlemen, Master Johann Sebastian Bach!" A smattering of (generally) positive acknowledgement crackled through the crowd as Bach took a characteristically stern bow.

I was actually somewhat intrigued by the dour-faced Prussian composer, so as soon as the applause died down, I grabbed two fresh chalices of wine and approached him.

"Mr. Bach...Mr. Bach, please, a moment?"

He turned toward me with a look as if his teeth had been grinding a lemon to a pulp for the past several hours.

"Yes?" he replied.

"That was a...err...wonderful performance," I hoped my feigned exuberance was believable enough, especially through the intermediary of the holotran affixed to my neck, "Really, top drawer."

"Thank you," he nodded.

"Might I ask, do you play the harpsichord much anymore?" I offered him one of the chalices, which he accepted and drained more readily than even Bloomington had, though without the general lack of manners and composure.

His body language didn't offer so much as a hint of a reply.

"No, no. Mostly I fight with that damned old fool Ernesti about some idiotic idea of his or another. The balance of my days are spent teaching the boys at the St. Thomas school not to screech quite so badly while singing. My evenings are composed of," he motioned in a wide arc around his head, "Events like this. Weddings, funerals and the like. Little time for practice, so everything you heard was God-given talent.

And here I thought that God wasn't wrathful, I thought.

"Why take the extra work? Love of performance? The need to energise a crowd?"

The glare remained on his face, even through the thinnest of chuckles, "My boy, you think an old man like me needs the 'thrill' of a performance to get the blood flowing any longer? No, no, the reality is that my salary here in Leipzig is rather meager—mere hundreds of Thaler per year, less than two per day. My poor Anna is a wonderful singer," the composer finally lit up as he mentioned her name, though his expression darkened quickly, "but currently between patrons. So, I take these events as a way to pay the bills."

"But…you're *Bach*!" I couldn't help but exclaim. "You're a genius! Your music will reverberate through the years like…like Mozart or…" I realised that I had made an error by mentioning a composer who hadn't yet been born, "…Beethoven."

"Ha! The deaf fellow in Bonn? Don't get me wrong, Mr.—"

"Templeton. Phineas Templeton." I stuck out my hand to be shaken, but Bach disregarded it.

"Mister Templeton. By the way, where are you from?"

"England, sir."

Bach nodded, "The clothes were a dead giveaway. But your German is absolutely impeccable, especially for an Englishman."

"Thank you," I said, though I wondered how he perceived my speaking voice: was it similar to when I spoke the King's? Or some autotuned bastardisation that made me sound like a cold, murderous German robot? Though judging by the attitudes we had witnessed around town, such a tone wouldn't necessarily be all that out of place.

He shook his head, "Don't get me wrong, Mr. Templeton, the deaf lad shows promise. And yes, perhaps my music is more popular currently in England than it is here. But the truth of the matter is that the art isn't the hard part. It's the critics like Schiebe, the political horseshit that I have to go through to maintain my rather modest position, *that* is the tough part of not only my job, but my work. I take it you understand the difference?"

I nodded. All too well. "A job is something you do for money. Work is something you do because you *need* to do it, lest you go mad from not doing so."

The corner of his mouth upturned into the faintest hint of a smirk. "Very good, Mr. Templeton. Dare I say I couldn't have said it better myself. Yes, that's exactly right—my work suffers because of all of the tiresome excrement that I must put up with on a day-to-day basis at my job."

He drew closer to me and whispered, "Want to know something few others do?" he asked. I took this as my cue to break out the "Live Long and Prosper" hand symbol, though I did so cautiously. I allowed my contorted hand to linger in front of him for several moments before the quizzical look on his face alerted me to the fact that he had absolutely no idea what I was showing him. I quickly ran my hand through my hair.

Bach remained crouched over, intent, yet guarded. "I would love nothing more than to piddle around with the harpsichord or the violin all day, Anna accompanying me with song, my spirit free to soar and write and create."

"So why not do it then?" I asked, innocently enough.

"How could I ever afford to do so? If it's not a bill, it's a creditor. I must survive, dear Templeton. Do you have any idea how difficult it is to find a good benefactor these days?"

"Some," I replied, absolutely stone-faced. A servant came by with more goblets, and Bach grabbed two more.

"Very well then, Mr. Templeton. I must be going so that my wife doesn't throw me out in the cold this evening," he smiled (*actually* smiled!) and gave a courteous bow which I returned. "Thank you for the conversation. And please do spread word of my level of play throughout all of England."

Are you really that unconcerned with your legacy? I thought.

"I will," I said.

He drained the goblet in one draught once more, and walked that precise, mechanical German walk out of the courtyard.

CHAPTER TWENTY-ONE

The rest of the evening was rather uneventful. Mother continued to blather non-stop about her life since she had left me with Father all of those years ago. Bloomington drank far too much wine, though his "condition," if you can call it as such, continued to improve with each chaliceful. Corcoran (I think) feigned interest in my Mother's exploits, if only to be able to lord his flirtation with her over me in the coming days. And Manyx constantly drew attention to himself with his awful, condescending grunts and snorts, which made me partly want to pop him one in the nose, much as I had Bloomington, to see if it may alleviate the annoying artist's apparent "sinus problem."

Speaking of which, Bloomington's face is completely healed, I thought. I found it odd, given that it had only been three or four...or five(?)...days since I had introduced his face to one of the most dangerous pairs of hands to ever grace Eton.

The other invitees enjoyed themselves with various dances and parlor games, including one particularly intriguing diversion whereby the best man "kidnapped" the bride and hid her in a secluded part of the estate for the groom to find. I found the practice to be quite whimsical, and thought it added a competitive edge to the festivities, though I certainly recognised the potential for abuse among more lascivious best men.

There were (mostly boring) speeches which I attempted to wash out of my brain with the fairly weak wine. But after several hours there were no more speeches to give, no more games to play. Even in eighteenth century Germany, when the help started to clean up, it was the universal signal for "party's over."

I embraced Mother (or, rather her, me) once more.

"So good to see you, Fin," she said. I couldn't tell if her tone was practised or earnest.

"Indeed, Mother." I still wasn't on-board one hundred percent with the woman. It was a lot to ask of me to be so after one night where she showcased her primary character trait to be self-absorption.

"Don't be a stranger when you get back, okay?" At least in this sentiment, she was sincere.

"I'll look you both up." I didn't know if it was a lie or not.

"Well, we'll be two years older, anyway. Though it may seem like tomorrow to you. You did say earlier that you're scheduled for return tomorrow, correct?"

To be perfectly honest, I didn't remember. It seemed like the kind of "cover-my-ass" response that I may give, so I nodded.

"Oh, I do wish we had more time to catch up." She kissed me on the cheek before she gave Corcoran a lingering kiss on the lips. Bloomington received a light hug.

I certainly don't, I thought.

I moved over toward Manyx and affected a smile.

"Nice to finally meet you, Manyx." I offered a hand, which was met with a loud snort and a too-long pause before he offered a brusque handshake in return.

"Oy," he huffed. I took it as a "yes."

Once pleasantries had been exchanged, we retraced our steps through the beautiful Leipzig streets and toward the gate through which we had entered. It was a chilly, crisp spring evening, though our many layers of shirts, cummerbunds, and overcoats provided ample warmth, and of course an opportunity for increasingly large sweat stains to appear under Bloomington's arms. I shook my head as we exited the city and walked in the general direction of the craft.

"Well, that was somethin', Doc. I think your Mom may be a little sweet on me," Corcoran said with a smug smile.

"Couldn't be any worse having you as a stepfather than that Manyx fellow," I said, just over my breath enough so that the Commander could hear.

The sun had set, and darkness rapidly fell over the German countryside. We picked up our pace and spread out a bit so that we had a better shot of finding the cloaked vessel.

"Mother*fuck*!" Bloomington yelled as a metallic "PING" filled the dusky sky.

"You too, now?" I deadpanned.

"That fucking *hurt*," Bloomington rubbed his forehead.

I cautiously made my way over to his position and searched for the hand panel. I found it, and we piled into the craft, exhausted from the day's festivities, and eager for another night's sleep.

I must say, I was getting rather used to sleeping in the command chair in "full recline" position. Though I never can sleep on airplanes or the like, I had insisted on the chair being able to convert into a "lie-flat" option, despite the protestations of my Benefactor.

"What the hell do you need that for, Phineas?" He said on more than one occasion, usually as his secretary, Helene, busied herself fetching us tumblers of scotch and bringing paperwork over for my Benefactor to sign.

"Why the hell not?" I asked in reply, as I raised the glass of Macallan Eighteen toward him.

"It just seems so...excessive," he would say as he turned his attention toward Helene, who must've been quite the looker back in the day, but whose salt-and-pepper hair and emerald green eyes made her attractive in a Angelina Jolie (or Helen Mirren, for your era) sort of way.

"Compared to the rest of the multi-billion dollar time machine that you're so graciously financing?"

"I just don't see—" almost on cue, Helene spilled the scotch all over my Benefactor's lap.

"Oh, clumsy me," she cried.

"Nothing of it," my Benefactor waved away the slight, as he so often did. I at least usually threw her a dirty look, lest she obtain the idea that such an indiscretion was acceptable the next time she served me a drink. "Very well then, Fin. Fully-reclining chair it is."

In hindsight, perhaps my Benefactor was being a horse's arse. The old bird must've known full well that I would end up sleeping on that chair, and wanted to make me as uncomfortable as possible.

Fucking tosser, I thought.

As I settled into the seat, I thought of the cool, pastoral scene in the surrounding countryside.

"Computer, three hundred sixty degree view, please. And increase external microphones." The walls disappeared and the cacophony of insect and animal noises filled the ship. I sighed as I luxuriated in the command chair, and looked around in the darkness, barely able to make out silhouettes of trees in the moonlight.

"Come on, Doc, turn that shit down!" Corcoran yelled from the bunk.

"Computer, increase volume by 50%." I decided to have a little fun with the Commander as I plugged my ears with my fingers and the din grew relentlessly loud, as if we had shrunk down to insect size and the various grasshoppers and other little beasties were speaking directly to us.

I swiveled the chair around to face the bunk. As Corcoran appeared in the doorway, he held his sidearm toward the ceiling.

I shot up in the chair, "Computer, cancel external microphones!" I barked above the noise. Immediately, the cabin went quiet.

"Glad we're on the same page," Corcoran threw me an annoyed smile as he re-holstered his weapon.

Though it took several minutes for my heart rate to return to normal, I engaged the proximity alarm and added a force-field this time, "just in case." I drifted off to sleep, and dreamt of Bach pounding away on his harpischord. He offered me his spot in his seat, and though I had never played the harpischord or even the piano, I felt as if I somehow knew exactly what I was doing. I cracked my knuckles and pounded on the keys...but no sound came out of the damned thing. I tried, over, and over again, only to find the same result. Bach's laughter filled the room and I reached for my sidearm.

I leveled the weapon at the musical genius and fired two shots, which passed through him harmlessly and only increased his laughter. I turned the barrel of the weapon toward myself and looked down it with one eye, hoping to ferret out the problem. I heard a loud "BANG" and woke up with a jolt.

I looked around the cabin, though only the usual ambient lighting from the kitchen was visible. I heard another noise, this one a loud "CLANG," also from the kitchen.

Though in hindsight it seems ridiculous to do so, I pulled my sidearm and crept toward the source of the sound. I got closer and closer until I was at the edge of the cockpit. I loaded my body like a spring, ready to uncoil and confront whatever creature was responsible for the din.

I leapt toward the kitchen...and immediately smacked right into the force field I had erected the night before. The perimeter alarm claxons sounded, and the cabin plunged into red light.

"Computer, cancel proximity alarm and force field," I yelled over the screaming sirens.

The cabin went quiet once more, albeit momentarily.

"What the fuck?" Bloomington cried from the kitchen as another pot spilled onto the floor. "I'm just tryin' to make some eggs!"

"I...uh...sorry old boy," I said as cheerily as I could manage. "Bad dream spooked me, and I set up the perimeter alarm after the good Commander brandished his weapon at me last evening."

"With good reason," Corcoran emerged from the bathroom, dressed in his eighties civilian clothing, though he still was towel-drying his hair. "Those bugs were loud as shit."

"They were a peaceful backdrop to an idyllic spring evening," I said.

Corcoran nodded at Bloomington, "Not when you have an irrational fear of bugs like Bloomy over here. Isn't that right, Steve?"

Bloomington drew his mouth taut for a moment before he offered a curse series of nods.

"Well then, I do apologize Bloo—Steve," I reconsidered with a warm smile.

"No problem," He offered his own wan smile, "Just don't fucking do it again, dick."

"Noted," I said with a nod.

We cooked up some eggs (which actually were quite delicious; if there was one thing Steve Bloomington knew, it was food) before we started our usual morning rituals. Part of my routine included consulting the list of places memorialised on the tablet to see if I could utilise my smart specs in the next time period, or if I would be stuck with my perpetually irritating contacts. I pulled up the copy of my Benefactor's instructions and read the next entry aloud:

"17-6-691: Jerusalem: Corner and Deal With T V"

I frowned; there were certainly no eyeglasses in seventh century Jerusalem. Though I found it odd that this would be our (I apologize…"my") third visit to the Middle East, I relished any opportunity to travel there given the state of the entire area in my time period. I (obviously) had never been to Jerusalem as an adult, nor had my father taken me there as a child. The closest we ever came was sketching the broad outlines of our mythical "holiday to Egypt" to see the pyramids, a trip which, as I've mentioned, never quite came to fruition.

Of course, in 2032 such a vacation would be impossible, but I could still see *this* Jerusalem, ancient Jerusalem, and hope to extrapolate it out to the various poorly-rendered holoconversions of some of the two-dimensional stills that memorialised the town before the worst occurred.

"Awesome," Bloomington somehow had sidled over my shoulder as he read my tablet.

I instinctively clutched the device to my chest, "I very much doubt that the 'T V' is the same 'TV' with which you're so familiar and fond."

Bloomington shook his head, "No, I mean, sorry. It's just—that tablet is the coolest thing I've ever seen."

"Really?" I asked.

"Sure. Though everything got a little fuzzy there for a while in Chichen Itza, I remember seeing it and being insanely jealous. I didn't realize just how cool it was, though."

"It's pretty standard, really," I feigned boredom despite the fact that I was pretty "geeked" on it, as well. "You know, glass holodisplay, tactile input up to a meter, sixteen terabytes of RAM, 256-core pre-quantum processor, waterproof, shock proof, pretty much everythi—"

"What kind of games does it play?" Bloomington asked.

I sighed as I pulled up the simplest game I could think of (solitaire), in the hopes that it would bore Bloomington enough so that he would leave me to plot the time jump. The solitaire "tabletop" popped out of the screen as the tablet dealt out the cards.

"Whoa—too fucking cool!" Bloomington exclaimed. He grasped one of the holographic cards in his hand and moved it up to the ace row. "You can—really? Really? That is un-fucking-believably awesome. You can move the cards like they're real cards!"

"Mind-blowing, I know," I deadpanned. "Almost as 'cool' as the real thing."

"Totally," the sarcasm was lost on Bloomington. "Can I—would you mind if I play a quick game or two?"

I thought about what was on the tablet. Other than my bank information, which couldn't be accessed without an internet connection, anyway, I didn't recall anything that rendered it a security risk.

"Not at all," I said. Bloomington beamed as he clutched at the device, but I held it firmly, much to the indignation of Bloomington. "But not until I've plotted the time jump."

Bloomington first scowled, then pouted, "Fine. But as *soon* as—"

"As *soon* as I plot the time jump!" All I could think was that Bloomington was as lucky that I wasn't as trigger-happy as Corcoran, lest he find out what it feels like to die twice in one week.

Bloomington scampered away, presumably giddy to soon be able to play the simplest card game imaginable on such a high-tech device. I shook my head as I keyed in my home coordinates, more out of a sense of duty at this point than anything else. I let out a "harumph" as for the first time in my travels, the computer spit out the dreaded "0.1%." Not that I had expected anything above 20% or so, but zed-point-one percent? I thought it rather the slap in the face by the computer to be so dispiriting.

Then I dialed in December 21, 2012, Montauk, Long Island. "0.8%."

Is the computer trying *to drive me utterly mad?* I thought. I realised how ridiculous that sentiment was, and worried that my descent into lunacy had already begun.

Finally, I set in the prescribed course of Jeruselem, 691 A.D., and *Presto!* "99.9%" once more.

"Bloody unbelievable," I said, with mock astonishment.

"Can I have the tablet now?" Bloomington asked impatiently.

I sighed and handed the device to him. You would've thought I had given him ten million dollars cash and thrown him a parade.

As I turned my attention back toward the flashing red "Engage" icon popped up, and as we were all well-rested and fed, I decided there was no need to dally.

"Time's a wastin'" Corcoran echoed my sentiments from the dining area. I smiled at the Commander's assertion and pushed the button, sending us hurtling through space and time once more.

CHAPTER TWENTY-TWO

To say that the sight of the Earth hanging majestically in the distance was becoming more than common would be an understatement. Dare I say that after so many jumps to so many places offering little but pain, suffering, and re-opening of old wounds, I was beginning to hate all of these so-called "different" Earths. It wasn't so much the people that were indigenous to any given time period; it wasn't their fault that they tended to be such a tiny, disgusting, hideous lot regardless of era or geography.

Rather it was the time travellers that we encountered who embarked on such an enterprise *for pleasure*! If only they knew how damned we were, in possession of our own machine, yet unable to travel at our own discretion!

I suppose it was akin to those old stories about a father catching his son smoking cigarettes (which, thankfully, my father never did; had he done so, I imagine the penalty would've been for pilfering his fags more so than any sort of sense of dereliction of morals) and forcing the lad to smoke an entire carton.

If that was the case, consider me ready to spew at this point in our journey, so close to the end, yet still with one more jump *after this one* before I could finally head home, and perhaps regain some fractional amount of normalcy in my life once more.

As the small, blue orb continued to grow larger, and the autopilot guided us toward our intended destination, I made the customary request of the computer for era-appropriate garb. It produced three outfits from the glove box, each of which appeared to be a simply-dyed tunic and an accompanying wrap of sorts of a different drab color, which fastened around the front, and three pairs of simple, lace-up sandals. I selected the one sized for me, and called Corcoran and Bloomington over to receive their costumes.

"It's a dress!" Bloomington snapped.

"I don't think it's half as fancy as those getups from last go-'round," Corcoran said.

"I find it rather freeing," I said as I slipped the outfit over my head and secured the wrap around the front. "Rather like a kilt."

Truth be told, I had never worn a kilt, but I assumed that my companions would assume that I had done so.

"You Brits and your crazy customs," Corcoran shook his head. Apparently I had been correct in my assumption.

Corcoran arranged his holster so that his firearm was readily accessible under the wrap, and I attempted to do the same, though my own shoulder-holster was either improperly fitted and jostled around my midsection, or I had lost quite a bit of weight, which was entirely possible; with the rapid shifts from day to night and back again, our eating habits had become less than regular.

We descended once more toward that familiar patch of land somewhere northwest of the rhino's head that was the Arabian Peninsula. As similar as this planet looked to any of the other Earths we had visited through the ages from thousands of miles into space, there was something "off" about the landscape toward which we were being slowly led, almost as if it was somehow tainted in a fundamental way.

I commanded the ship to cloak as the computer landed the craft outside of a city that was much larger than either Nazareth or Nicaea, the only other measuring sticks I had for the era and area. The computer brought us to a dusty little patch in the "shade" of a rather sparse mulberry tree outside of the city walls.

"Oh Steven, aren't you forgetting something?" I asked as I held out my hand. Reluctantly, Bloomington offered me my tablet back. "That's a good lad now," I said, perhaps too paternalistically.

"Computer, open the door," I said, as the gangway descended and we made our way down it. "Everyone remember where we parked."

"'Least we have a landmark this time," Corcoran offered Bloomington a nod as he jostled a mulberry branch. Bloomington was surprisingly not pissy, and merely nodded silently in reply.

As I looked around, I noticed that the landscape wasn't nearly as harsh and unforgiving as the almost Martian-like surface near Nazareth. If that area could best be described as "dusty brown," then the area surrounding Jerusalem was "brownish green," with more than a smattering of trees and shrubs that agreed with the town rather well.

We followed a nearby path into the settlement, which actually could be better described as a proper city, large and bustling enough to rival even 18th-century Leipzig. Though the familiar, short, unappealing individuals still roamed the squares and pathways, the variation in their garb and manner was remarkable. Groups of Jews passed by groups of Muslims, and not only acknowledged one another, but also exchanged pleasantries! I could hardly believe my eyes; it was a sight I hadn't seen for some fifteen years outside of the most progressive remaining pockets of American soil.

We passed a small Christian church adorned with a crude, wooden cross. Though the building was sparsely-attended, it was if not admired, then at least acknowledged by the groups of Muslims and Jews who passed by.

"Marvelous," I remarked, wide-eyed. Through my studies, I had learned that the Umayyad Caliphate was a particularly religiously tolerant bunch, but forgive me if I allowed the all-out religious wars of my own time to colour my skepticism somewhat. If only those factions could see what I currently witnessed!

But they will, I thought. And for the first time over the course of many jumps, hope filled and warmed a too-dormant cavity in my chest. Perhaps we had been sent back to see some time travellers discover this camaraderie for themselves. Perhaps the world leaders of the various factions spawned from the initial limited engagement

236

would call a cease-fire, lay eyes upon what true tolerance and co-existence could look like, and call off their bombers and drones.

The recognition must have flashed across my face, as Corcoran interrupted my "We Are the World"-inspired reverie.

"You know who we're here to see?" the Commander asked.

"Perhaps," I replied.

Corcoran waited a beat before he raised his arms to his side and shrugged, "Okay then, so Doc *maybe*, *sorta* knows where we're headed. How 'bout you, Bloomy?"

Bloomington was too busy staring at the various temples and shops, mouth agape, to notice.

Corcoran snapped his fingers in front of the rotund scientist's face, "Hey, flytrap, you hear me?"

Bloomington shrugged, "Your guys' guess is as good as mine." It was the first time in a while that his tone had lacked the tell-tale condescension, the jaded irony that had so come to mark the man.

"Well that's just peachy," Corcoran's lips formed a mock grin. "So we're just takin' a break here in the Mideast, then? Wandering around without any kind of idea of what we're supposed to do."

I stopped and turned to chastise the Commander, but as I opened my mouth, I realised that the man was correct. We had no leads on this one; even the initials "T V" were so cryptic as to defy any sort of insight. Though I knew some (at least an "Avi-acceptable level" of) ancient Hebrew, it would be nearly impossible for me to convert the primitive Hebrew alphabet printed on the signage to the King's.

"I'd say that's a good place to start," Bloomington said. He pointed toward a large structure being erected near the center of town. Though it was several blocks away, it towered over the city, and the shape of the tall dome atop it was rounding into—

"The Dome of the Rock..." I said, with more than a little wonder. Of course! The proverbial spark in the powder keg that had set off the whole mess in the Middle East to begin with.

Corcoran nodded toward the structure, "You know it?"

I weighed the pros and cons of telling them what they had to look forward to upon their return to the future, and decided that it wouldn't hurt them to know exactly the type and texture of shitstorm into which our civilisation was about to plunge itself.

I took a deep breath and sighed, "The Dome of the Rock was—is, in your time—one of the most holy places in the Muslim religion." I had heard the reports on the various news stations enough to repeat the spiel verbatim, though I found it somewhat distasteful that my hyper vigilant subconscious chose to focus in on such a fact after I had delivered the first sentence. "Muslims believe it was built on the very spot where the prophet Mohammed ascended into heaven. Unfortunately, that same spot is atop the so-called Temple Mount, which housed both King Solomon's original temple and its successor.

"As tensions rose between the two religions through the years, the site of the Dome of the Rock's construction became a bit of a sore spot for all religions involved. The Muslims obviously regarded the site with the utmost reverence. For years, though, a number of Jews wanted to relocate the Dome to Saudi Arabia, and rebuild a new version of Solomon's Temple atop the Mount.

"Fanning the flames somewhat were the Evangelical Christians, who believed that in order for their *rapture*," I hope my level of condescension wasn't too apparent, "to occur, Solomon's Temple must be rebuilt. As the Arab spring happened, and the protests that erupted a year later—"

"Cliffs notes is fine, Doc," Corcoran said.

I scowled at him sideways, but thought the better of chiding him and continued, "Perhaps three or four years after you left, on June 6, 2016, someone detonated a crude nuclear device inside the Dome of the Rock. The Muslims immediately blamed the Jews for destroying one of the iconic buildings of their entire religion, while the Jews pointed the finger at the Muslims as the only ones who would have access to the Dome during that time of day. Not to mention that the explosion took most of Jewish Jerusalem with it."

I paused and looked at my audience of two, whom I was pleased to see now paid me their full attention.

"Tensions boiled over, and while it's unclear who started what, before any of the Western powers could intervene diplomatically, the entire region was plunged into all-out war. Within forty-eight hours, and without any clear warning, both sides had gone nuclear, the Muslim nations having obtained nukes from Iran, or Pakistan, or maybe they even bought them from the Neo-Soviets…err…'Russians.'

"Battle lines were drawn, countries were forced to take sides, but not even the United States or, God save us, the U.K., were able to intervene before the damage had been done. Tens of millions across the Middle East, dead. Those that remained had hideous deformities, and roving gangs and lawlessness ensued. The area has practically been turned to glass, from Jerusalem to the Arabian Peninsula and beyond.

"Unfortunately, though the war officially 'ended' in 2028, tensions still run extremely high in my time. Muslims and Jews almost universally now despise one another, and refuse to speak, even in America. Countries on both sides continue to fight in their outer spheres of influence, though thank God the Chinese, Russians, and Americans have had restraint enough thus far to use their nuclear arsenals for deterrence instead of as offensive weapons. In short, gentlemen, it's a fucking mess."

I had turned to face the building that would start it all as I continued my little soliloquy. I slowly moved to eye Corcoran and Bloomington, and while the latter's mouth now was apparently busted at the hinge so widely it hung agape, the look on Corcoran's face was far more grave and disturbing. Gone was any semblance of the charismatic rake that I had come to know fairly well over the course of the last week or so, replaced with eyes somewhat too wide with a quality that didn't sit well on Corcoran's chiseled face at all:

Fear.

"That good enough for the 'Cliff's Notes,' Commander?" I asked.

Ricky nodded wordlessly as he let what I had said sink in. He took one step forward, followed by another. Despite the rather awkward sandals we all wore, Corcoran built up speed and didn't stop at a jog, but rather continued until he was at an all-out sprint. He kicked up dust as he tore through the streets and alleys of Jerusalem toward the monument under construction atop the temple mount.

I looked at Bloomington, and though his dread registered with me, I paid it no heed. I knew I was the only one of us who could keep up with the Commander, and I lurched forward into my own full gallop; I cared not if Bloomington followed. A heavily-armed and unhinged Ricky Corcoran in seventh-century Jerusalem was the last thing I needed weighing upon a thoroughly beaten-down conscience at present.

Thankfully, I was able to track the strewn pedestrians and dust trails until we reached the "wall" that signified the Temple Mount. I found Corcoran as he stared upward toward the thousands of men that must've been working on the project as they laboriously carted lumber, stones, and porcelain toward the top of the platform. To us, it must've seemed like the most intensive public works project ever, all of these undersized, yet somehow powerfully burly fellows carrying materials up, lodging them in their intended places, and constructing what otherwise seemed impossible without all manner of bulldozers and cranes and other heavy machinery.

"Spectacular," I said.

"What a fucking crock," Corcoran ruined the mood a bit.

"Beg your pardon?" I asked.

Bloomington scuttled up, somehow caked with dirt while the Commander and myself remained relatively clean.

"You heard me. *This* is the reason World War Three starts? *This* is the reason you're so...and pardon me for saying so, but...'fucked up,' Doc?"

I didn't know how to respond, so I merely stood, stone-faced. I looked at Bloomington, who was still panting, mind you, for guidance.

"Pretty...fucked up...Doc..." Bloomington heaved between breaths.

I was somewhat peeved because I had only allowed the Commander usage of the honorific "Doc" because of his own accomplishments, but I decided to let it slide...just this once...

"Well...yes. I suppose it never came to the fore previously—"

"Let's blow the fucker up *now*." Corcoran interrupted.

"Pardon?" I asked.

"Let's blow it up now. Save the trouble."

"And here when I think you're finally starting to get the hang of how space-time actually works, you say something as thoroughly asinine as that," I said. "Blow it up now? It survives! What happened, happened, remember? The Dome of the Rock *will* survive. It *will* be destroyed by an unnamed terrorist. And it *will* start a massive, world-wide conflict." For some reason, I was still loathe to use the term "World War III" with Corcoran and Bloomington, even though that was almost assuredly what the conflict had become.

"We can't just let *that* happen," Corcoran gave a sweeping wave to the edifice under construction. "Millions dead? I know you haven't been in a war, Doc, but I sure as shit have. Millions is a huge number. Mind-bogglingly huge. We're talkin' holocaust. And you're content to just let it go? Because 'what happened, happened?'" All of the affected Southern accent and charm was vacant from his voice.

I didn't even skip a beat, "Sadly, yes. Besides, purely academically, assume that we can change the past, against every shred of evidence we've uncovered thus far, despite all of the time travellers traipsing through history, using it as their own personal holiday. What's to say that destroying the Dome of the Rock now wouldn't create an even larger, more hateful and deep-seeded conflict?"

Corcoran's gaze burned on the building under construction as if he was attempting to focus on it to the point of immolation.

"Besides," I continued, "We aren't here to destroy the Dome of the Rock. We're here to 'corner and deal with T V.'"

Corcoran frowned, "There's no way that the Dome of the Rock is called 'T V' by someone?"

"You're stretching, Ricky," Bloomington interjected.

Corcoran took a deep breath to settle himself and nodded slowly.

"Okay then," he took several steps toward a crowded shack on the other side of the street.

"Just where do you think you're—"

"I need a drink," Corcoran's rakish grin reappeared momentarily before it faded away once more. "We ain't got anywhere else to go, right? No other leads? Maybe someone at the cantina'll know something."

I was somewhat thrown by Corcoran's ability to turn his folksy accent back on with almost Burnham-like command, but shrugged it off; he had clearly been caught up in a moment of intensity, which had caused him to perhaps drop his guard. Dare I say that in some of my own baser moments, I similarly start rolling my "r"s and lengthening my "a"s like a proper Yank, so his behavior didn't seem particularly without precedent.

Bloomington and I exchanged worried glances for a moment before the round little man shrugged and shuffled his filthy feet behind the Commander, and I followed suit.

Corcoran's comparatively large frame easily carved its way through the tiny pasties and he settled in at the bar, with Bloomington and I close behind. The room was small, with short ceilings and an odd, almost cellar-like odor, despite the fact that the watering hole likely often baked in the midday heat.

"Barkeep," Corcoran said. A burly man with curly, almost-black hair and a full beard waddled over toward him.

"Yes?" the bartender responded.

"What do y'all have here? Beer, or wine, or—"

The bartender shot out a hand to grasp the Commander by the top of his robe, but Corcoran was ready. He sidestepped the barkeep's attack, grabbed the stout man's arm and twisted. I heard the sharp "crack" of breaking bone, followed by a loud crash and thud as Corcoran used the man's momentum to carry him through the air and into a rather poorly-made table, of the type that looked as if it could be a part of the Trent Albertson collection.

"The Vizier! Get the Vizier!" the bartender cried in pain as he writhed on the ground.

"What is this? *Aladdin*?" Bloomington asked.

242

The bartender was not amused, "The Vizier is a mountain of a man, and strong as an ox as yourselves. He has dispatched a half-dozen men twice as large as you, using only his amazing magic."

It took a few moments for me to connect the dots, but when I did, I didn't waste any time.

"Yes. Get your Vizier. We wish to challenge his honor." The bartender and several onlookers stared at me, as if they wished me to continue. "He's a smut-nosed prillyhen. A festooned poppydrake. A frilly-arsed—"

"A cocksucker." Corcoran said, without so much as a smile.

"Or that," I said. Though I was loathe for the Commander to use such homophobic language, apparently the slur hadn't been lost in translation, as half the bar seemingly sat still in shock for several moments before their surprise turned to anger.

I figured this was my cue to unholster my sidearm, though Corcoran beat me by several moments.

"Magicians!" The bartender hit the ground with his good arm several times in agony as his other arm hung lifeless. "Stand clear of them!" The crowd gave us space as Corcoran and I took turns training our Barettas on them. After several moments, and I suppose satisfied that no one in the bar would try anything funny, Corcoran looked down at the bartender.

"Why'd you attack me, anyway?" he asked.

"Infidel! You dare to ask for unholy alcohol? So close to the spot where the Prophet ascended to heaven?"

I shot an ugly look at Corcoran, who just shrugged in response. Apparently not all of the town's inhabitants were quite as enlightened as progressive as I had thought.

"Do you have coffee, or tea…or anything?" Corcoran asked.

The bartender pointed to a bucket of murky liquid behind the bar and a smaller piece of pottery containing what appeared to be loose-leaf tea.

"I think we're good," I offered, thankfully before Corcoran could respond in the affirmative.

"Who *dares* disturb me during this most important phase of—" a "taller" man strode through the entrance toward the front of the bar, though he was still roughly Bloomington's height and general body shape. This man's face was scrunched, almost as if it had been punched in, and pocked with freckles that belied his red hair underneath. His eyes were narrowed and his hand moved toward the space between his washed-out, red tunic and the navy blue frontpiece he wore.

Corcoran and I both instinctively trained our weapons on the odd-looking little man, who most certainly didn't appear to be even my equal in terms of physical ability, let alone the Commander's.

His eyes locked on Corcoran's and his expression changed. The man's eyes went wide with fear, despite the two undersized guards who followed him. I found Corcoran's own countenance to be suitably menacing for the situation.

"Oh, thank you, oh your merciful Eminence! Thank you Vizier of Viziers!" the bartender practically cried with joy. "These men—"

"Oh fuck!" The red-haired little man bolted from the door as he motioned for his guards to follow.

Corcoran waived his gun around the room briefly, in no mood to trifle before he leaped over the protesting barkeep and followed this "Vizier," with myself and (barely) Bloomington in tow.

CHAPTER TWENTY-THREE

"Fuck!" The nasally voice punctuated the din of Jerusalem's streets as we pursued the Vizier. Despite his size and stature, the Vizier was remarkably quick and agile, and scampered up a ladder leading to several connecting rooftops. The Commander didn't hesitate to follow, and adroitly navigated the ladder as I suppose any ex-Navy SEAL might.

I stopped short of the lattice for a moment. It may be the proper time to mention that through all of our travels, this was the first time my fear of heights had come into play. I suppose that as a general rule, buildings were shorter in the past, but I hadn't really thought about it until this very moment. You see, I'm fine with heights as long as I'm enclosed in some sort of structure or craft, hence my lack of apprehension at the numerous times I had soared far above the Earth and into space, even when three-hundred-sixty degree view was engaged.

But take away the comforting walls, even when climbing the first few steps of a ladder, and I become a sniveling mess. There's something so terribly *naked* about the whole situation, to feel the waves of vertigo as I look up and see the top of whatever I'm about to climb.

Unfortunately, I had neither the time nor the luxury to entertain such thoughts for more than a fleeting instant. I was firmly secure in the thought that this Vizier character may not only be central to our task in this timeline, but also that he may serve some sort of larger purpose in our ridiculous little mission.

I took a deep breath and started to climb. "Don't look *up*, Phineas," I told myself. For whatever reason, I was the opposite of most individuals possessing my particular phobia, and was particularly bothered by seeing what awful heights await me as opposed to the terrifying altitude from which I could fall to my utter doom. In hindsight, I suppose there's likely something poetic to be said about such a condition, but just dwelling on the moment even now makes me dizzy and nauseous.

Somehow, I eventually summited the terrifying ladder, and rejoined the chase along the bank of rooftops. Corcoran gained on the Vizier, but the clever little man continued to leave obstacles in his wake; an untethered clothesline here, a discarded storage basket there.

Corcoran remained resolute; by the time we reached the end of the rooftops, we were back toward the outskirts of town. There was no ladder for egress. Instead, the Vizier jumped off the building and into a pile of straw on the ground. His guards turned to face us. Each man wielded a scimitar-esque sword.

The Commander raised his weapon in the air and fired a warning shot. To their credit, the quaking guards stood their ground as we approached.

"Don't make me…" Corcoran shouted before he stopped, aimed, and unloaded a round in each man's outside leg. The force of the slug turned each man toward the outside as they cried in pain.

"Sorry," I offered to the men without stopping as we galloped by. Thankfully, they didn't recover until Bloomington, who brought up the rear, as usual, had passed.

We tumbled into the hay below. The Vizier was perhaps two hundred metres ahead of us, and was already passing through the gates of the city. I dusted myself off, though the Commander didn't bother with such decorum, and I think Bloomington would need a power sprayer to "dust himself off" so caked with grime was he.

We gained ground on the Vizier, who dispatched two more guards from near the walls to deal with us.

"Un-fuckin'-believable," Corcoran said as he raised his gun at one of the men and pulled the trigger. The guard recoiled in pain; though Corcoran hadn't aimed for a vital organ, the wound appeared in the man's stomach, which I imagine would lead to an unfortunately painful death in this day and age. The rest of the guards thought the better of challenging us and dispersed behind the city walls.

I gritted my teeth and increased my speed to an all-out-sprint. I wasn't so much mad at the Commander for dispatching the poor guard, but rather at this "Vizier," who appeared to be yet another meddlesome time traveller, content to trade the lives of these poor souls to save his own hide.

The Vizier climbed one of the hills outside of town, and we closed within perhaps fifty metres. The red-haired little man wildly fired off cover shots, which I think only increased the anger of the Commander and myself.

Finally, when this Vizier turned around once more, either for want of ammunition or to dedicate himself to getting away, Corcoran bolted forward, like a cheetah stalking a gazelle. Ricky lunged for the man's legs in what would've been a fantastic rugby tackle.

The Vizier collapsed in a heap. He grabbed a handful of sand and threw it in Corcoran's face. The Commander recoiled for a moment as a smirk crept over the Vizier's countenance. The Vizier pushed himself up and took a step...only to find himself unable to move.

I must admit, dear reader, I had closed the gap and grasped the man's ankle myself. He looked back in terror as I pulled myself toward him.

"Say goodnight, darling," I said with a grin as I landed a punch that made my earlier assault of Bloomington seem like a pat on the nose.

"Ow! Fuck!" The man cried out. I frowned; I had expected to knock him out with that one blow, so perfectly-struck had it been. I hit him once more, only to more protestations.

Finally, a fist came out of nowhere and connected with the red-haired man's jaw, and he crumpled to the ground, out like a light.

247

The Commander shook his hand for a moment before he wiped his brow on the sleeve of his robe.

"That's for the SAND IN THE FACE!" He screamed at the man as he gave him two well-placed kicks in the ribs.

Bloomington huffed his way over towards us and stomped the man awkwardly three times.

"And that's...for almost... giving me...a FUCKING ...HEART...ATTACK!"

"Well, gents, I think he's out," I said. "I suppose you didn't bring any kind of restraints with you?"

"Oh, I'm sorry, Doc. Fresh outta cuffs. I didn't expect to be chasing slippery little bastards all day long in the goddamned desert heat."

"We could just wait for him to come to," Bloomington offered.

"And then what? Replay this little scene over and over again until we somehow can restrain him? I think not," I said.

"Come on," Corcoran said. He already bent over to grab the man's arms. "Let's carry him back to the ship. You have some rope, dontcha Doc?"

"What kind of a time traveller would I be if I didn't?" I asked, hopefully able to hide my genuine concern that I may not have rope back at the ship.

We spent most of the rest of the day into the night carting the zonked-out Vizier back to the craft. I was amazed that the man remained out for so long, to the point where I'm now almost convinced that he faked at least a portion of his unconsciousness. I suppose it didn't help him any that Bloomington would run up to him and knee him in the head intermittently when we refused the pudgy scientist a rest break.

Thankfully, what few travellers crossed our paths acted as if nothing was out of the ordinary as these three giants carted another giant across the landscape. We arrived at the mulberry tree that marked the craft's location when it was nearly dark. I fumbled around in the low light for the hand panel and lowered the door. Corcoran and Bloomington moved to bring the little man aboard.

"Stay here," I held my hand up to them.

"What? Why?" Corcoran asked.

"I'm not taking any chances on letting that…that 'thing' aboard my time machine."

Corcoran and Bloomington looked at each other, shrugged, and set the man up against the tree. They had long since disarmed him, but much to Bloomington's chagrin, Corcoran still refused to give him the sidearm, and instead kept it for himself. The Commander now trained both pistols on the Vizier, eager for the slightest twitch so that he could inflict further pain upon the man.

Fortunately, I had remembered to throw some rope in the glove box and triumphantly emerged from the ship wearing a million-dollar smile on my face.

Corcoran was still all business. He grabbed the rope from me and hogtied the little bastard. When he was finished lashing him up that way, he propped him up against the tree and tied the rope around him and the tree several more times.

"I think he's secure," I said.

Corcoran turned to look at me, "You sure?" he asked.

I didn't dare question the Commander, especially when in one of his moods, and instead watched him finish tying up the Vizier.

"I'll take first watch," Corcoran said. "Doc, you take next. Bloomy, you take third. I'll start a fire—we all sleep out here."

"Commander, I assure you, I have no plans to abscond with the ship in the dead of night—"

"Oh, I trust ya, Doc. It's him," he nodded toward the man tied to the mulberry tree, "I don't trust. If he starts to rustle, we need all of our guns out here, ready to go."

I nodded as gravely as I could manage given the circumstances, after which Corcoran got up and began to gather firewood.

"Watch him for a minute, will ya?" He asked.

"Sure thing," I said. Once the Commander had created a rather impressive fire, I found a cozy spot a good distance away and drifted off to sleep. I had one of those dreams where I was falling endlessly, though I seem to remember that what I was falling through was a never-ending time-travel vortex.

I was jostled awake to a beautifully clear night sky for several moments. As uncomfortable as the contact lenses may have been, especially after sleeping in them for several hours, a few blinks yielded sharp colours and the stark contrast of twinkling stars set against the night sky. The fire offered the only light pollution for miles; I was even able to make out the Pleiades and the dark violet, cloudy strip of the Milky Way.

"Your watch, Doc," the Commander said.

"He's still out?" I asked. I had fully expected the man to wake up at some point during the Commander's watch.

"Yep—or he's fakin'. Look alive, will ya, Doc?"

I nodded and took my place seated in front of him, gun pointed toward the Vizier, whose robes were now thick and brown with sand and dirt. I had nothing with which to otherwise occupy myself, so I studied the man's features, which were somehow younger than I expected. As such, it was all the more revolting that a young twenty-something fellow so carelessly and callously disregarded human life as when he used those unfortunate guards as little more than human obstacles to impede our progress.

More than anything, I wondered what we'd find when the man finally came to. Would he yield a new piece of the puzzle? Something to bring everything into sharp focus? Or would he just end up being another temporal tourist? A meddler, one of the stains on the timeline I had come to loathe?

I'm also ashamed to admit that the other thoughts that danced through my mind were contrary to what I had told the Commander. I *was* entertaining my own ego in considering whether to simply leave Corcoran and Bloomington behind to deal with this mess, to make the next jump myself and thereafter arrive safely back in my own time period. It was a primal, base instinct, one that didn't sit well in my gut, but one that my pride demanded that I debate internally nonetheless.

If I could leave them here, I thought. *Lost to history. Then* I *could become the great Commander Corcoran, the first to invent time travel.* I didn't know if it was the lack of sleep or time disassociation that gnawed at my sanity, but I almost rose from my perch several times before I finally realised that, handsome though I may be, certainly *someone* who worked on the project with Corcoran and Bloomington would recognise that I was an utter fraud, even twenty years after the ostensible "failure" of their experiment, should I return to my own time period.

As I simultaneously pondered these and several other more mundane physics concepts related to my eventual goal of developing the time travel technology further to be utilised in interstellar travel, the sun peeked over the hills in the distance. I turned to gaze at the magnificent sunrise, and when I moved to turn back to the mulberry tree, a hand grasped my shoulder.

It understandably startled me, and as I grabbed for my sidearm, I noticed that our prisoner was still lashed to the tree. I looked for the source of the hand, and found the Commander.

"Mornin'," he said, in somewhat better spirits than the previous night. He held a mug outstretched toward me. "Earl Grey, right? Scalding hot?"

I took the mug apprehensively. "How'd you know...?"

Corcoran shrugged, "Got it off the ship last night, and cooked it up this mornin' myself. Better be what you like—that's all you got." He pointed at the prisoner, "I see our little princess is still out like a light, bless his heart."

"Didn't move a muscle all night," I nodded.

"Let's change that, *shalln't we?*" The last two words were said in his ever improving, mocking English accent. This time, it was even close enough to force a chuckle from my still-stiff upper lip. Corcoran grinned as he wandered over to the Vizier. "Hey...Poncho..." Corcoran raised his voice at the man.

"What?" Bloomington asked from behind a log on the other side of the fire.

"Not you, Bloomy. I'm talking to this piece of shit who made me kill an innocent man." Still no movement from the man tied to the tree. Corcoran wasted no time; he raised the back of his hand above the man's head and thrashed it down upon his cheek. The Vizier's skin cracked as his eyes jumped wide awake.

"Fuck!" He yelled his familiar refrain.

"Rise and shine, asshole," Corcoran said to the redheaded young man.

The little man narrowed his eyes momentarily at his unknown abuser. His eyes focused on Corcoran, then went wide with fear.

"Whoa…Commander Corcoran? Is that you?"

"How in the sam fuck do you know who I am?" Corcoran asked.

"The news…that famous interview…everyone thinks you're a hero," the Vizier's mouth curled into a prickish little smile, "'Cept for me of course."

"And me?" I asked the man.

"His boyfriend?" The red-haired man laughed maniacally as I sighed at the juvenile insult. Corcoran slapped him across the face once more.

"Ow…fucker!" the red-head spat out again.

"Let's try this again," Corcoran said. He pulled his Baretta from its holster and trained it on the man. "Who the fuck are you, and why the hell have you time traveled back here?"

"I could ask the same of these two," he nodded at myself and Bloomington in turn. "And why are they along with the great Commander Corcoran? Maybe you should untie me first, and then I'll tell you everything you want to know." The red-haired man wheezed an odd, almost gargling laugh.

"I have a better idea. How 'bout you answer every question my colleagues and I have, or I start turnin' your legs into swiss cheese?"

"How 'bout…fuck yourself?" the nerdy little redhead said, a bit too aloof.

"I don't have time for this shit," Corcoran said. He casually aimed at one of the man's legs and fired a round. Instantly, the Vizier's tunic brightened and reddened around the wound.

"Fuck! FUUUCK! Oh my God, oh my God!" he screamed similar obscenities for several more moments before he calmed down.

"I'm not fuckin' around, hoss. You answer my questions...now."

"Okay, okay! Fuck, it hurts. Do you guys have any medigel?"

"Fresh out," Bloomington shook his head. I could tell he relished being able to play the role of the badass, assuredly an uncommon occurrence for the portly little scientist.

"We do have medical supplies, and can tend to your leg once you comply with the Commander's wishes," I said, fully ready to allow the little shit to bleed out.

The redhead nodded as tears began to well in his eyes. He shook them out and the green orbs returned to their beady little selves.

"My name is Skylar Osborne, but anyone who's anyone where I'm from calls me Kayoss. With a 'K' and a 'y,' but I guess I don't have to explain everything to you fu—" Corcoran cocked the pistol again, "—ffffine gentlemen. I'm from the year 2041. Cedar Rapids, Michigan. Now, can you please untie me?" Kayoss squirmed under his restraints.

"Why'd you come back in time?" Corcoran asked, unfazed by the question.

The man sighed with exasperation. "I have a lot of powerful friends, you know. Hacker friends that know all kinds of information about you, Commander. Information you'd never want to see the light of day." I thought he was overplaying his hand a bit, especially given that Corcoran wasn't exactly in a glad-handling mood.

"Dead men tell no tales," Corcoran responded, with just the right amount of bravado.

"Kayoss" gulped. "Don't you get it, man? The war? The Dome of the Rock?"

"We're all quite familiar," I nodded at my companions.

"It's the ultimate troll!" He gargled again. His laugh really did sound like a sewer drain after a particularly nasty downpour.

"Pardon?" This time Corcoran appropriated one of my favourites.

253

"My buddies and I, we like getting people wound up on-line. Trying to find that one, sweet tender spot that'll set 'em off and jab at it a few times with insults. Get morons nice and riled up. We have our site where we coordinate our little attacks, and report back on all of the fucking idiots we've trolled in a given day.

"When we heard about deregulated time-travel, we got our hands on enough cash through some fairly nefarious means that I'm still not at liberty to discuss," a short gargle, "and we sat around and thought, 'what can we do that would be the ultimate troll?' Like, historically?

"So it came down to assassinating Archduke Franz Ferdinand, assassinating Kennedy, pretty much a lot of assassinations, but we aren't the killing types, you know? I urged them to think bigger, to think what could possibly fan the flames historically, make us famous.

"For a little while, some of us wanted to try the 9-11 thing," I cringed with utter disgust and nearly was sick, "but that would involve killing ourselves, and how could we brag to each other if we were dead, you know?

"I knew we were on the right track, so I thought what's the biggest fucking shitty thing we could possibly start? What could really make people angry. And, obviously, the answer is World War III. So we started planning how to blow this fucker," he nodded toward the Dome of the Rock, "to kingdom come! But, again, suicide and whatnot—we had to scuttle it again.

"So why are you here, then?" I asked.

"He still doesn't get it! You must be a fucking—" Corcoran pistol-whipped the scrunched-faced little man before he could finish, though this only brought a smile to the Vizier's face. He gargled and coughed a few times before he continued. "Why go to all of the trouble of blowing the thing up, why get all of the explosives and whatnot when you can go even further back, and make sure that the building is placed in the one spot where it would be sure to start World War III?"

"You're a fucking psychopath," I could tell the Commander wanted to strike the man once more, but he was worried that he might knock him out.

"How did you do it?" I asked.

"Isn't it obvious?" More gurgles. "Bring a gun back, you tower over everyone, before long I had 'converted' to Islam, and was one of the Caliph's most trusted advisors. I convinced the Caliph that *this* was the spot where the Prophet ascended into heaven. And I mean, shit, for all I know, it was." A broad, evil smile washed over the Vizier's face, "though something tells me a few million more will be joining him in 'ascending,'...oh...in thirteen hundred and fifty years or so, give or take."

"That's totally fucked," Bloomington's face was growing red. Despite his own nerdishness, it was apparent that he was far better than to lower himself to Kayoss's level.

"Millions dead. Millions." Corcoran shook his head.

"I know, right! Years of war! Wall-to-wall news coverage! Famine, disease," that smile returned to his awful little face, "In short, utter chaos."

Corcoran pulled out a knife and held it in front of the man.

"You don't scare me with your guns and knives, Commander. I know my history. The damage has already been done. What can you do to stop it? Remember, what happened, happened, right?" I reached for my sidearm; if Corcoran wasn't going to shut this little bastard up permanently, I'd be more than happy to.

I thought for a solid ten seconds Corcoran was about to skewer Kayoss through his right eye. Thoughthe smart-assed little redhead shit sweated and shook a bit, the entire time his lips curled into a goading, teasing smile, almost as if *daring* the Commander to cut him.

At the last moment, Corcoran relented and instead cut the ropes that bound him.

"Ricky? What are you doing?" I asked.

The Commander pulled Kayoss' gun from his makeshift waistband and threw it fifteen feet away from them.

"Take it," Corcoran said. "I ain't gonna shoot an unarmed, defenseless man. So take it, you sack of shit, and I'll be happy to let you meet your maker. Though somethin' tells me that won't be happening unless your miserable soul was forged in the fires of hell."

As that evil little impish grin came over Kayoss's face once more, it occurred to me that the "Vizier" was still doing rather well for a man who had been shot in the leg minutes before. I surveyed his wound and noticed the blood from his tunic seemingly was disappearing from the fabric, and seeped back into his body.

"I'd be delighted to," the agile, nerdy little fellow grabbed two handfuls of sand and cast them in the Commander's face as he leapt toward the sidearm. Kayoss greedily seized upon the weapon, cocked it, and turned to fire at Corcoran.

What happened next is almost like a holovid in my mind, in the sense that I remember as if it happened to someone other than me. Since my hand was already on my weapon, I pulled it from its holster and released the safety. Any tremors that I had initially experienced while brandishing the Baretta were gone; I steadied my hand and squeezed the trigger three times.

What a perfect right triangle, was all I could think as I saw the three holes that I had formed in Kayoss's midsection. He fell onto the ground. His body still heaved as his hand waved for the gun that now sat tantalisingly close to him. His teeth were a twisted, broad smile, his eyes wide with fury as he slowly dragged himself toward the gun.

I was frozen by fear, paralyzed that I had actually shot another human being, as despicable as he may be. As Kayoss reached his goal, I thought that he was about to exact his revenge upon me for my display of "bravery," however misconstrued it may have been, only moments before.

Kayoss's hand brushed the metal of the gun. I was utterly powerless, so helpless despite my inherent advantage.

Suddenly, a large boot crashed down on Kayoss's hand.

"Eh, eh, eh," it was Bloomington. He wagged a finger at the red-haired troll.

A gun appeared beside Kayoss's head, held by a dusty hand.

"Go to hell," Corcoran spat the words at the troll as he pulled the trigger.

Twice.

CHAPTER TWENTY-FOUR

I fell to my knees in the sun-baked sand, utterly in shock. As my shins hit the ground, my hand involuntarily relaxed and my gun tumbled perhaps three feet away from my body.

"Yeah! Regenerate that, motherfucker!" Bloomington yelled.

Corcoran engaged the safety on his firearm and re-holstered it. My face must have been a mess of shock and incredulousness, as Corcoran took one look at me and jogged over.

He placed a firm hand on my shoulder.

"Thanks Doc. You saved my life, and for that, I'll owe ya' one forever."

I was still frozen with fear as a million emotions scattered through the prism of my mind. Relief at having the wherewithal to respond to a threat so quickly, horror at having taken another human life, shock at exactly how the scene had unfolded, and curiosity that I had experienced the proverbial "out of body experience," especially at such a crucial juncture in my life. There was something deeper and darker present, though. A feeling that I couldn't yet put my finger on, yet somehow rung my soul like a gong. It shifted my insides around to my core.

"Look," Corcoran knelt down so that his eyes were at my level, "you did what you had to do, Doc. Nobody's gonna blame you for that. I know, you're probably a swirl of emotions right now. None of 'em probably feel very good. Just remember: *I* killed him. Not you. This one's on me. Now, that's not to say that you didn't put one hell of a pattern into the little prick, but—"

I shook my head, "No. It's on me. And that's okay. What is a bit troublesome, though, isn't that I feel guilty for having killed *this* person. Rather it's that I don't." I distinctly remember that the words came out almost as if I was a robot, emotionless and matter-of-fact.

Corcoran nodded, "And that's fine, too. He was an awful person—one of the worst imaginable. Just…just a…" Corcoran searched for the proper word for a moment, "…a jerk. I've killed plenty of bad people in my day. And plenty of good ones, too. Sometimes, there's one who's so deplorable that you don't think twice about it at the time."

"What do you mean?" I asked.

"What?"

"At the time?"

"Oh…" I imagine that he was considering whether to tell me about the horrible nightmares that I'd soon experience, though truth be told (and as will soon become clear), I'm not certain if this was the event that triggered them. "Well…it's like this." He launched into a five minute diatribe about knocking over peoples' houses to build a road, and how it's necessary, but thoroughly distasteful. It was a screed that I found neither particularly helpful nor pertinent to my current circumstances, but I nodded along nonetheless.

"Got it?" Corcoran asked.

"Thank you," I mustered a weak smile, "That was very helpful."

"All right, if you two are done with your little therapy session," Bloomington predictably butted in, "We should be ready to jump again, right?"

I thought for a moment before I nodded my head.

"Then let's get the hell outta here and make the second-to-last jump already…well, third-to-last for the Commander and me, I guess."

I was about to interrupt Bloomington to correct him before I realised that he was absolutely correct. This time period had proven so physically and mentally taxing that I had forgotten that we were nearing the end of our journey.

As much as I had come to respect the Commander (and, grudgingly, to a much lesser extent, Bloomington), the maelstrom of emotions inside my head was cast aside for a moment as the relief of being so close to accomplishing our checklist of tasks washed over me. For wasn't that bloody list the chief engine of all of our troubles and sorrows? Wasn't this little game the source of so many tears? I would be happy to cast it off like the heavy paper shackles that it had become.

And I was eager to meet my Benefactor once more to show him just how awful the whole experience had been.

I must admit, my fantasies grew darker with each new terrible experience I was forced to endure. Initially, I hoped only to bend the Old Bird's ear a bit, give him a proper tongue-lashing for the awfulness for which he had been the architect.

But as I was pushed further and further away from my baseline sanity, either through these errands or as a side-effect of the time jumps themselves, I began to entertain scenarios where I'd pummel the old codger, or even return to that dark, out-of-body place psychologically where I could use my firearm against my Benefactor, and send him straight to hell to commiserate with Kayoss and the other odious time travellers that he had likely minted.

Despite all of these thoughts, I opened my mouth and was only able to utter two words, with a nod:

"Quite right."

"Somebody give me a hand with the body?" Corcoran asked.

"Pardon?" I said.

"The body? We can't really just leave him here." Corcoran said.

"Of course. I'll ready the on-board morgue." I said.

"The ship has a morgue?" Bloomington asked.

"No, you dolt! Of course not!" I felt bad as I lashed out at the portly little scientist, but it was good to have a pressure valve for my emotions at the moment. "I'll tell you this: that…that 'thing' certainly isn't coming aboard my ship."

Corcoran nodded, as if he understood what I was going through. He casually squatted down over a patch of earth next to the body and scooped out several handfuls of dirt.

"Shallow grave by the mulberry tree it is, then." Ricky said.

I felt bad for the Commander and soon joined him in this endeavor. Thankfully, Bloomington put what little social awareness he had at all into the task, as well, and we had the man buried within the hour.

"All right," Corcoran said. He dusted off his hands and wiped his brow, "I need a shower." He sauntered toward the gangway (which was still open, since I hated finding that hand panel without the aid of my smart spectacles), and boarded the ship, with Bloomington and myself close behind.

We took our turns cleaning up in the head and dressed in the comfortable, casual eighties clothing that Burnham had so graciously provided us. I must admit, before the trip, I was a "khakis and corduroys" fellow, but those denim jeans were actually rather comfortable and familiar, especially after I wore them several times, and *especially* compared to the coterie of near-dresses and horrific pantaloons to which we had been subjected.

As I toweled off my hair, I realised that I had forgotten to shave for…what had it been? Several days now? Regardless, the stubble was beginning to assert itself over the usually clean lines of my face, and though it may have been prudent to keep such a growth around for our little jaunt into ancient Jerusalem, I decided the better of keeping such an anachronistic fashion choice around for our jump to…where was it again? Somewhere far more modern, I was sure, but I double-checked the image in my tablet for peace of mind.

"6-2-1943: Paris: Seek out VS"

Of course! World War II-era France.

Perhaps we'll have to take out an Allied convoy of medical supplies, or firebomb a church full of schoolchildren, I thought. Forgive me for such macabre attempts at gallows humor, dear reader, but I was becoming sick of the negative images and experiences associated with time travel. Oddly enough, the only truly positive experience I had enjoyed was visiting with Burnham, who had proven to be a fraud and flim-flam artist of the highest aptitude, though, to be fair, my fond memories of the period may have had more to do with my rendezvous with Cynthia than any philanthropy on the part of that drug-addled con man.

At any rate, my suspicions about shaving were proven correct: as unhygienic as I may claim the French are from time-to-time, anything more than one of those dainty whisps of a mustache would have seemed dreadfully out of place.

Adding to my dilemma was the fact that I usually maintained a strict ritual with regard to my own personal care: always shave first, shower second. For whatever reason, it felt "cleaner" to me, as if I could wash away whatever scum the various shave-gels (hasn't been much innovation in that regard since your own time, save from the various razor companies adding ever more blades to their cartridges, I'm afraid) left behind.

As I approached the head, I weighed the various benefits of shaving, then washing my face to remove that abhorrent residue, or taking another shower, whatever Bloomington and Corcoran may have thought be damned, when I heard my two companions in the midst of a heated conversation through the door of the quarters directly opposite the W.C.

I immediately damned my obsession with soundproofing (so as the better to blunt my sleep-crippling hyper vigilance) as all I could hear were the raised tones of Bloomington and Corcoran's voices from the far side of the room. I pressed my ear up against the door and made out little more of the conversation, though I heard a pointed "wrong!" at some point by Bloomington, and a "Fine!" from Corcoran.

I heard the Commander's voice more distinctively through the door as he approached.

"Do whatever you want, I don't care…Specialist…" it was the first time I had heard Corcoran allude to Bloomington's lower rank in days.

More pressing, though, was the need to extricate myself from this rather compromising situation before Corcoran opened the door. Thinking quickly, I dropped the only thing in my hand, the shaving cream, on the floor toward the head and fell to my knees.

Corcoran opened the door as I pawed for the "dropped" bottle of shave gel. He shook his head and frowned.

"What's *your* problem now?" Corcoran asked.

"I just dropped the shave gel," I said in my most non-threatening tone possible.

Corcoran uncharacteristically threw his hands up, "Isn't anybody *not* a fuckup on this spaceship anymore?"

I looked at the Commander, as even keeled as possible, "It's a time machine."

"What?"

"Not a spaceship. A time machine."

"But…we go into space to make the—" Corcoran grabbed his hair and pulled it with exasperation before he shook his head and took a deep breath. "Never mind. I'm sorry, Doc. But have you ever been in a situation where someone was tellin' you what to do, and you didn't want to do it, but somethin' outside of your control was practically forcing you to?"

"You mean like the past week-and-a-half?" I deadpanned.

Corcoran finally offered a grin, "Somethin' like that. Well, Bloomy and I are havin' a bit of a disagreement."

"Anything I can—" *help you with?* I completed the thought in my head.

Corcoran cut me off, "'Fraid not. Mission stuff, the…" he took another deep breath and sighed, "…log entries I've been makin'. Bloomy wants me to make some changes that I don't want to, but I practically *have* to if I'm gonna adhere to our orders."

"And you're worried that these…changes…will have a negative impact on you and your superiors' opinions of your performance."

Corcoran's drew his lips taut and wide as he nodded, "Exactly."

My astute powers of deduction were able to reason that perhaps this little argument had something to do with me, and my inclusion in the reports that Corcoran would eventually turn in. Why else would they have had such a meeting in the privacy of their cabin, away from my prying ears? Combined with Corcoran's promise to me to put me in his report, I figured that Bloomington was being a wet blanket about mentioning my involvement at all, sticking to the rules and regulations and whatnot.

I sensed an opening and decided to plead my case, "Well, you *are* the Commander, aren't you?"

"Sure am."

"So don't you ultimately have some kind of...discretion...to include and exclude what you wish?"

Corcoran shook his head, "If only it was that simple. Sorry Doc, 'fraid I can't tell you anymore. It's just..." he looked up for a moment before he leveled his eyes with mine, "Some things just are out of our control sometimes."

I nodded gravely. "Well Commander, I understand completely. Control is a funny thing, you know. One minute you're cruising through time, thinking all of history is your oyster, ready to be explored. Then you find out you're not in a time machine, a 'spaceship,'" I nodded at him and received a hint of a smile for my trouble, "but rather on the most diabolical railroad of all time, forced to traverse a track you never wanted to and see terrible, awful things that question your faith in humanity."

"That's—wow, Doc," Corcoran's eyes grew wide with astonishment, "So what do you do? How do you cope?"

"Scotch," I grinned. "Whisky. And hope. Hope that I can someday get back home. And hope that I—*we*—get all of the proper credit we deserve."

I believe it was at this moment that Corcoran saw through my little ruse and allowed himself a soft chuckle.

"Well, if you're offerin', I'll drink to that!"

It had been far too long since my last draught of the Macallan eighteen year, and I needed no further prompting to grab a couple of glasses and pour two neat splashes into them.

I heard the tell-tale "whoosh" of the bunk door opening, "Doc's fixin' drinks if you want one." From the bar, I couldn't make out Bloomington's reply.

"Aw, come on—let's live a little. Couldn't ya' use one after dealing with that bastard outside?" the Commander asked.

This sentiment must have proven agreeable to Bloomington, who waddled out of the room. He took the bottle out of my hand, looked at me with suspicious eyes, and poured himself a glassful before he took it down in several gulps, and retreated to the bunk once more in a huff.

"I thought *I* was having a bad day," I said. The Commander and I shared a laugh over the sentiment; though it was true, there was something ominous about the look that Bloomington had given me. Though I would normally attribute such a characteristic to his lack of social graces, there appeared to be something behind the glare, though I couldn't put my finger on it as of yet.

I tipped the glass and took down the (rather healthy) swallow. I savored the flavors of caramel and the waft of smoke as the warm liquid passed my gullet. I ambled over to the control panel and, as had become customary, plugged in the coordinates for my time as well as Bloomington and Corcoran's. Neither percentage displayed warrants a mention so infinitesimally small were they.

I raised my eyebrows knowingly at the console before I dialed in the proffered coordinates. The also-familiar "99.9%" flashed on the screen, along with the red "engage icon."

"Everyone ready?" I called to the back of the ship, remembering how I had apparently "startled" Bloomington previously as he shaved, despite any discernible sensation of motion within the craft as it moved.

I didn't hear any objections, so I pushed the button and the ship took off.

264

"Computer, three hundred sixty degree view, please." I suppose the computer may have been happy at the rare display of courtesy and politeness I exhibited toward it.

The walls faded away to reveal the full landscape around us. I took one more look at the mulberry tree, the final resting place of the most odious time traveller whom we had met to date.

Yet as I studied the shallow grave, something was off. The mound appeared to be far shorter than I had remembered leaving it, and the fresh, loose earth atop it was less compacted than I recalled.

I shook my head, but when my eyes had refocused, we were out of range of the tree. We hurtled toward space for what would presumably be my second-to-last time jump, hopefully for a good long while.

And I was left to silently wonder if the Vizier was dead after all.

CHAPTER TWENTY-FIVE

My relief escalated after we emerged from the vortex and I realised further that I would no longer need to wear those bloody contact lenses for the rest of the expedition. As poetic as it had seemed earlier to preserve those millions of years worth of grains of dirt and muck for experimentation's (and, honestly, posterity's) sake after I had removed the first pair of lenses, I now wanted nothing more than to forget the last several time periods, and was more than ecstatic to practically rip the little plastic discs out of my eyes and discard them in the bin.

As I placed my spectacles comfortably on the bridge of my nose, we already had entered the atmosphere and were beginning our descent toward the continent. A squadron of planes flew in formation some distance beneath us, and I realised that we were likely already visible to any other aircraft, and even potentially the radar of the day.

"Computer, engage cloaking device," I said. Thankfully, the craft had enough power, and confirmation of our cloaked status appeared on the right console.

We descended toward the pastoral farms of rural France, and for once I was happy for the reminder that we were back in civilisation. The rolling hills and carefully-carved out rectangular parcels of various sizes and colours nearly made me forget that this civilisation was currently embroiled in one of the ugliest, most racist, bloodiest conflicts that the world would ever see.

We cruised on approach toward Paris, and in short order the familiar sights of the Eiffel Tower and Champs d'Elysees came into

266

focus. One thing that stood out was the Nazi flag that sat atop L'Tour Eiffel. It waved sinisterly over the city, and allowed not only every Frenchman to know who watched over him constantly, but also provided all of Europe with a preview of what lay in store should any of the remaining allied countries fall.

"You're welcome," I muttered at the city, a special sentiment I imagined countless Brittons had wanted to direct at the French of this era through the years.

We settled down in the middle of a grassy park that I didn't immediately recognise, and, much to my pleasant surprise, one that didn't appear to be particularly infested by Nazis. An odd patrol would skirt around the area from time-to-time, but otherwise we were in a blissfully forgotten corner of Gay Paree.

I fastened my holster around my torso and concealed it under the camo jacket from our forays into the Yucatan. I walked toward the gangway, and was about to command the computer to open the door when I heard a voice.

"What're you doing?" Bloomington asked.

"Whatever do you mean?" I asked, somewhat annoyed by the rotund little scientist.

"I think he means why are you going into 1940s Paris dressed like Marty McFly at a 'Nam rally," Corcoran said.

I looked at my clothes and saw that I had indeed forgotten to change, and was still wearing the comfortable t-shirt and blue jeans. Not to mention that I hadn't put two and two together regarding the camouflage jacket, and the potential military overtones associated with such a getup.

"I, uh…" I thought briefly about breaking out the old, "Just testing you guys!", but decided that it was far too ridiculous for even this scenario. Instead, I shrugged and marched over to the glove box, more embarrassed than anything else.

"Computer, 1940s-era France appropriate garb." There would be no "please" this time.

The little vacuum-packed clothing file whirred to life, and produced three rather dapper three-piece suits, one brown, one light grey, and one charcoal pin-striped, with matching shirts and ties, as well as well-polished shoes and tasteful-looking spats.

I surveyed the sizes and tossed the appropriate suit to each fellow. I had been hoping for the pin-striped number, but it apparently belonged to Corcoran, and I had to settle for the light grey ensemble.

"From the Al Capone collection, I assume?" Corcoran asked.

"Derringer, I believe," I deadpanned.

We dressed quickly and exited to a rather dreary day, the type of day that seemed fitting given the Nazi occupation. As sparse as the red swastika'd arm bands and goosestepping pairs of boots were in this part of the city, it still gave me the willies to be in a point in time where such an evil, ugly ideology could not only take root and survive, but also flourish and spread across some of Europe's most vibrant cultural centers.

Perhaps the most troubling part of it all was that in my time, nearly one hundred years later, the world hadn't learned its lesson. People continued to kill others based on nothing other than the religion under which one decided to live his life. Little was different in 2032 other than the manner in which both sides decided to meet their ends. Though being vaporised in a nuclear blast was hardly pleasant, for my money it was quite a bit less dehumanising than the atrocities that these Nazi monsters committed.

The end result's the same, though, I thought, more than a bit influenced by the dreary scene.

Then, it dawned on me: the firepower of whatever Nazis with whom we may come in contact would, for the first time, likely be somewhat greater than the sum total of our two pistols. I held up my hand to the access panel and re-entered the ship. I unlocked the armory and grasped the prototype laser pistol. It felt surprisingly light, if a bit unbalanced, in my hand. I decided to holster it, and placed my Baretta inside my waistband, nestled against the small of my back.

I opened my jacket to show Corcoran the laser pistol safely lodged in its holster. I felt like a futuristic Elliot Ness, displaying the laser gun to a gangster to indicate that I meant business. Instead of showing any kind of respect or fear, Corcoran merely nodded matter-of-factly.

I closed the ship's door and we took in the verdant landscape, dotted with a smattering of trees to provide some much-needed height to the otherwise pleasant little park. It was the first time I had smelled anything clean and modern since, ironically, I had been at Chronobase Alpha some sixty five million years ago (I didn't count St. Louis since the simultaneously pleasant and revolting smell of the brewery pervaded the entire landscape). The few trees meant that only the odd chirp of a songbird here or there shattered the otherwise eerie silence that hung over the scene like an ominous cloud that had strayed a bit too far from the heavy, grey banks above.

A woman in a suitably drab, neutral brown outfit walked along one of the paths not but thirty feet away from us. Her nose was pointed skyward in that perfect French manner that simultaneously caused me to both deride and desire her. I patted the holotran on my neck and thought of what exactly I should ask her. "Pardon me, darling, we're three time travellers trying to figure out what the devil this eccentric billionaire's clue means. Do you have a moment to help us?" probably wasn't the best way to go.

To my shock, Bloomington of all people waddled over to the woman and struck up a conversation.

"Pardon, madmoiselle," I looked for the tell-tale patch on Bloomington's neck, but found none.

Could it be? Could he actually have spoken perfect French?

"My friends and I are looking for perhaps a place with French food and wine as fine as you are beautiful," *my* holotran had adjusted, and made it seem as if Bloomington was speaking in English once more, but his mannerisms were far more polite, his demeanor more gentlemanly than I had ever seen previously. His voice gained a rich baritone quality that made him seem positively adult; to be fair, it was probably the first time that I realised that the man truly *was* an adult, and not some Peter Pan-inspired perpetual adolescent.

The woman laughed and blushed, "Oh my!" Bloomington grasped her hand and brought it to his lips to give it a genteel kiss.

Corcoran and my jaws may as well have had weights attached to them.

"Well...it depends on what you seek..." the woman was suitably cryptic before she tilted her head to one side, "You men are foreigners, no?"

"Americans," Corcoran answered. I wondered if she heard the reply in English or French.

"Oh! I see..." The pleasant surprise was evident on the woman's face.

"He's British," Corcoran stuck out a thumb at me.

"Oh...I see..." her tone was somewhat less-than-enthused.

I wanted to trade barbs with the tart, but thankfully Corcoran intervened.

"Looking to keep a low profile, if you catch my drift," Corcoran whispered.

The woman nodded, her eyes wide. She looked around for several moments before she whispered back, "The Earth, Candlelight Cafe, even The Dragon's Tears sound like places that may interest you."

It took me a moment to realise that the rather inelegant sounding establishments likely rolled off the tongue in her native French.

"Merci, madame," Bloomington kissed her hand once more. She couldn't help but giggle like a schoolgirl, despite being roughly the same age as myself and the Commander. "We shall be enjoying a drink at the Candlelight Cafe. I expect to see you there once you are free, that is so long as your mother will let you out!" Bloomington added a smile that I considered downright creepy, but one that this woman must've found charming, as she laughed again.

"You are too much! Perhaps I will. Good luck, gentlemen," she locked eyes with Bloomington and blew him a kiss before she walked through our little group. Perhaps thirty feet down the path, she turned and made eyes at Bloomington once more before she waved at him over his shoulder.

I could've knocked Bloomington over with my pinky. He sighed a self-satisfied breath as he stared dopily at the retreating woman.

"What the fuck was that?" Corcoran beat me to the punch.

"What? Sometimes it pays to pay attention during French class in high school." Corcoran and I looked at each other and shrugged. "Fortunately for you two, I spent a semester abroad here in college."

"You didn't find this pertinent to explain to us *before* we got here?" I asked.

"I discussed it with the Commander!" Bloomington looked toward Corcoran, who smiled a helpless grin and shrugged once more.

"So neither of you found it—"

"I was gonna tell ya' once we got in the city," Corcoran said. "Unfortunately, Casanova over here got distracted as soon as we got off the ship, so I didn't exactly have any time, okay?"

I shook my head and maintained a stony expression that I hope indicated disdain, even as I chuckled inside at how much the three of us kept using the excuse that "we didn't have enough time," even though we were travelling in a bloody time machine.

"Anyway," Bloomington shot Corcoran and me a particularly nasty and over-exaggerated eye-roll, "I think we're up in Parc Monceau, which is in the northwest part of the city. I think some asshat [*there's the old Bloomington,* I thought] told me that the Candlelight Cafe was some kind of an underground base during the war, or led to a tunnel or somethin'. I dunno. After chatting…err…'confirming which kindsa places we should be looking for' with that hot chick, I think it's our best bet, right guys?"

I nodded without looking at the Commander. He did the same.

"Great!" Bloomington could hardly hide his glee. "Let's go then. This way, fuckheads!" He waved us onward, and practically skipped down the path. It was as fast as I had ever seen the little ogre move, but Corcoran and I still tottered along behind him at an artificially retarded pace.

We eventually emerged on a street that, though far from "bustling," was somewhat abuzz with foot traffic. Unfortunately, three Nazi officers were among the throng of people; I had to physically steer the otherwise oblivious Bloomington away from them.

We made a roundabout path through the plaza and came to a bank of row buildings with stonework foundations and recently replastered exteriors. One of the edifices was a light rose-coloured shade pocked by patches of unfinished white plaster, and had a sign with a picture of a candle upon it, and "Cafe Chandelles" written in pretty, flowing script.

Bloomington pointed at the sign perhaps over-emphatically; I had to reach out and pull his arm down, lest he attract undue attention.

"What the fu—?" Bloomington began to raise his voice, but I clasped my hand over his mouth, and brought the pointer finger of my free hand to my lips to signal quiet. The shorter scientist nodded in agreement and raised his eyebrows with a head bob toward the sign once more.

We entered the establishment to find it rather empty, aside from two exceedingly French-looking "gentlemen" seated in a booth in a corner, smoking like furnaces as they muttered unintelligible French at one another. The room was dark and cozy, made all the more so by the candlelight that danced off of the box-like booths and along the shabby, splintering bar.

A (and I'm usually loathe to use this word with regard to women due to the ire it normally inspires, but it really is the best adjective to describe her) handsome fortiesh woman with a decent-sized mole on her right cheek leaned up against a support beam past the booze, at the far end of the bar. She eyed us with suspicion as Bloomington plodded toward her. Corcoran and I tried to appear as nonchalant as possible behind him.

"Hello, miss," Bloomington said with a smile. "We would like a bottle of your finest wine, please."

The woman stared at Bloomington for a moment. She took a long drag off of her cigarette and blew a large cloud of smoke in Bloomington's face.

"Have a seat," she said as she turned toward a spiral stone staircase at the far end of the bar.

"Friendly enough," Corcoran said with a smile. Bloomington didn't take the sleight in stride.

We sat at one of the booths in silence for several moments before the woman reemerged carrying a bottle of unmarked red wine, and three less-than-spotless wine glasses.

"Thank you," Bloomington muttered. The woman poured out three healthy portions of wine before she retreated to her former position along the upright beam and lit another cigarette.

"To one hell of a journey," Corcoran offered as he raised a glass.

"And to its conclusion," I completed his toast (or so I thought) and took a healthy portion of the wine in my mouth. It was actually surprisingly good, as far as French wines go. Though I tend to downplay my American ancestry, during the course of my work across the Atlantic at Hopkins, I had developed an affinity for richer, bolder cabernets in the Napa model, as opposed to the "understated," rather chalky-tasting French reds. This wine had much better mouthfeel, much more substance, much more—

"And, here's to Bloomy over here gettin' laid for once in his life," I nearly spat out my wine as the Commander made his snide remark.

"Fucker!" Bloomington looked ready to hit his superior, but he must have remembered the licking I had given him back in Mayan times, and reasoned that the Commander could likely work him over far worse than I had.

As if to underscore that last point, Corcoran offered Bloomington his usual rakish grin, followed by an expression of mock surprise.

"What? All I said was I hope the guy gets some ass. She was a looker, Bloomy. Way out of your league."

"Will you shut the fuck up?" Bloomington was growing rather red. I found it funny that his bulbous little head was beginning to look like a radish atop his rotund body...which I suppose also looked like a much larger, well-fed raddish that could feed twenty families of rabbits for weeks.

"Aw, come on now, Bloomy, just bustin' your chops. I think she was into ya."

"Really?" Bloomington's hostility melted away almost immediately. "You think so? I think she's pretty great, too."

"You spoke with her for what, three minutes in the park?" I asked before I downed another large draught of wine.

"And you talked to that old chick in St. Louis for what, an hour or so—?"

"I *beg* your pardon?" I was close to belting the insolent little shit on the spot. "Cynthia's no...no common French whore!" Regrettably, my gaze turned toward the smoking woman up against the support beam behind the bar at that instant. If she heard me, she offered no indication.

"Neither is...my girl!" Bloomington was starting to raise his voice once more, though I nearly laughed in his face when I realised that he hadn't even gotten her name.

"Goddamn it, enough!" Corcoran hit the table once, hard, and shook the accoutrements set atop it. He stared at each of us with laser-like intensity for a moment before he relaxed his jaw to form his trademark grin, "There's plenty of women around here for all of us."

I affected a smile in the hopes that Bloomington would see it as a peace offering, "I'll drink to that."

Bloomington broke his brood as well, "Me too." We clinked glasses once more and drained nearly half the bottle.

The front door flung open and two immaculately-uniformed Nazis waltzed in the bar as if they owned the place. They sang some damned awful German folk song that hurt my ears; their singing was so off-key and screeching that even though the words were being translated into English, I couldn't understand what in God's name it was about.

One of the men had a face that was long and lean with a hook nose. He was perhaps ten years older than I, though surprisingly undecorated given his advanced age. The other man was blonde, blue-eyed, and likely stepped out of one of Hitler's recruiting posters. I mean that quite literally; I believe he was the model for the recruiting posters we had passed on our way to the bar.

"Well, Rolfe, let us celebrate!" the older man removed his hat to reveal a horseshoe of grey male-pattern baldness. "My treat."

"Thank you, Colonel Schaffer," the handsome younger man responded.

The older man's smile hardened into a scowl as he pounded on the bar, "Bar wench! Give us your finest bottle of whiskey. Two glasses."

The woman blew a cloud of smoke out of the side of her mouth. "Sorry, no drinks without pre-payment," the woman answered with the condescension usually reserved for beggars and vagrants. It was especially odd given that we hadn't paid for our own bottle of wine ahead of time.

The older officer's eyes bulged with surprise before he let out a forced chuckle, "Surely, fraulein," *Must be that the holotran can only handle one language at a time,* I thought, "you would not refuse service to officers in your Fuhrer's employ?" He patted the luger in his holster for effect.

Without thinking, I got up and interjected myself into the situation. Corcoran followed close behind; his hand already reached toward his jacket.

Unfortunately, the old Nazi's reflexes were still those of a man many years his junior. In one motion he spun and brought the barrel of the luger to rest next to my forehead. Judging by the fact that Corcoran hadn't already dispatched this man, I figured that "Rolfe," or whatever the younger officer's name was, had his own sidearm trained on the Commander.

I raised my hands and slowly turned to face the Nazi bastard. Though I was certainly fearful, my fear was somewhat buffered by the numerous times my life had been in danger over the past few days, as well as my hatred for all things Nazi.

"I'm not looking for trouble," I said.

"Apparently you found it," the Nazi officer said. "Though I must admit, your German is quite excellent for a foreigner. You aren't citizens of the republic, are you?"

I shook my head. I wasn't going to give this Nazi dog the courtesy of a response in his native language.

"French? No, your face is far too taut and angled. American? Doubtful. Though these two," he motioned at my companions, "play the part of fat little American *piggy* and OSS officer rather well...you have the lean face of...a Britton?"

"Don't answer him, Doc!" Corcoran yelled. For his troubles, both the older officer and Rolfe unfastened the safeties on their most hideous-looking pistols.

"Ah, a physician!" the German's expression brightened. "A doctor, are we now? We could use another set of hands at our field hospital near the western front..."

"What makes you think that I'd work for you?" I offered.

"It's amazing what a man will do to save his own skin when threatened, isn't it, Rolfe?" he asked the junior officer. The younger man didn't so much as flinch. The older Nazi moved the gun under my chin, "Especially in such an unpleasant way as being shot like a common dog—"

He stopped and ducked his head down to my neck level. My breathing increased in rapidity, though my bodily functions were somewhat more under my own control than they had been when I was being chased by dinosaurs.

"What is this?" When the older officer had brought the luger to my chin, I had straightened my neck somewhat, inadvertently revealing the holotran beneath my lapel. "Who exactly are you? Where are your papers?" He pulled the holotran off with his off-hand.

"Inside my coat pocket." I thought I was done for when he heard me speak the King's, but thankfully no shots were fired. I slowly reached toward the laser pistol I had fitted comfortably against my ribs. The only thought that consumed my mind at that moment was that I had little or no shot of taking down both this older Nazi and the younger one who currently held my comrades hostage. It was extremely likely that at least one of us would leave this room in a box.

I secretly hated myself for hoping that it was Bloomington.

My hand inched closer to the prize. Slowly, steadily, I kept it firm, unshaking, in an effort to not betray my thoughts. *Calm now, Fin. Easy does it,* I thought.

"Halt!" the older German shouted. It may as well have been a gunshot. "Err bekomt sie," he nodded toward Bloomington, who was perspiring like a water buffalo, or "only slightly more than usual."

Bloomington looked to Corcoran for approval, and received a nod in return. Steven slowly made his way toward the older Nazi and me. Rolfe kept his pistol trained on Corcoran; it was rather clear that the men didn't regard the bumbling, pudgy scientist as nearly as much of a threat as the Commander and myself, perhaps with good reason as Bloomington continued to shake as he drew near.

I hoped that my coat was open to the proper angle so that Bloomington could see the laser pistol inside. I nodded as if to indicate that the "papers" were indeed in my inside coat pocket. Bloomington outstretched a tremulous hand toward my chest and—

He reached past the pistol and into my pocket. I shot him daggers, practically willing him to just grab the damnedable gun already!

"Coat pocket?" he asked.

"Somewhere in there…" I kept my voice as even as possible through gritted teeth. He fumbled around in my jacket for several more seconds; I no longer felt the cool metal of the luger as it had grown warm against my skin.

Suddenly, as sure as I would've bet on my life that the Nazis were about to waste the lot of us, Bloomington raised an eyebrow. His expression changed from one of deep-seeded fear to a mischievous, dare I say Corcoran-esque glare.

"Found them!" He exclaimed as he unholstered the laser pistol. Corcoran and I ducked as he held down the trigger and a barrage of laser fire shot entirely through the older Nazi and into the bottles of liquor behind him (with a rather satisfying, classic laser "pachoo!" noise, if I do say so myself). Rolfe fired two shots, high, as Bloomington hit the floor. I grabbed for the pistol in the small of my back and levelled it on the blonde Nazi. I fired two rounds, though I'm afraid that Corcoran had already unleashed his own pattern into the younger man's chest before my slugs found their mark. The powerful man's dying body somehow pulled the trigger several more times and scattered gunfire about the room until he fell, lifeless, in a pool of his own blood.

CHAPTER TWENTY-SIX

"Eat laser bolt, you Nazi shitfaces!" Bloomington screamed at the corpses. We checked around to make sure that none of us had been hit by the wild final twitches of "Rolfe's" horrible existence, and saw that the only (still regrettable) casualty had been the bottle of expensive scotch that the barmaid had been carrying to the soldiers (Macallan, unfortunately, I believe), which now was little more than a dripping neck of jagged glass.

"Took you long enough," I couldn't help but complain to Bloomington. I attempted to nonchalantly dust myself off and straighten my tie, though I fear the end result appeared somewhat less calm and cool than I would have hoped.

"That's for giving me shit about my special lady," Bloomington said. "Maybe next time you'll be nicer."

I could have strangled the man at that moment, but thought the better of it since he had just saved both of our lives.

"Heads up next time would be 'preciated," Corcoran scowled, "But that was one hell of a job, Bloomy." He grinned and extended his hand toward the portly scientist, who grasped it heartily. I got the sense that whatever tension had caused the riff between the two the previous evening had finally dissipated.

The older Nazi was carved clear through by several small, straight holes, each one cauterised by the bolt as it had entered and left. The younger one was riddled by bullets, though Corcoran put one more in the man's head just to be certain that he was dead.

Upon this final gunshot, the door to the back of the pub flew open and a middle-aged woman ran out to survey the carnage. I expected her to be furious, but her eyes were sunken and kind, as if she had been up far too many long nights already but couldn't care less about enduring another. She crouched and cradled the old German's head in her hands as she took first his pulse, then Rolfe's.

She sighed, not with any derision at us, but rather more as a release, a pressure valve of sorts.

Equally curious, the Frenchmen in the booth in the corner continued their muffled conversation, as if nothing had happened at all.

"Etes-vous temps voyageurs?" She asked.

"Beg your pardon?" I replied. Without the holotran, my pigeon-French was virtually useless.

Her lips tightened into a kind smile as she offered the familiar Vulcan hand symbol to which we had become accustomed. Though I had thoroughly had it with all manner of time travellers, something was different about this woman. She merely nodded at me and pointed to the bodies, still smiling.

"Il lever," the woman pretended to grasp two imaginary poles and lifted her hands up before she pointed at the bodies.

"I do believe she wants us to carry the bodies," I said.

"'Course she does, Doc—she just said as much!" Corcoran said.

I decided that it would take too long to remind the Commander that I was without use of my holotran for the moment, and instead crouched at the legs of the older Nazi and, along with Bloomington, lifted him into the air. His lifeless corpse was surprisingly heavy, at least to us. Frustratingly, the Commander and the kindly woman had no trouble moving Rolfe's even larger body.

We carted the corpses through the door through which the woman had emerged and down a staircase to what appeared to be a dusty storeroom. A few bottles of wine stood upright on a simple shelving unit, and though a simple lightbulb dangled from a chain at the bottom of the staircase, a candelabra curiously stuck out of the right side of the cool stone wall.

The woman dropped her half of Rolfe, which hit the ground with a simple, disconcerting "thud." She pulled on the candelabra and the back wall and the shelving unit swung ajar. We jimmied the bodies through the opening and into the other side.

What we found was straight out of *Hogan's Heroes*. Perhaps half a dozen people, men and women, dressed in drab, inconspicuous attire feverishly shuffled all manner of papers and worked two antiquated radios in one of the far corners. Next to the radios was another, longer tunnel, which, presumably, was also obscured by a secret door that now swung open.

The woman walked over to a box and knelt next to it for a moment. She emerged with a plastic-wrapped patch that she threw at me. I'm proud to say that I caught it, and recognised the tell-tale shape of the holotran immediately. I wasted no time as I unwrapped it and placed it on my neck.

"Better?" The woman asked.

"Quite," I replied with a nod.

"So, it appears we share a common origin," the woman said. Her English was impeccable, or I should say the holotran's translation was.

"Somethin' like that," Corcoran nodded.

"Your names?" It was a nurturing suggestion more than a command.

"I'm Doctor Phineas Templeton," I extended a hand toward the woman.

"Very pleased to meet you, Doctor." She took it warmly, with just the right amount of pressure.

"These are my colleagues, Commander Richard Corcoran and Specialist Steven Bloomington."

"Commander...Specialist..." She took each of their hands in the same warm, yet firm, manner with which she had taken my own. Corcoran appeared to be irked for several moments; perhaps he was peeved that this woman hadn't showered him with adulation as nearly every other time traveller on our journey had previously.

I like this woman already, I thought.

"And you are…?" I asked.

"Violette Segal," the woman smiled once more. "Pleased to meet you gentlemen. What brings you to this time?"

"You don't know us?" Corcoran asked. I was glad the Commander finally got a taste of what it felt like to be me in all of these time periods.

Violette shook her head, "Can't say that I do, Commander." Corcoran bristled once more.

I practically clasped a hand over my own mouth to prevent from laughing with glee, "We've been on a long and exhausting scavenger hunt of sorts through time—"

Violette looked around the room. We were beginning to get some curious looks from her compatriots, so she grasped my arm and indicated that we should follow her to a more secluded tunnel within the complex.

"Now, you were saying, Doctor?"

I explained the situation to the kindly older woman as quickly and concisely as possible given the circumstances, which must have taken a good half-hour or so. It didn't help that Bloomington or Corcoran would often "butt in" to correct some otherwise meaningless detail.

"And so now you're here to…do what, exactly?"

"Likely to meet with you. Your initials *are* 'V.S.,' correct?" I asked.

She nodded silently.

"Then perhaps it would help if we asked you some questions. Maybe we can ferret out our precise purpose from your responses."

"I shall do my best, Doctor."

I began to ask a stock "when are you from?"-type question, but the Commander preempted me.

"Hold on. You *really* don't know who I am?" Corcoran finally expelled the words that had been gnawing away at him for the past half-hour.

"Commander, of course I know who you are. I also know that you're a very private man—downright reclusive when I'm from. There was a big parade when they announced time travel had happened, and was to be deregulated, and of course you gave that famous interview—" I did my best to steady my involuntarily rolling eyes, "—but to be honest, there's not that much to know about you, and I cannot *know* you. So though I'm very grateful for your contributions to our society, forgive me if I'm less than starstruck at making your acquaintance."

"If only *we* could know this 'reclusive' Commander Corcoran," I muttered.

"Hey, you're the old codger yellin' at kids for throwin' rocks," he shot back.

I pushed my glasses up on my nose, "At any rate, perhaps we should start with a little bit about you. When are you from? What did you do? Why did you come back here?"

Violette laughed, "Always the same questions!"

"I apologize, Miss Segal—"

"Please—Violette. And no need to apologize—I just find it funny that any number of time travelers have been through here, and each one wants to know the same few things about me." She chuckled once more. "Very well—I came back from the year 2040. I was a nurse in the French army, and a damned good one at that. Always prided myself on volunteering to go to the forward areas; Syria, Saudi Arabia, Israel; post-radiation control, of course."

"Of course…" Bloomington said, perhaps a bit too sarcastically.

"When the U.S. Government legalized time travel and effectively ended the war, they—"

"Ended the war?" I asked.

She nodded, "Once the Americans had future firepower at their disposal, they were pretty much able to dictate terms to the rest of the world. Fortunately, there are still enough people in power in that country with old-fashioned ideas like 'liberty' and 'egalitarianism' to ensure that—"

I saw Bloomington open his mouth to interrupt, but I cut him off, "It's *not* a form of government run by intelligent birds, Steven."

"I…uh…knew that," he replied, unconvincingly. I could only imagine the picture he had formed in his head.

Violette could hardly contain her laughter as she continued, "Ensure that the new *pax Americana* was mostly civilised, much as the Chinese and Russians didn't care for it. Once the war was over, though, the French government forced those of us who had stayed in the service for a number of extra years into retirement.

"At first it was enjoyable: long days out on the beach in Cannes, basking in the glow of happy young people a quarter my age..."

Sounds dreadful, I thought.

"But after several years, I felt so damned useless. I wanted to help people once more. I yearned for the kind words of those I had helped, the smile of a child whose suffering I had helped ease if only a bit.

"So I cashed in my pension, bought a ticket to Baltimore, and decided that I could best be of service in the second most horrific time in history. When these Nazi monsters traipsed around my wonderful homeland, taking what they pleased, executing people for...well..." she looked upward, "...you saw above. Though I regret that Johann and Rolfe were so stupid as to force you gentlemen into such a tough spot."

"You knew those guys?" Bloomington asked, though I noticed he glanced in my direction to gauge my reaction, and perhaps to confirm that his question was not, in fact, stupid.

"Of course! They came by the bar most days to enjoy a few glasses of whiskey. Pleasant men. Not good men, mind you, but pleasant enough, most of the time."

"Sorry we had to waste 'em," Corcoran offered.

Violette shook her head, "Don't be. Ultimately, they were Nazis. Who knows what kinds of atrocities those two were capable of? And even if not, they were getting to be a bit of a pain in my ass," she said.

"Asking questions?" I (somewhat ironically) asked.

"Something like that," she responded. "When you're running a French resistance outpost in a secret room under your bar and trying to shuttle Jews out of France, it's better not to have a couple of nosy Nazi officers poking about most of the time." Her expression turned dour for a moment, "Unfortunately, the Germans will be back in another day or so. We need to pack this room up and shuttle the equipment elsewhere, somewhere safe."

"Do you know of such a place?" I asked.

"No, this is the only resistance base in the entire city," Bloomington replied for her, sarcastically.

Violette smiled once more, "Your friend is correct. We have several more outposts around the city, all connected by a secret system of catacombs and tunnels. It will be tough, but we will cope."

I met the woman's kind eyes and couldn't help but break into an earnest smile of my own.

"Something on your mind, Doctor?" Violette asked.

"Pardon my manners, but it's so refreshing to finally meet a time traveller who's up to some good in the past."

"What do you mean?" she responded.

"It's just...our last several jumps have been filled with all manner of self-absorbed and downright *nasty* individuals, travelling through time for their own selfish ends. It's nice to see someone so committed to doing good."

"How? By condemning Nazis to death? Make no mistake, Doctor, I'm not terribly proud of that aspect of my existence in this time period. It's a necessary evil to take the lives of a couple of them every now and then, but an evil nonetheless.

"And aside from that dreadful fellow you met in Jerusalem that you spoke of earlier, how can you say that none of the time travellers that you've met have done good? Victor Burnham was a con-artist and a drug addict, but did he not positively impact countless lives through his philanthropic pursuits? Your mother and her artist...boyfriend, or whatever; they travelled through time to be inspired by some of the greatest artists of all time. Will that not lead this 'Manyx' character to create new and wondrous works of art upon his return? Even Mr. Fleener is helping to advance humanity's understanding of the sciences by mentoring young Newton. And that's to say nothing of Trent Albertson, who—"

"Whose name will be invoked in the service of every major war from his death onward!" I interrupted.

"Who will set an example of love and mutual respect that will echo through the ages, and provide countless amounts of comfort and guidance for those most in need of it." She narrowed her eyes at me somewhat. "None of us are completely free of faults, Doctor Templeton. And none of us, save perhaps that dreadful Kayoss you described and the unfortunate Fuhrer that I now face, are completely rotten to the core, though obviously they convinced a number of individuals that what they were doing was right, no matter how horrible and misguided they both were."

"How can you say that at a time where evil is so prevalent?" I asked.

"And good more so!" Violette didn't so much raise her voice as she did her tone.

"Tell that to the folks in the internment camps," Corcoran offered.

"As I said before, nothing is perfect. Not even your beloved America," Violette said.

"Don't look at me," I replied in my most affected aristocratic English accent. Everyone ignored my attempt at humor, so I waved it off. "Let me ask you this, though: if 'what happened, happened' is true, and the past is set in stone, why come back at all to help anyone?" Before I had finished asking the question, I already knew the answer.

"Who would help them otherwise? You don't see me trying to assassinate Hitler; those fools—and they *do* exist—are condemned to be discovered or killed or God-knows-what by the Nazis before they accomplish their goals. No, far better to get a Jewish family to safety or help the Allies with intelligence from here than to try to influence larger events in history for that exact reason. I may not march into Berlin with the Allied forces, but I'll know that I did my part, preordained as it may have been, to help these people through such a horrible time."

"A far better answer than I could've ever hoped to provide," I said. Though you may have divined that I have a penchant for speaking out of both sides of my mouth at times, I genuinely meant this. I would be lying if I said that an undercurrent of utter nihilism hadn't slipped into my worldview over the course of this oddest of weeks (or had it been longer now? At some point I'll have to sit down and figure out exactly how much time passed, to the hour). It was somewhat comforting to see someone as kind and bright as Violette confront that fact head on, disregard it, and try to improve things for those less fortunate.

"I have a question," Bloomington raised his hand. I dreaded the next words to come out of his mouth. "We met a woman, a few years younger than you, out in Park Monceau earlier today. She's the one who directed us here. Beautiful, smart, funny, with the most beguiling accent. Auburn hair, the cutest little button nose—"

Violette smiled, "You must mean Marie. She's been taking long walks around that park ever since her husband—" the expression on Bloomington's face indicated that if the next word out of Violette's mouth was anything other than "died" or "left her," he may well off himself.

"—Left her for another man. Helps her clear her head, she says. I hope she wasn't too unfriendly."

"She was a delight. An absolute goddess." Bloomington breathed a sigh of harried relief. "She said she'd maybe meet me here later for a drink, do you think—"

Violette nodded, "Marie will see the signal and know to meet up at the rendezvous point." Violette's sentiments must have averted what I thought was the very real possibility of Bloomington's pending heart attack. I found it odd that he hadn't been a fraction as nervous when he confronted the Nazi officers that had trained their guns on us mere hours before.

Just then, a rumble shook the ceiling of the underground chamber. Violette sprung into action with the vigor of a woman half her age.

"What's that?" Corcoran asked.

"The signal," Violette replied, nonchalant. "Come. Grab what you can and follow me through the tunnels. The bar is being torched to the ground—too risky to leave it standing." I half-wondered whether the muttering Frenchmen would bother to get up from their booth, but thought the better of asking as much given the circumstances.

We each grabbed a large boxful of equipment and followed Violette down one of the longer tunnels that branched from the main chamber. Violette waited until everyone was clear and casually tossed something into the room behind her before she slid a door shut. Seconds later, we heard a loud "Boom!" followed by a "crash" behind us, and realised that she had destroyed the room with a grenade.

"No goin' back now," Corcoran nodded.

"Can never be too careful, Commander." Violette responded.

Corcoran raised his eyebrows at me, but his thoughts were written all over his face: "You got that right."

We carted the supplies for what was likely no more than a couple of miles, though in the darkness and dankness of the tunnel, and with the occasional rat that scurried past, it seemed much longer.

"All we do now is carry stuff and shoot people!" Bloomington said.

"Welcome to the resistance," Violette offered.

"Come now, Steven, isn't this what you had in mind when the sheet said we were headed to Paris?" I asked.

"Not exactly," Bloomington replied. "But I'd gladly trudge through ten rivers of shit for one evening to get to know Marie." The oddest part about the man's comment was that there was no smart-ass sexual undertone, no crude subtext. Bloomington *genuinely* wanted to spend time with this woman, rats and supplies and Nazis be damned. After how crass he had been, after all of the insults the man had suffered at my (and the Commander's) expense, there was something touching about seeing his more human side, a selflessness that cannot be truly appreciated without first witnessing such overindulgent selfishness on the part of the same individual.

Eventually, one of the other resistance members came upon a large steel door (not unlike the one that cordoned off my laboratory from the rest of the world) and rapped several sets of rhythmic knocks on it. The door swung open to reveal a gaunt, extraordinarily French-looking fellow smoking a cigarette.

Now all he needs are a baguette and a beret, I thought.

The man locked eyes with Violette, who nodded at him, and he finally waved us all inside.

This room was similar to the previous one, if a bit more "lived-in" and well-lit. We placed the boxes along the side wall as more resistance members descended on them and began to unpack. Even Bloomington worked without complaint; he conversed freely in French with everyone else, his usual temerity replaced by the good-natured, confident fellow I first saw in the park.

As I hoisted a large radio out of one of the boxes, someone tapped me on my shoulder. I instinctively turned around and found Bloomington's mystery woman, presumptively "Marie," staring at me.

I was so shocked that I dropped the wretched radio on my feet.

As I stood there, still in two of the three pieces of the suit, mind you, and grabbed at my spats, I let out a string of expletives that would've made Bloomington blush.

I finally composed myself enough to speak clearly, "Err...pardon me, madame, but—"

She was all business, "Where is your friend? The charming, powerful gentleman with the impeccable French?"

Before I could answer, Bloomington swooped in on one knee, grabbed her hand and brought it to his lips.

"Ah, young lady, so you return! Though this is quite a ways away from the Candlelight Cafe."

"Apparently someone knocked over one of the candles," she smiled, her expression already much brighter. "Pity—was always a favorite place of mine."

"Ah, indeed. Mine as well. Come, my dear—" Bloomington rose to his feet and offered her an elbow, "—I have something to show you. Did I mention that I almost went to medical school in my younger and more vulnerable years?" She wrapped her arm in his. Bloomington yanked in his elbow and brought her closer. For some damned reason, "Marie" found this to be particularly charming, and giggled like the world's eldest schoolgirl. They left the room through one of the tunnels (which I would later come to find was the exit). We saw neither hide nor hair of them until the next morning.

When my foot had recovered from that damned radio and we had finished unpacking, I must say that the new resistance outpost looked downright professional. I asked Violette if there was anything else we could do to help.

"For now? No. You are free to stay here and I would ask that you confine yourselves to this room or the bar above us, but obviously I cannot hold you against your will. If you wish to return to your ship, you're obviously free to do so. There is a tunnel that will lead you to the park where it sits. I can show you—"

"Now, just hang on a minute, darlin'," Corcoran turned the charm up to "eleven." "Here we are in beautiful Paris, the City of Lights, albeit with a honest-to-God Nazi occupation goin' on, but still…we're supposed to stay inside at some stuffy bar?"

"I assure you, Commander, you will likely find that the club upstairs is more than adequate for whatever diversions you may have planned. And if you require accommodations for the evening, we are happy to provide them down here, " Violette answered. "But, as I said, if not, you're free to leave."

Corcoran raised an eyebrow at me, "Well then, Doc, *shalln't we?*" As practised as his mocking British accent was becoming, I now failed to find the humour in the affectation.

We walked up the stairs, not quite knowing what to expect as we plunged through two more sets of false doors (conveniently triggered by false candelabras in both cases), and emerged into a rather raucous cabaret theatre, complete with a chorus line of shapely, full-figured women predictably performing the can-can to cat-calls and wolf whistles from the crowd.

Corcoran and I looked at each other.

"Well, Ricky, though you didn't get your burlesque house in Leipzig—"

"I know, Doc. This oughtta make up for it." The grin on the Commander's face slowly morphed into a thousand-watt smile as his head bobbed with each extended leg.

"Careful, Commander," I warned. I pointed out several of the tell-tale red arm bands of Nazi officers in the crowd.

"God damn Gerry fucks!" Corcoran hissed with genuine anger. "Ruinin' all my fun." For a moment I thought he was going to pull out both pistols and start shooting up the German officers like a real-life Yosemite Sam, but thankfully the Commander's more civilised sense of decorum prevailed over his baser urges.

"Oh, I doubt we need to worry too much, Commander. Just don't attract too much attention to yourself and you'll be fine." He nodded at me. I smiled a knowing grin. "Need anything from the bar?"

"I thought you'd never ask."

CHAPTER TWENTY-SEVEN

Sadly, there was to be no "Cynthia" at this particular place of if not ill, then "questionable" repute. Corcoran chatted up two rather lovely young French ladies for several minutes. I decided to have a bit of fun with him and pulled him aside.

"Oh, for Chrissake, Doc—"

"For Trent's sake?" I corrected him with a sly grin.

"Fuck off. Can't you just please butt the fuck out and leave me alone?"

"Yes, they *are* rather lovely young ladies, aren't they?" I pretended to eye his targets. "Voluptuous. Beautiful. Not some little waifs who would fly away like so many sex symbols of your time, am I right?"

"Sure are. Now if you'll excuse me—" he moved to push me out of the way.

"There's just one thing that you may be interested to hear," I said.

"What? That you've decided to tell Hans, Fritz and the gang over there that you've found their Jewish boyfriends?" He nodded at a particularly Aryan-looking circle of large, surly German officers.

Though I found his joke to be in poor taste, I still chuckled for effect, "Always the jokester. No, I was referring to the infamous Parisian syphilis outbreak of 1943."

Corcoran stopped and turned to face me. "The what now?"

"Syphilis? Nasty business, that one. Can drive a perfectly normal man completely—"

"I know about syphilis, Doc. What's this about an outbreak, though?"

"Oh, there's probably no need to worry. I'm sure cabaret workers are generally a 'low-risk' group. And whatever medieval prophylactic devices they may have here surely will protect you, despite their somewhat spotty track record."

For a moment, I thought I had taken the jest a step too far when Corcoran leaned toward me and sneered. A second later, though, he brought his hand to his face and whispered.

"You…uh…have a rubber on ya?"

"I'm afraid—"

"Right…in the ship."

"In the ship," I confirmed his guess a half-beat after he had said it. Corcoran frowned and marched toward the secret entrance to the resistance's lair below.

"Where the devil do you think you're going?" I asked.

"Seein' if Violette has any medigel to go along with those holotrans." He started to walk again, stopped, and turned back toward me, "Who woulda thought I would be sayin' that when I got in that time machine a coupla' weeks ago?" He asked.

"Who would have thought you would say that sentence, either?" I replied.

Corcoran shook his head and continued on toward the secret entrance. I actually admired his ingenuity; why wouldn't a nurse from the future have a stash of medigel from which to draw? The true question was whether or not she was willing to allow Ricky Corcoran access to her supplies just so he could enjoy some French companionship for the evening, even if there was, in hindsight, a good chance that the women were Violette's own spies.

I ordered a scotch and found that one thing that the Germans allowed in clubs that their officers frequented was fine scotch. It was something else, really; German officers recreating not but twenty feet above a major resistance hub. Spilling God-knows how much intel to these well-trained cabaret girls in exchange for what? Sex? Maybe with some, but probably the vast majority were not, in fact, prostitutes.

Love? Could these Germans be so naive? No, they did so for the reasons any red-blooded man will tell a remotely attractive girl anything: acceptance. A desire to please. Demonstrating social proof, et cetera and so forth. That innate human want to be adored by another, or even many others, so deep as to betray awful national secrets, horrifying truths that the Nazi state held so dear.

I generally kept to myself and enjoyed the show, though please dispel any visions you may have of a lecherous older scientist bent over in a drunken stupor, tongue unravelled on the table while ogling the beautiful women onstage. No, after about my third or fourth scotch, my eyelids grew heavy, and I could only down another drink or two before I retreated to the relative security of the resistance bunker. I hadn't seen Corcoran either in the club or in the hideout, but I assumed that he was still trying to figure out a way around the mythical syphilis epidemic about which I had informed him earlier.

The "mattresses" that Violette had prepared for us were little more than large canvas sacks stuffed with straw, but I was so exhausted that it may as well have been a room at the Waldorf, albeit if that room happened to be the least-disturbed corner of the hotel's wine cellar.

I drifted off to what would prove to be the last good bit of restful sleep I would have for a while. I dreamt of that wonderful New Year's Eve I had spent with Cynthia, yet it wasn't New Year's Eve again. There was still a big to-do, and a countdown to *something*, but I couldn't discern what the devil it was. Any time I asked anyone, Cynthia, Burnham, even the Commander and Bloomington, they responded with sly, knowing smiles that threw me for a loop. A figure stood in the doorway of the room, and though I couldn't tell who exactly it was, as the count continued, "3...2...1..." the person took one step forward, and immediately the room descended into chaos, as the ceiling and walls began to crumble and fall around me.

I shot out of bed. Corcoran rubbed his head and sat up on the straw bag next to me. Bloomington was nowhere in sight. The sound of machine gun fire rattled around the stone walls of the room, and instantly snapped me out of what remained of my groggy reverie.

Corcoran had already unholstered both of his sidearms and scanned the room for any potential threats. I reached for my laser pistol, but Bloomington must've still had it, as I was forced to grab my Baretta from its spot nestled against the small of my back, which ached from bearing the force of the weapon as I slept.

As neither of us picked up any immediate threats, we rushed to the main chamber only to find Bloomington, of all people, at the bottom of the staircase leading to the cabaret, laser pistol in one hand, machine gun in the other like some kind of damned fool action star.

"Take that you Nazi assmonsters!" He screamed above the roar of his weapons. Violette and the other resistance members hurriedly re-packed the very boxes that we had unpacked the day before. We hurried over to her side.

"Status?" Corcoran asked coldly, efficiently, as only a true soldier might.

"The Nazis—they found our hiding spot. One of the cabaret dancers gave us up to one of their operatives."

So the espionage went both ways, then, I thought.

"Hey, little help over here?!" Bloomington shouted out in between volleys. "Commander! Doctor Templeton!"

Corcoran ran to Bloomington's side, and I followed closely behind. The Commander grabbed the machine gun from our portly companion and fired at the upstairs door whenever it opened.

I decided that I had enough gunplay over the previous several days, and instead jogged back over to Violette to see if there was anything further I could do to help.

"No! You've done more than enough already, Doctor. Take the Commander and make your way back to the ship through the tunnels." She handed me a hand-drawn map on a sheet of loose-leaf paper.

I nodded and turned to get Corcoran before I thought for a moment and faced Violette once more.

"What of Bloomington?"

"What?" Violette barely heard me over all of the commotion.

"Bloomington. My other...friend."

"He expressed his desire to stay here and help us fight."

"The hell he did!" I hadn't meant to say it aloud, but for some reason it burst out.

"You speak with him. We're happy to have the manpower, but only he can make the choice."

I sprinted back to Bloomington and Corcoran's position to find that the never-ending parade of Nazis (which, come to think of it, sounds like the worst possible theme park attraction ever) had momentarily halted. Corcoran and Bloomington both knelt on the ground and tried to catch their breath.

"Come now, gents, quickly. We must be off to the ship," I said.

Bloomington shook his head, "I'm not goin'."

"Beg your pardon?" I asked him.

"I'm not goin'. I'm staying here, with Marie."

"I hope you realise the full gravity of the situation, Steven. You will be placing yourself in mortal danger. There's no guarantee that ChronoSaber will be able to ever retrieve you, let alone—"

"He's a soldier, Doc. No need to lecture him like a child," Corcoran interrupted. He placed a hand on Bloomington's shoulder, "But Doc's right, Bloomy. I'll try to come back for you and Marie when I get back, but there aren't any promises that that's gonna happen. You sure you can live the rest of your life here if need be?" Corcoran was more sincere and serious than I had seen him since dealing with that awful little freak Kayoss.

Bloomington considered his superior officer's entreaty for five seconds or so. He stared first into space, then at the bullet-riddled door atop the steps. Finally, his gaze turned toward Marie, who was helping the French-looking gentleman whom had let us into the hideout the previous day secure some articles of equipment.

Finally, when I thought he would certainly reconsider and join us, he nodded.

"I belong here," he said. "With Marie. I'd rather die with her here than get whatever fame and fortune awaits back home."

Corcoran nodded gravely. I sat, utterly shocked, not only at Bloomington's decision, but also at the fact that any woman would find him anything but utterly repulsive.

"Steven, I—" I started to speak, but before I could get into any sort of a heartfelt "goodbye" or apology for maligning the man so much, he leapt to his feet, grasped my hand, and threw the other meaty arm around my back.

"Thanks for everything, Doctor Templeton," he said. "Nothing personal," he patted me on the back several times.

"Same to you, Steven," I said. My back pats were nowhere near as vigorous as his, but I figured that after all we had been through, they were well-earned, nonetheless. And, for the record, I suppose I likewise no longer bore the man any ill will.

The door atop the staircase opened once more, and Bloomington disengaged from our embrace to fire a fresh volley of laser fire at the incoming fascists.

"Commander," Bloomington offered Corcoran a nod. "I would hug you, but—"

Corcoran held up a hand, "No need, Bloomy. Take care of these Nazi pricks now, ya' hear?"

"Yes, sir!" Bloomington said, with perhaps a bit too much sarcastic enthusiasm.

"And Bloomy?" Corcoran paused for a moment, "That's an order."

Bloomington forced a small smirk before he opened up on the Germans once more. He must have found several targets, as only a hail of curse words descended down the staircase.

"Oh, wait, Commander?" Bloomington asked. "Can you leave the machine gun? We're kind of low on weapons."

Corcoran laid the automatic weapon down and took several steps toward me.

"Marie, honey," Bloomington yelled at the far side of the room. "Can you take the Commander's machine gun and help me MOW DOWN THESE NAZI ASSHOLES!" he screamed toward the top of the staircase. Marie scurried over to the portly scientist's side and picked up the dormant gun. The last glimpse I caught of them, both laughed with glee as they fired at the stream of Nazis that poured through the door atop the staircase.

Corcoran and I nodded a quick goodbye to Violette, and triggered the secret door that led to the catacombs.

CHAPTER TWENTY-EIGHT

I'll spare you the details of most of our journey through the "catacombs," as this section of the tunnels underneath the city was little more than an open sewer. It is worth noting, though, that for all of her virtues, Violette forgot to supply us with a light source, meaning that we generally had to navigate by whatever light we could glean from the tiny "skylights" in manhole covers and open sewer drains.

We didn't speak much on the way, other than to perhaps blow up at one another several times regarding forks in the road and that sort of thing. Eventually, though, the subject of Bloomington came up.

"Let it go, Doc," Corcoran said.

"It's just unfathomable to me that you'd want to stay in a time period devoid of so many wondrous technological advances for a woman that you met that very morning."

"Hey, the guy's in love—what can I say?" Corcoran replied. I was shocked by his nonchalant attitude about the whole matter.

"You just lost your chief scientist and colleague!" I said.

"What's the big deal? You're the one who runs the ship, and once we get all square, I can come back and get him 'tomorrow,' if need be. It's not like he's lost somewhere in time, unknown to the rest of history."

"Haven't you paid any attention at all? Time travel is a tricky business! Rather inexact, what with all of the quantum computations and—"

D.J. Gelner

"He made a decision, Doc. Now he has to live with it." A solitary ray of light streaked the Commander's face. Though I expected a pronounced scowl, he merely leveled his eyes at mine.

We continued more or less undisturbed until we came to an outtake grate perhaps two or three hours later. We had no way to pass it other than dive under, which would have been far more unpleasant if I hadn't already been coated in roughly fifteen different kinds of shit.

As I plunged in, I discovered that we had veered away from the sewer some time before, and I found the cool, relatively clean water to be rather refreshing on my weary, filth-caked skin.

We emerged from what was little more than a glorified creek on the far side of the park from whence we had landed. Though the park was as barren of Nazis as it had been upon our arrival, Corcoran and I both thought the better of arousing the suspicions of any onlookers by sprinting through the park in waterlogged three piece suits on an otherwise sunny, pleasant Parisian day.

We reached the clearing that housed the ship, and I pressed the button on the temple of my smart spectacles (which I was grateful for now more than ever) to reveal the craft's location. There it was, undisturbed; it sat blissfully silent in the warm, fragrant air of Paris in springtime.

I placed my hand upon the plate to lower the gangway, and we both hurried up the ramp and into the ship, whereupon I shut the door straightaway.

I allowed the Commander the first shower, and followed soon thereafter. As I towelled off my hair, and dressed in a fresh, crisp suit, provided by the QC, I checked the power levels, which read "Nominal—Ready for Time Travel." I jokingly keyed in the coordinates for the jump back to my time—

Then I realised it; this time, it was no joke. The display read those fantastic numbers that had guided me to so much hatred and sorrow, so many jumps to exotic locales. At that moment, they were the three most hated and loved numbers I had seen in my life:

300

"99.9%"

Home! I thought. In all of the action over the past two jumps, I had forgotten that it was finally time to return to my "given" time. I didn't dare to check to see if Corcoran's time would come up similarly; I was worried that even the slightest change would erase those wondrous numbers from the screen, and trap me in this awful little piece of history.

"How's it goin'?" Corcoran's voice startled me.

I tried to hide my enthusiasm as best as I could, "Fine, thank you. Are you ready to see the future, Commander?"

"Beats the hell outta all the places in the past we've been," Corcoran said with a tight smile.

"Despite the devastating, 'ended,' yet on-going World War, I think you'll find America to be quite pleasant in 2032."

"Here's hopin'," Corcoran nodded. A sly smile crept across his face, "Any chance I could pick the victory music?"

I considered his request for several moments. I was ready to blast the latest technorock hit from Clive Henrickson, but I figured that since the Commander would be able to avail himself of all the modern classics soon enough, I'd throw him a bit of a bone on the way back.

"Very well," I said. I hit the "music" icon on my tablet and allowed him to scroll through the catalogue, which I must admit was quite extensive.

"Okay...okay...no...no...let's see...HERE WE GO!" Corcoran exclaimed as he tapped the tablet's surface with great force.

As the first few notes started playing, I realised I had made an egregious error. A song that I would later learn was called "The Show Goes On," by some fellow named "Lupe Fiasco" blared over the loudspeakers.

"What in the devil—?" I asked.

"Hey, they used to play this after Rams games," Corcoran said with a wink.

"Why were you a fan of the Los Angeles...oh, that's right. They were in St. Louis for a few years there, weren't they?"

"And you claim to not be a sports fan," Corcoran said with a grin.

"Living in Baltimore, it's hard *not* to know who the Ravens beat up on every weekend," I replied. It was true; inevitably during my "office hours" with my colleagues, some neanderthal dolt or another would bring up the American football contest in town that weekend and (I imagine to wind me up a bit) try to solicit my opinion on the ultimate victor.

"There's a little bit of autotune in this one, but I like that it's not overproduced, you know?" Corcoran said.

"Commander, forgive me if I don't discuss the various merits of using autotune or not in—"

"Isn't it nice to hear the artist's natural voice, though?" Corcoran said. "There's somethin' pure about it, you know? You can really hear the raw emotion—"

"If I wanted to hear emotion in a singer's voice, I would listen to something from...oh, I don't know...Barbara Streisand?" Corcoran smirked and I realised that being from 2012, his attitudes toward the stereotypes accompanying listeners of Barbara Streisand may not have been as "enlightened" as most people in my time, "or...err...Frank Sinatra?"

Corcoran smiled, "agree on the Chairman. No one could quite belt 'em out like him." Suddenly, Corcoran furrowed his brow as he scrolled through the contents of my playlist and jabbed at another icon. "Maybe this is a bit more your speed, Doc."

Thankfully, that "noise" that had been on the loudspeakers was replaced by the beginning of "I've Got the World on a String." I breathed a sigh of relief as I unconsciously began to bob my head with the music.

To my shock, Corcoran followed suit. We caught each other's glances and broke into a smile as we began to sing the words together. As we got into the song more, I couldn't help but be a bit touched. The Commander and I had struck up quite the little friendship over the past who-knows-how-many days. Two men, who couldn't be any more apart, brought together by these ridiculous errands, this wild goose chase. Somehow we found some common ground in all of the travails and awfulness through which we had been. I chuckled a bit at the absurdity of it all, though Corcoran must have realised that he was in an even more absurd position; about to experience the future, first-hand!

I hit the red "Engage" icon and we continued to belt out the song, all pretenses at modesty thrown to the wayside. We ascended through the clouds and into the heavens above just as the song crescendoed into the thrilling climax. As it came to an end, we hadn't made the jump yet, which allowed the Commander and I a couple of rather awkward moments.

After several seconds of uncomfortable silence, Corcoran pointed back toward his quarters, "I'll...uh...go work on my report some more," he said.

"Indeed—I had better focus on piloting this damned thing," I said, even though I had every intention of allowing the computer to handle those duties unless the moon decided to make another surprise appearance.

After another ten minutes, the tunneling lasers engaged, and sent us into the wormhole for what I thought was to be my final time.

There was no boredom during the jump this time; I was as giddy as a child on Christmas morning. We emerged from the tunnel of wondrous colour as the Earth hung, as it always did, in the distance.

The ship approached the blue marble at a much faster rate than that to which I was accustomed. Keep in mind, this was in spite of all of the space junk and debris that surrounded the planet, so forgive me if I was more than a bit "on edge" as we approached the Western Hemisphere.

Apparently, the computer was on a mission, as it expertly dodged every obstacle that modern Earth threw at it. I looked down at what I expected to be a sick planet in my time. A decent chunk of its surface rendered useless by nuclear war and fallout. Warring nations constantly threatening to finish the job. The Middle East a—

Patch of lush, green life? I thought as I surveyed the familiar shape of the rhinoceros's head butting into the Indian subcontinent. I wiped my glasses and blinked my eyes to ensure that my senses didn't presently deceive me, but it was true; that "barren wasteland" looked now vibrant and verdant, even if from thousands of miles away.

"That's odd," I muttered. I allowed myself the possibility that it was simply the "fallout scrubbing" that was going on in the area, using various encouraging genetically-modified crops to take in and process the nuclear waste and replace it with oxygen, but that program had only begun a year ago, and was constantly being sabotaged by all three sides of the conflict.

The craft continued to build up speed toward the east coast. Though we felt no momentum, I was beginning to feel rather alarmed at our approach. The ship continued to dodge satellites, aircraft, and other time machines, which performed their own—

"Other time machines!?" I couldn't help but exclaim.

"What's that, Doc?" Corcoran asked from his quarters.

"Uh...nothing, Ricky. Nothing at all." I hoped my fake grin showed in my tone.

The ship flew in amazingly quick spurts and bursts. It changed directions on a dime without slowing down. Eventually, the Chesapeake Bay came into focus, though I was shocked by the dozen or so other saucers outside of my window.

"Dear God," I whispered to no one in particular. "What have we done?"

CHAPTER TWENTY-NINE

As we hurtled toward the ground, I was sure that my Benefactor had played one final cruel joke on us. "Nothing personal, Fin," he would say. "Just had to tie up the loose ends."

I gripped the armrests of the command chair with white-knuckles and prepared for the inevitable crash. We descended toward a garish, glass-and-stainless-steel eyesore of a building that was some eighty stories high in the middle of what only vaguely reminded me of downtown Baltimore.

The ChronoSaber tower from the video in Dinosaur times! I thought. I was certain it would be one of my last.

At the very last moment, as my survival instincts kicked in, and I shut my eyes and tensed all of the muscles in my body, I felt...nothing. I slowly opened one eye, then another, and saw that we had landed in a field across from the new stainless steel-and-glass building. I checked the readouts on the dash: "Time Jump Successful," the screen flashed, though I wanted nothing more than to put a fist through the panel since something had obviously gone very wrong.

Corcoran picked one hell of a time to emerge from his quarters. He cocked his pistol and placed it in his holster, as if nothing out of the ordinary had occurred in the slightest.

"Miss anything?" he asked.

"I'm...uh...not quite sure..." I replied. I fumbled for my own sidearm and was shocked to find that it was of the conventional variety, and not my prototype laser pistol.

Damn! Bloomington has it! I cursed my own carelessness at my oversight. I attempted to hide my frustration as I casually chambered a round and placed the Baretta in my own holster.

"What is it?" Corcoran asked.

"Let's take a look around, shall we?" I said, hopefully more "British Indiana Jones" than "inept Marcus Brody," as brilliantly portrayed by Denholm Elliot. Though I somewhat preferred his turn as "Coleman" in *Trading Places*, but I suppose that's neither here nor there at the moment.

Now where were we...ah yes! I ordered the computer to lower the gangway, and we descended it like a couple of astronauts setting foot on an alien world.

And how strange it was! It was as if the Inner Harbor had grown and swallowed the rest of the city whole. Litter and graffiti were nonexistent, and though vagrants still milled about, they quietly went about their business without so much as bothering anyone else. Notably, several more well-to-do pedestrians stopped and dropped $50 bills into the empty coffee cups in the bums' outstretched hands.

"So this is the future, is it, Doc?" Corcoran said as he took out his gloves.

"What in God's name are you doing?" I asked.

"What?"

"The gloves—it's the middle of July in Baltimore!"

"Yeah, and I'll bet you all have about fifteen different superbugs from antibiotic-resistant bacteria that'll kill me right quick."

"Well, well...the great Commander Corcoran, a germophobe!" I teased him a bit.

"Guess you learn somethin' new every day," Corcoran said, without a hint of emotion.

I couldn't help but gaze across the street toward the giant skyscraper that dominated the skyline. In front of it stood a large glass obelisk dominated by the holographic "ChronoSaber" logo with the stylized clock face from the holovid. Underneath the logo was a scrolling line that read as follows:

"Welcome to ChronoSaber, where our business is to make sure you have the time of your life," I thought the copywriters should be fired for that one. "Come inside if you no longer wish to experience," the font changed subtly; apparently this was a "fill-in-the-blank" of sorts, "July 6, 2042."

Like the video I had seen, it was all a bit corny and thus not nearly as funny as I imagined the writer had initially thought it, but—

"2042!" I couldn't help but hide my shock.

"Yeah?" Corcoran said. "Isn't that where you're from?"

"2032!" I screamed at him.

"Oh," Corcoran said.

"How could this happen!?" I cried at no one in particular. I turned to re-enter the craft.

"Whoa, whoa, Doc, where ya goin'?"

I didn't reply as I marched up the gangway and fiddled with the controls.

"Computer! When you told me 'time jump successful,' what did you mean by that?"

The response flashed up on the screen near-instantaneously, "Jump to July 6, 2042 successful."

"What did I enter as the coordinates?" my first thought was that I had somehow made a mistake in keying them in.

Another quick message, "July 6, 2032, Baltimore, Maryland, USA."

"Why, then, you damnedable bucket of bolts, are we in 2042, *exactly ten fucking years later?!*" Though Corcoran had made his way back onto the ship by now, I'm sure he would have heard me were he still outside the vessel.

This time, the computer thought for a moment.

"Access Denied. Result is within acceptable measure of error," the words flashed across the screen like a gut punch.

0.1 percent! I thought.

"Now see here, you scurrilous rogue—*I* am your master. *I* created you. And you will tell *me* exactly what is going on here *RIGHT*

307

FUCKING NOW!" To drive the point home, I pounded several times on the display; I doubted the computer could feel pain, but I thought it best to let the wanker know that I meant business.

Instead of insulting me or…shocking me, I suppose, or otherwise attacking me, the computer calmly brought up a map of downtown Baltimore, circa 2042, and zoomed in on our position. The building across the street from us flashed and a red, circular indicator surrounded it.

"One Chrono Place," the words flashed beneath the image. And without saying a word, I finally understood.

"This isn't over, computer. I'm not finished with you."

The computer thought for several more moments before the most curious phrase flashed up on the screen.

"Goodbye, Finny," it said.

"Fuck off, ass!" was all I could mutter under my breath.

"What'd it say? Where're we goin'?" Corcoran asked.

I knew the answer. I hated that I knew it, but I knew it all the same. It was the final insult, the last joke that was to be played on me…at least as "Doctor Phineas Templeton." What was about to happen was going to strip away my humanity one way or another; so utterly fed up was I that I knew that where I was going, I would either emerge a murderer, having crossed the line into dispatching a person in cold blood, or that I, myself, would leave the room in a coffin.

It was a fitting end for such an awful journey. Push a man, then push him some more, then see if you can finally push him to that darkest of places, deep in the cockles of his soul that had been exposed to too much harsh light over the past several weeks, where he dared not to tread formerly, but a place to which he had become all too accustomed.

"We're going," I said, "to meet the person pulling the strings."

"But how do you—"

"We're going to meet my Benefactor."

CHAPTER THIRTY

I was a man on a mission as I jaywalked across the street, oblivious to oncoming traffic. Horns must've honked, and perhaps the Commander even offered some apologies between his pleas for more information, but I gave no reply.

We marched through the courtyard in front of the tower single-mindedly. Four officers, dressed in the same camouflage outfits as the soldiers at Chronobase Alpha, guarded the entrance. I mentally prepared myself to dispatch them with my sidearm if need be, but thankfully they simply moved off to the side and saluted as the Commander and I passed by.

Inside the lobby, a set of metal detectors was guarded by two more soldiers. I stepped through one of them and heard the loud "beep" indicating that there was metal present on my person. Despite my all-consuming rage, I had been so trained by the invasive security measures deployed by TSA that I dutifully emptied my pockets, including my holstered sidearm, and walked through the machine once more.

"Thank you, sir," one of the soldiers said with a smile. "Have a nice visit to ChronoSaber." He nodded at Corcoran, "Commander, you can go right on through, of course."

I grabbed my pistol and snapped the holster around my torso once more. We proceeded to the bank of elevators in front of us.

"Sir...sir, please!" Another soldier chased us down and held something toward us in his hand. I grabbed for my sidearm very slowly, anticipating more trouble.

"Sign in, please," he said, and extended a tablet. I dutifully placed my thumb on the indicated spot and my picture and a short biography flashed on the screen before large red letters flashed up.

"Proceed to Floor 88," the tablet read.

"Wow...big meetin' with the boss, I guess," the soldier said. He eyed Corcoran and a wave of understanding washed over his face. "Oh, Commander, of course—you know the way. Right on in!" he pointed at the open elevator doors on the right side of the bank. To get at them, we circumvented a fountain that, I didn't realise until later, was identical to the one in the lobby of Burnham Harrington.

The elevator controls were a scrollable touchscreen, and, as expected, the eighty-eighth floor was represented by a wide horizontal button at the top. The doors shut almost immediately, and the Commander and I were treated to a holographic representation of downtown Baltimore, which was actually a pretty damned accurate representation of the freshly-made city I had only briefly been able to survey.

Corcoran sniffed the air, "Is that...vanilla?" he asked. I stared him down silently for several moments to let him know that his attempt at lightening the mood had fallen flat. He simply shrugged and looked forward once more.

After one of the quicker elevator rides that I had remembered (though it may have been a function of not having used one in quite some time), we emerged in a room that was identical to the posh, richly-appointed sky lobby in Burnham Herrington all of those years...days...whatever...ago. Even down to the "click-clack" of old-fashioned Macs and the eighties-ish look of the two receptionists.

"What a mindfuck," Corcoran let out with wide-eyed wonderment.

I marched up to the receptionist's desk and waited for her to notice us. After several moments, she hung up the phone, sighed, and looked at us.

"May I help you?" She asked, as if bored from working at a *time-travel agency!*

"Phineas Templeton, here to see my Benefactor."

"One moment," she replied.

"Anywhere I can take a leak?" Corcoran whispered at her.

"Commander! At a time like this? When we're so close to—"

"When *I'm* so close to pissing myself?" Corcoran hissed back at us.

"Around the corner to the right," the receptionist answered.

Not but thirty seconds after the Commander ran off, an elderly man stepped out into the room from behind the corner to the left of reception. It took me a moment or two, but I recognised the large, almost Borgnine-esque face that I had seen days before, weathered by the scourge of time.

"Garrett," I whispered.

"Expecting someone else, Doctor Templeton?" he extended a hand. I ignored it.

"Where is he?" I asked.

"'He' isn't who you want to meet. I assure you that I—"

"You're a sham—a front! Take me to him," I pulled my suitcoat back to reveal the sidearm in my holster. "Now."

Garrett raised his hands and widened his eyes, "Okay, okay...you're the boss..." he said. "But don't say I didn't warn you."

I pulled the gun out, but I'm not sure the secretaries even noticed. Even if they had shrieked, I wouldn't have heard it so focused was I on dealing out retribution to my Benefactor. The old bird was going to answer my questions, let me know *why* this had to happen. Why to me?

And then, he was going to pay.

"Send the Commander back when he's finished, would you?" Garrett asked over his shoulder, almost *politely*. I assume the receptionists nodded in the affirmative.

We transversed the same hallway that Corcoran, Bloomington and myself had days ago in St. Louis toward the familiar mahogany door. Instead of the "Victor U. Burnham—Principal," nameplate, though, there was none.

Garrett opened the door, and to my surprise, there was my Benefactor, seated in the chair that should have been Burnham's.

"Ah, Finny. So good to see you, my boy! Come in, come—"

"Spare me your pleasantries, old man," I pushed Garrett forward to reveal my Baretta and aimed it directly at my Benefactor's forehead. His secretary, Helene, was the only other person in the room, and instinctively took several steps back.

"Helene, I'm sorry you have to see this," I said to the attractive, middle-aged woman with salt-and-pepper black hair, and those piercing green eyes. Surprisingly, she was more steely and determined than the old buzzard was.

"My, my...it appears that we found the big boy guns on the ship..." the old man said. His hair and beard were all white and remarkably full, though I owed that to being able to travel through time at will, and procure the latest and greatest hair care and beauty products to—

My stomach dropped. The faintest dawn of a realisation crept over me. Though there was still a healthy layer of fog overlaying it all, my brain whizzed and whirred as the cogs and synapses fired, and attempted to make sense of the thoughts that swam through my brain. My knees wobbled as I staggered over toward a chair and sunk into it, gun still outstretched at my Benefactor.

"Why am I in 2042?" I steeled myself. "The computer said—"

"A computer that I procured for your benefit, and perhaps modified to suit my own...proclivities..." The old man said with a smile. "Helene, be a dear and get the good doctor a whiskey, will you? I think I see the faintest hint of an epiphany forming in that overpowered mind of his." The older woman professionally sashayed over to the bar and dropped two oversized ice cubes into a whiskey glass. My mouth began to salivate with the tell-tale "plink, plink."

"What's your poison again? Macallan Eighteen?" The old man nodded at Helene, who continued to dutifully prepare my drink. She brought it over to me and I took a large draught; I wanted desperately to feel the slightest burn in my throat, something that I could focus on as an anchor in my reeling head.

Helene walked over to my Benefactor and smiled at him for a quick second.

"Thank you, dear," he said. "Now, where—"

312

She slapped the man forcefully across the face.

"I said we keep it up until no longer is necessary, Jacob. Now, I think we owe the good doctor an explanation," she said in her harsh English tone, as she patted the man on the cheek twice. At first it was barely noticeable, a speck of red in a sea of white beard that gradually grew larger with each passing second. Eventually the convulsions began, and the first hints of spittle formed at my Benefactor's mouth.

"What..what's going on?" I asked. "Stop that!" I pointed the gun at Helene, who smirked and shrugged. "No...he's mine. I need answers! Why did you!"

My Benefactor's body fell in a heap on the desk, eyes open, not breathing.

Helene shook her head. "He always thought he was smarter than he was. Thought that some day, I'd grow careless and make that one fatal misstep that would allow him to take control of this operation. Unfortunately," the smirk on her face turned downright evil, "*He's* the one who forgot to take his medigel this month."

More synapses fired in my mind, "You...Helene. You're—?"

"The puppetmaster? The one actually pulling the strings? The one who sent you on your little scavenger hunt? Don't act so shocked, Phineas!" Her smile turned into a scowl as she pounded the table. Both Garrett and I jumped, I out of my seat, and Garrett in place. "Ask yourself, was there ever a meeting with him where I wasn't present? Didn't it ever strike you as odd at how clumsy I was at opportune moments, how he'd change his tune after I so 'carelessly' spilled scalding coffee on him? Isn't it odd that such a ditzy secretary could keep her job for so long? Despite your *incessant* eye rolls and 'harumphs.'"

"I just thought he was rogering you on the sly..." I couldn't help myself.

At least she laughed at the joke, even if her chortle was a bit on the devious side, "There's that English wit! 'He's too awkward to get with her,' they all said. Or even worse, Victor said, 'He's a homo.' Pardon the phrase, but those *were* his exact words."

Another piece of the puzzle locked into place, but I decided to play dumb.

"Get with whom?" I asked, innocently as a child might.

Helene smiled, "I think you know the answer, Phineas. Much how you know why this office looks like this today. A stolen glance in a lobby just west of the Mississippi…"

"You!" I couldn't help but blurt it out. In hindsight, I wish that my excitement had led me to pull the trigger then. "It was you getting out of the lift at Burnham Herrington!"

She rolled her eyes, "For being one of the great geniuses in all of history, you certainly can be a bit slow to put two and two together. Yes, 'twas I, that 'stunning' creature that you saw leaving Victor's offices on New Year's Eve."

"What were you doing there? How did you get back?"

"Isn't it obvious? Getting decorating tips. Visiting an old friend." she quipped before she put both hands on the desk and narrowed her eyes, "Ensuring that he was prepared for your visit, and knew the full magnitude of why you were there."

"But…the cocaine…with Bloomington…" My head began to reel.

She laughed wickedly, "Ah, you *still* don't know how medigel works, do you? That's right—it's 'from' your future. My future, too, though now it obviously can exist wherever in the timeline one may have brought it, so long as the universe will allow it." I swallowed deeply as the realisation continued to percolate.

"How should I put this?" She continued. "Once medigel is in your system, it stays there for thirty days, repairing any damage that's done, and slowly working its way out. As it's still in your system, it *craves* anything to fix in the body, especially the deleterious damage caused by alcohol and other drugs. When the medigel doesn't find these things, it buzzes away, entering the brain and leading to some, at times, *erratic* behavior, like with your friend Steven Bloomington," she said. "But, with the proper amount of toxins in the body, you become good as new. Fortunately, Victor knew this but you did not, so he forced himself to ingest a bit too much pharmaceutical grade cocaine to induce a heart attack, and leave you even more puzzled than when you arrived in his time period."

"Well, that puts the most *burning* mystery in my mind to rest," I said.

"Sarcastic little shit," she hissed. "Haven't you figured it out yet, Doctor? Why I would send you through time, an errand boy, with a special forces operative and another scientist?"

"The best...damned...reality show in history?" I loosened my tie and took another swig of scotch.

"Each jump, designed to accomplish a given goal," she ignored my barb. "From destroying your confidence in the sciences with Newton, to scaring you shitless with the dinosaurs, and even letting you know that your actions had real consequences with the Mayans."

"So the past *is* changeable then?" I asked.

She laughed her evil laugh once more, "How perfectly *adorable*, isn't it, Zane?" She smiled at Garrett, who politely excused himself and left the room. "No, my dear Finny, it most certainly is not. Not at all. Once you actually *went* to those places, you fixed your 'present' self's place in the timeline. You didn't find another version of yourself or the Commander, or anyone else coming to warn you about any of the events about to occur, did you?"

I cocked my head and struggled for a response, but could only manage a swallow.

"The truth of the matter is that Trent Albertson was absolutely correct. What happened, happened. But the harsh reality is that it's not just 'the past'— it's *all* of time. Past, present, and future. It has happened. It is happening, right now. And it *will* happen, exactly as it should. There is no changing *any* time, since it is *all* history, from a far enough point in the future.

"But still, *someone* had to go and 'create' the history that we now so..." she waved an arm around the plush environs, "...enjoy. At some point, you still had to actually travel through time to all of those locales and do exactly what you were supposed to do, what you *always* did. And the best part of it all, the part that you didn't even consider until just now, just this moment..." she levelled those stark green eyes at me.

"...Is that *you* made it happen."

"No...you set us on the track. You told us where to go—" I stammered.

"And you interpreted things as I thought you would. As I *knew* you would. Each step leading you down a darker path, ensuring that some day ChronoSaber would come to fruition, and that all you see around you would become *mine*."

"Impossible," the realisation hit me like a ton of feathers, each one individually harmless, but collectively crushing. "But then—"

"Yes," she licked her lips. It was almost as if she was getting some kind of weird sexual pleasure out of my realisation.

"If future technology...can be brought...to the past..." I had a bit of trouble forming the words.

"Go on—" she said, breathlessly.

"Bloomington didn't invent time travel, did he?" I blurted it out. "Neither did Corcoran!"

She nodded.

"It *was* me. *I* invented the time machine, after all. And *you* brought it back to them, didn't you?"

"Bravo," her voice was low and husky. I half expected Helene to break out a cigarette. "But don't go patting yourself on the back too hard. Where do you think that your quantum computer came from? You certainly didn't build it, nor will you. The truth is that once time travel has been deregulated and popularised, *all* future technology is available from that point forward. Medigel, holotrans—these aren't from a mere five or even ten years in your future, but are the result of long stretches of breakthroughs in research that have been brought back—"

"Technology..." it was barely a whisper as I released it into the world, disregarding her diatribe. "So then why is there no medigel in *my* time?"

"You're missing the point!" Helene shook her head. "There likely *is*. But the reason it hasn't been manufactured is a combination of many factors, from lacking the technology to reverse engineer such advanced parts, to reliance on other advanced technologies to enable their usage. You saw exactly 'why' bringing technology to the past could be so problematic when you had such a devil of a time showing those savage Mayans anything on your tablet.

"As for anything that slips through the cracks," she turned toward the window, "the universe has a funny way of taking care of things. Like why we can't go back and assassinate Hitler, or with that poor fellow that met the business end of one of Constantine's guard's pikes. *That* professor had a handgun, but he was utterly powerless because the universe, history, *God*; whatever you want to call it wouldn't allow it to happen. *Couldn't* allow it to happen. Because, my dearest Finny..." Helene turned to face me and put both hands on the desk. She bent over to reveal a good amount of (still shapely, mind you) cleavage, "...it...*didn't*...happen!"

I was beginning to see what she was getting at, but, "What did..." I felt a dull pain begin at the base of my skull and moved my hand to rub it away, "...what did Corcoran—?"

"Haven't you figured it out yet?" Helene interrupted. "Why the Commander's 'bathroom break' has taken so long?"

"Ricky...would never..." My head was now fully spinning, as if I had polished off a whole bottle of whisky.

She chuckled, "Oh, but he would! He never told you his mission, did he? Such a pity that a 'brilliant' scientist such as yourself couldn't figure it out before, hmm? How's the scotch, by the way?"

I eyed the half-empty glass of whisky on the armrest and mustered up barely enough strength to knock it to the floor.

"The Vizier?" I asked, barely a gasp.

"How else was Ricky going to find out about the extent of the war? To realise how devastating it would be? To make the choice that he had to?"

"France?" I croaked out.

"Can't have the Nazis winning *that* war, now could we? ChronoSaber wouldn't do too well under a fascist regime. Those two officers you three dispatched were far more crucial to the German war effort than even Violette could imagine. Not to mention all of the yeoman's work that wretched little Bloomington put in after you two left."

"And…now?" I asked.

"I think you very well know, 'what now?'" she said. "'Now,' the Commander returns to the past a hero. A time travelling commando, adored by all for ending the war, or I should say ending the fighting, a fine surrogate for you and all that you've accomplished. And you…well…without your time machine and my support, what exactly do you have?" She had slowly made her way over to me and grabbed me by the cheeks like an overbearing aunt might.

"But—"

"I know, I know…'but if he returns to 2012, how does no one know about him?' I said he returns to *the past*, not 2012…"

For whatever reason, the words still didn't register, though, as will soon become clear, they should have. I blame whatever she used to spike my drink.

"Why…harm…me…?"

"Jesus Henrietta Christ!" she exclaimed.

"Trent…Albertson," I could barely whisper.

She smirked, "Speaking of which, are you even sure that he's really Jesus Christ? Maybe he's a mascot, a flunky we pay to parade around as much," Her face drew taut and grave before she broke into a smile. "Or maybe he was telling the truth, and his whore of a grandmother wasn't influential enough to prevent his stoned escapades. It's of no further import to you."

"You…bitch…" I croaked at her.

"Where were we now? Ah, yes. Why leave you stranded in the future? Why, Phineas, my dear, this is why it's a good thing that you stuck to your science and didn't take your father's advice to go into business. If you ran the most successful business in the world, a company with a monopoly on a luxury industry with the highest market cap and insane margins, would you want the only person in history who could conceivably launch a competitor running around in the past, stirring shit up? Hmm?

"I've given you enough poison to kill you. It really would tie things up rather nicely. Unfortunately, I have a sneaking suspicion that it won't fully work out."

My mind flashed back to Mayan times, and I was suddenly glad that I had to tear the packet of medigel open with my teeth and ingested some of the pineapple-tasting goop.

"Better for you to be here, under my finger, where my operatives can keep tabs on you, in whatever alley you choose to rot away in for the rest of your miserable days. Even the mere mention of your name in the history books may lead some other fabulously wealthy individual to track you down and offer to bankroll you, hence why I must withhold the recognition that you so desperately seek, leaving you safely anonymous."

Her smile brightened, "The beauty of it all is that I know that you never do form a competitor. You couldn't have—the universe simply won't allow it. It hasn't happened, nor will it. The universe has forgotten you, given up on you, left you as a sacrifice to the greater good. But just to make sure, I'll keep tabs on you, and ensure that you never amount to anything again..." she brought her lips tantalisingly close to mine. Though I was repulsed, I couldn't move.

"...Personally."

At that moment, I could barely form a coherent thought, yet I knew. Somehow, I had always known.

She was right.

That's why she had sent me to Nicaea to witness the academic run through like a kebab, no matter what he had brought back with him. *That's* another reason we were forced to pursue the Vizier, and to see what chaos our run-in with the Mayans would bring about. History *was* fixed—it was fixed against me! No matter what I did, I would be lost to history, not even a footnote in the Commander's daring tale of survival.

My last thought before everything faded to black was simple, yet somehow poetic:

This may be my last thought...ever...

CHAPTER THIRTY-ONE

I awoke propped against a wall with a splitting headache. A pedestrian flung several coins at my face.

"Poor guy," the woman said as she slinked by (with a rather well-toned behind, might I add).

The cool breeze blew on my face and shot up. I felt for my sidearm, but found none. I rifled through my pockets, but they were empty. My tattered suit added to the fiction that I was, in fact, a derelict.

I looked toward the end of the wall against which I sat, only to find two ChronoSaber guards talking into their earpieces, as if to underscore Helene...excuse me, "My Benefactor's" point. Pardon me for failing to interchange the two during our tale, dear reader, but I'm still struggling with the full magnitude of the realisation myself.

They may be watching me, I thought. *But eventually, they'll slip up, get careless.* It didn't dawn on me until later that the last man who had said that, my erstwhile Benefactor, Jacob Harvey, ended up dead by poison tack to the cheek.

I stood up but didn't bother to dust myself off. An empty cup sat next to me, filled with bills and coins. I greedily emptied the haul into my pockets. A glass holosign in front of the building practically exploded with flashing colour.

"Museum of Unnatural History," the sign read. Though, admittedly, by any other standard, it was a stately-enough looking building, and apparently a proper place of learning, and not some disreputable "Ripley's"-type freak show.

I looked past the end of the museum only to see the ChronoSaber tower a block away.

Maybe it's still here! I thought. I felt on my face for my glasses (which my still-paralytic facial muscles could not discern due to the continued blurriness of vision I experienced) and found them. As I raced toward the open space opposite the tower, I pushed the button on the temple of the smart specs to reveal the location of the time machine.

Thankfully, they still worked.

Not even a second later, I was sorry that they did.

The ship was gone.

I slowed to a trot as I approached the green space, which seemed oddly out of place. I noticed a sign in the corner closest to me that I had either not seen previously, or had subconsciously ignored. As I read the words upon it, the pallor drained from my face.

"Richard J. Corcoran Park," the sign read.

"No...no...it can't be..." I rushed back toward the ChronoSaber tower. This time, the guards leveled what appeared to be LR-15s on me, and though a mature T-Rex could suffer their bolts relatively unscathed, I feared that my somewhat softer skin may not fare as well.

Thinking quickly, I instead bolted for the museum, up the steps and to the ticket window.

"One please," I emptied my pockets into the automatic ticket machine, and it spit out one ducat, along with several bills that I hadn't the time or care to collect. I sprinted into the "museum," which was really a long row of holodisplays. I settled behind the first empty one and it began its pre-canned spiel.

"Welcome to ChronoSaber's Museum of Unnatural History," a warm female voice greeted me. "In these displays, you will find all recorded information about time travel as we know it through..." a short pause was followed by a somewhat more mechanical tone, "July 7, 2042." A canned graphic of a cartoon cake with ten birthday candles flashed in front of me, followed by the sound of a noisemaker and then a slightly varied rip-off of the "Happy Birthday" song.

Cheap bastards… I thought.

"Welcome to the tenth anniversary of time travel! As you know, per an agreement between ChronoSaber and the U.S. Government, the full archives of time travel files could not be opened until ten years after the return of the first time traveler, Commander Richard J. Corcoran. We are pleased to announce that he returned safely ten years ago yesterday, on July 6, 2032. As a result, you are among the first people to have access to these exciting archives!"

I looked around at the rather sparse museum. Perhaps a couple of "media types" browsed alongside me, but I was surprised that there wasn't a larger crowd perusing the displays.

"Of course, you can always access the archives on your mobile device at www.chronosaber.com/ttarchives."

Of course… I echoed the computer's voice inside my head.

"How may I assist you?" The computer asked. At least this one had the chutzpah to talk to me to my face, and not hide behind a console like that insolent little shit of a ship's computer aboard my now-stolen time machine.

"Narrative account of Commander Corcoran's successful first time jump."

The computer thought for an instant before a holovid materialised in front of me.

"Commander Richard J. Corcoran," a picture of the Commander, if cleaned up a bit, flashed up in the display. "An American hero like no other.

"Born in what is now O'Fallon, Missouri in 1973, Commander Richard J. Corcoran succeeded in life despite numerous early hardships. His parents—"

"Computer, fast forward to details of time travel voyage," I said. Hopefully my tone conveyed my annoyance.

"Commander Corcoran left Montauk Naval Base on December 21, 2012 with Mission Specialist Steven Bloomington, in an operation known only as 'Project Omega.' Unfortunately, Specialist Bloomington was lost in action when marauding ancient warriors ambushed the duo," An artist's (or I should say "cartoonist's") rendition of a caricatured Corcoran and Bloomington firing guns into a circle of stereotypical "native warriors" came to life on the screen. "Though both fought valiantly, Bloomington was unable to fight off the advancing horde—"

"Fucking liar!" I practically yelled it at the display. "Where am I in all of this?"

"You are currently in level one, main gallery," the computer replied in its even tone.

"God damn smart ass!" I shouted, and started to get odd looks from the guards. "Please...continue..."

"After fighting off the natives, Commander Corcoran jumped to several other locations, in search of Project Omega's true objective: advanced weaponry for the United States military.

"Having succeeded in his mission, Commander Corcoran returned in his time machine, though due to the early uncertainty with plotting time travel, he landed some twenty years later, some three hundred miles south in Baltimore, Maryland."

"What a fucking coincidence!" I yelled once more.

"There, he met with ChronoSaber founder Zane Garrett before being rushed into quarantine. After being released from quarantine, Corcoran granted a single interview request, to CBS's Lara Logan, some five years after his return before he disappeared into seclusion once more."

The computer pulled up the interview footage. After Corcoran (who didn't look a day older than when I had last seen him) attempted to charm the (still rather stunning, might I add) Ms. Logan for several minutes, the conversation turned toward the topic in which I was most interested.

"Commander, you've been very reluctant to speak publicly about what you've termed your time travel ordeal," Logan said.

Corcoran forced a weak smile. Gone was the rakish charm that I had come to expect from the man, replaced with a vulnerability, almost a weakness. He took a deep breath.

"Well, Lara, you know I can't get too much into that. The military still has a gag order on us for another five years. Not to mention that…" he looked into the distance for a second. *His twang…it's gone…* I thought. *Another huckster. Another charlatan.*

"…I'll tell you one thing: one word I've grown to *hate* through all of this is 'hero.' I'm not terribly proud of what I've done. Good men have been lost along the way, not only to this world, but to history. That, in and of itself, is a great tragedy.

"But the greater tragedy is this idea that time travel will become a panacea to live fantasy lives or change the world, damn what the scientists say. It's not. It's just another way for folks with enough money to be foolish enough to think that they can leave their mark on history. And the shitkicker of the whole thing is that all the while, no matter how hard you try to change it, no matter how powerful you think your grip is on the situation, history will end up leaving its mark on you."

Though the image of the Commander began to tear up, I couldn't help myself. I balled my hand into a fist and struck the display, full force. It splintered somewhat, though I think the sharp "crack" that I had heard was one of my metacarpals. My expression, though, remained taut and unchanged.

The crack of the display aroused the suspicion of the guards, who spoke into their headsets and jogged over to get me. I instinctively reached for my holster, content to go out in a blaze of glory, only to realise that I no longer had my sidearm. I played the gesture off as if I was dusting myself off. I raised my hands as the guards approached.

"I'm leaving…I'm leaving…" I said. I backed toward the entrance several steps before I launched into a full-out sprint out of the door.

I ran until I found myself once more in Richard J. Corcoran Park. The guards must have been content to have run a dangerous derelict out of their jurisdiction, and didn't pursue. I fumbled with my glasses once more to ensure that the ship was actually gone. As the glasses changed their tint, I still saw no sign of the craft.

I did, however, find a curiously-shaped package with a red bow stashed behind one of the legs of the park's sign. A letter was attached to the bow with the word "Doc" printed in block letters upon it.

I tore open the letter and forced myself to read it aloud in my trembling hands, though at some point my voice started to sound like the Southern twang I knew so well.

"Dear Doc,

I suppose between ChronoSaber and the museum, you figured out the gist of things. I stole the time machine. If you haven't put 2 and 2 together on the how yet, I guess I better get to it from the start.

No doubt you've met that weird lady with the black hair named Helene, who apparently runs ChronoSaber. Garrett's just a patsy. She cornered Bloomy and me and the rest of the scientists as we were studying the wreckage of the Roswell craft and offered to help us complete it sometime in 2012. Budget was tight back then, and she offered her services gratis, so I asked, 'What's the catch?' She said, 'you'll meet a foppish Brit scientist along the way. He'll rescue you at a certain point in his travels. Use these,' and she handed me my gloves, 'electrostatic gloves to get his handprint, which you'll need to commandeer his craft. And use this,' she handed me my (pretty sweet-looking) I-Pod, 'to record everything he says.'"

*Dear God, no…*I thought.

"She said to me, 'Earn his trust, get him to open up, so that you can eventually cobble together the phrase, 'Computer, transfer all voice control to Commander Richard (or Ricky) Corcoran.'"

My head reeled as it all came together. *Damn my photographic memory!* I thought. Flashbacks overwhelmed me, first all of the times I had addressed the computer. Then I was back at Burnham's party speaking to Corcoran, *"I'm afraid it's terribly boring, really, compared with your story. Father transferred to England when I was still young…"* Then I was back in the cockpit before our final jump, *"If I wanted to hear emotion in a singer's voice, I would listen to something from…oh, I don't know…Barbara Streisand?"* Then after that fight Corcoran had with

325

Bloomington, *"Some things just are out of our control sometimes,"* it was Corcoran's voice, but I followed with, *"Well Commander, I understand completely.* Control *is a funny thing, you know."* Finally, my mind raced to the first time I had met the Commander, in the jungle outside of his crashed spacecraft. *"Commander* Corcoran? *Commander* Corcoran!" I had said. *"Like I said, you can call me Ricky,"* he flashed a smile. *"Indeed I can,* Richard." I said. *"Ricky,"* he said one more time. And for the first time, all of those little half-smiles and grins made a lot more sense. *"Commander..."*

I forced myself to continue reading, despite the tears that boiled off my face and onto the sheet below.

"As you've likely guessed, I wasn't putting together a report—I was splicing up your audio. That thing had a hell of a recorder on it, and awesome battery life. You should really think about picking one up.

When I finished up in the john at Chronosaber, you were already gone. I rushed back to the ship and got the stash of cash Burnham had given us. I got some funny looks for trying to use paper currency at some places, but eventually, I bought up plenty of goodies to take to the past—medigel, holotrans, half the shit in the Apple store, and even lifted one of those laser rifles off of a guard.

I played the message to the computer, and sure as shit, it worked. I tried to get back to 2012, but the computer locked me out, forced me to go back to 2032. I think I've seen you jump this thing enough that I can do it myself now.

I left you this note because I felt bad. There are still forces at work that you can't even comprehend. I'll honor my word as best I can, and hopefully get you in the history books someday. I'm really sorry for the ill I have caused you—it was the most despicable, yet ultimately most necessary thing I've ever done. To know that bringing these things back to 2032 will end what's left of the war is the only thing that comforts my dark conscience even now, before

I've made the jump. I imagine the feelings will just grow worse with time.

As a peace offering, I left you this. I know how much you enjoy it, so don't go wasting it all at once. It'll hopefully ease the sting a bit, and get you through the next few weeks.

Do what you gotta do. I give you my solemn promise, not only as an officer in the U.S. Navy, but as an honorable man, that our paths will cross again, and I will do my damnedest to ensure that you suffer a better fate, live a better life, when they do.

Until then, though, I offer my deepest apologies.

Sincerely,

Your Friend Ricky"

Still holding the letter, I unwrapped the package, my face angry and harsh. I tore the paper to ribbons, only to find the one thing that I didn't want to see at the moment. For as sweet as it was, and how much it had helped me through this journey, even it had betrayed me when I was most in need.

The tell-tale label of the Macallan Eighteen glared back at me, mocking me for my solitary vice that I had tried so desperately to control through the years, nay ages. Each word an embossed dagger to the heart as I read the label aloud:

"*The Macallan. Highland Single Malt Scotch Whiskey. Aged 18 Years,*"

And a single phrase, printed in ink, across the bottom of the label:

"*Special Limited Release—Vintage 2014*"

CHAPTER THIRTY-TWO

I laughed and rolled like a buffoon, for at that moment, was I little better than one? I had been utterly had, a jester for the court of infinite time, a simple pawn in a chess game played in four dimensions.

All had been for naught! The months and years of my life disappeared in one moment as I first crumpled Corcoran's letter, then thought the better of discarding it and began to eat it; quite literally, I shoved the paper down my gullet. The first reading had so burned those words into my soul that I could recite them, start-to-finish, by rote five minutes afterward.

I laughed like a maniac through the streets of Baltimore for weeks on end, fluttering to-and-fro mad as a hatter in June, trying to shake ChronoSaber's goons all the while. It was a laugh I've never been able to replicate before or since; one minute light and relishing in the absurdity of it all, the next dark and sinister, and hoping for nothing more than to wring the life out of Ricky Corcoran, to clasp my hands around his neck and dig in for his dear life, which should be mine, mine, MINE!

I rushed across a bridge (The Richard J. Corcoran Bridge, to be exact!) and hustled to my lab, only to find any trace of it bulldozed from Hopkins' campus. Another park, a green space that would never spill the secrets it once contained.

I heard the sideways comments of "proper" individuals; "Gone mad with the time sickness, he has!" They'd exclaim in hushed tones. More than a few passers-by took pity on me and threw me a spare twenty or so, told me to get help and get clean. But my mind was finally clear as a whistle in springtime, sharp as a T-Rex tooth! Oh, the jokes that time—nay, the universe itself!—could play on an unsuspecting time traveller!

Then came the mourning period; why did history and creation smile on people like Ricky Corcoran and Trent Albertson and leave true genius in the gutter to rot, a festering sore on a foreign time? I asked myself this question millions of times under countless bridges and overpasses, and still couldn't find an acceptable answer.

"Haven't I done everything you asked me to?" I asked to the sky one particularly dark and rainy evening. "Didn't I follow the rules? What more do you want? My life? My soul? Take them! They're yours! I submit, existence! I kneel before thee, a man, broken!"

There was, of course, no response. There was never a response, though my experiences dictated that someone was most certainly listening somewhere out there. How else could my grotesque existence so nicely and neatly package things up for all of the others around me? Was that not "fate" or "God" or "the universe," or whatever else you wished to call it?

I began to cobble the events of my life together, to try to place exactly where or when it had gone wrong, and realised that my life's story was actually rather exciting. I began to forego all of the bottles of scotch that my take as a panhandler usually brought (all the while saving that "special" bottle of scotch Ricky had left for the perfect time) and instead saved up for a budget-level tablet and keyboard to memorialise this manuscript that I have written these many months now.

I scrounged up enough to have this tale couriered to the time right before Corcoran was set to take off on his nefarious mission, to out him for the fraud that he is before harm could befall all who had suffered the slings and arrows of time travel, including myself. I gave the courier strict instructions to provide this manuscript in whole to some talentless hack eager to make a name for himself as ebooks were beginning to come into fashion, where my scrawlings need not pass through the watchful eyes of editors or publishing houses to reach the masses. As I said before, the odds are 99.9% that I have already failed; the book is, as far as I know, not a best seller. But as we have seen before, even that 0.1% can be enough to otherwise alter the flow of history, for better or worse.

So I ask you, dear reader—did I accomplish my goal? As you'll recall, it was to provide the God's honest truth, as much as that can even exist any more, and recount my tale. To expose the fraud Corcoran for the liar and cheat that he is. To out my Benefactor, Helene, who may or may not be destined to become one of the most ruthless businesswomen of all time.

But to most importantly to give credit where credit is due—to ME! The true creator and all-knowing father of time travel! The man who hath suffered insult and apathy silently for far too long.

Several of my contemporaries (and by that, I now mean Clarence and Mason who live under the bridge [that very same Corcoran Bridge, mind you] with me) have asked "would I do it all over again?" Sadly, the answer is "Of course." Not because I want to or I think it's somehow been a worthwhile learning experience, or a way to foster personal growth.

Rather it's because the universe demanded as much. It gripped me by the collar and cast me about, its own personal plaything, the one piece that it could move all throughout the space-time continuum. And perhaps most importantly, the only piece with the natural curiosity to listen to what it had to say, to comply with its every desire, no matter how absurd those desires may have been, and dutifully take my established, "rightful" place in this completely wrong-minded history.

We ride the current of time during our brief stay on this planet, completely at its whims. Even when it appears that we have craft to navigate its rapids and eddies, know that it is the mighty river that ultimately commands us through our lives. All we can do is grab a paddle and attempt to stay out of the more dangerous parts, all the while casting caution to the wind.

Or is it? Wait—I have it! One final jump to change it all! No more Corcoran Park, no more bridges bearing That Man's name, just one simple final jump that will provide me with the peace of mind I need to survive. I'll get the money somehow; just no more drinking for a little while longer, no more sweet, sweet anesthetic blissfully rescuing me from this awful existence. I could even stow away! Give the guards the slip—that shouldn't be too hard. They're beginning to get downright complacent when it comes to me! Where will I go? Past? Future? Does it matter? My past to change this future, or this future to escape my past? The point is to be the one place in time where everything is as it should be. No more time travel, no more insanity. No more narrow escape from death at the hands of a T-Rex, all those years ago. Or was it days? I don't even fucking know any more!

Here comes the laughter again, washing over my soul, cleansing it, clearing it, and wiping it clean! Yes, that's my medicine now! How daft! How mad! How utterly droll!

Now, now, Finn, get a hold of yourself. Cling onto that last nerve for dear life. Cage your unbound mind and make it your friend once more.

There's work to be done.

CHAPTER THIRTY-THREE

It was a rare sunny day in London, or at least as sunny as the notoriously dreary city got on a thoroughly autumnal Sunday in November. A man in a rather plush, black cashmere topcoat and fedora carried a small boy on his shoulders. His eyes were haggard and bag-heavy, the result of far too little sleep and perhaps a few too many cigarettes in his off-hours. These were the times that made it all pay off, though; the transfer to London, all of the long nights and moronic traders with whom he dealt, even his wife's departure to be with some awful street artist she had met in some long-haired part of the city.

It was all worth it for moments like these. The man stared out at the still-new London Eye and winked at it. Though it never returned the gesture, the man often liked to imagine that it did.

"Candy Floss! Two pounds fifty!" A vendor cried from a nearby cart.

"Papa! Papa! Please?" The boy asked.

The man pretended to consider the question for several moments before he "capitulated," and nodded with approval.

"Hey now, bub. 'At'll be two pounds fifty." The vendor said.

The man rummaged through his thick wallet. He thought that he would have to clear it out one of these days, but when would he ever find the time to do so? He plucked out a five pound note and handed it to the boy on his shoulders.

"Go ahead, Finny. Give the nice man his money."

The boy extended a cautious hand toward the vendor, who eagerly took the bill from him.

"Out of foive," the vendor motioned toward his cash box.

The man extended a waving hand, "Keep the change."

The vendor smiled, "Thank you, sir. Always been a fan of da Yanks, I have. Even now, a year on from 9-11, I think you're doin' quite well, if I do say so myself, despite what a wanker that President Bush of yours may be and 'dis noise about Iraq 'ee's makin'." He handed the boy one of the cones of spun pink sugar. Immediately the lad tore into it like he hadn't eaten for days.

"Tyrannosaurus Rex—RAWR!" the boy yelled as he took a massive bite of the sugary treat.

The man chuckled. "Easy now, Finn—you don't want to eat it all right away."

"But Daaaad! It's so gooooood!" The boy protested. The man shook his head and grinned. The candy floss vendor bid the two adieu as they continued their walk near the river.

"Papa, why did you give that man extra money?" The boy asked.

"What do you mean?" The man responded with an impish grin.

"The candy floss was two pounds fifty, and you gave him five pounds. You paid double what it cost."

"Not bad for a six year old," the man said, barely able to contain his pride. "Sometimes, Finn, those who are fortunate like to give a little extra to those who work hard and aren't as fortunate."

"Why?" the boy asked.

"Because, we want to reward hard work, Finny. It's tough times out there."

"But that man just stands there with the candy floss all day, guarding it." The boy said.

"From hungry little boys like you?" The man dipped down and the boy squealed with delight as he clutched his beloved candy floss to ensure that it didn't go flying. "I'd say that's hard work."

The boy laughed. They came upon an alley, and a shadowy figure sat up against one of the brick walls. His long hair was dark and unkempt, and an equally untamed beard covered his face, yet somehow added some slight distinction to the prematurely wrinkled skin that surrounded his eyes.

"Spare change, pop?" the bearded man asked. He smiled from ear-to-ear.

"Now Finny, that's a bum," the man said. "You work hard because you don't want to end up like him."

The bum smiled and locked eyes first with the man, and then with the child that sat on the man's shoulders. The smile waned for a moment as the bum's eyes widened, and the faintest hint of recognition washed over his face. Dimples pushed at his high, gaunt cheekbones as the grin returned in full force.

"Come along now, Finn." The man put his wallet away and walked off.

The bum's smile lingered for quite some time after the encounter, despite the man's not-so-subtle dig at his expense. The vagrant's eyes glazed over as foot traffic continued on the narrow cobblestone street in front of him.

So many people flittering to-and-fro, and for what? He thought. *What good will it do them?*

The drifter reached several times to his right, and eventually grasped his target; a brown paper bag, which obviously holstered a bottle of some type of alcohol. The bum took a deep draught on the bottle until his tongue stopped dancing with the telltale burn of its contents.

The bum removed the bottle from its bag and looked at it, baffled. He turned the container upside-down and a couple of drops fell from its mouth, onto the cobblestones below. He jerked the bottle up above his head, eager to catch one more taste, no matter how small, of the fine liquor.

There will be other bottles, the drifter thought. *Next week, then.*

He placed the bottle next to him gingerly, as if putting his prized possession on display for the rest of the world to see. The bum knew it didn't matter; likely some street sweeper would break it or think it a novelty gift if he came upon it.

But to the vagrant, it was a link to his past, how he had arrived here, and the reason that he found it so important to make his way to this end of the alley every week so that the same man could embarrass him in front of his child.

Most of the passers-by ignored the vagrant, though the occasional good samaritan offered him a low-denomination note, they didn't so much as make eye contact with the pitiable homeless man, who eventually picked up the empty bottle, sunk back into the alleyway, and half-passed out against the wall of a building.

Had passers-by stopped to look, they would have noticed something very odd indeed; the bottle was no cheap paint-thinner of a gin, but rather carried the familiar label of Macallan eighteen year scotch whiskey.

If one were to examine the print on the label, he would have seen something even odder, especially given that it was just past the turn of the millennium:

The Macallan

Highland Single Malt Scotch Whiskey

Aged 18 Years

And a single phrase, printed in ink, across the bottom of the label:

Special Limited Release—Vintage 2014

The bum sighed, a mix of contentment and exasperation. He stared half-awake at the rarely-abundant London sun and searched for some semblance of familiarity, something that he could latch onto after the chaos that had marked his life thus far.

"You know, there's a fine for littering, dontchya...?" A long shadow settled over this most truly homeless of men. The voice certainly wasn't that of an Englishman, but was more familiar, American, downright folksy.

The hobo unpocketed a pair of too-fancy spectacles and desperately rubbed the lenses free of soot and residue. He squinted at the pale sunlight and, though he was close to the point of seeing double, made out the form of an athletic-looking fellow. This man wore sunglasses, and the hair was a bit longer, but its sandy-blonde texture and the well-crafted jawline gave the stranger away almost immediately.

"You...huh...Comman....Commanduh...Cor...Corcor—?" the panhandler asked, though in his drunkenness, the sentiment was barely recognizable.

"Come on, Doc," the stranger knelt to the hobo's level and extended a hand. "We've got work to do."

COMING SOON

Corcoran Was a Time Traveler

Stay Tuned for Updates:

Follow D.J. on twitter @djgelner

E-mail D.J. @ djgelbooks@gmail.com

Check in at www.djgelner.com for more details

ABOUT THE AUTHOR

D.J. Gelner is a sportswriter, radio personality, and attorney. He worked at a large law firm for several years before shifting his focus to writing full-time. He lives in Clayton, Missouri with his dog, Sully.

ACKNOWLEDGEMENTS

Writing this novel has been an amazing experience. It's not the first novel I've written, but it's the first one to be released, and as I've always said, a novel not able to be read by all is no novel at all. It was also extremely fun to write; for his many faults, Doctor Templeton is a great character with whom to share one's head (see, writing as him is a tough habit to break). I only hope the good doctor made you think and chuckle (hopefully in that order) as much as he did me.

I'd like to thank first and foremost my loving parents, Dennis and Pat Gelner. Mom and Dad, I love you both very much, and I truly wouldn't have been able to write this book without your allowing me to use your house as my office for so many days this summer and fall. Not to mention, you know, all of the years of private school, college, law school and whatnot for which I can never truly repay you, but thank you nonetheless. To preempt any questions, no, Phineas's parents are not modeled after my own. I do like to think, though, that my affection and love for both of them matches Finny's own admiration of his father.

To my brother, Grant: you're more of an inspiration to me than you can possibly know. Thank you so much for always being there to listen to me gripe, or to offer insights on life, my books, or just random stuff about sports. I always know that when I have a chance to hang out or talk with you, I'll come away from the conversation with a smile on my face. I love you, man. Oh yeah—also, thanks for the excellent Orion's Comet logo; it really is great.

Thanks to my beta readers, Sara Eagan, Chris Burke, and Lauren Clasen, who gave excellent feedback on ways to improve what was a relatively rough first effort. You guys are awesome; I doubt this novel would be nearly as enjoyable or make whatever sense it does without your input, especially on the ending.

I'd like to thank Jenga and Sully for being such excellent writing partners; you guys are the best co-workers I've ever had (no offense intended to any of my other former co-workers).

Thanks to Derek Murphy for the great cover design on both the digital and print editions of this book; I think it's a really top-notch cover in both forms of media.

I also owe a hearty "thank you" to all of my teachers through the years, good and bad, for helping to make me the writer that I am now. I think two deserve special recognition as far as helping guide me toward fiction. One is Mrs. Maggie Eisenberger, who first nurtured and encouraged my interest in fiction in second and third grade. Though many were short, fifteen page "choose your own adventure" tales about dinosaurs and more still were recounts of my yet-to-be experienced exploits to come in the NHL, Mrs. Eisenberger always offered kind words of encouragement. She even went so far as to send off some of the hockey stories to the Blues, which prompted a visit from Blues announcer John Kelly, a highlight of my young life, which showed me how rewarding fiction can be.

The other is Dr. Richard Sandler. I had Dr. Sandler for English my senior year, and he always had a creative essay option at the end of the books we read, as well as a short fiction "workshop" portion of the class at the end of the year. It was the first time I wrote fiction that would be read aloud, and I have to say, putting myself out there for the first time was a big step on the path that has led me here. To you both, I owe you debts of gratitude that I fear I can never truly repay.

Also thank you to Adam Carolla, Bill Simmons, Alison Rosen, and Pete Holmes; though you don't know me, your podcasts helped me get through many a long brainstorming walk. In return, I've added a few Easter Eggs here and there in the book that I hope your fans are "hyper vigilant" enough to catch.

To everyone who has offered words of encouragement as I've written this book (or any of my other stuff), even so much as a facebook "like," thank you. You have no idea how much your support means to me. Also, to those of you who have doubted me or expressed derision, even something as little as a raised eyebrow or cross-eyed glance when I mentioned that I planned on becoming a novelist, thank you as well, for giving me a different form of motivation to keep going and improving my writing.

And finally, thank you for taking the time to read this book. I hope that you enjoyed it enough to continue along in the series; I currently have a couple of novellas planned between this book and the second one, so be on the lookout for those shortly. I can't do this full-time without folks supporting my work, and all I can do is try to write stories that are worth the price you paid.

Though this is a big first step on my journey as a writer, it's exactly that; a first step. Now comes the hard part: writing the next book, and hoping that it's as fun for me to write as it is for you to read.

Again, my most sincere thanks.

-D.J. Gelner
January 1, 2013

Printed in Great Britain
by Amazon.co.uk, Ltd.,
Marston Gate.